Cures for Cash

Where would you go if traditional
medicine was out of reach?

Cures
for
Cash

Lynne Martin

iUniverse, Inc.
Bloomington

Cures for Cash

iUniverse books may be ordered through booksellers or by contacting:

iUniverse
1663 Liberty Drive
Bloomington, IN 47403
www.iuniverse.com
1-800-Authors (1-800-288-4677)

ISBN: 978-1-4697-9985-8 (sc)
ISBN: 978-1-4697-9984-1 (hc)
ISBN: 978-1-4697-9986-5 (e)

Library of Congress Control Number: 2012904732

Printed in the United States of America

iUniverse rev. date: 3/20/2012

DEDICATION:

I would like to dedicate this work of fiction to my husband. He's suffered through the highs and lows of a full-time writing career, the unavoidable damage by household pets, and most of all...my indifference to the world when I'm in the midst of a new project. He is strong, he is supportive, and he is irreplaceable.

I would also like to pass a genuine thank you to my editor, and friend, Anne M. Younger www.iwriteanything.com. The only woman I trust to cut a beloved character, or chop one of my favorite scenes, in any and all of my projects.

Chapter One

"Toto, I've got a feeling we're not
in Kansas anymore."

—The Wizard of Oz, *1939*

Justice stared down at the admittance form and nervously debated how in the hell he was going to fill in all the empty blanks. Penciling in his name and home phone number alone had taken him longer than most. Justice was the type of man who worked with his hands and usually left the books and pencils to his wife. Unfortunately, he'd made the trip to the medical clinic on his own. Now he was now forced to complete any necessary paperwork somehow, without his wife's assistance.

"Done with my board?" the muscle-bound attendant demanded from his chair.

"Not quite," he answered back, forcing himself to rise to his feet and make his way across the clinic's floor. "I… I'm just not really good… you know, good with…"

Tony leaned across his desk and snatched the clipboard from the young man's outstretched hand. After scanning the nearly empty form, he picked up his own pencil and began quizzing the potential patient. "Mallory is your last name?"

"Yup," Justice answered, pivoting his head side to side to see if anyone was eavesdropping on their conversation.

"What's your address?"

Gaze shifting to the ceiling, Justice repeated his complete street address and zip code from memory, quite pleased with his mental accomplishment.

"Surgery?"

"Yes sir," Justice vigorously nodded his head, silently offering a prayer that the doctor would take care of everything during this initial visit.

"I mean what kind of surgery? I got to write out a description for the doctor so he knows what kind of procedure you're looking for."

Justice knew exactly what he wanted done, but was by no means comfortable enough to describe the details to a total stranger.

"Listen up. You've got two choices, bud," Tony explained in the same monotone voice he reserved for all the Changeroom's un-cooperative patients. "You can either fill in the blanks yourself, or explain it all to me. Which is it going to be?" he demanded, offering Justice his own pencil.

"I want to be fixed. We can't afford no more children," he admitted with a sigh.

"VAS... EC... TO... MY," Tony spelled out as he completed the form. "How you paying?"

Without hesitation, the young man pulled out a rolled wad of twenty-dollar bills wrapped with a single elastic band.

Tony penciled the word *cash* into the final blank. "Now sign this." He pushed the clipboard back across his desk.

Justice obliged as if following his boss's instruction down at the greenhouse.

Ripping the single page off the clipboard, the clinic's attendant shoved it into a recycled manila folder and motioned for the young man to return to his seat. "Grab a chair. I'll call you as soon as the doctor's ready."

Gratefully returning to the waiting area, Justice slumped down into one of the plastic patio chairs, releasing a huge sigh of relief.

"Hey bro," a hooded teen called out from across the waiting room. "Nice *gansta roll*. What'd ya do, roll up on your mama?"

"Hey buddy, stuff a sock in it," Tony yelled out across the clinic's floor.

"Chill bro, just checking out white bread's roll."

"Mind your own business," Tony barked for the last time before rising up and heading back between the clinic's swinging doors.

"You've got to try and relax." Dr. Clifford attempted to soothe the patient on his table, worried that her continual fidgeting might hamper his ability to balance the collagen injections in her bottom and top lips.

"Howww's it wook," the woman managed to force out through her numbed tissue. "Need morrre?"

Dr. Marcus Clifford, the Changeroom's sole owner, chief surgeon, supply clerk, and after-hours janitor, stood back and assessed his patient's symmetry. "I could possibly add a little to the upper right," he turned to pick up a mirror, "but I think you should have a look first." The doctor took a moment to stretch the aging muscles in his lower back.

Taking her time with the hand mirror, turning her face first to the right and then to the left, the patient carefully appraised her new look.

"Now, you understand that your lips are somewhat swollen from the procedure," the doctor warned. "But after twenty-four hours, the resulting fullness will be permanent."

"Wooks good," she smiled, the puffiness of her swollen mouth giving her face *cartoonish* features. "Howww bout?" she pointed to her bumpy and obviously disfigured cheekbones, "da wessst?"

"The rest of your face is a whole other problem." Dr. Clifford set down his syringe, adjusting his bifocals as he leaned in for a closer look. "The lumps are dissipating a little," he announced, gently pressing down on the fluid-filled pouches. "Maybe in three or four months we'll be able to do something. Right now, I think we really have no choice but to wait it out. Alright?" he asked, looking into her eyes for confirmation.

Silently nodding her head, the patient set down the mirror and began to prepare for her departure.

"I just have to ask you," the doctor couldn't help but speak his mind. "Why'd you let some quack inject your face with God knows what? You know you could have ended up in hospital with a range of conditions brought on by blood poisoning, and toxemia, and…"

"Doc pwwease," the woman attempted to silence him with a wave of her hand. "He wass cheeeppp," she slurred.

"I understand. Cheek implants are upward of three thousand dollars, collagen injections somewhere in the neighborhood of fifteen hundred, so the doctor you picked probably just injected saline for a couple hundred cash. But I must tell you, his symmetry was all off." Dr. Clifford slowly moved his head, continuing to appraise the lopsided bumps now adorning both her cheekbones. "I can't understand his logic regarding the positioning."

"First off," Tony interrupted the conversation, "she ain't talking about a doctor. She's talking about that nut that works out of the gym on fourteenth, and I bet it isn't salt water either. I heard the guy's injecting motor oil instead of collagen or saline."

"You know this guy?"

Tony set down the folder and snapped on a pair of rubber gloves before beginning a quick clean up of the empty syringes and dirty gauze littering the stainless steel tray. "I don't know him, I just know *of* him," he answered without lifting his face from the task.

"But why motor oil?" Dr. Clifford struggled to comprehend the information.

"Doesn't absorb easily into the surrounding muscle, stays liquid, and it's dirt cheap."

Leaning in for a third time to inspect his patient's distorted facial features, the doctor couldn't help himself, making a verbal prediction before he realized what he was saying. "If you don't have this foreign material removed as soon as possible, I'm afraid your appearance and your physical health are only going to worsen."

"Howww?" she demanded, not sure whether the doctor was genuinely concerned about her physical well being, or just pumping her for further business.

"Well, it appears that the motor oil was injected at varying depths and locations on each side of your face. That's one of the reasons you're finding the swelling and plumping of surrounding tissue totally uneven."

"Sooo," the patient mumbled, attempting to pucker her newly injected lips in the handheld mirror.

"So, if you don't have it all removed from your face as soon as possible, you might…"

"Nnnough!" She threw down the mirror. "Goin' hooome," the patient abruptly announced, then turned and marched out of the surgical room.

"Don't worry about her, Doc." Tony finished his clean up. "She's a crack ho who works the street, and a couple c.c.'s of motor oil in her cheeks is really the least of her problems."

"We've both had a hell of a day. Why don't we take one more and then call it a night?" Martin suggested, leaning against the counter as he stripped off his rubber gloves.

"We've got a vasectomy that you could wrap in twenty minutes. Want it?"

"Why not?" Dr. Clifford shook his head. "Two hundred bucks is two hundred bucks."

"That's right," Tony agreed. "And tonight, on the way home, I'll stop by the mall and pay the clinic's late phone bill," he promised, realizing that the elderly doctor was much too tired to personally make the stop.

Julia dug both plastic bottles out of her knapsack, and unceremoniously dropped them on the bathroom counter. After quickly unscrewing the first lid, she swung the open nozzle up toward the running tap. Testing the water temperature with her fingers, she decided the water was sufficiently warm, and filled the clear plastic container.

"Julia. Hey Julia? It's me, Keith," her male co-star abruptly shouted from outside the bathroom door. "Do you know where that Serena chick is hiding her ass?"

"Well, she sure as the hell ain't in here with me," the young woman yelled back, simultaneously wiggling out of her tube dress and g-string underwear.

"Serena's first up, and the little bitch is AWOL. Now the director's ready to whup her ass, and everybody's blaming me for holding up production. Could ya help me find her?" he called out one last time before disappearing back down the hallway.

"Amateurs," Julia hissed, slamming her plastic bottle back

down on the counter before yanking a clean bath towel out of her knapsack.

Wrapped in bleached white cotton, Julia angrily threw open the bathroom door and marched down the hall to the basement stairs. Determined to find the bitch and get the day's shoot back on track, she headed for the one place she thought she might be hiding.

"Serena, are you in there?" Julia pushed open the furnace room door.

Unwilling to answer, Serena fumbled with her lighter in a vain attempt to ignite the moistened end of her freshly rolled joint.

Julia stood her ground, repeatedly blinking to adjust to the low light. Finally comfortable with her surroundings, she carefully dropped to a crouching position and evaluated the darkened shapes occupying the opposing corners. "Look kid, I'm just here to help you out. But if you'd rather I just piss off and tell the director where to find your little ass himself, then I'll go."

"Don't leave me," the girl managed to croak out from behind the furnace, forcing herself to rise on unsteady knees. "I've never done this before, I've never..."

"You're not a fucking virgin, are you?" Julia demanded; standing to her full height as she adjusted the towel wrapped snugly underneath her arms. "Cuz trust me honey, this ain't the time or the place to pop your cherry."

"I'm not a virgin," Serena barked back, some of her strength returning as she stepped forward to defend her position. "I showered, and shaved, and brushed my teeth, but the make-up lady said I was supposed to go clean up. I don't know what else she wants me to wash." The girl threw her hands up in the air.

"How old are you?" Julia demanded, hands on her hips.

Serena stood her ground, eyes never leaving Julia's face. "I've already been on my own for three years," she brazenly announced, unsure whether she was speaking to a friend or a foe.

Not satisfied with the answer, Julia began to think aloud. "Well, nobody works around here unless they're at least seventeen. The director's pretty careful about that shit since he was nailed with statutory two years ago. So tell me, you been seventeen for a couple months, or you're gonna be seventeen in a couple years?"

"Six weeks," Serena chuckled to herself. "That's when I met Keith, a month and a half ago, at my seventeenth birthday bash."

"What a gift," Julia muttered under her breath.

"Is the director really pissed at me?"

"Well, he ain't sending you roses. Hell, what'd you expect? It's time to shoot, and you're not ready. Exactly what's the hold up again?"

Finally succeeding in her repeated attempts to light the joint, Serena yipped with excitement when the tip finally ignited into a small orange flame. Quickly sucking up the acrid smoke, she inhaled as deeply as her lungs would allow, only opening her eyes after circulating the smoke through her nose. "Want a drag?"

Accepting the joint, Julia pinched off one side of the rolling paper between her fingernails and repeatedly sucked small drags from the unfiltered tip. "You really don't have a fucking clue what the problem is, do you?" the veteran croaked while holding the smoke down as long as humanly possible in the confines of her lungs.

Shaking her head side to side, Serena chose to accept Julia as her friend and honestly admitted her ignorance. "I don't have a fucking clue what that lady wants."

Joint finished, the roach ground into the concrete floor of the furnace room, Julia grabbed Serena by the hand and dragged her up the basement stairs. Sequestered once again behind the bathroom door, she turned to face the questioning eyes of her young protégé. "I'm not much good at explaining," Julia admitted, "so I think it'd make a lot more sense if you just saw what I was doing and did the same."

Nodding, Serena watched as her tutor picked up an empty

plastic bottle, filled it with warm tap water, and then shoved the nozzle straight up inside her vaginal cavity.

"Make sure you get it all the way up inside before you squeeze," Julia warned, "or trust me, it'll just end up running all down your legs."

Serena continued to nod.

Julia set the empty bottle back on the countertop before dropping down to the toilet seat and releasing all the liquid back into the bowl.

"You're cleaning out your twat, right?" the young girl's face lit up in excitement. "That's what she wanted me to do?"

Reaching for the toilet paper, Julia patted herself dry before rising back up to her feet. "Can't blame them, who'd wanna go down on a dirty box?"

Serena picked up the bottle and turned toward the tap, shoving the plastic under the faucet to rinse off the nozzle before refilling the canister. "We don't use soap or nothing else?"

"Soap?" Julia shrieked. "Never let anyone tell you to douche with soap. You'll burn for days and the guys will hate you. They said it's like going down on a box of Tide. But if you're just off your rag and feel a little dirty, put about an inch," she pointed to the bottom of the bottle "of vinegar in with the water and that'll really clean out any leftover blood or lingering smell."

"Thanks," Serena smiled, twisting the nozzle back down on the filled bottle. "My turn?"

"And don't use my bottle," Julia snatched the container from Serena's fingers. You can buy them cheap at any dollar store." She turned and pulled a new container from her own bag.

"Thanks," she accepted the gift. "I'll get you another one as soon as I can."

"Well then, you better get at it," Julia encouraged her. "Hey, are you booked for anal, too?"

"Yeah, I think so," Serena shyly admitted as she ripped open the package before unscrewing the lid. "They said it was an extra hundred bucks."

"Well then you better hurry up with that." Julia waved her hands. "You're going to have to douche your ass, too. Don't want any of the guys dipping in and pulling out a chocolate bar, do you?" She winked.

Nodding her head in agreement while attempting to comprehend the analogy, Serena followed suit and awkwardly bent her knees. Nervously gliding the unforgiving plastic tip up past the fleshy tissue of her vaginal lips, her fingers bore down on the thin walled bottle, flooding her innermost cavity with clean, warm, tap water.

———————

The kids had almost finished cleaning their plates and were already clamoring to be excused from the kitchen table, when Annette finally realized that her husband wasn't coming home for supper, again.

"Chocolate cake," all three begged in unison.

Annette relented, sending the children to their playroom with the evening's desert.

"Smells good," her husband suddenly called out from the front door, making a beeline straight toward their bedroom. "Guess you ate without me," Wally announced before disappearing out of his wife's sight.

"You never called; I didn't know how long to wait," she bluntly stated, desperately trying to filter out any pangs of disappointment from her voice. She called after his retreating back, "I saved you a plate of extra crispy chicken though. Want me to nuke it?"

"Sure, sounds good," he called out from behind the bedroom door.

Annette quickly re-set her husband's place at the kitchen table, complete with a separate fork for his salad, and one or his desert.

"Kids sleeping?" Wally asked. He casually patted his wife on her bottom as he squeezed past her. He reached into the refrigerator door and pulled out an open bottle of white zinfandel.

"They're watching a movie in their playroom. So," she stalled for a second as the microwave announced its completion, "how come you didn't call? I was starting to get worried. It's nearly eight, and you said you were only working a half day this Thursday."

"I was." Wally focused his entire attention on the supper his wife had placed before him. "Then Billy came to me. He was having trouble with the new sales contracts, and before we knew it, it was already five o'clock. Then he insisted on buying me a beer as a thank you, and voilá, it was nearly eight o'clock."

"Well, next time just call, alright?"

"Alright." Wally agreed, picking up a chicken leg and biting down through the lingering crispness.

Deciding to finish off the bottle of Zinfandel, Annette poured herself a glass and joined her husband at the table. "You seem to have taken Billy under your wing. I hope your boss is willing to compensate you for all the extra hours."

"You know sales," Wally reminded his wife of fifteen years, "It's all in the numbers, and that's all management cares about. It boils down to the monthly sales sheets. How many funeral packages did I sell, and how many extras did I manage to tack onto the price? Basic salesmanship, Annette, you know the drill as well as anyone."

Downing the last sip out of her glass, she rose from her chair to rinse her stemware before loading it in the dishwasher. "I'm not trying to give you a hard time, Wally." She shook her head. "I appreciate it that you're not hanging around the lounges, sipping cocktails with twenty-something secretaries, but…"

"But what?" he demanded, the greasy chicken beginning to

churn in the pit of his stomach as it mixed with the half glass of ice cold wine.

"But not knowing is really hard. Planning a life with a husband who doesn't know day-to-day what time he's going to be home really sucks. I can't count all the dinner invitations I've passed on these last couple of months. You know," Annette waved her finger toward her husband's face, "pretty soon they'll stop inviting us."

"Well, I'm home now." He abruptly stood up, pushing his dinner plate toward the center of the table as he turned and stomped off.

Annette busied herself with cleaning up the remnants of supper for the second time while Wally retreated to his den. Smart enough not to jump into the shower the second he walked in the door, Wally reverted to plan B. He slid open the bottom drawer of his desk and pulled out a supermarket container of disposable wipes and began his clean up. Starting with his neck, he wiped off any lingering traces of saliva or manufactured scent, the pre-moistened wipes erasing his lover's tracks. Continuing down his chest, Wally slid his right hand down into his suit pants, twirling his fingers into the solid matt of pubic hair adorning his penis. Bringing his fingers back up to his face, he was instantly rewarded with the pleasant memory of his afternoon encounter.

Although their passion had been all-consuming, unfortunately, the latex condom he'd worn had shielded the skin of his own penis from any direct contact with his lover. Wally could only pick up a medicinal scent; hints of the spermicidal foam lining the prophylactic that now coated the head of his own penis. Any lingering enjoyment would have to be garnered from his pubic hair, and obsessively, Wally's hand dipped down to stir up a second helping. But all trace of their tryst was gone.

Chapter Two

"What we've got here is a failure to communicate."

—*Cool Hand Luke, 1967*

When she could no longer afford the daycare bills after the birth of her third child and chose to stay home, Annette Freeman had quickly mastered the art of compromise. By no means had she ever deluded herself into thinking that balancing their household expenses on Wally's single income would be an easy feat. She just hadn't been prepared for the inconsistency of his sales commissions.

"Don't ever marry a salesman," her mother had warned. "One month you'll be eating the chicken, and next month you'll be eating the feathers!"

Well, they hadn't actually needed to rip open any of their down comforters, but she had made a couple trips to the local food bank when Wally had blanked a month. His base salary only managed to cover the mortgage and utility payments, but the other necessities like groceries and gasoline tended to be more of a scramble when there were no commissions to pad the account.

"I'll make it up next month," had become a hollow promise, and Annette just wished that Wally would admit that he wasn't cut out for the sales game. In the last twelve months, she'd seriously considered taking a part-time job, but with a house to run, three children under the age of ten, and limited computer skills, the marketplace wasn't exactly clamoring for her return.

As the years passed, Annette's entry-level secretarial skills had become obsolete. She'd heard through the grapevine that her previous employer had already terminated her position, since the company now subscribed to a central twenty-four-hour answering service with a floater visiting the office once a week to manage the company files. She'd been so busy raising her family that she'd lost touch with the latest software. The thought of competing with twenty-something college grads was daunting, to say the very least. Armed with these realities, Annette had chosen to focus her energy on her husband's career, devoting any spare time to studying the written art of salesmanship in an attempt to hone Wally's skills. She wouldn't say the effort had been fruitless; she just hadn't been able to measure her results with any financial gains.

"That's all of it," her oldest announced, lifting the plastic hamper to dump the contents without directly handling the soiled laundry.

"Did you check the upstairs bathroom?"

"Mom, what about Colin? Why can't he help with the laundry?" she whined. "It's my last day of summer holidays."

"He can, and he does," Annette reasoned with her daughter. "But *this* Friday, I've asked *you* to help. So will you please go upstairs and bring down the hamper from the bathroom?"

"Okay," Monica groaned, spinning on her heel to head back up the basement stairs.

"Me help," a tiny voice announced from somewhere behind

the trash bags, full of empty juice boxes and soda cans. "Me wanna help, too."

Annette stepped around her piles of soiled laundry and lifted her youngest daughter Tammy up and over the wall of recyclables. "You can help Mommy with the soap," she promised, plopping her daughter down on top of the dryer.

"Soap, soap," her two year old repeated; the latest trick in her arsenal as she attempted to master the English language.

Bending down to complete the final sort, Annette's hands reached out to grab an armload of bedding, her eyes suddenly drawn to a succession of streaky brown stains. "Looks like Daddy left skid marks again," she muttered aloud, shaking her head while reaching for the spot remover.

Wally's bowels had been acting up for a couple of months now, resulting in a multitude of symptoms, all seemingly resulting in varying degrees of diarrhea. No matter what she cooked, or how many antacid tablets he ingested, Wally was continually plagued with watery bowels. Once or twice a week, Annette still found herself waking to the aftermath of soiled sheets.

He'd stopped by the medi-center twice on his way home from work, and both times the doctor had just reassured him that he just needed to relax and stay away from spicy foods. Annette had responded by parking her recipe for curry chicken and hiding both jars of salsa. But it didn't seem to matter; Wally still turned in early most nights complaining of stomach aches while continuing to soil their marriage bed.

———————

Jogging down the concrete maze of university sidewalks, Freddy Nally was finally able to catch a glimpse of the eastern lecture hall. A newer building tucked in the rear of the campus, it seemed impossible to lose sight of that three-story structure, but somehow, Freddy always managed to get lost.

The campus map had been of little help, especially since Freddy realized he'd left his last copy lying somewhere in the jumble of sleeping bags that temporarily substituted for a sheet set on his bed. With few other options, he had given up, thrust his arms into the straps of his knapsack, and taken off running. Every pedestrian he stopped had been just as lost as he was, so Freddy opted for his back-up plan. He trotted around the campus ring road, and scanned his surroundings visually to spot the eastern lecture hall. Fifteen minutes later, sweat already beading on his forehead, he ran through the building's main doors and stumbled into the anatomy lecture hall.

"Take a seat. Any one will do." The professor stood at the podium and shuffled his notes. "We've got a lot of ground to cover on the skeletal system, so let's quiet down and get to work."

The students quickly pulled out their writing materials before stowing their knapsacks and coats under the seats of their folding lecture chairs.

"Today, we're going to begin by covering the structure of cartilage," the professor announced, his eyes never wavering from his notes.

Freddy flipped open his clipboard, and scribbled *Anatomy 101* and the date at the top of the page, ready to record his lecture notes.

Dr. Goldman motioned for his teaching assistant to dim the lights, then turned on the overhead projector, and finally raised his head to address the assembled crowd formally. "I assume you've all pulled the notes and diagrams for today's lecture off the class website?"

A small percentage of the four hundred students sitting shoulder to shoulder in the lecture hall verbally moaned their regrets, having forgotten altogether, or simply misplaced the papers in route.

"This is not high school," the professor admonished them. "Mommy and Daddy aren't here to remind you to take your books to school. If you want to succeed in medical sciences, you're going to have to take care of yourselves."

A murmur and rustle of papers moved through the auditorium as the unprepared students sought help from their more obliging neighbors, who shifted position to share the material.

Forced by his late arrival to squeeze into one of the back rows near the aisle, Freddy, unfortunately, was not able to share anyone's notes. Pressing down firmly with his pen, he scribbled a huge reminder for himself to pull all the notes for next class.

"All right students," Dr. Goldman announced. "We're going to try something a little different for a few minutes before we jump into the lecture. I want everyone to stand up."

Half the class immediately rose to their feet; the rest were somewhat embarrassed and a little apprehensive about the idea.

"It's not a request. So everybody stand!" the professor barked into the small microphone pinned to his shirt. This time, everyone obeyed his command; the remaining students jumping to their feet to join their vertical classmates.

Stepping around his podium, the doctor slowly sauntered across the stage, enjoying the freedom afforded by his wireless microphone. "After each statement, if you fall into the category I've just mentioned, please just take a seat. Once seated, remain so until we're finished. I think you'll all find this little experiment quite interesting." He exchanged knowing glances with his assistant.

"Alright class, here's the first one," he began. "How many of you were class valedictorians back in your local high schools?"

A surprising percentage proudly thrust their arms in the air, waving their hands as if frantically flagging down a taxicab.

"Sit down," he commanded the students, motioning for them to take their seats before he continued with his explanation.

"Unfortunately, people have been filling your heads with the idea that you're smarter than everyone else for so long now, you probably believe you're something special. So like I said, sit down."

A hush descended on the entire lecture hall as the students reluctantly dropped into their seats.

"Number two," he loudly announced. "Any of you under the age of eighteen? I want you to sit down too."

Another small group returned to their seats.

"You're too young. You don't have a clue about who you are or what you want to do with your lives. Come back when you're at least a couple of years older," he shook his head at the mere thought of seventeen-year old anatomy students.

"Now number three. Anyone whose parent, spouse, or sibling is already a doctor, sit down."

The whispers were audible; students feeling compelled to announce their family connections to neighboring classmates.

"You're probably here for the wrong reasons," he simply stated, moving on to his fourth point without further clarification. "Number four. If English is your second language, and I don't care how bilingual you think you are," Dr. Goldman added as an afterthought, "sit down."

This brought some heated murmurs from the floor, two Asian students actually raising their hands in disagreement, stubbornly refusing to take their seats.

"Trust me people," the professor spoke from over twenty-five years of experience. "You'll be much too busy translating phrases back into your native tongue to properly memorize them. A full-blown case of information overload as you unconsciously study in two languages."

The two students relented and dropped their hands.

Returning to his podium, the doctor glanced down at his notes. "Number five. Anybody one hundred percent financed through student loans, grants, or any other kind of government funding; take a seat. You'll quickly realize they don't pay enough and you'll need a part-time job just to survive. That part-time job will kill you when combined with your full-time studies."

Only a few students sat down, the boy standing next to Freddy looking positively ashen as he reluctantly dropped down into his seat.

"Number six, ladies and gentlemen. Anyone here who lives farther than four hours away, and just relocated to this city to attend university? Take a seat. I hate to be the bearer of bad news, but the commute and the loneliness will probably break you."

Glancing down the front rows toward the stage, Freddy was surprised that he was still standing, guessing that at least half the students had already taken their seats.

"Number seven," he continued with his little experiment. "All you part-timers take a seat. You're got to find yourself a new hobby, and personally, I think you've been watching way too much General Hospital and Grey's Anatomy."

A small chuckle escaped the student body as everyone nervously latched onto the professor's lame attempt at humor.

"Number eight. Anyone here a newlywed? Married less than twelve months? Well, take a seat. A newlywed can't have both, so make a choice. It's an undergraduate degree in medical sciences, or it's your marriage. Trust me; it's a choice you don't want to have to make with a baby on the way and your spouse talking to a divorce lawyer."

Freddy was surprised at how many people dropped out of the running, shaking their heads in disbelief. One girl, only three seats to his right, slumped down in a huff and crossed her arms in a brazen show of defiance.

"Number nine. Any of you parenting a child under the age of six? Well, you know what to do."

"Why?" an anonymous voice called out from the floor.

"One simple word. Responsibilities. You'll be torn, too busy to spend the amount of time necessary to master the course materials. Too many obligations. And to be honest, when your kids are that young, they deserve your full-time attention."

Quickly attempting to tally the remainder of students still standing, Freddy was caught off-guard when Dr. Goldman left the stage and marched partway up the center aisle.

"Number ten," he announced from his position on the stairs. "If you already have a part-time job, or you're planning on picking one up, sit down. Your time will be divided, and you'll never make up the lost hours." Turning to make his way back to the podium, Dr. Goldman motioned for his teaching assistant to join him up front. "Quan, could you please tell the class how many times you were forced to take the entrance exam, drop classes, and then reapply, before you were accepted into this program?"

"Three times," the TA leaned toward the professor's lapel and proudly announced into the mike.

"Ladies and gentlemen, this brings us up to magic number eleven. If any of you have *never* failed at anything in your life, whether it is a class, a job, or maybe even a relationship, then sit your butt down. You don't know anything about defeat or loss, and medicine is as much about learning from our failures, as it is about celebrating our accomplishments."

Freddy was absolutely shocked. He, and a few other students scattered through the lecture hall, actually were still standing.

"Now, have a look around you. I count about thirty-five or forty of you still on your feet," he proclaimed with an all-encompassing wave of his arms. "By my calculations, that's about right. Ten percent of you will make it. Ten percent of you will actually finish med school, survive your internship, and become licensed, practicing physicians. Now everyone, take your seat," he nodded as the remainder sat down in their chairs, murmuring their personal opinions regarding the unsettling results.

"One more thing," the professor shook his finger at the assembled class. "Before one or two of you *eager little beavers* runs out of this class and heads straight to the dean's office to file a conduct report, let me first clarify a couple of points," he picked up his water bottle and squeezed a mouthful of liquid down his throat. "By no means am I suggesting that those of you identified in any of the categories are guaranteed to fail, no more than those thirty or forty of you who are left standing are guaranteed to succeed. I was just making a point. Learn from me. I'm your Anatomy 101 professor, but I'm not a fortune-teller. You *will* make your own destiny."

Now everyone," he announced with a loud clap of his hands, "let's get back to the skeletal system starting with the three types of cartilage. Anyone know why hyaline cartilage has a glossy appearance?"

No one spoke; everyone was too busy shuffling through papers and debating their own longevity in the program.

Chapter Three

*"You don't understand! I coulda' had
class. I coulda' been a contender.
I coulda' been somebody, instead of
a bum, which is what I am."*

—On the Waterfront, 1954

Standing motionless in front of his refrigerator's freezer compartment, Dr. Marcus Clifford debated whether he should defrost a small portion of breakfast sausage or a few strips of sugar-cured bacon; a treat only afforded on Sunday mornings after a grueling workweek. Unfortunately, he had also been lax with his exercise routine, and now Marcus felt the first pangs of guilt begin to surface at the mere sight of the highly processed meat. Years before, in an attempt to offset his life-long love of comfort foods, he had taken up power walking. Lately, despite his best intentions, fatigue always seems to override his plans.

"Bacon," he finally muttered with a shake of his head. He yanked out two individually wrapped portions and transferred them to the microwave's turntable.

"Coffee on?" a female voice called out, her leather bottomed house slippers slowly shuffling across the kitchen floor.

"Tea, I think," Marcus answered, suddenly mesmerized by the spinning slices of pork as they began to bubble between the multiple layers of paper towel.

Teresa filled the copper kettle and set it down on the stove before taking a minute to search for her purse. "I'm going out of town next week," she announced as she struck a match and ignited the tip of her cigarette.

"Where to?"

Flicking her used match toward the drain in the kitchen sink, Teresa popped the cigarette in her mouth to free both hands for setting the table. "My mother's really going downhill, and I think I'd better drop by and see how she's doing."

"Good idea," he agreed, gingerly transferring the greasy strips to the waiting fry pan. "You taking the bus?"

"Yup. I'm not going to take a chance driving. I don't think that old clunker of mine has five hundred miles left in her. Don't wanna push it and have her die on the side of the highway, two or three hours out of the city."

Marcus agreed, realizing that if nothing else, his girlfriend was definitely practical when it came to money matters. "Boiled, fried, or poached?" he continued with his brunch preparations.

"Neither. I spotted some tomatoes in your crisper and I'm just gonna slice them up and enjoy a good old bacon and tomato sandwich."

"Now that sounds good," Marcus agreed, throwing all caution to the wind as he envisioned adding a thick slice of Colby cheese to the bacon and tomato before sandwiching them between slices of lightly toasted sour dough bread heavily slathered with deli mayonnaise.

"I'm not sure exactly how long I'll be gone," Teresa jarred Marcus back to the conversation at hand, "but I promise to phone you as soon as I'm settled. Probably stay with my sister and her husband, but I'll be damned if I remember what cell number they're using these days."

Marcus trusted that Teresa would call, as much as he trusted that the sun would shine. She had been a regular fixture in his life since they had met at his clinic. More than just depending on her to meet his sexual needs, he actually found himself longing for her company whenever their jobs kept them apart.

Teresa still resided in the same halfway house where the police officers had taken her on the night of her last beating. Her role was no longer that of resident. She now held the salaried position of day intake worker. She used her experience as an abuse victim to help the battered and broken women who found the strength to step through her door.

Teresa's ex-husband had never allowed her to drive a car, or carry any measurable cash, so when she finally fled, she had stumbled blindly from her doorstep toward the first light she saw burning in the night.

Since the midnight clerk at the gas station had hidden the blood-soaked woman in the backroom before calling the police, Teresa had finally been able to break free. Many years of physical and mental abuse had definitely taken their toll on her self-esteem, but on that last night; she knew she had only one choice… she had to run. Teresa hadn't been fighting for respect or common decency; she had been fighting to save her very life.

When he met Teresa, Dr. Marcus Clifford had been volunteering his clinic's limited services for years, providing medical care to the shelter's clients one afternoon a week.

Teresa's first appearance in the clinic has been a difficult experience for her. She'd lived most of her adult life hiding the evidence of her beatings, so it had taken days of cajoling and hours of heartfelt testament from her fellow residents before she had finally joined the small group of women on their weekly trek. After a twenty-minute walk, and a cup of the clinic's free coffee, they waited patiently to have their physical wounds checked by the doctor. The psychological scars, unfortunately, were left untended.

The afternoon of Teresa's first visit, the doctor had noticed the women hanging around the coffee pot. Taking a break to grab his lunch, he took off his lab coat, sat behind the reception desk, and watched the ladies nervously assess their surroundings. It was abundantly clear from their demeanor that they all had experienced abusive relationships. Their collective reaction of fear towards any stranger approaching their tight circle was as strong a testament to their physical abuse as much as the fading bruises marring their bodies. Still, they were here at the clinic, a trip that obviously forced them to step out of their temporary comfort zones in a positive attempt to rejoin society.

These women deserved encouragement for their strength to persevere, and with this thought in mind, Martin decided to introduce himself, even before the women had finished taking their brief turns on his examination table.

Inexplicably, he found himself drawn to one woman in particular. Maybe Teresa reminded him of a girlfriend from his youth, or a lover from days long past. At any rate, Martin found himself desperately wanting to move past the confines of the doctor/patient relationship.

A free cup of coffee down at the clinic turned into a five-dollar latte at a local Starbucks. Within a handful of dates, Marcus and Teresa discovered that they had common interests. They also found common ground and great comfort in their mutual acceptance of each other's past heartbreak. This was the exact medicine a fifty-one year old housewife needed to begin healing and the perfect morale boost for a sixty-two year old doctor needing to resurrect his personal life.

Knees knocking and arms twitching at her side, Julia realized that it was time to stop smoking *rock* and bring herself down to a manageable high. She was scheduled to work again later that night, and showing up this strung out might actually land her ass on the unemployment line. And the last time Julia had checked, there was still no unemployment compensation for out of work porn stars. Since her only *other* chance for employment was a starring role in a local snuff film, she decided to force herself to come down and try to sleep.

Unfortunately, the only way to come down immediately off a cocaine-high was to shoot heroin. It was a volatile balance, the opiates in the heroin counteracting the stimulants of the rock cocaine. A minute miscalculation and she could overdose. It was a gamble Julia had been taking for years, and the odds were starting to pile up against her. Forcing herself to rise, she stumbled over a few empty wine bottles and moved toward the CD player. She switched off the music, and flicked the television to the morning news. As the chirpy weather girl began her report, Julia began rummaging through a pile of trash in search of her surgical tubing.

"I think I might need to come down, too," a young girl's voice called out from the corner recliner. "Can you hook me up?"

Julia tripped over a remaining party guest sleeping on the floor, angrily shoving the man's legs out of the way. Eventually hitting her mark, she dropped back down onto the faded upholstery to cook up her shot of heroin.

"I don't work 'til eight tonight, what about you?" Serena asked, still hanging out at Julia's apartment ever since showing up for the party Thursday night.

"Yeah, me too," Julia agreed. "I think they said we were shooting at eight, but I don't exactly remember where. Do you?"

"My purse," Serena nervously nodded toward the bedroom. "Wrote everything down and shoved it in there."

Since Julia reasoned that three or four hours of sleep would probably be enough to get ready for the night's shoot, she yanked open the tubing she'd just used to tie off on her left arm and sent the warmth of the heroin into her bloodstream. "Just one more hit on the stem," she promised her houseguest, as she picked up the glass crack pipe, crusted with the brownish residue of the drug.

"Party on!" Serena whooped, secretly relieved that her hostess wasn't ready to end the night and was willing to smoke a little more rock. Serena rose on wobbly legs, her naked torso fully exposed as the silk kimono she wore fluttered open at her sides.

Passing the dope back and forth, both women continued inhaling the smoke until the rock had totally burnt away, leaving only a thin film of burnt drug coating the swatch of tin foil.

"You really got nice tits," Julia complimented the young girl. "When I was you age, mine were fine, too," she cooed. "But you know," she shoved her hands under her twenty-seven year old breasts and lifted them upward toward her chin, "time sucks."

"Keith said my nipples are too light for film, they need a little color," Serena dropped her own head down to survey her own chest. "Keith said he knows a tattoo guy that can fix them right up, put a little color round the points," she circled her index fingers around her pinkish areolas.

"That'll work," Julia agreed, "but better than color them up, why don't you do something a little special. Maybe pierce them. You could run a nice gold chain between your nipples; maybe jazz it up with a few little jewels or charms. What you think?"

"I like it. I like it a lot," Serena hopped up and down on the edge of the couch, almost landing on the back of some poor guy's head.

"Where do I go? How much is it gonna cost, cuz I'm not really all that flush right now," she nervously giggled.

"Fuck cost, we can do it ourselves," Julia announced, the idea seriously beginning to take root the second after she made the offer. "All we need to do is make sure our needle is sterilized; and that you're really numbed."

"I'm... like... seriously numbed."

"I meant your tits," Julia shook her head. "Now go to the kitchen, grab two ice cubes, and rub them back and forth over your nipples until they're all melted."

Teetering off toward the refrigerator, Serena busied herself with an open bag of ice while Julia pulled an old sewing needle out of the hanging drapery. Casually running the stainless steel through the flame of a lit candle, she suddenly fumbled, dropping her needle down amongst the piles of week old trash littering every inch of her coffee table. Shaking her head in frustration, Julia decided that the needle was probably sanitized enough anyway. She blew out the candle before it accidentally set her rental house on fire, and picked up the needle and brushed away the flakes of tobacco and the greasy potato chip residue now clinging to the metal shaft and then stumbled toward the kitchen.

"I can't feel a thing," Serena announced.

"Okay. Stay put. I'm coming to you."

Standing at the kitchen sink, Julia pinched Serena's left nipple and aggressively pulled it away from her chest. "You ready?"

"Bring it on, bitch!" Serena growled through gritted teeth.

Forcing the needle through the young girl's nipple from right to left, Julia stopped mid-pierce, lifting her face to check the response of her patient. "You fine? Not gonna faint or anything, are you?"

"Fuck me. That really hurts," Serena wailed; her face flushed in response to the sharp stab of pain. "But... I'm... okay," she announced through several deep breaths. Recomposed, Serena turned her attention back to the task. "What's wrong? Why don't you pull it though?" she asked, with her eyes shifting back and forth from the needle's midway position to Julia's down turned face.

"I gotta put something in, you know. Kinda like sleepers when you get your ears pierced."

"Well, what we gonna use?" Serena began to whimper, terrified by the sight of blood as it began to drip down the needle toward the exposed eye.

Quickly extracting a gold hoop from her own ear, Julia flashed the nickel-sized circle in front of Serena's eyes. "You can borrow these." Without further delay, she pushed the needle through the far wall of the nipple, immediately threading the gold hoop through the freshly lacerated tissue.

"Holy mother of Christ," Serena swore. "That fucking hurts like hell."

"Done," Julia announced, standing back to take a good look at her handiwork. It looked damn good, and as soon as all the bleeding and redness had subsided, she knew the kid would wanna thank her. "So, ready for the other?"

Wiping the tears spilling out of the corners of her eyes, Serena forced out a nervous little laugh. "I think we're gonna need a little more rock before we continue on with this party."

Julia nodded her agreement, led the way back into the living room, and twisted the lid off a new vial. Dumping the rock cocaine out onto the cluttered table, she motioned for Serena to kneel beside her as they prepared to numb their mutual pain.

Chapter Four

"Yo, Adrian!"

—*Rocky, 1976*

Shopping on a Sunday afternoon proved to be a little more difficult than Justice Mallory would have ever imagined. Because he usually attended church with this family, he'd always assumed that stores in his neighborhood would be relatively empty on the Lord's Sabbath, since most God-fearing Christians would be gathering their families for worship.

Justice couldn't understand how this one day of the week had evolved into the most profitable shopping day. This was supposed to be a day of rest, and if you weren't obligated to work, a good family man's objective should be to lead his loved ones in prayer. It was an obligation, an oath that Justice had sworn to God, in the presence of family during his marriage vows, and then again at the baptism of both his children. It was a promise he had taken to heart.

Reluctantly arriving at his destination, Justice squeezed his truck into one of the few available spaces in the Walmart parking lot, and very carefully ejected himself from the bench seat. Still extremely tender from his Thursday night vasectomy, he slowly shuffled toward the entrance doors, painfully aware of the healing incision on his testicles.

When a runaway shopping cart forced him to sidestep suddenly, Justice clenched his teeth to stifle the searing pain, tearing like rockets through his groin. The jerking motion had taken his breath away, akin to being gored by an enraged long horn steer on the underside of his crotch, and until he was able regain his focus on his surroundings, he wasn't moving another inch.

"Hey buddy, what's the hold up?" a young guy barked from somewhere behind his back. "You stuck in glue or something?"

"Something," he moaned in response, wiping his forehead before continuing with his shuffle toward the automatic doors.

"Welcome to Walmart," a hostess chirped in his direction, offering all who entered the use of a shopping cart.

Deciding to take her up on her offer, Justice found that using the cart made him a little more relaxed, offering an impromptu wall of protection as he plodded up and down the superstore's aisles.

He'd been walking for fifteen minutes, zigzagging back and forth, still unable to spot the racks holding men's underwear. Quickly running out of time and energy, Justice relented. "Excuse me," he called out to another shopper moving toward him near the back of the store. "Do you know where, uh... uh, where the shorts are?"

Raising his eyes toward the ceiling, the man turned on his heel and began scanning the overhead signage. "You talking swimming trunks or underwear?" he simply asked.

"Underwear," Justice nervously confirmed with a nod of his head, and then he gingerly turned to see if anyone else was catching their conversation.

"It's right over there," the guy announced and pointed to a hanging sign. "See? Men's underwear," he read.

But Justice couldn't see. The words *men's underwear* could have been written in hieroglyphics, for all he knew. He was functionally illiterate; a specific term assigned to men and women who somehow reached adulthood, but still managed to raise families, earn a living, and continue to function in the world, even though they were unable to read even the simplest words.

Looking toward where the man was pointing, Justice was grateful when he noticed a red banner wrapped around one of the poles. "By the red sign?" he asked.

"That's the spot," the man nodded his head.

Once again alone with his cart, Justice stared at the metal shelving, row after row, filled with hundreds of packages of men's underwear. He rarely shopped for his own clothing since he had moved from his mother's house straight into his wife's apartment. Justice wasn't exactly sure how to find what he needed, as he looked at the packages.

The doctor at the clinic had given very explicit instructions to wear snug jockey shorts with a good support pouch for at least two weeks. Because of this special requirement, Justice pulled himself up off the couch to take care of the task. Since he planned to head back to work on Monday morning, he already realized that better underwear was truly a necessity. His testicles were still throbbing from the slight jostling he had received in the Walmart parking lot.

He picked up the first package and looked at the sealed underwear showing through the plastic. He liked the navy color but was unsure of the size or cut. On the back of the package, he was disappointed to see nothing but a jumble of letters and numbers. He put it back on the shelf, picked up another brand, and quickly flipped the plastic-wrapped briefs. This time he was rewarded with a picture, the outline of the underwear, emblazoned in black.

"That's good," he mumbled, and set the package in the basket of his cart, while he carefully dug in his pocket for his old underwear tag. After retrieving the torn swatch, he carefully matched the word *medium* to the glossy advertising on the package.

With his eyes flitting back and forth, he searched for the obvious bumps in the letter M, one in the front, the second in the back. Two rows later, Justice was finally satisfied that he'd found the right diagram in conjunction with the correct size on three individual packages. He tossed the underwear into his cart, turned, and slowly made his way toward the cashier, confident that his trip had been a success.

———————

Bending over the metal barbell, Tony continued to set the adjustable weights, oblivious to the group of young women congregating in the far corner of the gym.

"That's him," one girl whispered to another, as she watched Tony grunt through a rep of ten squat thrusts. "I heard that he worked out here, and I'll bet you twenty bucks that's him!"

"How do you know it's really him?" another girl challenged. "There are a lot of guys in here with jet black hair, big muscles, and armfuls of tattoos."

"Jail tats," the first girl immediately corrected her friend. "They're different. Jail tattoos are usually smudgy, only one or two colors, and they tend to bleed out at the edges. Kind of like really cheap lipstick, if you know what I mean?"

Each nodded, all turning in unison to analyze Tony's artwork.

"You're right, that's him," Karen nodded her head.

Now that they'd established Tony's identity, it was time to make a decision and nominate a delegate.

"He looks mean. I don't think he's going to be very happy if someone just waltzes over there and interrupts his workout."

"What do ya think he's gonna do, bite your head off in the middle of the gym?" one of the women teased. "Grow up. He's either gonna help or not. He's not going to blast any of us clear across the floor."

Tired of all the bickering, Karen held up her hands. "Alright, I volunteer. I'll go over there and break the ice."

The other five girls instantly stopped arguing among themselves and focused their full attention on Karen.

"Watch my back!" were her last instructions as she made her way across the floor. The closer she moved, the larger he looked. By the time Karen was only a couple yards from Tony, she realized that the guy was over six and a half feet tall, and probably weighed more than two hundred and fifty pounds. He looked menacing, she'd give him that, but they were in the middle of a public facility. She'd be fine.

"You lost?" Tony suddenly growled, never missing a rep as he continued with his routine.

"No, I was just…" Karen stalled, reaching down to pick one of the smaller free weights off the metal stand. "I was just looking to work on my biceps," she blurted out, curling the ten-pound weight up toward her shoulder.

"Then don't bend your wrist. Lock it so it's in line with your forearm," he barked through a succession of deep breaths.

Turning to evaluate her own movements, Karen took his advice, instantly rewarded with a warm pull in her upper bicep. "Guess I don't know a lot about weights," she snickered, right arm beginning to weaken after only six reps.

"Pull four more, and then change to your left," Tony ordered, setting down the barbell before moving over toward the leg press. Adjusting the weight to two hundred pounds, he continued working on his upper quadriceps.

"My name is Karen," she suddenly announced, unwilling to allow their limited line of communication to evaporate suddenly.

"Tony," he offered in a one-word reply.

"Nice to meet you," Karen offered her best smile. "I have to be honest, I'm actually more the aerobics or spin type."

"I know," he responded, eyes never losing focus on the metal checker plate underneath his size fourteen sneakers.

"How'd you know?"

"Muscular calves, underdeveloped arms, and makeup," he summed up brusquely.

"You're good," she laughed, genuinely amused with his observations.

Moving on to the next piece of equipment in his routine, Tony continued his workout as if Karen was an annoying child, set on following him around the playground.

"Well, what else do you know about me?" Karen couldn't resist.

"You drew the short straw."

"Really? What makes you say that?"

Tony paused exercising and turned his head toward the group of young women anxiously huddled together across the room. "You're the one who came over here, so I assume you drew the short straw."

Hands suddenly on her hips, Karen found an untapped well of courage and drank deeply. "I'll have you know I volunteered!" Her voice and posture challenged his interpretation of the afternoon's events.

"Fine, you volunteered," he turned to continue with his routine.

"I volunteered," Karen repeated for the second time, suddenly finding herself at a loss for words.

"Well then, why don't you cut to the chase so you and all the other little *Desperate Housewives* don't miss out on your class," he strongly emphasized the words.

Karen sucked in her breath, as anger began to boil behind her calm exterior.

Tony decided to get right to the point and end their impromptu conversation. "Yes, I work at the Changeroom. No, I don't remember the names of any famous patients. Yes, the doctor is properly licensed, and finally no," he summed up in a flourish, "the doctor won't come to your house for a little Botox party. Now, are we done here?" Tony reached down to grab a towel from his gym bag. "I'd like to hit the shower but I'm afraid you're just gonna follow me in there, too."

"Don't flatter yourself. I hear that men with huge muscles are usually trying to compensate for other shortcomings." Without waiting for a reply, she turned on her heel, and stomped off to where her friends anxiously awaited her return.

"What'd he say?" the group of women chorused as they crowded around Karen.

"He's just another *steroid puppy!*" she hissed, infuriated that Tony had been able to guess the nature of her visit. "I have a feeling that he's nothing more than the clinic's janitor."

"I don't think so," one of the women argued back. "From what I hear, he's more like the receptionist, bouncer, and doctor's assistant, all rolled into one. I wouldn't be surprised to find out he's a licensed nurse or something like that."

"A nurse?" Karen pondered the last statement, trying to imagine Tony gently encouraging some fragile old lady to swallow her prescribed medication.

"Whatever. I'm done with him. You wanna take another shot, find yourself another volunteer. I'm hitting the steam room."

"What about class?"

Karen just shook her head, too wound up to concentrate on the advanced aerobics scheduled to start at the top of the hour. "Tomorrow," she offered in compensation. "I'll pick it up in the a.m."

Watching the girls grab their bags and trot off, Karen wondered just what she'd been thinking. Had she been absolutely insane? How in the world could she have expected a total stranger to just open up about his personal life? Lord knows, she would have acted the same way if some idiot tried to befriend her for no apparent reason. Hell, the last time a guy tried to be so overly friendly; she'd lied and told him she was a dyke.

Concluding that she should apologize for her bad behavior, Karen grabbed her belongings and scanned the gym's floor for any sign of Tony. Within a minute, she realized he'd already left. As she turned to move toward the showers, she was shocked to see him sitting at the juice bar, chatting up some silicone-pumped Barbie doll.

He hadn't seemed to be the type of guy who would be interested in *the plastics*, women so surgically enhanced that the only original parts on their body were their fingerprints. But then, how well did she know a man she'd only casually spoken to for a couple minutes?

"Shit," Karen cursed, when she realized that Tony had probably felt her staring right at him. As he started to pivot on his barstool, she realized he might recognize her as the woman who'd approached him on the floor. She'd be lucky if he didn't call over the manager and have her barred for stalking him. After dropping into an open chair and grabbing a menu, Karen hid her face in the laminated pages as she scrambled to come up with a secondary plan.

"Looking for me?" Tony demanded. His arms were crossed over his massive chest as he towered over her table.

"Oh, hi." She smiled her most innocent smile. "I, uh, I felt like a little guava," she lied through her teeth. The explanation sounded weak in her own ears.

"You're more persistent than most," Tony announced, not budging an inch.

"Well," Karen opted for the truth, "I actually just wanted to apologize. It sounds like you get a lot of unwanted attention, and I'm sorry for the intrusion. I know how I feel when guys walk up to me uninvited and just start chatting me up."

Tony dropped his arms to his side, caught off guard by Karen's honesty. "Trust me lady, I can handle anything you can throw in my direction, but I'm not mad. I'm just…" it was his turn to search for the appropriate words, "amazed at your persistence."

"That's the thing with us desperate housewives. We don't like to give up."

The tough veneer actually cracked for a split second and Tony allowed himself to smile, his face instantly softening into a wry grin.

"Well," Karen announced as she rose to her feet. "I'd better get moving and let you get back to your date."

"She's not my date," he announced, unsure why he'd felt compelled to clear up the misunderstanding. "She's just an ex-patient."

"Figured so," she couldn't help but smile.

"Can I buy you that guava?" Tony suddenly asked, not very good with the subtleties of casual dating.

Karen sat back down at the table, and motioned for Tony to follow suit. "I'd really prefer a strawberry smoothie," she confided as the waitress neared their table.

Drinks ordered, Karen was suddenly unnerved by the silence, wondering who was going to brave the gap.

"Tony," a voice politely beckoned from behind their backs. "How have you been doing?"

"Dr. Hood," Tony jumped to his feet to greet the elderly gentleman. "I'm fine, sir. How have you been?"

"I'm sorry to interrupt you, but I was wondering if I could bend your ear for a couple of minutes?"

Quickly excusing himself from the table, Tony joined the gentleman. As they stepped away from the juice bar, they continued to whisper in hushed tones.

Karen thought Dr. Hood appeared to be at least seventy years old—with graying hair, slow movements, and deliberately placed steps. Tony in turn was treating his visitor with respect. He quietly nodded his head as the doctor spoke and didn't interrupt until the man had finished each statement. Just as she debated whether she should excuse herself and allow Tony some measure of privacy, Karen was surprised by his sudden return.

"I'm sorry, I have to run," he announced, throwing a ten-dollar bill on the table to cover the two smoothies. "I'm really sorry, but this can't be avoided." Without another word, he turned and left the table, joining the doctor as they headed straight for the gym's side exit.

Chapter Five

*"Listen to me, mister. You're my knight in
shining armor. Don't you forget it.
You're going to get back on that horse, and
I'm going to be right behind you,
holding on tight, and away we're gonna go, go, go!"*

—On Golden Pond, 1981

Stuffing the soiled linen down into the plastic hamper, Tony continued to busy himself with a few mundane tasks while Dr. Martin Hood carefully finished dressing his wife's atrophied limbs.

"I picked the blue cotton house dress," Martin gently explained, always mindful of Olga's fondness for natural fabrics and cool colors. "Not too tight," he reminded himself, consciously omitting the first two buttons at the nape of her neck.

Watching the tired old man bend over the inert form of his wife, Tony shook his head in awe, humbled by the retired doctor's endless commitment to the care and well-being of his charge. Olga had been stricken with a terrible condition that not only caused hideous growths to form on her skull and surrounding facial tissue, now the condition also seemed to rob her of her intelligence. Still, Dr. Martin Hood had pledged the remainder of his days to her care. The man had given up his career and his freedom to make her final years as comfortable as possible. His commitment saved Olga from placement in an institution. Her life there would have consisted of invasive physical exams and tissue biopsies, as researchers studied her to locate the illusive link between normal and abnormal cell regeneration. Her condition was a medical mystery and he had saved her from this clinical torture—his level of commitment almost too much for Tony to comprehend.

"Blll… luuu… uuue," Olga slowly repeated, a thin line of drool running down her chin.

"Blue," Martin repeated, smiling to confirm her limited attempt at speech. "Your dress is a very pretty blue."

Over the last couple of years, Dr. Martin had asked Tony to visit the house at least fifteen or twenty times, yet, it was still unsettling for the younger man to be in Olga's presence. The woman somehow reminded him of a nursery rhyme gone terribly wrong.

Humpty Dumpty sat on a wall; Humpty
Dumpty had a great fall.
All the King's horses, and all the King's men,
couldn't put Humpty together again.

In Olga's case, it unfortunately looked as if all the King's men had made the attempt working blindfolded without a map.

The results were anything but pretty. There were lumpy growths protruding at the oddest angles, distorting her facial features, pulling and straining the soft tissue covering what remained of her natural bone structure. Her mouth hung agape, and her nose cartilage had shifted considerably to the right, giving her whole face a melted and twisted appearance that was very disturbing. Tony had long given up trying to look Olga in either of her eyes. He usually found his gaze focused on one of the reddish protrusions extending through her patchy white hair, and was able to avoid her watery stare.

   As husband and principal caregiver, Martin did what he could to compensate for the disease's rampant progression by scheduling quarterly surgical removal of the growths. He ordered his medical supplies through his old colleague, Dr. Clifford, at the Changeroom, and performed all the procedures on his dining room table. But the battle still seemed to be never ending, since new growth always sprouted on alternate areas of her skull. Tony had been present for one of the operations, when Martin requested Dr. Clifford's surgical assistance. It had been traumatic for all of them, to say the least. At the end of that last procedure, Tony had made both men swear never to ask him to assist in a surgery again.

   "She'll be fine now," Martin said as he pulled the knitted afghan to cover Olga's shoulders. "Why don't you finish up with the sling?"

   Tony moved toward the bed and evaluated the overhead pulley system. Originally installed upstairs in the master bedroom, Martin eventually had to move Olga downstairs to the living room; his arthritic knees had become more and more of a problem. Tony had helped with the move, and was confident that the equipment had been properly installed. "I just don't see why it slipped," he said. He picked the sling off the living room floor for a closer inspection. "There was no reason for it."

   "We were just lucky that Olga dropped onto the bed and didn't fall head first onto the wooden floor," Martin said, "She could have broken her neck on impact."

   Tony bit his tongue and gazed at the twelve-foot windows that were now shrouded in heavy drapery, permanently shut off from the outside world. Dr. Hood and his wife weren't living—they were just biding their time until one of them died. For both their sakes, Tony hoped Olga would be the first to pass away.

———————

After forcing his fingers into the stiff leather of his work gloves, Dr. Clifford slowly dropped to his knees and surveyed the mess. Mindful of possible contamination from sharp edges, he carefully swept the shards off the concrete sidewalk, dropping the broken beer bottles into the garbage bag where they joined used condoms, and a discarded crack pipe.

It was Sunday afternoon, and cleaning up outside the Changeroom's entrance was a common practice. The job was usually part of Tony's list of duties, but Marcus found himself filling in while his assistant lent a hand across town.

Only hours before, Martin had stopped by the clinic in a panic, frantic about nearly dropping Olga. He insisted that he needed Tony's help to fix the overhead sling. Marcus tried to calm his old friend down, and offered him a chair and a cup of coffee, but there was just no placating the man; he was on a mission. The best Marcus could do was to point him in the direction of the local gym.

Watching the esteemed doctor pleading for help had been disheartening; such a proud man now reduced to caring for a wife who continued to live in a near-vegetative state.

Many years ago, in what seemed to be another life, all three had held respected positions in the same hospital. Dr. Martin Hood was chief of staff in the cardiac care unit, and Olga Heinz was head duty-nurse. Dr. Marcus Clifford rounded out the group as head of the research department. Together, their education and experience had been invaluable assets to the hospital, but times had changed as they always do, and they'd all been replaced.

Marcus had been the first to leave; forced to take over the reins of the Changeroom after his uncle's untimely death. A temporary leave to support his extended family quickly backfired, as his once proud name became irreparably tarnished. The mere association with the underground, pay-as-you-go clinic finished his career with the University Hospital Research Department. After a single month, not only was Dr. Clifford no longer welcomed in his own lab, but funding for all three of his research grants just seemed to evaporate. No one was willing to have their research dollars connected with the man who was privately referred to as the *Slum Doctor*. His brilliant career was tainted by his family's legacy, the pay-as-you-go basement clinic, favored by the community's sex workers, drug addicts, and criminally prolific gang bangers.

As Marcus's personal finances dwindled, so did his marriage. His wife's interest waned in direct correlation to the zeros in his shrinking bank accounts. So with his research career over, his marriage finished, and his fate apparently sealed, Dr. Clifford gave up the fight and permanently transferred his shingle to the Changeroom's front door.

He lost contact with his peers as the years progressed. It was only by chance that Marcus ran into Olga in the waiting room of his own clinic. She'd purportedly been researching a project of her own and had been just as surprised by the coincidence.

They'd exchanged pleasantries, caught up on a few past events, and then parted ways. Weeks later, after Olga was violently mugged in a city park, and then suffered the onset of her untreatable condition, he found himself drawn back into Martin's life.

Dr. Martin Hood had been the first to renew contact. After resigning his position from the University Cardiac Care Unit, he called Marcus at his clinic to request a list of medical supplies to treat his long-time love in his home.

Marcus had happily obliged his old colleague. The resulting reunion was bittersweet as both men worked side by side to unload the clinic's van, packed to the ceiling with black-market medical supplies.

Over the years, their tight circle of friendship had grown to include Tony. His practical knowledge of carpentry, mechanics, and everything electrical proved invaluable. He'd been a great help with the construction of Olga's living environment, and his ability to keep their joint project a secret had endeared him to them all.

Marcus tied up the garbage bag, and slowly turned to walk down the basement stairs and back through the clinic's front door, when he suddenly realized that his pathway was blocked.

"Doc?" a young kid questioned with a single word.

"I don't keep any drugs in my clinic," Marcus lied, suddenly afraid that this little introduction might be leading to hold-up, an event he wasn't prepared for without Tony's protection.

"My bro's hurt. Needs your help," the hooded kid with his face shrouded in shadow motioned to the waiting car parked at the curb.

As he inched his way back toward the clinic's door, Marcus scanned the concrete steps for any sort of a weapon, something to protect himself if the rest of the gang jumped out of their ride and rushed him.

"You gonna help him?" the kid demanded, stepping up to yank on the doctor's sleeve in an attempt to hurry him along.

The youngster couldn't have been more than nine, maybe ten years old. With his face still hidden by the grey cotton hoodie, he nervously shifted his weight like a boxer preparing to punch.

"Take him to emergency, I'm just a clinic," Marcus tried to explain. "They'll be able to help him out."

"Open your door," the child barked in the gruffest voice he could muster. "We're coming in."

Ready to argue his case, the doctor instantly changed his mind, his flood of courage dissipated at the sight of the handgun whipped out of the youngster's waistband.

"What's... what's the matter with him?" he asked the kid, his eyes never moving off the firearm barely poking out of the kid's baggy sleeve.

Without a reply, the young felon waved his friends over, his neck swiveling as he scanned the city sidewalks for any sign of interference.

A group of young teenagers exited the car, and walked over en masse, supporting an injured boy in their midst.

Shaking his head, Marcus turned and unlocked the basement door, praying that he'd live to see another day.

―――――――――

Tony fiddled with the sandwich that Martin had prepared to thank him for his help. He took a deep breath and shoved the bread into his mouth. With no appetite, his stomach churning from the medicinal odors; it would take superhuman strength to get the entire offering down his throat.

"Would you like a beer?" Martin asked his guest, not sure whether Tony even liked the taste of brewed hops.

"Yes," he jumped on the idea.

Unscrewing two caps, Martin walked over to the kitchen table and gently set both bottles down. "You're going to have to excuse my manners. I find that I never entertain anymore. Heck, my nephew left the half case of beer when he stopped by over a year ago to thank me for paying his tuition."

Tony just nodded and grabbed his bottle, filling his mouth with liquid in an attempt to force down his last bite.

"I was hoping Marcus would have stopped by. I haven't seen him in weeks, but I guess he's just so busy."

"Just call him," Tony offered with a shrug of his shoulders. "I know his girlfriend Teresa is out of town, so he could probably use a little company."

His turn to taste the beer, Martin grimaced after only one sip, his palate more accustomed to the sweet taste of a well-aged sherry. Setting the bottle back on the table, he folded his hands in his lap. "I think it's great that Marcus has found himself a lady friend. No one should be alone; it's not healthy."

"Not even you," Tony added, gratefully wiping his mouth with a paper napkin as the last bite made its way down his esophagus.

"I have Olga," Martin gently reminded him. "I'm never alone."

"That's true, doctor," Tony sadly agreed, not sure how much company Olga could be in her condition.

"How about you, Tony? I still don't see a wedding ring on your hand."

"Just haven't found the right mix of brains and beauty yet."

"Well, take some advice from an experienced old man. Don't wait too long to find someone to spend your life with. Olga and I wasted too many years sneaking around behind closed doors because neither of us wanted to jeopardize our careers with a public relationship. I was a fool, Tony, and every day, I pray for just a couple of those moments back."

Tony let out a sigh, unable to find the words that might bring the doctor some small measure of comfort as he rose from his stool. "You both take care of yourselves and call me should you ever need anything else."

Martin thanked him for the tenth time, reluctantly leaning against the front door-jam as he watched his solitary guest return to the outside world.

———————————

Pulling on a second pair of rubber gloves for better protection, Dr. Clifford examined his patient. As per his instructions, the boys had stripped off the victim's jacket and shirt, exposing the through and through gunshot wound. The bullet had pierced the deltoid muscle of his right shoulder, but appeared to have missed the humerus bone. He wouldn't be one hundred percent sure without an x-ray, but he was confident enough to continue with his treatment.

"Anyone pick up the casing?" he asked, continuing to debride the edges of the wound.

"Why? You wanna pass it to the cops?" the eldest of the group shouted out, jumping up from his seat in the treatment room.

"No, no cops," the doctor reassured the kid. "I was just wondering if you knew the caliber, maybe picked up the shell. This information helps me. If I know what size of bullet, then I know what kind of damage we're looking at on the inside," he explained in a matter of fact tone without raising his head.

"I can't feel my hand," the victim finally mumbled, the first words to cross his lips since entering the Changeroom.

"That's normal." The doctor turned his head to look down into the kid's eyes. "You're experiencing nerve shock, one of the ways your body helps you deal with all the pain. Let's just check to be sure." He turned his attention down to the boy's fingers. "Can you please open and close your hand for me?'

The boy complied, his fingers easily making a fist.

Turning his attention back to the boy's shoulder, the doctor continued to probe the wound.

"You carry a cell phone, Doc?" the supposed leader asked from the foot of the exam table.

"No," Marcus shook his head.

"You want one, Doc? Maybe a new iPhone? "

Marcus began to relax enough that he allowed himself to smile. He completed his last suture before lifting his head. "Here's the way it goes, boys. All treated gunshot wounds have to be reported to the police, but since I'm really not open today, and you're not going to be writing me any kind of personal check, I won't be filing any report."

All five boys began smiling, nodding and jostling each other as they digested the doctor's point.

"Swallow these." He handed the victim two pale yellow tablets before turning to fill a paper cup with water.

"What is it?" the boy asked, looking first to his leader then over his shoulder at the hovering doctor.

"Biaxin," he stated. "It's an antibiotic. It'll help your body fight off any infection."

Silently nodding his head, the oldest, and obvious leader of the group, signaled for his wounded friend to follow the doctor's orders and swallow the pills.

"I've put another six pills inside this envelope," he said as he handed them to the kid. "Take two tonight, two tomorrow morning, and two tomorrow night before bed. Understand?"

"Yes," the boy nodded, accepting the small brown envelope as Marcus began to set his right arm into a white cotton sling.

Turning toward the leader as if addressing a parent, Marcus continued with his instructions. "In ten days, the stitches will need to come out. Just snip the top open with a pair of nail clippers, and then pull them out with tweezers or clean needle nose pliers. You can take care of that?"

"Yup."

"And if the edges get red and puffy or start leaking pus, you'll have to take him back to a doctor. You wouldn't want him losing his arm, would you?"

Everyone shook their head in unison as they watched the doctor finish up, pulling his rubber gloves off before dropping them down into the open can.

On impulse, Tony decided to first swing back around to the gym on his way to the clinic, but he debated whether it was worth running inside to check out the juice bar. Realistically, he knew there was no way in hell that the woman he'd just met would be waiting for him at their table. He'd left her there hours ago. Hell, if she had been still sitting alone, he would probably turn and run the other way; since that had all the earmarks of stalker behavior.

He slammed on the brakes anyway, and gave in to his curiosity. After grabbing the first available parking spot, he locked his car and quickly made his way inside. He felt unsure what to do and was suddenly struck with a serious case of nervousness. Stalling, Tony found himself leaning over the receptionist's desk to make idle chitchat with a woman he usually found quite obnoxious.

"Back for seconds?" the woman teased. "You already worked out once today, didn't ya, big boy?" she continued to joke around, her tone bordering on shrill.

"Just checking for something I might have forgotten. Did anybody happen to turn in a… a new red towel?" he settled on the obscure item.

"No, but maybe you wanna come back here," she motioned to the storage room door behind the front counter, "and help me go through the lost and found box?"

Tony realized it was time to move along; the receptionist was beginning to misread his presence as possible interest. "Flag me down if you find anything," he smiled. "And just for the record, last time I checked, the lost and found box was still kept at the membership desk."

With his confidence returned, Tony finally made his way to the juice bar. He grabbed a stool, ordered his usual strawberry/kiwi refresher, and glanced around the room. The table he had previously shared was vacant, covered with a few empty glasses, and discarded sandwich wrappers. There was no sign of the woman anywhere so he instructed the bartender to pour his order into a to-go cup.

This was nuts. Who was the stalker now?

He reached into his pocket to retrieve a five-dollar bill, and tossed the cash down beside his drink, just as a finger lightly poked him in the back.

"Hi there. Looks like we both had the same idea," Karen flashed Tony her most brilliant smile.

"I just wanted a juice," he stumbled, thrusting his paper cup out toward her chest.

"Me, too," she nodded, lifting her drink up from her side and wiggling it slowly in front of his face.

"I thought you'd be gone hours ago."

"I did. I mean, I was," she babbled, "but the guilt of blowing off my class was starting to gnaw on me. So I came back and picked up a later class, and then I was just cooling off before heading out," she summed up in a flourish, nervously blotted at her left cheek with the cotton towel. "Anyway, I saw you sitting here, and voilá, I decided to say hi. So, hi."

"Hi," Tony answered back, desperately hoping his face wasn't as red as hers.

"Can I sit?" Karen motioned toward a vacant seat.

"Oh shit." Tony jumped to his feet. "Sure. I'm sorry, let me help you." He reached over to yank out the stool, but his sudden burst of energy almost ripped the upholstered seat right off the metal stand.

When they finally sat shoulder to shoulder at the bar, neither knew what to say. It was difficult carrying on a conversation with a total stranger when you weren't able to see the other person's face, or gauge the response to any of your comments.

Tony suddenly realized that turning sideways on the barstool to face his guest might be the only way to continue their conversation, so he put both hands on the bar and shifted his weight.

Unfortunately, Karen had come up with the same idea at the exact same time. As her left leg slammed into his right, their kneecaps actually came together in an audible thud.

"I'm so sorry." Tony reached out to grab Karen's upper thigh, hoping that their collision hadn't physically caused her any pain. "Are you alright? I didn't mean to ram your leg with mine. I was just turning to face you." He searched her eyes for any sign of tears.

"Me too." She pursed her lips, working hard to suppress a giggle. "Hitting your leg was like slamming into rock."

"Thanks." Tony sheepishly nodded his head. "I work hard at it."

"How about mine?" Karen teased, dropping her eyes to Tony's right hand still gripping her left thigh.

"Oh fuck," he swore, yanking his hand back as if he'd just touched a sizzling hot plate. "I… I'm sorry. Again." He spun back toward the bar and grabbed his drink.

Readjusting her position on the stool, Karen took a succession of deep breaths, fighting to control her urge to laugh. Once she was sure she could speak without embarrassing herself, she blurted out the first statement that came to her mind. "Bet you wish this bar served alcohol right now!"

"You got that right, but I think we can make do," Tony announced, picking up his paper cup for another quick drink.

Karen followed suit with a succession of small sips.

Carefully spinning his upper torso without moving his legs, Tony pivoted in an attempt to face his companion. "I also wanted to say that I was sorry for running out on you this afternoon. But some things in life are just beyond our control."

"No need to apologize… again," Karen emphasized the word with a quick smile. "It's not like you stood me up on a date."

After a quick glance back at the bar, Tony suddenly turned back toward Karen's stool. "Do you wanna go out on a date with me?"

Touched by the simplicity of his request, Karen felt herself strangely drawn to the man. They knew nothing of each other, but then, that was the whole point of dating. "I have an idea," she said, "How about we each answer one question about ourselves. Then, if we're still interested, we can make a date."

"Sounds fair," Tony agreed. "You go first."

"Alright. Mine's pretty simple. Are you married or currently involved with a significant other?"

"No," he frankly replied.

"Okay," Karen smiled. "Your turn."

"Welllll," he dragged out the word. "Why did you want to know if I worked down at the Changeroom?"

Karen caught herself before spouting off some lame excuse, and opted for the truth. "For years, my friends and I have been hearing gossip that there's an underground clinic where you can have almost anything done for cash. Word is that you work there. I was just trying to get to the bottom of the rumors."

Taking a split second to debate her answer, Tony downed the remainder of his drink. "Yes, I work at the Changeroom. As for the fees and the procedures performed, well, that's all at the doctor's discretion."

Karen nodded, silently assimilating the information.

Tony felt his courage dissolving with every second on the clock, so before another minute passed and he totally lost his resolve, he turned back toward Karen. "Now that you know the truth, do you still want to go out on a date with me?"

"Yes," she smiled. "But can we please go someplace where they serve *real* drinks?"

Tony nodded his head in agreement, as he pulled out a pen and paper from his pocket. He wasn't about to trust his memory when it came to this woman's full name and phone number.

Chapter Six

"You can't handle the truth!"

—A Few Good Men, 1992

As she watched her father shave, Monica debated just when would be a good time to interrupt his concentration. She knew he hated to be bothered when he dressed for work, but there just didn't seem to be any other time. He was either working late at the office, or going to bed early with a tummy ache. He never just sat in the living room and talked anymore. She missed his company.

"What do you need, Monica?" her father asked, liberally dousing his damp face with aftershave.

"You smell nice," she smiled, enjoying the masculine scent as it wafted round the room.

"Thank you, baby. Is that all you wanted?" He dropped the hand towel into the sink and reached for his favorite comb.

"No, actually, I have something for you," she smiled, whipping out a computer-generated invitation. "My ball team is having a father/daughter game this Friday. We're gonna have a wiener roast afterwards. Can you come?" she pleaded, her tone betraying her nervousness. "I looked at Mom's calendar, there isn't anything else written down that day."

Wally accepted the folded paper from his daughter, and laid it gently beside the sink without taking a moment to open the fold. "Daddy's really super busy at work right now. I'm training a new guy and it's taking a lot of my extra time. Can't your mother go?"

"It's a *father/daughter* game," she mumbled, fighting the tears that threatened to spill down her cheeks.

"You know, if Daddy didn't work so hard, you wouldn't even be able to play ball in the first place. Money doesn't grow on trees, honey."

Monica turned and walked out of the bathroom, her question answered.

Wally quickly finished his morning routine, already running fifteen minutes behind schedule. Rushing down the stairs, he couldn't help but notice the smell of pancakes, fully aware that his wife would expect him to sit and grab a quick bite. Refusing would just escalate into an argument, possibly dragging on longer than it would take to scarf down a plate. He really had no option. So, bearing his time constraints in mind, Wally blew into the kitchen and grabbed an empty plate off the table.

"I call the first stack," he said and leaned in to peck his wife on the cheek as she flipped the cakes filling the griddle.

"Alright, they're all yours," she relented, loading the vertical pile onto his plate. "Did Monica find you? She's been pacing back and forth since the minute you turned on the shower."

"Yes, she did." Wally returned to the table, covering his stack with syrup. "Something about a ball game on Friday night? I can't commit that far in advance; you know my schedule."

"So, what'd you say to her?"

"He said no." Monica slid into her chair, eyes downcast as she refused to look her father in the face.

"I didn't say no," he corrected his ten-year-old before shoveling in his first bite. "I'll just..." He picked up a glass of juice to wash down the sticky pancake. "I'll just have to wait and see how things play out on Friday afternoon."

Still stationed at her stove, Annette couldn't help but shake her head. She heard the disappointment in her daughter's voice, her pain evident as she sat motionless in her chair. "Monica, what time is the game, honey? Maybe if your daddy knows everything in advance, he can plan better."

"I'll run and get the invitation," she jumped up from her chair, thrilled to have a minute of her father's attention.

"More?" Annette set a fresh plate down in the middle of the kitchen table.

"I'm stuffed," Wally announced, dropping his cutlery to the center of his unfinished plate. "And honey, don't build up Monica's hopes. Chances are I won't be able to make it. Better if she deals with it right now."

"Better for who?" she mumbled as Wally straightened his tie and marched out the front door.

"Mom, can you come up here?" her eldest daughter's voice called out from the upstairs washroom.

"I'm coming," Annette shouted back, quickly setting up her two youngest with pancakes and juice as they scrambled to take their seats at the empty table.

"Mommy!" her daughter's voice rang down the stairs. "I really need you."

Running up the stairs, Annette's nose was assaulted by the overwhelming stench.

"I didn't mean to," Monica wailed. "I just reached for the invitation, and I knocked it over." She began to cry. "Now Dad's never gonna show up at my ball game. He's gonna be mad for sure."

Leaning into the ceramic sink, Annette immediately saw the broken neck of the cologne bottle. The sink was flooded with amber fluid, a large quantity had obviously absorbed into the hand towel her husband had discarded into the base of the bowl.

"Go eat your breakfast," Annette urged, manually spinning her daughter around by the shoulders. "Mommy will clean up the mess and meet you at the table," she promised her.

"But the bottle. It's Daddy's favorite," Monica continued to wail. "He wears it every morning."

"Don't worry, I'll replace it. Daddy will never know," she promised.

Monica finally heeded her mother's instructions and tromped down the stairs, wiping her nose on her sleeve as she joined her siblings at the breakfast table.

Annette quickly closed the bathroom door to contain the overwhelming stench, flipped on the fan, and propped open a window. She was not totally disappointed by the accident, since she found her husband's cologne to be a little too musky in the first place. She carefully picked up the broken bottle and poured the remaining liquid out. After stowing the glass pieces and the hand towel in the garbage, she quickly noted the brand name, and then tied up the plastic garbage bag. After she scrubbed the sink, she realized that this mess wouldn't disappear in an hour. She planned to open all the doors and windows to flood the house with fresh air as soon as the kids left for school.

———————

Running yellow lights and taking every shortcut he could think of, Wally somehow managed to make up the time he'd lost when wolfing down his wife's pancakes. By eight, he finally reached the office and was able to slide into his desk just as his telephone began to ring.

"Wally Freeman," he announced into the phone line.

"I hate weekends," the voice purred. "Two days without your touch is way too long. How you gonna make it up to me?"

"Any way you want," Wally whispered back into the phone. "I couldn't get out of the house fast enough. Wouldn't you know that of all mornings, Annette decides it would be a good idea to make a batch of..."

A short cough on the line immediately suspended Wally's train of thought.

"Do you think we could possibly talk about something besides your wife and her home cooking?"

"Sorry, I didn't mean to be a jerk. I just wanted to explain why I was late."

The phone went silent.

"Are you still there?" Wally whispered; his heart pounding as he realized the error of his ways. "Please talk to me," he begged. "I need to hear your voice. I've been waiting all weekend just to hear from you, too."

"Well then, be a little more sensitive, please."

Exhaling, Wally sunk back in his chair, not realizing that he'd actually been holding his breath. "Can I buy you lunch, a long lunch? Maybe eight inches worth of lunch?"

"I have a massage at one, but maybe after work, if you're still in the mood."

"I'm always in the mood," Wally cooed. "Aren't you coming in today?"

"I called in sick. The daily grind is really starting to get to me. Actually, come to think of it, I'm more of a freelance kind of worker. You know the type. I can only produce when my muse strikes."

Being struck by a muse wasn't a luxury Wally could afford these days. His extracurricular activities were draining every penny he could spare. With the mounting bills for back-to-school clothes and supplies, he was starting to feel like he was swimming in quicksand.

"I don't know how you do it," Wally sighed. "If I miss just one day, that's just less money at the end of the month and more bickering."

"Well, I've always relied on the kindness of strangers."

Wally laughed, reminded of a line from *A Streetcar Named Desire*. "That must be my problem. I don't know any kind strangers."

"You're too melancholy for me, baby. I'm just going to say good-bye and get on with my day. You call me after work, alright?"

"I promise," Wally vowed, hanging up the telephone just as the other desks in the office bullpen began to fill with his co-workers.

———————

Freddy found that balancing an open textbook on his knees while trying to drink a large coffee and inhale two glazed donuts on a moving bus wasn't as easy as he thought. The bumps in the road jostled the Styrofoam cup, and when he wasn't blowing the flakes of sugar off his pages, he was wiping the burning droplets off his hand.

"What you studying?" a young lady sharing his bus seat leaned in to ask.

"I'm a student in the College of Medical Sciences. I want to be a plastic surgeon."

"Wow," she giggled. "Never hurts to know a plastic surgeon. My name is Amanda."

"Freddy," he smiled back, suddenly drawn to the girl's perfect features. "I don't think someone like you needs any kind of surgery."

"Maybe not now," she argued her point, "but my mom says gravity is cruel. It's the one thing a woman can't run from."

"Touché," he grinned, closing up his anatomy textbook. "What do you do?"

"I'm a model. Well, I'm *going* to be a model. Right now, I just answer the phones at a tile and flooring shop, but I've dropped my pictures off at over a hundred photographers. Mom says I'll catch my break if I don't give up." She nodded to herself, smoothing out the pile of manila envelopes stacked on her knees.

Exiting the bus, Freddy and Amanda each took their turn to step out onto the concrete sidewalk.

"I'll see you around," she called over her shoulder, sashaying down the street and eventually disappearing around the corner.

Dropping his cup and donut wrappers into the garbage, Freddy slung his knapsack over his back and began the final trek to his first class. Twenty minutes and only one wrong turn later, he found himself at the right door. He was getting better; the campus wasn't as daunting as it initially appeared during the first week.

Grabbing a seat, Freddy pulled out his notes and prepared himself for the lecture. Waiting for the professor to appear, his mind wandered back to his chance meeting on the bus earlier.

The girl's skin had been absolutely flawless. Her pores were almost invisible, the tone and skin color akin to alabaster. She was as close to a living doll as he'd ever met. And her mouth, it couldn't have been prettier if painted by a master. It had just the right fullness and curvature, without being *porn-star* pouty. He'd only glimpsed her teeth, but they too appeared ideal.

Oblivious to the professor standing at the front of the auditorium, Freddy only clued into the class beginning when the lights dimmed and diagrams began to project on the screen above the professor's head. Still unable to focus on the lecture, Freddy returned to his daydreams.

Her body looked toned; as least, her legs were in great shape from what he'd been able to see as she'd walked away. The calves were well defined, that youthful firmness that was so easily attained with minimal maintenance. But he'd have loved to get a better look at her breasts, to see if they were in proportion with the remainder of her body. There was absolutely no reason why they should be drooping on a teenage girl; his only worry was that they were disproportionate, or worse yet, asymmetrical. The rest of her body was relatively curvy, so for appropriate proportions, she needed to be carrying a large B or small C cup. Those dimensions would fill her out to the desired hourglass figure for the perfect woman.

Freddy was still daydreaming when the professor moved on to the second part of his lecture.

After she had dropped the kids off at school, and opened every window in the house, Annette decided to slip out and replace her husband's cologne. She had noticed a sale on kid's sneakers at the local Kmart, so as soon as she found the right sizes for her growing children, she thought she would drop by the cosmetic department and pick up another bottle.

An hour later, pushing a cart full of toilet paper, the kids' favorite cereal, and two dozen boxes of instant macaroni, Annette made her way to the cosmetics counter. Quickly dismissing the discount brands, she moved toward the locked display case. Up and down the rows, she scanned the bottles for just the right name.

"Can I help you?" the sales girl politely interrupted.

"Yes." Annette welcomed the young girl's assistance. "My daughter knocked over my husband's cologne this morning, and I thought I'd just stop by and replace it."

"Fabulous," the girl chirped. "What's the name?"

Opening her purse and pulling out her wallet, Annette retrieved the pink post-it glued to her grocery list. "Dolice & Gabannas," she slowly stumbled over the foreign words. "Drecars, the three point, two ounce size.

"Dolce & Gabanna?" the girl repeated with the correct pronunciation.

"Sorry, I'm not really sure how to say it," Annette explained, passing the girl her handwritten note.

"It's D & G's, Drakkar. You were close enough," she announced, passing back the note. "But I'm sorry, ma'am. We don't carry it anymore."

Sighing, Annette bent down to pick up her purchases. "Do you think they'll have it at Walmart? I was going to swing by on my way home."

"I doubt it, but I can't say for sure," the girl shook her head. "If I had to guess, I'd say your best bet was one of the boutiques downtown."

"Really? That's odd. I didn't think they'd carry brands like that."

Stepping around her main counter, the girl bent down to retrieve a fragrance manual. Scanning the lists until she finally located the desired page, she motioned for Annette to step over and have a peek.

"See here?" She pointed. "Dolce & Gabanna, three point two ounce, three hundred and ninety-five dollars."

"What?"

"That's why we don't carry it anymore. It wasn't a big seller. Personally, I find that mid-range colognes, especially those in gift boxes with soap or deodorant around the forty to fifty dollar mark are our best movers."

Annette wasn't listening. She was trying to digest the information.

Chapter Seven

"All right, Mr. DeMille, I'm ready for my close-up."

—*Sunset Boulevard, 1950*

"Kill the lights. I'm not fuckin' wasting anymore wattage on this piece of shit!" Manny barked from his vantage point.

"I'll be fine, just give me ten," the actor begged, struggling to extract himself from a tangle of naked bodies in a desperate attempt to plead with the director. "I just popped one about half an hour ago." He made a V-shaped symbol with the fingers of his right hand. "Should kick in any second, man. Please don't kill the shoot, I really need the bucks."

"Listen, you little shit." Manny closed the gap to hiss directly into the kid's face. "I need the cum shot. What you gonna do about that? You think your magic Viagra is gonna be able to save your ass today?"

When she realized they were all taking an unscheduled break,

Julia extracted her head from a crotch, and wiped the salvia off her chin with the back of her right hand. She repeatedly flexed her lower jaw in an attempt to work out the cramps.

"Ya think we're gonna finish?" Serena whispered as she struggled to wiggle out from under the pair of male thighs wrapped firmly around her neck.

"Only if lover boy can blow his load."

As Julia settled herself on the edge of the foam mattress, Serena slowly snuck back across the floor to grab her cigarettes. Both were mindful of the argument heating up in the basement's far corner.

"I don't give a fuck how bad you need the money," Manny continued to rant. "I want the money shot! And unless I get the shot, we're all fucked! Do you understand me, you little shit?"

The groan was audible, the remaining actors all verbalizing their displeasure.

"I'll do it," one of the veteran performers jumped up to his feet; cock still rock hard in the palm of his right hand.

Manny pushed the kid aside and stepped over to his latest volunteer. "I like you, Tyreek. You're always ready with the right attitude. But am I the only one who sees the fucking problem here?" he yelled, throwing his hands in the air.

Everyone stopped whatever they were doing to focus their attention on the matter at hand.

"You're black, and the kid's fucking white. We ain't filming a documentary for PBS, but I still think people are gonna notice different colored dicks! Don't you?" he shouted, pushing past another one of his *cocks for hire*.

Manny's younger brother slowly walked up beside the director, and carefully summed up their situation. "We have two choices, man. We can wait for the kid to blow his load, which could be hours if you count the number of dime bags I saw on the floor, or we could re-shoot with Tyreek in the lead. What'd ya think?"

Manny crossed his arms at his chest and ran the day's tally in his head. Five hundred for each of the five actors, another four hundred for film, light bulbs, and the new extension cord. Two hundred and fifty for set rental, and finally another hundred and fifty bucks for lube, batteries, and a set of clean sheets. That was thirty-three hundred dollars, down the fucking drain unless they were able to wrap the shoot.

"We need a Plan C." He uncrossed his arms and stared right into his brother's eyes, "Cuz your Plan A and Plan B aren't worth shit!"

"Well," his brother reluctantly sighed, "we could always fake it. Remember the time that big fucker nearly overdosed. We finished that shoot."

Evaluating his options, Manny decided that Plan C was actually his only option. "You think you can find what you need here?"

"Somebody's gotta have an extra. Give me ten minutes."

"You've got five. Now get everything ready, I'll educate our little star."

Within half an hour, not only was Manny ready to film his cum shot, but everyone was back sucking and fucking right on schedule.

"You! New girl! Move out of the shot." He waved his hands in Serena's face. "Julia, you're gonna bring this home for me, alright baby?"

"Sure Manny, I can do it," she nodded her head, confident that she could see a sweet little cash bonus on the horizon.

"Alright people," the director clapped his hands. "We're gonna wrap this up right now. You understand what you have to do?" He walked up to his young star, rubbing the kid on the back as he looked down toward his crotch.

"I'll do it if you think it'll work."

"It'll work, just do it like we showed you." He turned to walk out of camera range. "Now everybody shut the fuck up and listen to me. When I give the cue, the cameras gonna pan around the room, so I want everybody really into the moment. You hear me, Julia?" He changed his mind and walked back over to the bed. "I want you to be sucking the kid off like it's the last cock left on the face of the earth."

She nodded, taking a second to look up into her partner's eyes and wink.

"Then," the director continued to instruct, "the camera's gonna pull back to where I was standing, and that's when I want my cum shot. Make it good, sweetie." He smiled at Julia one last time. "We're running out of time, and I really need you to help me put this one in the can."

"Got it, Manny." She tucked her hair behind her ears while quickly repositioning her knees.

"Alright, boys and girls, let's make it hot," he yelled, backing out of range before signaling for the camera to roll.

Within seconds, the action was in full gear, everyone back in their original places. Still slightly miffed that she'd been pulled from the big finale, Serena couldn't help but evaluate Julia's performance out of the corner of her eye.

"That's it, take it all," the lead actor coaxed, words gurgling up from the back of his throat as Julia repeatedly managed to engulf his entire shaft in the cavity leading down her throat.

"Couple more thrusts," Manny called out from the sidelines, not at all concerned with the camera picking up his voice, since all speaking parts during the acts of sex would be dubbed in during editing to accommodate direction from the floor. "Now... cum!" he yelled, "let her have it all over her face!"

With the camera now framing only Julia's head, the actor began a succession of rapid squeezing motions, releasing spurts of cloudy liquid from the tip of the plastic enema bulb hidden in the palm of his right hand.

Closing her eyes to the oncoming fluid, Julia compensated by opening her mouth, purposely allowing the creamy rivers of goo to run haphazardly down her chin.

"Hold it, hold it." Manny held the shot. "Make it good," he encouraged the kid. "Clench you ass muscles like you're blowing your load and loving it."

The kid followed the director's instructions, obviously a better actor than anyone had originally anticipated.

"Now put a few drops on the head." He instructed the kid to spread a gob of milky mixture on his cock before the camera finished the sequence, with a final close up.

"Alright, everybody else," Manny signaled, waving the two main stars out of the wrap-up shot while the camera scanned the bed to catch the surrounding action.

Bending to grab the first available towel Julia could find in her duffle bag, she began carefully cleaning her face, mindful not to smear her eye make-up, incase Manny needed any final takes.

"Now everybody make nice and kiss... and... we're done." The director joyously smacked his brother's shoulder. "We did it. But don't move yet," Manny called out to his crew. "Just hang on for a sec until I check it out. Nobody fuck off yet until I see the playback."

As the director took five minutes to view the final scene through the camera's viewfinder, Julia took the opportunity to wrap her body in another clean bath towel.

"It looked good from where I was," Serena smiled, sucking heavily on a cigarette while standing butt naked on the edge of the set.

"Yeah, I think it'll work," Julia agreed, her attention suddenly drawn down to Serena's nipples. "You feeling any pain?"

"Little, why?"

Dropping her head down only inches from the young girl's breasts, Julia carefully surveyed her own handiwork. "I don't like the way your nipples are healing. They shouldn't still be leaking blood. The piercings should have sealed by now."

"Oh, no big deal," Serena waved off the attention. "I think they were just overly chewed," she nodded her head toward Tyreek as he bent down; carefully pulling his jogging pants up and over his erection.

"Funny how long those pills last," Julia couldn't help but notice. "But then I guess how else is a guy gonna keep it up for a two or three hour shoot?"

"That's a wrap!" a voice commanded from behind the camera, "Now grab your cash and hit the fucking bricks so we can get outta here, before I get charged double," Manny yelled at his actors as they began shuffling toward his younger brother. "And give Julia an extra hun," he called out. "The bitch earned it."

Slowly pulling the flatbed wagon, Justice carefully picked up the pots of petunias and began loading them side by side for transport. Forced to lift each potted plant by the plastic rim, he moved with precision, always careful not to over-lift and strain his incision.

"Hey Mallory," the supply supervisor called out over the hedge. "Come here for a second. I need your help."

Making his way toward his boss, Justice instantly noticed the truckload of compost slowly idling by the potting shed. "I don't have a shovel with me," he called out. "Should I go grab mine?"

"Don't bother." Eli waved him over. "Just hop in the truck."

Circling the greenhouse's ring road, Justice watched his boss scan his clipboard.

"Says here you're on light duty for the rest of the week. What ya do, throw out your back?"

"No." He scrambled for a plausible explanation.

"Well what?" His boss pried, unwilling to let him off the hook.

"I had surgery. You know… on my male parts."

Shifting gears before pursuing his line of questioning, Eli slowly bounced the truck over the Texas gate. It was a feature recently installed at all the entrances, promising to protect the maturing beds from any damage caused by foraging wildlife.

"Mallory, you telling me that you had a vasectomy?"

"Yep." Justice nodded his head, eyes still focused on the passing scenery. "So where we taking this load?"

"I thought you was one of those really religious kind of guys. Aren't you and your wife supposed to keep popping them out?" he teased, unaware of just how painful a nerve he'd inadvertently touched.

"You worry about your kin, and I'll worry 'bout mine," Justice firmly ended the line of questioning.

The remainder of the drive was completed in silence; both men seemed lost in their own thoughts until arriving at the ornately decorated gates. "Jupiter Greenhouse," the driver shouted into the estate's intercom. "We have your load of compost."

Justice waited patiently for further instructions, watching as his boss scribbled the time and date on the delivery order.

"Their own staff is supposed to be on site to unload. Guess they don't trust us little peons to shovel their precious dirt," he snickered to himself. "Love to know what a high-class gardener like them gets paid for a gig like this." He motioned to the well-manicured lawns. "Bet they ain't breaking their back for nine fifty an hour."

Nodding his head, Justice silently agreed. If the grounds proved to be just as lush as the front entrance, they'd really be something to see. Rolling down his window, he leaned his head out and inhaled a giant breath of air, taking the time to decipher the aromatic scents.

"Marigold and mint," he proudly announced, the yellow blooms commonly planted to discourage insects from entering domestic herb gardens. "I wonder if we'll be able to see their whole set up," he spoke aloud, longing to glimpse the designer gardens of the rich and famous.

"Mallory, I never met a man who likes flowers as much as you. Sure you're not gay?" he teased for the hundredth time, always suspicious of a man who knew more about flowers than any broad he'd ever dated.

"Just cuz I appreciate horticulture, doesn't mean I butter my bread on the wrong side."

"Well, you're shooting blanks now, aren't you," Eli teased as he shifted the truck into gear and began inching through the slowly opening gate. "You're not much use to yer wife now, are ya? You tell her if she needs a real man, just give me a call."

Leaning over to give his boss a friendly punch on the shoulder, Justice stopped cold and just pointed. They had entered one of the most beautiful estates in the county, and without realizing it, they were experiencing firsthand what very few had ever seen.

"Holy cow," Justice muttered, never a man to use the Lord's name in vain. "There must be at least twenty thousand dollars worth of shrubbery lining this drive."

"No shit," his boss echoed his thoughts, judging the double rows of junipers flanking the driveway to be at least fifteen feet high, running at least a quarter of a mile up the property. "What'd I say this guy's name was again?" He reached down to grab his clipboard.

Scanning the delivery order while slowly making his way up the drive, Eli nearly yanked his foot off the gas when he finally located the name. "Justice my man, we're in the company of royalty. Ya know who lives here, boy?"

"No." His eyes never left the moving scenery as he soaked up every aspect of the professional design.

"Well, this is the home of Manfred Louis II. He's the guy whose dad won that big lawsuit against the power company. Said they were electrocuting his cows and making the baby calves all distorted and deformed. Don't you 'member reading any of this in the paper?"

"No," Justice answered, still caught up in his visual exploration.

"Well," Eli summed up his history lesson. "His dad got millions, maybe tens of millions, all from the power company. Then, I heard Manfred and his old man both married playboy bunnies and it was party time every night, except..."

"Except what?" Justice finally gave Eli his attention.

"Except the old man decides to get divorced, but before the paper work is final, his wife drops dead from some kind of drug overdose. Pretty suspicious, hey?"

"Living outside God's circle of love." Justice shook his finger. "That's what happens when you're chasing the almighty dollar. It takes over your whole life. I bet these people have never been to church one single day in their lives. If you ask me, I..."

"Whoa boy." Eli pulled the truck to a stop. "We're here, so zip your lip. Nobody wants a sermon come Monday morning."

Justice heeded his boss's warning, standing by in silence as a group of estate employees overtook the delivery truck like a swarm of ants. Within ten minutes, their cargo was unloaded, and they were politely being ushered off the property.

"Thank you for calling Jupiter Greenhouses," Eli sang out, throwing his clipboard between the bucket seats before climbing back into the cab of the truck.

Justice gave a small wave, too uncomfortable to shout out any goodbyes.

"Don't you just wish that you and your wife could live up here with your kids?" Eli dreamed aloud. "Shit, if I could marry me a playboy bunny, I'd stay faithful and happy for the rest of my life.

You could take that to a bank," he swore, shoving the truck into first
gear and slowly making his way back off the estate.

Lost in their own thoughts, both men rode back to the greenhouse
in silence. Eli daydreamed of everything he longed for to make his
life complete; Justice worried about everything he might have lost
in his quest to make his life simpler.

———————

As he slowly opened the pizza box, Marcus couldn't help but grimace
at the greasy slices staring back at him.

"Enough for two?" Tony called out, taking a minute to wash his
hands before joining the doctor at his desk.

"Oh, please," he groaned, "pull up the chair and rescue me from
my imminent heart attack."

Accepting the invitation, Tony plopped down in a guest chair
and prepared to dive into the box.

"How can you look so excited about such a disappointing
meal?" the doctor asked honestly, continually surprised by Tony's
unwavering appetite.

"Didn't pay for it," he mumbled through bites, "so how can it
be disappointing?"

Tony's matter of fact attitude had to be one of his most redeeming
qualities. His spirit of take-it-as-it-comes had helped Marcus through
some of the worst times of his life. After being forced to take over the
clinic, Marcus had stood by and helplessly watched his wife, Susan,
walk out on their marriage. Tony had summed up her departure in
one simple sentence. "Well, that's one less person for me to call when
you finally die."

The simple absurdity of the statement had been like a slap in
the face. It had jolted Marcus right out of his self-pity party, and

from that moment on, he had been able to deal with the end of his marriage without falling into a deep pit of despair.

"Oh, I forgot about this." Tony dug down into his coat pocket. "This was left for you at the front door when I opened up this morning."

Even before Marcus opened the small brown paper bag, he knew it was a cell phone, courtesy of his weekend warriors.

"May I?" Tony asked, picking up the small note as it flittered to the floor.

"Help yourself," the doctor shrugged, turning over the cell phone as if inspecting a brand-new surgical instrument.

> *"Dear Doc. Thanx for the sewing. Its for you. Dont worry about the bill. Weel keep it loaded 4 ya. This is not paymint for the medasin."*

Tony turned the note over in his hand before looking up to catch the doctor's eye. "No signature, but I have a funny feeling you know exactly who the author is of this fine piece of penmanship."

Marcus just smiled, and dropped the cell phone back into the bag before setting the gift down into his desk. "Not a group I'd want to encourage—or anger, for that matter. Let's just hope this was a one-time emergency, and we won't have to deal with their problems again."

Tony nodded, piling one piece of pizza on top of the other to make their consumption that much more efficient.

"One of these nights, we're going to have to do something about that leak in the back sink," Marcus said between bites. "I thought I saw a silverfish come out of a crack in the lino, and you know how I hate those little buggers."

"Well, then pick a night," Tony surrendered.

"How about tomorrow? You can have a peek at it tonight before you leave and pick up whatever you need on the way in to work tomorrow. Then Tuesday night, we can tackle it together after closing."

Wiping his face with a paper napkin, Tony wrinkled his nose, an expression the doctor had rarely seen before. "Tuesday won't work for me. I think I'm gonna have a date."

Wiping his own hands with the remaining napkins, Marcus suddenly realized the new expression was one of uncertainty. "New girl? Anyone I know?"

"No way." Tony shook his head. "She's not a *wanna be* who dreams of looking like someone else. She's never even been a patient here at the clinic."

"So we've established what she isn't," Marcus teased his friend. "Why don't you tell me what she is?"

"She's different." He shrugged his shoulders. "I don't know how to explain it. I just think she's different.

Marcus prayed she was different; not the usual women Tony met who just wanted to use him for a free breast enhancement or a couple rounds of Botox.

Chapter Eight

"E.T. phone home."

—*E.T. the Extra-Terrestrial, 1982*

"Yes, my classes are very stimulating," Freddy said on the phone to his mother while simultaneously attempting to adjust his computer's settings.

"Are you coming home for fall break, dear?"

Surprised that she was even aware of the university's fairly new semester schedule, he quickly scrambled to uncover her source of information. "You been playing on the internet again, Mom?"

"No dear, I haven't been on the computer ever since your younger sister came home and told me I'd infested it with *cookies*, whatever in the heck that means. I honestly have no clue what that girl was rambling about. Anyway, I heard about fall break when I was visiting your Aunty Elaine. She's planning a special dinner for her daughter, and I..."

Freddy suddenly realized that he was shit-out-of-luck. His virus protector wouldn't allow him to make too many adjustments without voiding the protection. Now, where in the hell had he left his copy of Norton? Did he pack it, or was it still at home somewhere under his desk?

"Are you still there?" his mother sharply demanded.

"Sorry, just checking through my mail," he lied, pushing his chair away from his kitchen table.

"So, does it sound good?" She pressured him for a reply to her offer.

"What day was that?" Freddy began to fish, hoping his mother would quickly recap her plans.

"That's a Friday, dear."

No help, he'd have to try something else. "Who else is coming?"

"I already told you. Weren't you listening, Fredrick? There'll be Aunty Elaine's family, the Patricks from down the street, and of course your sister, and us," she summed up in a flourish.

As he poured a glass of cranberry juice while cradling the cordless phone in the crook of his neck, Freddy decided it was as good a time as ever to take a little evasive action. "You know, Mom, I take my first set of midterm exams right before fall break. The whole idea of time off is to regroup and rest. You know, take it easy?"

"Yes, I know, take it easy," she answered, not the least bit swayed by his reasoning.

"So, if I have to get on a bus and ride across state, I'm not really resting, now am I?"

"You weren't paying attention, were you?" his mother demanded, her patience beginning to wear thin. "I've arranged a ride for you with Elaine's daughter. Your cousin will pick you up and bring you home, so you don't have to worry about some horrible bus ride. How can you say no?"

How could he say no? He wasn't sure, but he was going to keep trying.

"When was the last time you called your sister? She told me she hasn't heard hide nor hair from you in weeks. Reaching out a little to family wouldn't hurt you, Fredrick."

God, how he loved these little family chats.

"One more thing," his mother rambled on, "Jennifer called again."

"You didn't give her my number, did you?" His voice suddenly leapt up an entire octave.

"I don't understand what the problem is? Jennifer was your girlfriend for the better part of two years. Why are you so adamant about running away from her now?"

Dropping back down in front of his computer, somehow comforted by the mere proximity of his laptop, Freddy hung his head in defeat. "I'm not running away from Jen, Mom. It's just over, and rehashing everything isn't going to accomplish a thing. Can't you get it?"

"Watch your manners, young man. This is your mother you're speaking to, not one of your schoolmates."

"I shouldn't have said that," he apologized, generally sorry that he'd even taken the initiative to answer the phone. Freddy handled nearly all of his communications either via text messaging, or Skype. He only relented and ordered a landline at his mother's insistence. She wasn't going to hear of any such nonsense. As far as Lucy Nally was concerned, the internet was not an adequate form of communication. She was determined to be the kind of mother who could reach out and touch base with her son whenever she wanted; not sit back and wait for some stupid little envelope to fly across the screen of the family computer to let her know she had a typed paragraph waiting for a reply.

"Jennifer sounds so lost, honey. Maybe you could drop her a card with a little note. You know, just kind of reach out to her, in friendship."

"Maybe, Mom. That sounds like an idea."

"Let me get you her new address," she offered, setting down the old wall mounted phone before Freddy could get in a word.

"She's moved upstairs from apartment number three to apartment number twelve in the Wilfred Albert residence hall. Let me see if I can find the rest of the address," his mother shouted into the air while digging through her collection of papers.

"Mom, Mom, it's alright. I know the address," Freddy repeatedly argued into the phone the moment his mother picked up the receiver. "I have it from the mail you forwarded to me, remember?"

"Do you think I bother you?" his mother suddenly blurted out the question.

"Mom, where's this coming from?

"Your sister said that sometimes I force myself on her. Do I do that to you, too? Do I invade your life, Frederick?"

"Mom, I really have to study. I've got a pile of notes to decipher, and it's already seven o'clock. Can we maybe do this another night?"

"Yes," she chirped, somehow comforted by the change of topic. "I'll be looking forward to seeing you at fall break. Take care; and we all love you, sweetie."

"I love you too, Mom." Freddy gratefully hung up, vowing never to answer the landline again.

––––––––––––

Wally watched the bullpen slowly clear of bodies, and anxiously waited for his small window of privacy. He had about half an hour, before the swing shift started filling the desks, and in those thirty minutes, he planned to finalize his plans for the remainder of the evening.

"Night, Freeman," the last voice called out before clearing down the hall.

Standing up and walking around his desk, Wally quickly checked the empty halls. When he was confident that any remaining managers were sequestered behind their office doors, he turned and trotted back to his workstation. Carefully dialing from memory, Wally's eyes darted around the room while he waited for the phone to be answered.

"The party you have reached is presently unavailable. Please leave your name and number and your call will be returned as…"

Wally hung up the phone and quickly redialed the number.

"The party you have reached…"

He dialed for the third time.

"The party you…"

That was it; he'd had enough of this bullshit! He was a grown man and he was damned if he would sit in an empty office afterhours and play a high school version of telephone tag. He was going home to his family. They'd be thrilled that he was home on time for dinner, and with a little coaxing, he was sure his wife would be up for whatever he suggested after the kids were asleep in their beds.

But there was only one problem. He didn't want anything from Annette.

"One more time," Wally muttered to himself, quickly dialing the number before his resolve faded.

"Hello baby," a sultry voice finally replaced the monotone of the answering machine.

"What were you doing," he demanded, adopting a tone as if speaking to one of his own children.

"Why?"

"Well, for starters, I must have phoned you at least ten times. You know I have a limited window for privacy."

"Don't whine, Wally. It doesn't become you."

His earlier frustration at not being able to make contact now boiled over into hostile resentment. "I just phoned to say I'm going home to see the kids. Haven't been spending enough time with them lately, so I thought I'd stop by my house and have a quiet family supper." He brandished the information like a weapon.

"Well, well. Doesn't that just sound like a little slice of heaven."

Wally felt his confidence suddenly evaporating.

"You know, I was actually thinking of doing the same, except my parents are spending the next couple months in Las Vegas. They keep inviting, and I just keep putting them off. But now that you mention it, it might not be a…"

"Baby, that's not what I meant," Wally scrambled to slap a band-aid on the hurt feelings. "I was just feeling a little put-off. Like my call wasn't important."

Only silence greeted him on the line.

"Can we please get together? I don't care where," he offered, willing to drive across town if necessary.

"I don't know. I'm not really feeling all that sociable right now."

Suddenly, all Wally wanted was to meet up. He couldn't imagine having to go home and face his wife. He'd beg if he had to; he didn't care. Their relationship was almost becoming an addiction, and he couldn't imagine another twenty-four hours without his fix.

"Alright, I guess we could meet for a drink. How about Maxwell's?

"I'm still in a suit and tie from work. I didn't bring a change of clothes. You know I'm gonna stand out. Hell, the bartender's gonna think I'm there to check his liquor license."

"Look Wally, if you wanna blend in so bad, why don't you just pack up your little brats and take your whole damn family down to McDonalds for a Happy Meal?"

Decision made, he unknowingly bowed his head. "I'll be there in half an hour."

"Make it an hour. I still have to blow dry my hair."

Hanging up the phone, Wally collapsed into the upholstery of his vinyl chair, exhausted by the mere act of making plans.

"Wally Freeman, is that you on the phone?" a man's voice called out from down hall.

"Yes sir, it is," he answered back, instantly recognizing his supervisor's head poking through the bullpen's door.

"Good, come here," he motioned. "I have something I need to talk to you about, and now I won't have to chase you down tomorrow."

He reluctantly followed.

"Have a seat, Freeman."

Wally's head began to pound. Not usually prone to migraines, he suddenly felt as if the top of his skull was visibly pulsating.

"Let me get to the point..." His boss stopped mid-sentence to light a cigarette; obviously choosing to ignore the office's no smoking policy. "You've been drawing a salary bonus each pay period for your work in our trainee program. Unfortunately, upper management is not satisfied with the results and has decided to discontinue the program."

"You can't." Wally leaned forward in his chair, both sets of knuckles turning white under the pressure. "My family counts on that extra pay. Is there maybe something else I can do around here to earn that check?"

Chugging down a swig of black coffee between drags on his cigarette, his boss seemed to be searching for just the right words. "You've been here just over two years, this fall. Am I right?"

"Sounds right."

"Well, you were hired and then trained to be a salesman. Nobody ever promised anything about bringing you on as a fulltime trainer for a monthly wage. We hired and trained you to make sales—to bring up the monthly bottom line. Am I right?"

"I know, and I really appreciated the opportunity that I was given, sir."

"Well, that's all fine and dandy. But I'm a little concerned about your future. I've been sitting here all afternoon trying to figure out how to justify even paying your base salary. And to be honest with you, son, I haven't been able to come up with a decent reason."

"You're firing me?" Wally jumped to his feet, the colors in the room beginning to spin.

"Sit down, sit down." His boss motioned from behind his desk. "I didn't say I was going to fire you today. It's just that your totals for the last quarter have been really low. Actually, you've got the lowest totals for any of our salesmen, day and night shifts combined," he admitted with a shrug of his shoulders.

"But, I was…"

"I know, I know." He ground out his cigarette just in time to light another. "You've been busy training, and that's why you've only sold twelve prearranged funeral packages in the last ninety days. Am I right?"

"Absolutely, sir."

"So, let's just stop dwelling on the totals from last quarter." He pushed the manila folder to the side of his desk. "What are we going to do about this quarter?"

Once again, Annette had fed the kids and cleaned up the kitchen before her husband was anywhere to be seen. It was getting so bad that he didn't even bother to call anymore, his absence had somehow become the norm.

"Mommy," a voice called out from the basement playroom.

"Monica won't let me watch Tree House. I always watch my show before bed."

Leaning over toward the basement railing, Annette began to yell, "If I have to come down and settle this little squabble, the television is going to be shut off and you can all go straight to bed!"

Silence.

Satisfied that she had thwarted the conflict, Annette went back up to the master bedroom. She wasn't sure what she was looking for or why she had chosen to start in their bedroom, but something told her it was as good a place as any.

Opening the small notepad she'd grabbed off the fridge, she began to jot some ideas down. The first clue would definitely have to be the Dolce & Gabbana cologne. What married man working on commission and struggling to make ends meet spends three hundred and ninety-five dollars on cologne? It just didn't make any sense. Unless...?

Annette jumped off the bed and rushed down the stairs to Wally's den. After flinging open the bottom drawer where he kept folders of their monthly bills, she scooped up the last six months and dropped down into his chair. Page by page, she slowly scanned the papers, looking for any other signs of extravagant spending.

Half an hour later, not only had she failed to locate a receipt for the cologne, she actually hadn't spotted anything out of the ordinary, Wally's desktop now littered with utility bills, grocery slips, and gas receipts. He had clipped together all the slips of paper according to method of payment, but they held no discernible secrets. Embarrassed by her motives, Annette quickly reassembled the files, and stowed them back into their respective slots.

"What ya doing?" Monica asked from her vantage point in the den's doorway.

"Sorting papers. Is everything alright?"

"Daddy called. He's working late—again," her daughter sarcastically tossed in as an afterthought.

"I didn't hear anything." Annette stopped and looked toward the desk's phone.

"I was talking to my friend. He came through on the other line."

"Okay," she nodded, turning her attention back to the remaining files.

"Are you going to tell Dad about Friday? Cuz the coach says as long as he's there by six, he'd probably be fine."

"I'll tell him, sweetie," Annette smiled back in an attempt to encourage her daughter. "I just hope you're not too disappointed if he can't make it."

"I'll be fine, Mom, don't worry about me."

Annette *was* worried about Monica, just as she was worried about all her children. The last few years had been rough on them all, but knowing that she and Wally were struggling through it together had somehow given her the strength to carry on. She honestly didn't know what would happen if it all turned out to be a lie.

Sucking back the vodka and orange soda now sloshing around in his travel mug, Wally continued to fight the late afternoon traffic. Everyone was in a rush, gunning their motors and honking their horns; they all inched forward street by street in an attempt to make their way back to suburbia.

Without looking at his watch, he already knew he was forty minutes late. Ignoring strict policy against ever making personal calls on his company cell phone, he'd intermittently kept dialing ever since he'd left his work.

"Come on, come on," he growled, praying that the phone would magically start flashing and vibrating to alert Billy to his call. But it was no use. Nobody was going to hear a cell phone in a crowded bar. He'd just have to get his ass down there as fast as possible.

"Five bucks," the bouncer demanded, not even bothering to look Wally in the eye.

"I'm not staying," he tried to explain for the second time.

"Five bucks, or fuck off!"

Fishing out a handful of singles, he threw his cash on the coat check counter and made his way inside.

Country music poured down from wall-mounted speakers, as Wally squinted, as though closing his eyes would somehow block out the mind-numbing guitar riffs. He walked the main floor and scanned the faces of the happy-hour patrons.

As he crossed the empty dance floor and made his way into a new station, one of the waitresses shouted into Wally's face, "Manager's in the back." His business attire obviously sending her the wrong message.

Wally ignored her as he had most of the other patrons' stares, and frantically continued his search. Table after table of jeans clad, beer swilling, good ole country boys filled the saloon floor. For the life of him, he couldn't imagine why he was jeopardizing his marriage to hang out in a place filled with men and women whose idea of dressing up was to brush the mud off their shit kickers. It was definitely time to leave.

"Looking for me?" a familiar voice whispered in his left ear.

Wally's heart began to pound, his back snapping straight as if zapped with ten thousand volts of lightening. "Billy." He spun around, instantly yearning to wrap his arms around his young lover and lose himself in his unending desire.

"What the hell took you so long?" the young man demanded, his hands now resting on his slender hips.

"I got called into a meeting with management. They're cutting my training bonus immediately. I'm back to base plus commission," he complained, watching Billy's eyes wander with lack of interest. "Do you know what that means? In one afternoon, I've lost a third of my wages."

Reaching out and gently brushing the lapel on Wally's suit jacket, Billy slowly lifted his chin, and leaned in as if asking for a kiss. "Let's get back to my table."

Spell broken, Wally shook his head and began to take stock of their surroundings. "I guess you're right," he conceded, not the least bit comfortable with the neighboring table's attention.

Settled in the back of the country saloon, Wally quickly climbed up on an empty stool, and purposely positioned himself so his knee could rub Billy's thigh in the shadow of the tabletop.

"So, how do you like this place? I was thinking about making it our new meeting spot." Billy couldn't help himself from teasing.

Wally motioned the waitress over, and quickly ordered two Bloody Marys with salted rims.

"But I'm drinking beer," Billy announced, obviously intent on making a scene.

"Fine," Wally muttered through clenched teeth. "Please bring us two Budweisers instead."

"And two glasses of tomato juice," Billy smiled. "We just love tomato juice." He reached up and gently stroked Wally's cheek.

Making notes on her pad, the waitress shook her head and left the table, wondering if she'd get paid for the beers before one of the regulars opened a mess of hurt on the two pretty boys.

"Why we here?" Wally demanded under his breath. "This isn't exactly the kind of place I had in mind."

"You said you're always afraid of running into someone who might know Annette. Well, I think it's safe to say you're covered in here."

Scanning the room, Wally released a deep sigh. "I guess, but why a country bar?"

"I can't resist a cowboy in tight jeans," Billy slipped his hand under the table and gently rested his fingers on Wally's right knee.

Heat rising up from his chest and pooling in the redness of his cheeks, Wally unconsciously shifted his weight back and forth on his barstool. His need to be intimate with Billy began overriding his common sense, and before he realized exactly what he was doing, he'd clamped his hand down over his lover's fingers and was grinding Billy's palm into the meat of his own thigh.

"I just wanna be with you. Can't we leave?"

"Our drinks are here. Let's enjoy," the twenty-four year old announced, instantly taking control of the situation.

When Wally reluctantly stood to extract one of the few twenty-dollar bills remaining in his wallet, he couldn't help but notice the stares and whispers beginning to circle their table. "You know," Wally casually mentioned as he returned to his perch, "I have three quarters of a bottle of vodka left in my car and I was thinking a little road trip might be fun."

Slowly filling his glass with the chilled beer, Billy carefully added just the right amount of tomato juice to suit his palate. "For starters, you don't drive a car. You drive a family van. And second off, road trips are for high school kids."

Forgoing the juice, Wally downed a good third of his bottle, feeling more and more uncomfortable by the minute.

"Besides," Billy announced, "I wanna dance."

Wally's last swallow of beer froze in his throat.

He'd seen Billy act up before. He'd done it one night as they'd both sat together in a booth at a local steak house. When the waitress had innocently asked if they wanted separate checks, Billy had flipped his lid and decided to make a point. For the remaining half of their dinner, while Wally uncomfortably choked down his rib-eye, he had also fought off his date's wandering hands. Billy had suddenly been obsessed with letting every man, woman, and child know that they were a romantic couple. To this day, Wally still cringed every time he drove by that restaurant.

"Well, I'm not in the mood to dance." Wally rose from his stool, setting down the half-empty bottle of beer.

"You'd feel better if we had some shooters," Billy decided, quickly raising his hand to summon the waitress. "Can we order two *Buttery Nipples*," he winked at the young girl as if sharing some private secret.

"We're out of shooters," she bluntly announced.

"What?" Billy leaned around her shoulders to catch a glimpse of the heavily laden shelves mounted behind the bartender's back.

"That's fine," Wally nodded, buttoning up his suit coat as if chilled by a sudden rush of cold air.

"No, it's not!" Billy argued. "Then you can bring me a white wine spritzer?" He crossed his arms and glared at the waitress.

Turning toward Wally, hoping to make eye contact with any ally, the waitress dug down into her denim apron and extracted a ten-dollar bill. "Drinks are on the house," she dropped the money back down on the table, "but take my advice and hit the bricks."

"Like fuck," Billy sneered. "I came here for a good time, and I'm not leaving until I'm damn well good and ready!"

"Yes, you are," Wally argued, leaning over and hoisting his date off the stool and onto his feet. "Thank you for the beers." He nodded at the waitress, noticing a group of burly bouncers leaning against the shooter bar, ready to jump into the action at the slightest hint of a problem. "Keep the ten, we appreciate the heads up."

Just as Wally began to steer Billy across the floor and back out the saloon's main doors, the waitress suddenly had a better idea, only stopping a second to shove the ten into her apron.

"Go out the back door," she announced, pointing to a well-concealed exit, just eight feet from where they stood. "Less traffic," she offered with a shrug of her shoulders.

Without another word, Wally and Billy silently made their escape, obviously aware of the hostility beginning to brew in their wake.

Chapter Nine

"Fasten your seatbelts.
It's going to be a bumpy night."

—All About Eve, 1950

H e'd not only made Wally stop for clean plastic glasses, but had also demanded a bag of crushed ice and unsalted taco chips. Billy did not like giant cubes floating around in his drink or the after-effects salted snacks had on his tender lips. He was, by all accounts, extremely high maintenance.

"Do you think this is a good place?" Wally squinted through the windshield, trying to read the words peeling off the side of the dilapidated building.

"Sure, why not. If we're gonna run and hide like rats, might as well settle in and have a drink with them," Billy swung open the van door and slipped out into the darkened back alley.

"Billy, where you going?"

He never answered; he just took large gulps of his drink while curiously surveying his surroundings.

"Please come back inside," Wally pleaded, debating whether he'd need to step outside to coax his boyfriend back into the comfort of his van. "You're going to catch a cold," he warned, mindful of how much Billy detested a runny nose.

Without a word, Billy finally relented and hopped back inside, turning his body sideways to eye the box of windshield washer fluid still balanced on the padded backseat. "Wanna get more comfortable?" he smiled, setting his plastic cup down into the dashboard holder.

"Let me move that box." Wally instantly jumped into action, downing his remaining drink before jamming his empty cup between the seat and the floor mat.

Squeezing between the van's two buckets seats, Wally twisted his upper body sideways to snatch a quick kiss from Billy's lips. He then scrambled over the vinyl-padded consol and landing with a thud on the back seat. "Just a sec," he promised, planting both his knees on the bench seat as he lifted the cardboard box. "I'll just set it back here," he said with a huff, the air forced from his lungs as his solar plexus pressed against the upholstered back.

As a huge grin spread across Billy's face, he quickly shrugged off his leather bomber jacket and forced his own slender shoulders between the van's buckets. He threw his body directly on top of Wally's, effectively pinning him as he continued to struggle with the wiper fluid.

"Hey, let me turn around," Wally chuckled, instantly excited by Billy's unannounced attack.

"Stay still," he commanded. With his hands roaming up and down the curves of Wally's ass he yanked at the fabric of his suit pants.

With his breath now coming in ragged gasps, Wally dropped the case of fluid on the van's floor and waited.

It didn't take long for Billy to move his fingers up toward Wally's waistband, his right hand freeing the leather belt from the confines of the silver buckle.

Still facing backward, Wally searched for something to hold on to, finally settling on the seatbelts straps hanging off the bench of the third seat. He wrapped his fingers around the nylon, and braced himself, not even sure what he was preparing for.

After unbuttoning Wally's pants and then unzipping his fly, Billy roughly yanked the suit fabric and briefs down to Wally's bended knees. He paused for a second to rub the erection growing in his own denim jeans. Billy then abruptly reached forward through Wally's legs, and cupping his naked balls, he slowly began to massage them in the palms of his hands, well aware of his rock-hard erection pushing against the fabric of the seat.

"Your hands are so... so cold," Wally groaned, his voice almost failing him as he struggled to hold his position.

"Don't talk," Billy barked, pulling back his left hand to spank Wally's bare butt cheek roughly.

Dropping his head in a heated flash of pleasure, Wally began to bear down on the back of the seat, his teeth gnashing at the piped edging.

Billy took a second to fish a condom out of his front pocket, unzipped his pants, and freed his cock. He expertly positioning the latex sheath over the head before unrolling it down the length of his shaft.

Conscious of what was probably happening behind his back, Wally sucked in a succession of deep breaths. On one hand, he hoped that Billy would be gentle; on the other hand, he prayed that he would not. With no lubrication to smooth the entry, Wally couldn't help but shudder in pain; his spine arching as he threw his head back toward his assailant.

Billy continued to impale him forcefully with every single stroke, callously disregarding his lover's discomfort. There'd been no warning, and very little foreplay, just Billy's single-mindedness as he mounted an all-out attack. And tonight, he was taking no prisoners. "Take it all," he growled, as he clamped his hands onto Wally's shoulders, the grinding of his hips, forced his boyfriend's chest back toward the seat.

Billy's cock was tearing Wally in half; the un-lubricated entry ripped at the soft lining of his anus, his sphincter muscles holding tight without any warning from a lubricated finger or teasing tongue. Billy was anally raping him, and he was in agony. He was finally living out his wildest fantasy.

"Can you take it?" Billy shouted without missing a stroke, his own legs and back beginning to cramp in his awkward position.

"I... I... I..." Wally just moaned, unable to verbalize his feelings.

"That's what I thought you said, bitch," Billy groaned, his own climax nearing with every thrust of his hips.

Eventually, the jabs of pain in Wally's rectum had faded, replaced by a general numbness. Within three or four more strokes, the numbness had evolved; the sensations were now tickling his cock and rapidly igniting themselves into strokes of pleasure. By the time Billy was nearing explosion, Wally was grinding his ass back into his lover's pelvis, gyrating and rocking his hips for maximum penetration.

Billy had moved his hands from Wally's shoulders and was now firmly guiding his attack. Hands clasped on each hip, Billy pulled his cock all the way out and then forcefully plunged it back in, each time forcing his swollen head back through the tight opening of Wally's quivering ass.

"Fuck me," Wally finally groaned, "I can take it."

Throwing his head back, Billy began to release his load. As the tip of his condom filled with the pulsating bursts of cum, his body stiffened, ceasing to move. Still pressed up against Wally's back, he rode out the waves of his climax in silence.

When he felt his lover begin to explode inside his ass, Wally froze, already trained to hold still while Billy shot.

"Holy shit, that was good," Billy finally moaned. He carefully extracted himself, disgusted with the soiled condom hanging limply off the tip of his cock; he moved to stretch out the cramps in his legs.

When Wally realized that Billy had dropped down onto the seat, he unclenched his fingers, and flexed his hands as he clumsily spun around and dropped to sit beside him, his suit pants now falling down toward his ankles.

"What's that," Billy motioned toward Wally's erection, his sexual appetite obviously insatiable.

"It's for you," Wally whispered, his voice suddenly hoarse.

Pulling the used condom off his cock, Billy leaned forward and dropped it in an empty drink cup, amused at how it strangely adhered to the plastic sides.

"Do you wanna suck on me?" Wally asked, not sure if he was asking for more than he deserved.

"No," was his only reply. He obviously had another idea. Turning to face Wally, Billy straddled his thighs, slowly tilting his pelvis forward as he lowered his own body down on the top of Wally's swollen erection.

"My condoms are in the…"

Billy silenced Wally with a searing kiss, his tongue exploring the depths of his lover's mouth. "I'm gonna fuck you bare back," he announced, the words ringing in the confines of the van.

"But…"

"But what," Billy groaned, shifting the rim of his ass and setting it down just above the head of Wally's cock. "It's my ass, it's my risk."

Wally's head began to swim. He knew that the greatest risk for contracting sexually transmitted diseases fell on the receiver, their exposed anal tissue an easy absorption target for any lingering viruses. But there was still some risk for the giver, and he wasn't sure he was ready to gamble with those odds. "I'd still feel better if..."

All his protests were silenced the second Billy dropped down on top of his cock. Wally's firm shaft impaled his lover's anal tissue as the brute strength of the erect cock held the head straight upwards, forcing Wally's swollen penis directly into the twitching hole of Billy's ass.

"Oh God," Wally moaned, throwing his head back, his mouth agape as he struggled to suck in mouthfuls of air. He'd never fucked anyone before without some form of lubrication and the sensation was mind-blowing. Whether it was his wife, or a girl from his single days, the female vagina always tended to self-lubricate, making the passage easier, somehow more accommodating. But with Billy riding his cock, Wally seemed to be forcing a new passageway with every stroke.

Bracing his hands on the back of the van's seat, Billy continued with his ride, too wrapped up in his own pleasure to notice Wally's sudden revelations.

"It's soooo tight," Wally groaned, suddenly afraid that no other sex would ever feel as good again.

Billy just nodded, groaning his response as his own sticky cock bounced up and down off the muscles of Wally's stomach.

"Blow your load in me," Billy commanded, his position of dominance never wavering.

Wally obeyed, opening his eyes to enjoy every second of the moment as he threw his arms around Billy's chest and pulled him down hard onto his cock. Thrashing together, both men rode out the climax, bodies writhing together as Wally emptied his hot load into Billy's grinding ass. Oblivious to their surroundings, they both collapsed in a naked heap, hearts pounding, and lungs gasping for breath.

By the time they had regained their composure, and finished cleaning off their bodies with the box of his kids' wet wipes, it was nearly ten o'clock. After a quick drink to bask in the afterglow of their sexual acrobatics, Wally sped off to drop Billy at his apartment.

Home by eleven was much too late for a weeknight. The truth was, Wally actually worried about Annette's reaction. He would have some serious explaining to do, and by his calculations, he only had another ten short blocks to concoct the ultimate story.

―――――――――――

As Justice Mallory listened to his wife splash around in the bath, he knew that she was preparing her body, hoping her husband would be interested in warming their marriage bed.

So far, he had avoided physical intimacy ever since his vasectomy at the Changeroom. Unsure whether he it was pain or riddled with guilt, he just knew he wasn't interested in making love.

"Do you want me to save the water?" Sarah called out from behind the bathroom door.

"I showered," he sharply answered.

Wrapped in a floor-length bathrobe, Sarah Mallory stepped out of the bathroom to continue her evening routine.

"I think I'm going to make a pot of coffee," Justice announced suddenly.

Sarah quickly twisted her head toward her husband, surprised to see him rise and leave their bedroom. Justice stumbled into the kitchen, deep in thought, unaware that he was standing motionless in the pitch black.

"What's the matter?" Sarah whispered behind his back, having silently followed her husband through their apartment's darkened halls.

"I'm just not ready for bed. Thought coffee might, well…"

"It'll keep you up, is what it'll do. Let me boil you some milk." She stepped around him and reached into the refrigerator to retrieve the carton before flipping on the light switch.

He watched Sarah set a small pan on the stove, and then he relented and dropped down onto a kitchen chair. He was exhausted—physically and mentally—too tired to attempt putting his feelings into words. But he had to try; he needed to make Sarah understand. "When you say you always wanted a big family, how many did you exactly have in mind?" he asked.

"I don't know God's plans," she answered simply. "Time will reveal what he has in store for us. Be patient," she smiled, gently tousling his hair.

"You know, a lot of people these days are only having one child. We already have three. Guess compared to most, that's already a big family."

"Compared to most?" Sarah repeated. "Since when have we started comparing ourselves to *most*? We are not here to be the norm, we are here to please God; and through his wisdom, he will plan our family. God will decide if our number is three, or six, or nine."

"Nine kids?" Justice barked, the mere thought sending a shiver of fear up his spine. "Nobody can expect a man to raise nine kids in this day and age."

"Relax," Sarah attempted to soothe him with her calming voice. "I just picked a number out of the sky. I really don't believe God would expect you and me to raise nine children."

"He better not, cuz he'd have a pretty harsh surprise if he did."

"Justice Arnold Mallory," his wife said as she stepped over to deposit the cup of warm two percent milk on the table in front of

him, "We will accept and be grateful for whatever gifts God chooses
to bless us with, and we'll never question his divine wisdom. Will
we?" she demanded in a rhetorical tone.

Pushing his cup aside, he silently motioned for his wife to join
him at the table. "Sarah, you know what I make down at Jupiter
each month. There's only two guys making more than me, and one
of them is the owner's nephew."

"I've never complained."

"No, you haven't, but you and I both know the money ain't that
great. We're still living in a rental," he waved his arms toward the
apartment's living room," and it doesn't look like it's gonna change
real quick."

"We'll make do," Sarah rose from her chair, ready to lean over
and plant a loving kiss on her husband's forehead.

"But that's just it," he argued, rising up from his position to
prevent her show of affection. "I'm sick and tired of making do. Can
you tell me when we'll finally get ahead?"

Turning on her heel, she busied herself with the cleanup, and
struggled to understand her husband's sudden change of heart.
They'd always lived their lives by God's plan—material wealth was
never a dream they wasted much effort on. What in the world was
he suddenly talking about?

"I love our kids," Justice suddenly announced, as if his
commitment had ever been an issue. "It's just that I think our family
is big enough."

Sarah dropped her dishrag in the sink and quickly spun around,
the look in her eyes warning Justice that he'd triggered a sore spot.
*"And God blessed them, and God said unto them, be fruitful, and
multiply, and replenish the earth, and subdue it, and have dominion
over the fish of the sea, and over the fowl of the air, and over every living
thing that moveth upon the earth.* Genesis, Chapter 2, Verse 28," she
quoted, hands on hips, lips pursed in anger.

By the time she was twenty-two, Sarah had studied hard enough to memorize the entire book of Genesis. Without a doubt, Justice truly believed Sarah would conquer the remainder of her Bible before she died. After all, her mother had named her after Sarah, wife of Abraham, who lived a fruitful and God-fearing life until the ripe old age of one hundred and twenty-seven.

"You don't have to quote scripture to me." Justice moved back to the table and reluctantly took his seat. "I know as well as you do what it says. I've been living my life by the written word ever since the day I was born. Reading or not, I know the Bible, too."

"Then why are you questioning the teachings? Contraception is not an issue for us to discuss, Justice. God will take care of those decisions."

He wasn't talking about condoms and birth control pills, he was talking about his vasectomy, and he had absolutely no idea how to broach the topic. "Sarah honey, remember back when we had our son and the doctor asked us about circumcision?"

"Absolutely," she nodded, the mention of her first pregnancy ushered in a flood of pleasant memories.

"We never argued," Justice pointed out, "cuz we'd already made up our mind before you gave birth. We knew that our son was going to be circumcised."

"Genesis, Chapter 35, Verse 22," Sarah nodded. "Of course we knew what to do. The Bible had already told us."

"But that's what I'm saying. Where does the Bible tell us that we have to keep on having babies? We were fruitful; we multiplied. We have three great children, Sarah, and I really think it's enough!"

"You don't want me anymore?" the tears began to well in the corners of her eyes.

"Oh baby, that not what I'm saying." He jumped to his feet and rushed over to his wife's chair, pulling her up into his arms. "Look at me, Sarah," he coaxed, gently raising her chin with the fingers of his right hand. "I do want you. I want you when you're bathing the kids in your nightgown and it gets all wet," he shook his head. "I want you when I wake up in the morning and you're snuggled tight into my back. I want you all the time, but I'm scared to touch you, cuz Sarah, I just don't want to take a chance and get you pregnant again."

"But that's not our choice," she argued back, her wide-eyed innocence breaking Justice's heart.

"Yes it is, and I took care of it," he blurted out. "I had a vasectomy."

Sarah seemed to melt in his arms—not the warm and fuzzy kind of melting when a person is overwhelmed with waves of passion—she was melting as if fainting, the spirit draining right out of her body.

While brandishing his flashlight like a weapon, Wally continued to search the floor of his van, frantic to erase any clues as to his evening. Having already tossed out the plastic cups, the empty vodka bottle, and the dripping bag of ice, he was confident that he had accounted for most of the incriminating evidence. Scanning the carpet one last time for any lingering pieces of condom wrappers, Wally decided he'd done the best he could. He quickly jumped back behind the wheel, pulled out of the gas station, and drove the remaining two blocks home. After shifting the van into park, he took a deep breath and forced himself to gather his composure. He was about to walk into his house without so much as an empty file folder and try to convince his wife he had been selling pre-paid funerals. It was weak and he knew it.

He unlocked the front door, pulled off his shoes, and slowly began his ascent to the master bedroom.

"Wally, is that you?" Annette called out from bed, her back

propped up by a stack of pillows as she worked on the weekly menu plan.

"Sorry I'm so late, but I had to..." Wally stopped short, his sense of smell suddenly overwhelmed by the stench of their bedroom. "What in the hell stinks so bad?" He wrinkled his nose, rushing over to fling open the bedroom window.

"You can still smell it? I can't," Annette answered. "I thought I'd already aired it out."

"What is it," Wally gasped, fanning his nose with the palm of his hand.

"Monica accidentally knocked your cologne into the sink and the bottle broke."

"My cologne? What was she doing with my cologne?" he demanded, his good mood quickly evaporating.

"It was an accident," Annette reminded him. "And before you get all high and mighty, you might want to explain to me what you were doing with a four hundred dollar bottle of cologne, when we can barely afford to buy the kids new running shoes?"

Stopped short in his tracks, Wally stalled by stepping into the bathroom to survey the damage while his brain scrambled for a plausible answer. "It was a gift," he admitted, which actually happened to be the truth.

"A gift," Annette repeated, rising from underneath the covers to move closer to her husband. "Who gave it to you?"

"Billy, you know—my trainee? He gave it to me. Someone gave it to him and he couldn't stand the smell, so instead of wasting the cologne, he brought it to the office and told me to take it home."

"That's quite the gift," his wife muttered. "You know, I felt so bad for Monica that I stopped by the store to replace the cologne before you came home, and was absolutely shocked at the price. Who in the world spends that kind of money?"

"Not me. That's half a month's mortgage," Wally teased, enjoying their common ground.

"You hungry? I saved you a plate."

"Sounds great," he smiled. "I'm gonna grab a quick shower first."

As Annette left the bedroom to warm her husband's leftovers, Wally quickly closed the bathroom door and stripped off his clothes. Throwing everything in the hamper except his suit coat and pants, which he'd later toss in the dry-cleaning bag, he turned and moved directly into the hot stream.

The minute his hair and body were touched by the water, Wally could smell Billy's intoxicating man smell. The dampening of his skin seemed to release the scent of sex, rising up from the hairs in his crotch; the aroma instantly transported him back to his van. Within the blink of any eye he was there, bent over the seat as his lover's giant cock slammed into his ass, filling him with unspeakable pleasure.

"Don't start without me," Annette giggled, dropping her robe to the floor as she moved without invitation into the back of her husband's shower. "I didn't think you'd be up to sex after the hours you put in today, but by the look of things I was wrong," she giggled, slipping her dry arms around Wally's slippery chest.

Dropping his face to catch a glimpse of his own cock, Wally was surprised by his erection, positive that his body would be just as exhausted as his brain.

But not nearly as surprised as Annette, since the moment she reached out and lovingly circled her fingers around her husband's penis, it instantly began to wilt in her hand.

Chapter Ten

*"Louis, I think this is the beginning
of a beautiful friendship."*

—*Casablanca, 1942*

T ony stood in front of his bathroom mirror buttoning up his shirt, and for the third time that morning, he appraised his image. He wasn't a pretty boy by any stretch of the imagination, but he wasn't exactly unattractive either. He was rugged.

Years back, Tony had overheard a woman once describe him in that context and over time, it had just somehow stuck. Since he usually towered over most people at six foot four, and weighing in at a solid two hundred and twenty-five pounds, the average stranger regarded Tony as just a muscle bound brute. Very few took the time to ask him his opinion, and for those who did, his answer carried little weight.

His girth had come in handy on a few occasions when patients of the clinic had lost their cool or slipped into drug-induced frenzies.

Wrapping his burly arms around a tweaking speed freak had worked wonders; his human strait jacket was able to secure the patient while the doctor rushed forward and administered whatever sedative he deemed suitable.

His basic duties at the Changeroom had evolved over the years. He was originally hired to intake patients, and keep order in a somewhat chaotic environment, but he found himself slowly migrating toward a larger range of clinical responsibilities.

Tony DeMarco had never been formally trained in the medical field, but he still managed to exude a sense of knowledgeable authority over many of their walk-in clientele. Under no stretch of the imagination did he remind anyone of a doctor or a nurse; he was just a guy from their own neighborhood. Tony had grown up on the same poverty-stricken streets as most of the patients who walked through the clinic's door, and they all seemed to sense it immediately. He was one of them, and they respected him for it. This fact somehow managed to bridge the gap between Dr. Clifford's medical expertise, and the unusual wants and needs of their cash-paying clientele.

He quickly unbuttoned the cotton shirt that snugly covered his muscular back, stripped off the material, and tossed it down on his bed. Since he was planning to take Karen to a movie, he figured something with a little stretch might be a better idea. All he needed was to pop a few buttons on their first date and walk out looking like a caveman.

Showered, shaved, and finally dressed, Tony headed for the Changeroom. He planned to work until noon, the then he would head out and meet up with Karen. Nervousness didn't quite sum up his emotions. Experience had taught him that dating wasn't something he excelled at, and no matter how hard he tried. Tony accepted the fact that it would more than likely be their first and only date.

"Marcus," he called out. "It's just me."

"I was wondering what was taking so long. But now I have my answer," the doctor smiled; nodding his head as he quickly appraised his employee's appearance. "You have plans later?"

"Yes," Tony answered in a single word statement.

"Date?"

"Yep. A lady from the gym," he exclaimed with a sigh, suddenly wondering what in the world he was thinking. "I should cancel."

"Why in the hell would you do that?" Marcus teased, continuing with his task of sanitizing the examination table. "You can't spend the rest of your life working at the clinic and lifting weights down at the gym. Hell boy, look at the size of you," he raised his spray bottle and motioned toward Tony's upper body. "You're starting to look like... like a..."

Crossing his arms at his chest, Tony leveled a questioning look at the doctor, daring him to continue with his train of thought.

"Like a solid brick wall. How's a woman going to cuddle up to you when she can't find any soft spots?"

After dropping his arms and chuckling aloud, Tony walked over and poked his finger into the doctor's abdomen. "Looks like you're soft enough for us both, old man."

"Anyone there?" a man's voice called out from the waiting room, his footsteps quickly moving toward the procedure room's swinging doors.

"Stay put!" Tony barked. Suddenly all business, he turned and rushed off to intercept whoever had entered their doors.

"She needs a doctor!" the man demanded in a very deep voice, crouching over an unconscious form.

"What's the emergency?" Tony asked, forcing his hands into a set of extra large rubber gloves.

"She's unconscious, and she needs a doctor. Go get 'em." The man straightened his back, fists already balling up.

Sucking in a deep breath, Tony slowly moved across the floor, eyes quickly evaluating whether or not the man was brandishing any sort of concealed weapon. "You tell me what the problem is, and *I'll* decide if I'm gonna call the doctor," he firmly stressed his point.

"It's my daughter, Tisha." The man's resolve began to weaken, concern softening his voice. "She's a junkie, and I was trying to detox her. But it's ain't working." He suddenly reached up and wiped his eyes. "If I take her to the hospital, they're gonna call probation. They'll know she's violated again, and they'll put her back inside."

With the man's heartfelt confession still hanging in the air, Tony decided he trusted him enough to step forward and check out the patient,

"Tisha goes back in, and she'll be back on the heroin. I gotta keep her out or she's gonna overdose and die."

Tony quickly leaned in and checked her breathing. Shallow, but rhythmic. "Are you sure it's heroin?" he demanded, instantly concerned with the dry blood crusted around each of her fingernails.

"Why? You think I'm lying?" he shouted in amazement. "I'm telling you, my girl's a junkie. I wouldn't make that shit up. No father would!"

"Relax man," Tony straightened his back to face the father. "No one's calling you a liar, I just need to know if it's really heroin. That's all," he nodded, firmly patting the man on his shoulder. "Now help me carry her into the back."

As Dr. Clifford cautiously stood by watching Tony for any signals of danger, both men gently set the girl on the clinic's examination table.

"Overdose?" the doctor asked, immediately gloving up before taking any steps toward the patient.

"No. Forced detox," Tony bluntly stated. "Father says heroin, but I say not."

"But it is heroin," he continued to argue. "She told me it was. Why would Tisha lie?"

"She's a junkie," Tony stated in the simplest of terms, as if that was enough to explain the most deceitful of behaviors.

"Crack?" the doctor spoke aloud, immediately noticing the girl's bloody fingernails.

"That's my guess," Tony stepped past the father before moving in for a closer inspection. "Let's check out her arms," he suggested, drawing everyone's attention downward as he freed her upper limbs from her nylon baseball jacket.

"She's been so itchy." Her father shook his head, turning away as if sickened by the condition of her tattered skin.

"Cocaine bugs," the doctor confirmed, lifting up her right arm for a closer inspection of the bloody rips and tears.

"Bugs? Tisha's got some kind of bugs?"

"Metaphorically speaking." Dr. Clifford turned away to pick up his stethoscope. "Extreme withdrawal symptoms from a stimulant such as cocaine will sometimes manifest as a crawling sensation directly underneath, or at the surface level of the skin. Junkies will literally rip themselves wide open in an attempt to pluck out the bugs. Some have even been caught carving their limbs open with pocketknives or broken glass. It's quite a sight." He shook his head to clear the images.

"Heroin addicts can get itchy blood, too," Tony threw in as an afterthought. "But the scratching is not as severe, usually only leaving scabs or bruises. This is definitely more like cocaine bugs." He nodded to himself, confident with his preliminary diagnosis.

As the doctor quickly established Tisha's vitals, Tony began the tedious job of cleaning her wounds. Some already showing signs of infection, he wondered just how long her father had her stashed away under lock and key.

"Your daughter is extremely dehydrated," Dr. Clifford spoke

aloud. "She needs fluids and a massive dose of electrolytes. I assume she's been vomiting?"

"Everywhere," her dad confirmed.

"Tony, why don't you get the girl's history? I could really use a heads up for treatment purposes," the doctor suggested.

Finishing up with his last swab, Tony set down the bottle of alcohol and turned to the patient's father. "Let's go into the waiting room and grab some coffee. The doctor will take over from here."

Reluctantly following Tony's lead, Tisha's father found himself standing in the middle of the clinic's waiting room. Five or six needy patients already filled plastic chairs.

"I'll be with you guys in a minute," Tony announced to the anxious crowd. "Have a free coffee and just hold tight."

Since everyone appeared to be momentarily satisfied with the announcement, Tony turned his attention back to the patient's father. "Come have a seat at my desk," he said and motioned toward an empty chair.

"I don't have a lot of cash," the man announced. "I brought what I could spare."

"Well, then let's just fill out one simple form and figure out what kind of treatment you can afford."

Reclining in her bath water, Karen slowly raised each leg and dripped heavily scented oil drops down onto her wet skin. Still smooth as porcelain from the previous week's wax, she enjoyed the sensation as she slowly massaged the slippery bath oil round her muscular calves.

"How much longer?" a voice called out from the other side of the door.

She sighed her regret, dropped her legs back into the water, and sat straight up. "I'm done. You want the water?"

As her roommate stumbled into the bathroom, eyes still partially closed, hair stuck to one side of her head, she suddenly stopped to take stock of the situation. "Just you in the water?"

"Does it look like there's anyone else in the bathroom?' Karen couldn't help but tease Alicia.

"Fuck off," her roommate finally smiled, blinking her eyes as she fought to adjust to the florescent lighting. "I'll take a bath."

Rising up, Karen reached for a towel, wrapping herself in the cotton before stepping out onto the mat. "I'm going to make coffee. You got time for a cup?"

"Just one," Alicia answered, which usually meant she already planned to be ten minutes late for work. "So tell me, who's the guy?" Her roommate couldn't help but tease, eyes instantly noticing the open vial of custom blended oil lying empty at the side of the tub.

"First date. Not much to report at this stage." Karen wrapped a second towel around her head before reaching for her robe.

Alicia yanked her tee shirt off headfirst, and dropped it in the middle of the bathroom floor. As she turned, Karen noticed a fresh set of bite marks, high on her right shoulder blade. "You still dating that freak?"

"He's not a freak," Alicia laughed. "He's just an active lover."

"Maybe you should have feed the poor guy first." Before Alicia could answer back with a snappy retort, Karen strolled out of the bathroom. As she busied herself applying a complete layer of body lotion in her bedroom, Karen never noticed the man leaning against a kitchen counter, silently watching her re-hydrate her skin through the partially open door.

"You missed a spot," he snickered, turning to refill his empty juice glass.

"What the hell," Karen cursed, snatching up her discarded bathrobe off her bed attempt to cover her naked silhouette.

"Relax babe," the guy tipped back his chin to down his second glass of apple juice. "I'm not going to jump you. I was just waiting for Alice to finish in the can."

"Alicia," she articulated.

"Alicia," he repeated with a grin. "We're gonna grab a bite down at Denny's. Wanna tag along?"

"No, thank you," she quickly declined, carefully backing out of his line of sight.

"Suit yourself. I was gonna buy."

No longer interested in even making small talk, Karen tightly cinched the terrycloth robe around her waist and marched back into the shared bathroom.

"Good, you're back. Can you pass me my razor?" Alicia asked, soapy hand already reaching out from the edge of the tub.

"Why didn't you tell me he was still here?" Karen hissed, picking the razor off the edge of the bathroom sink and throwing it into the center of the tub.

"God, you're wound up tight." Alicia bent down to fish for the plastic handle. "What's up? Job interview? IRS audit?"

"Only the date," Karen reminded her roommate before dropping down onto the seat of the toilet. "He's kind of unusual, and I'm not really sure we have anything in common, but…"

"Unusual, like one-eyed unusual?" She asked for clarification.

"No, nothing like that. We just come from two different worlds. But he seems so honest, so straightforward. I'm kinda drawn to him."

"It's a date. Not marriage, right?"

"Right," Karen confirmed.

"Then pull your head out of your ass and try to enjoy yourself. And hey," a thought suddenly dawned on Alicia as she quickly swiped the razor over each of her soapy armpits. "I bought a new box of ribbed Trojans. You should try them. They're hot."

Nodding her thanks, Karen once again excused herself from the bathroom and quietly slipped into her own room. Alone, behind a locked bedroom door, she finally felt comfortable enough to drop her bathrobe. She stepped to the full-length dressing mirror, and began evaluating her naked reflection.

Her breasts were good, a firm C cup with nice pink nipples. Her sculpted shoulders and well-toned upper arms were also positive attributes, a definite asset in the summer, wearing tank tops and spaghetti straps. One hundred stomach crunches and two hundred daily leg lifts had produced washboard abs and tight inner thighs. All in all, Karen knew she was attractive.

That was, until one looked closer.

Since the sixth grade, when all the girls began sharing a communal shower room, Karen had noticed that she wasn't exactly built like everybody else. The right side of her labia minora was slightly enlarged, almost as if one lip was noticeably swollen or inflated. All three of her previous boyfriends swore it wasn't an issue, neither of them particularly conscious of the irregularity.

Karen didn't believe a word of what they had said. Whenever she took stock of her body, it was a deficit she couldn't correct. No amount of exercise would work it off and no amount of testimonials regarding its normalcy would change her mind. She was deformed, and that's all there was to it!

It haunted her. Whenever she worked out, she would reach a point where her muscles began to ache and she felt like pulling back. Then, she would visualize her deformity, and would keep going. It never failed to spur her on. She knew she had to be perfect everywhere else just to compensate for her one glaring inadequacy.

Bending to snatch a clean pair of bikini underwear from her laundry basket, she quickly stepped into the panties. What in the world had ever made her agree to a date with a physical specimen like Tony? She must have been momentarily insane.

Chapter Eleven

"Houston, we have a problem."

—Apollo 13, 1995

Rolling over in bed was usually little more than a subconscious act, yet this morning Serena was greeted with a jolt of pain so powerful it actually made her yelp out loud. Since she had passed out naked, face down on top of the blankets in Julia's bed, she had barely stirred during the last five or six hours. Somehow, she managed to adhere to the bedding in her sleep.

After sucking in a succession of deep breaths, Serena finally summoned enough courage to look down at her breasts, shocked to find fresh blood tricking down from her swollen nipples.

"Oh my God," she cried. She covered her aching breasts with a crumpled pillow. "Julia, are you awake?" she screamed, her voice echoing through the one bedroom apartment.

"Fuck me. What's going on?" Julia stammered, shaking her head as she sat up on the couch in an attempt to focus on her surroundings.

"It's my boobs," Serena shrieked, yanking the pillow away from her chest to expose the sight of her torment.

Julia reached for a cigarette, and took a minute to light a smoke before struggling to her feet. Slowly rubbing the sleep from her eyes while Serena nervously bounced on the balls of her feet, Julia finally felt coherent enough to chance a closer inspection.

"You've got one hell of an infection," she winced, wrinkling her nose at the mere sight. "Open the blinds. I need more light."

Tears running down her cheeks, Serena dropped the pillow and shuffled toward the living room drapery, carefully lifting her arms to yank them open. Shuffling back, she nervously sank down into the couch.

"Alright, let's see what we got," Julia motioned for her guest to wiggle in closer. With the fog clearing and her brain beginning to function on a normal level, Julia quickly realized this wasn't your average first-aid situation. "Looks like you've got a really, really, bad infection."

"And it's bleeding, too," Serena cried, as if Julia had been able to miss the obvious. "What do I do? It hurts?" she wailed, hot tears continuing to stream down her cheeks.

Her face only inches from Serena's nipples, Julia began to inspect the damage thoroughly. "I'm no doctor, but you better hit the medi-center. Looks like you might have blood poisoning."

"How do you know?"

"Look at your veins," she pointed to the faint red lines snaking away from the young girl's areolas. "You're in pretty bad shape."

Serena bowed her head, screwed up her courage, and gently squeezed her right breast with both hands. With a slight twist of her wrists, she was able to turn her nipple upwards toward the light. "It's dripping pus," she mumbled, shocked by the sight of her own body.

Julia snatched a tissue off the coffee table, and tentatively dabbed at the crusted scabs, instantly rewarded with a fresh rivulet of milky fluid. "Get dressed; you're going to see a doctor."

"I don't have any health insurance," Serena gently dropped her breast. "I can't go to any emergency room, and I ain't fucking heading down to the county hospital. They'll just make me sit for twelve hours before some fat old nurse lectures me on safe sex. I'm fucked," she began sobbing at full volume.

"Grab your shit," Julia finger combed her hair into a quick ponytail. "This place is for people just like you and me, and they *only* take cash."

―――――――

As he nervously paced the Changeroom's waiting area, Tisha's father adamantly refused to relax. He watched the patients come and go through the clinic's door, so he couldn't understand why his daughter's treatment was taking so long. "Hey Tony," he called out, taking three long strides toward the intake desk. "How's it going back there? Is the doctor almost done with Tisha?"

"Sit down, Jack. You're even making me nervous, man." Tony motioned again to the empty chair.

"I'm sorry, but I have to work the afternoon shift and I need to get Tisha home and settled before I leave. I'm seriously running out of time." He wrung his hands in his lap.

"Well, I told you ten minutes ago that Dr. Clifford wasn't going to release your daughter until he'd pumped her full of fluids. So as soon as the IV is done, you'll probably be ready to take her home. Just give him another fifteen minutes, alright?"

"Okay," he nodded his head, silently convincing himself that he'd be able to wait. "Can I ask you a couple questions?"

"Anyone else need to fill out an admittance form?" Tony shouted over Jack's head.

No one stepped forward.

"Shoot," Tony said as he leaned back in his chair and crossed his arms at his chest.

"Well, do you think a real junkie can actually clean up and quit shooting?"

"Sure, anything's possible," Tony assured the man. "Especially if she really wants it."

"What if she doesn't want it?"

Tony leaned forward while simultaneously lowering his voice. "You can't keep your kid locked up forever. Someone eventually will figure it out and blow the whistle on you."

"But…"

Tony held up his hand and instantly stopped the man's rebuttal. "Look, I know it's for *her* own good, and you're probably saving her ass from jail or the streets, but the law is the law. They'll eventually end up locking *you* away and setting *her* free."

The father rubbed his chin, scrambling to regroup his thoughts. "What about some kind of treatment like methadone or that new one, uhmmm," he struggled to recall the medicine's name. "Bupey… buprey…?"

"Buprenorphine," Tony corrected him, pulling open one of his desk's side drawers to extract a file. "It's not really that new, just another less harmful substitute for heroin. The addict still has to want to kick the habit. Besides," Tony reminded Tisha's father, "your daughter is a crack head."

"Heroin or cocaine. What's the difference? Dope is dope, right?"

"No man, it ain't." Tony shook his head, handing Jack a couple of government-sponsored pamphlets. "Heroin is an opioid. When you snort it, inject it, or smoke it, your brain changes the heroin into morphine and this gives the addict the desired high. Unfortunately, with time, they become immune, and the high is replaced by a crippling chemical dependency."

"Shit, you talk just like a doctor," he shook his head, staring down at the pamphlets as if they were written in Greek.

"Your daughter is addicted to cocaine. It's a stimulant and an appetite suppressant. When she injects it, snorts it, smokes it, or even inserts the rocks up her butt, she'll feel a euphoric sense of happiness and increased energy. You know, bouncing around the house like she doesn't have a care in the world?"

"Yeah, I know," he agreed. "When she was stoned, I couldn't even get her to sit down long enough to eat a bowl of soup."

"Well, that's the difference between coke and smack. One brings you down to a state of complete mellowness," he waved his palms horizontally across his desk, "and the other sets you off and flying."

Folding the pamphlets in half before stuffing them down into his shirt pocket, Jack turned his complete attention back to Tony. "Well, if they have treatments like methadone and that burey... whatever, for heroin addicts, what they got for cocaine?"

"Nothing really yet," he shrugged his shoulders. "They're working on a couple," his eyes dropped to scan his own file. "GVG, a drug used to treat epilepsy is in trials, and a couple others whose bloody names are too hard to pronounce. But as we sit here right now, we got nothing," he reluctantly closed his file. "I've heard good things about Cocaine Anonymous. You know, that spiritual twelve-step program?"

Laughing aloud, Tisha's father threw his hands in the air. "You think my Tisha's interested in sharing her story down in some church basement? The only thing on that girl's mind is her next fix. She lives and breathes dope. That's it, nothing else matters. Not school, not work, not even her baby girl." The man looked away, fighting to regain his composure.

Tony remained silent; from experience, he knew that a verbal response was not necessary.

"Do you know that when I found my Tisha this last time, she'd been sleeping under a hot air vent behind a drycleaners? I don't think she'd changed her clothes or washed her body in weeks. She stunk, Tony." He stopped to brush fresh tears from his eyes. "My little girl actually stunk up my car so bad that I had to rent a steam cleaner to shampoo the back seat." He put his hand to his mouth, compelled to make one final confession. "There were these little black beetles crawling around on her... You know what?" he pointed down toward his own crotch, "I think they were attracted to the blood, from her period." He lowered his eyes and his hand. "Have you ever heard of anything so disgusting in your life?"

Tony had, but it wasn't the time to share.

"I want my daughter back," Jack quietly moaned, "but don't know how to do it."

Tony noticed another patient's departure from the clinic's back room, so he gently pushed his chair out from behind his desk and stood up to straighten his legs. He casually slid a box of tissue in Jack's general direction. "McAndrews," he called out, scanning the room for the next patient.

"Me." A guy stood up, cradling what appeared to be a broken arm.

"Your turn," he nodded, leading the patient past his desk and directly into the back examination room.

————————

A twenty-seven dollar cab ride later, Julia and Serena extracted themselves from the back of the taxi and made their way down the steps to the clinic's front entrance.

"Where are we?" Serena muttered, cautiously looking back over her shoulder as she followed Julia in her descent down the stairs.

"It's called the Changeroom." Julia yanked open the main door.

"Cash talks, bull shit walks. Now move." She stepped aside to hold the door open. Motioning for Serena to grab a seat in a white plastic lawn chair, Julia toddled up to the front desk; casually shooting a quick glance at the man seated in the intake chair.

"Julia, is that you babe?" Tony smiled the minute he reappeared from the back.

"You bet your ass. How's the *Terminator* doing?" she teased with a wink, taking a second to run her fingertips casually down his left bicep.

"I'm fine, sweetie." He stepped forward, and gently ushered their conversation away from his desk. "What brings you down here? You feeling alright?"

"I'm tight," she smiled, porn terminology for feeling fine.

"AIDS test?" he guessed. "Need your work card updated?"

"No, it's a co-worker, my… friend, I guess," she stumbled to pin a label on Serena. "Her nipples are really infected. I think she might have blood poisoning."

When he turned back to his desk to grab a blank form, Tony immediately noticed that Tisha's father had moved off. Now standing alone by the coffee urn, he slowly sipped a fresh cup of brew.

"Fill out the basics." He handed Julia a clipboard. "You know the routine, so we'll skip the little interview. She got fifty bucks? Half for the exam, half for a prescription?"

"Covered," Julia nodded, accepting the pen and paper. "How long's the wait?" she inquired, already scribbling information onto the form.

"Give me a sec," he reassured her. "I think I can do a little shuffling."

By the time the worried father had loaded his weakened daughter into the back seat of his car, Tony had made room for Serena in his lineup.

"Thank you for everything," Jack rushed back inside to shake Tony's hand.

"Take it easy man," he nodded with a smile, knowing in his heart that the father's problems were far from over.

After dropping Tisha's form into the day's *completed* file, Tony motioned toward Julia. "All right ladies, first class seating in the back," he teased.

Rising to follow Tony, both girls' high heels clattered across the basement floor, neither aware of the stares following their departure.

"Nice outfit," Tony couldn't help but tease his old friend.

Glancing down at her black sequin tube top and silver spandex Capri pants, Julia couldn't help but laugh. "We were at a wrap party, crashed, and then came here first thing. Guess we forgot to change," she snickered, turning to catch a glimpse of Serena, who stood shivering in what appeared to be nothing more than a man's cotton dress shirt and four-inch pink stilettos.

"Dr. Clifford," Tony stepped forward to introduce the girls, "this is my friend Julia, and this is her friend, Serena."

"Nice to meet you," the doctor smiled, a little confused as to whether the women were Tony's visitors or the clinic's patients.

"Doctor, Serena has a possible nipple infection and was wondering if you would take a look," Tony explained, slowly ushering her forward.

With the confusion cleared up, the doctor looked around the room to see if Tony and his friend were going to leave before the examination. Once he realized that everyone was staying put and obviously not hung up on issues of privacy, the doctor gloved up and stepped over to Serena. "Why don't you have a seat, dear?" He motioned to the paper-covered table. "And unbutton your shirt for me."

Settled on the cold vinyl, Serena nervously looked to Julia for support. Julia reciprocated with her best supportive smile.

"May I?" Dr. Clifford asked before gingerly peeling back the cotton shirt.

"Sure," she suddenly looked away as the doctor leaned in for a closer inspection.

"Can you tell me what happened to your breasts," he asked, reaching for a cotton swab to move the swollen nipples gently.

"Well, I kinda… well, it was late… and uh…"

"Serena and I were cracked out and we pierced them with a dirty sewing needle," Julia summed up in flourish, turning to drag over an empty examination stool.

"Let's take your temperature." The doctor reached for his ear thermometer, worrying that the young girl might be on the verge of shock.

"So." Julia turned her attention back to Tony. "How's it hanging?"

Julia knew exactly how Tony was *hanging*, since they'd made at least a dozen movies together when he'd been in his early twenties.

Back in the beginning, Julia had been only sixteen years old when she'd broken into the porn industry. Armed with a fake ID, and a bottle full of her mother's stolen Valium, she'd found the courage to drop her clothes and allow men sometimes twice her age free rein over her body. By the time Tony had made her acquaintance, she was an eighteen-year-old seasoned pro, known for her ability to keep the camera rolling. Julia was a girl who could roll with the punches, literally.

Motioning for Julia to follow him out of the exam room, Tony abruptly turned down a back hall and led her directly to a private lunchroom.

"Replay?" she teased, alluding to more than one of their sexual encounters.

"The waiting room coffee tastes like slop," he casually explained, as he ignored her advance. He swung open a door leading into a small seating area. "Thought you might want something to drink while you wait for your friend, and I couldn't let you fill a cup with that other crap."

"Me and Serena haven't really known each other that long."

"She one of Manny's girls?" Tony bent over to pour two steaming mugs of almond flavored special roast.

"Looks like it's shaping up to be that way. But to be honest, she's not really that good. A little naive, if you know what I mean."

Adding cream with no sugar to both cups, Tony passed Julia a ceramic mug. "We were pretty green once, too. She'll wise up."

"That's the problem," she slowly raised the cup to her lips. "She's already filming hardcore, full anal, and still didn't know anything about douching. She's totally out of her league and only worried about the money. I'm afraid that girl is gonna say yes to something that going to fuck her up real bad without even knowing what it is."

"You're not her mother, you know," Tony reminded his friend.

"I know, but she's so damn young."

"Let's go back out front. Can't leave the natives alone too long or they'll riot," he joked about the clinic's clientele.

Settled back in the waiting room, Tony quickly excused himself to check on the doctor's progress.

Flushing the freshly lanced pus pocket with antibiotic solution, Dr. Marcus reached up to pull the rolling light stand as close as possible. "I'll be putting two stitches in each nipple, but don't worry, there shouldn't be any scarring. Breast tissue is remarkably resilient. Although fairly thin, it heals rather quickly. And let me know if you can't handle the pain. I've given you as much lidocaine as I dare with the drugs you've already ingested."

"Ouchhhh," Serena wailed, attempting to muffle her own cries by shoving a balled fist in her mouth.

"Half done." The doctor patted her shoulder. "You want me to take a break, or start debriding your left side?"

"Just... get it... over with," she whispered through ragged breaths.

"Another couple minutes and we'll be done," he gently promised.

"How ya doing, sweetie?" Tony seized the opportunity and stepped up, hoping his sudden appearance would take Serena's mind off the procedure.

"This really hurts," she cried, closing her eyes as the doctor finished lancing her left breast.

"Bet you won't pierce yourself again," he teased.

"No way," she tried to laugh through the tears. "Where's... where's Julia?"

"You can bring in her friend," the doctor spoke up, "We're almost done, and I think the patient might need a little help getting dressed."

Signaling Julia to follow him back through the doors, Tony stood his ground and waited for her to join him.

"She all done?"

"Just about," Tony nodded. "She's really crying a lot. Looks like a fair bit of pain."

"Couldn't knock her out?"

"Guess he was afraid that with all the other stimulants racing through her blood stream, anything more than a topical injection of lidocaine might be dangerous. You'd never know for sure if she was going to have a drug reaction and stroke out right on the table.

Grabbing Tony's elbow, Julia quickly spun him around. "I know we're both from the same neighborhood, but shit man, every time I come here you sound more and more like a fucking doctor."

"So I hear." He turned and steered Julia toward her reunion.

Chapter Twelve

"There's no place like home."

—*The Wizard of Oz, 1939*

As he sat, sipping his second cup of coffee at the kitchen table, Justice lost count of how many trips his wife had made down to the basement laundry room and then back up to their apartment. Whether or not her arms were laden with baskets, she still somehow managed to slam the apartment's door every time she went through it. He'd taken about all he could handle, and he'd be damned if he was going to spend his one day off listening to his wife stomp around their apartment. "Sarah, come here," he called out.

"What is it?" she barked back, head buried in the hallway linen closet.

"I said, come here!" he shouted back, leaving little doubt as to his intention.

She stomped into the kitchen, and Sarah threw her back against the far counter, crossing her arms as she waited for whatever her husband was ready to dish out.

"Come and sit." He pulled out a kitchen chair. "You look like you're ready for a fight, the way you're standing over there."

She was, and sitting down wasn't going to change her mood.

"Come, come," Justice encouraged his wife, pushing away the cream and sugar to make room on the kitchen table.

"What do you want?" she repeated for the second time. "Going to make another announcement? Maybe you've decided we're getting divorced now?"

"For Christ's sake, Sarah."

"Don't you ever take the Lord's name in vain in my house!" She stepped over and waved her finger in his face. "You may have abandoned your faith, but I will not!"

Jumping to his feet to meet his wife's eyes, Justice did something he'd never done in his entire life. He gave the woman a shove and kept walking.

Then it was his turn to slam the apartment's door.

———————

After locking the clinic's front door a good hour before, Tony had finally weeded the remaining patients down to one last broken wrist.

"Where's your cast?" Tony couldn't help but ask, remembering the guy's initial visit from the week before.

"Job interview, had to cut it off," he winced, rising from his chair to walk over to Tony's desk.

"Did you get it?"

"No." The young man slowly lowered himself into the intake chair. "Wanted at least a second-year electrical apprentice. Didn't seem to matter to that asshole that I've been pulling wire since I was a kid, and can change out an electrical panel with my eyes closed."

Shaking his head, Tony scanned his desk for a pencil. "Guess you can't write with your bum arm?"

"Nothing legible," the patient confirmed.

Tony copied down the man's information from the driver's license, and made a few final notes. "So you want another cast, Jimmy? Maybe one with a zipper?"

"That'd be handy," he agreed, turning his head to appraise the empty waiting room. "You know, I've never seen your clinic like this before. Usually you guys are stuffed to the rafters."

"Closing early today. The doctor and I both have other commitments," Tony briefly explained as he rose from his chair. "Sit tight, I'm gonna check to see if Dr. Clifford has time to cast you."

Tony was about to interrupt the doctor while he methodically collected all his metal instruments and dropped them one by one into a stainless steel bowl when he stopped for a second to watch the doctor work. Life would be much simpler if they could just afford a few of the basic medical conveniences. An autoclave would have been at the top of Santa's wish list. No more messy chemical sterilization; creating antiseptic tools would be as simple as filling the machine and allowing the pressurized steam to do the trick. Even a second hand x-ray would have been a bonus; the doctor would no longer have to theorize whether the injury was a multiple, hairline, or compound fracture. The list was endless, and unbeknownst to his employer, Tony spent a large chunk of his days off, scouring used supply stores and internet supply companies for any deals they could afford.

"Before you wrap up, do you think you have time to recast a broken wrist?"

"Are we sure it's broken?" the doctor asked, reaching down into a locked cabinet for a plastic jug of phenol.

"Yes. We casted the guy last week, but he cut it off before a job interview."

"Did he get the job?"

"That's funny," Tony snickered. "I asked the same thing."

"Well, bring him in," the doctor relented, setting the unopened bottle down on the counter.

"Want me to mix the plaster?" Tony offered, already quite adept at the procedure.

"Yes. But prep him first. I need to make sure we have enough cotton wrap before we start."

Settled on the examination table, sling off, and shirt removed, the patient watched Tony and the doctor both buzz in circles around his position. Thought they rarely spoke, and worked in the confines of a ten by twelve foot exam room, they never once even stepped on the other's toes.

"You know what you guys remind me of? You remind me of the Packers," Jimmy snorted aloud, "and it looks to me like your running plays out of some secret handbook."

Amused with the analogy, Dr. Clifford walked over and gently picked up his patient's arm, re-evaluating the break. "You're still pretty swollen Jimmy. If you cut this cast off, I can't guarantee how your wrist is going to heal. You don't want to end up on an operating table, do you?"

"No sir," he vigorously agreed. "This time I'll keep 'er on for the duration."

Tony approached with the bowl of plaster, while the doctor organized his strips of cotton.

"You'll have to take it easy for another eight to ten hours until this plaster cures, and Tony," the doctor called over his assistant, "I want you to show Jimmy how to fold a proper sling while I set up this cast. You could have choked yourself with that last contraption," he good-naturedly teased his patient.

"Hey doc, can I ask you a quick question?" Jimmy asked.

"Fire away," he answered, slathering the first layer of white plaster over the initial wrap of cotton.

"It's about my wife. She's not herself these days."

"How so?"

"Well, she forgets the clothes in the washing machine 'til they get moldy, and sometimes when she goes for groceries, she can't even find her own car."

"Memory loss can be triggered by a whole range of conditions. Sometimes it's as simple as the patient self-medicating when they unwittingly mix their prescriptions from different physicians. Other times, it can be as serious as Alzheimer's or arterial blockage. I can't even make a guess without a proper history and a battery of diagnostic tests."

"Should I bring her in?"

"Jimmy, I can't do anything here for your wife." Dr. Clifford took a deep breath and swallowed hard. "You're going to have to take her to a proper hospital with a full range of diagnostic equipment. I don't even have an x-ray machine here at the clinic."

"But last time she got lost at the mall, the cops did take her to county. They checked her out in emergency and couldn't find anything wrong."

Tony looked up from his task and caught the doctor's eye. They both knew that her examination must have been extremely cursory, at best. After taking her vitals, and giving her a quick interview to make sure she was lucid, Jimmy's wife would have been released under her own recognizance.

"Well," Tony scrambled to bring a little light to the situation, "why don't you gather up all your wife's prescriptions and bring them down to the clinic?"

"Everything," the doctor agreed. "Check the bathroom, her purse, her nightstand, and each of the kitchen cupboards. Bring every single bottle you can find, whether it's brand new or completely empty. Even bring the over-the-counter stuff. I'll have a look at it, and maybe it'll give us a few clues."

"That's it," Tony unhappily announced. "That's the end of our plaster."

Dr. Clifford slowly nodded his head, fully aware that now they'd be forced to order the newer, more expensive, fiberglass resin for casts.

———————

Without truck keys or his wallet, Justice was reduced to wandering the neighborhood, reminding himself not to linger too long in the park, lest someone mistake him for a pedophile.

After only thirty minutes, he desperately wanted to head home, but Justice couldn't imagine what he was going to say. He'd never done anything like this before, and honestly, he couldn't didn't think he would ever being mad enough to do something like it again.

Finally turning back up the block, he decided to bite the bullet and just head home. Better to confront his wife's rage than let her stew for another couple of hours. Time would only compound Sarah's anger, and if she were left alone long enough, she might even be tempted to call her sister in for reinforcement.

Justice marched up the three flights of stairs to their apartment, and tentatively tried to turn the knob. When it didn't budge, the realization suddenly hit him that he was locked out without a key. It hadn't occurred to him that he might be forced to knock, reduced to begging for entrance into his own home. "Sarah, I'm back. Can you open the door?" he called out in what he hoped to be a neutral voice.

Without a reply, the tumbler suddenly rolled over in the deadbolt and hurried footsteps retreated from the door.

"Honey, I'm coming in," he announced, not sure whether she

would greet him with a hug or a frying pan. The kitchen and living room were completely empty, with no sign of his wife or the kids; the only movement came from somewhere in the back bedroom.

"Sarah, can you come out here?" he shouted, down the hall. "I want to apologize for acting like such a jerk."

When their bedroom door finally swung open, his wife strolled down the hallway wearing a freshly ironed dress. Not only was she wearing one of her better dresses, she had pulled on a pair of pantyhose and quickly twisted her hair up and pinned it to the back of her head.

"Where are you going all dressed up like that, and…" he stopped to look around the room, "and where are the kids?"

"My sister took them for a couple hours cuz I have an appointment."

"What kind of appointment?" Justice continued his game of twenty questions.

"Bishop Connor's office just called me back to say that he had an opening this afternoon and would be able to see me."

As he opened the fridge to extract a carton of milk, Justice carefully debated his next statement. "Tell me something. When exactly did you call Father Samuels and tell him that you needed to see the bishop?"

"After you left," she admitted, with no apology in her voice.

"Call him back."

"Why?" She snatched the carton off the counter and stuffed it back into the refrigerator.

"Cuz I don't need the entire congregation knowing our business, that's why. This is between you and me!"

"And God!" Sarah retorted.

"And God, and God. Always God," Justice chanted, angrily throwing his hands in the air. "Sometimes I think there are three of us living here in this marriage."

"I don't think I know you anymore," Sarah cried, grabbing a dishtowel and pressing it up toward her eyes. "What's happening to you?"

"I'm living here in reality while you're off… off living in some kind of fantasy world," he began to rant. "In your world, a bunch of prayers are going to feed our kids and pay the rent. Isn't that what you think, Sarah? You think going to church and making confession is going to save us all. Well, damn you, it won't." He stepped forward and grabbed her arms. "If we kept on having babies like a good Catholic family, we'll be on food stamps within a couple years. Can't you see that?" He frantically searched her eyes for any sign of acknowledgement.

"I just can't understand why you're turning on us." She yanked her arms free and plopped down into a kitchen chair.

"Us?" Her husband took off on another tangent. "That's exactly what I'm talking about, Sarah. It's not supposed to be the three of us. You, me, and the Holy Spirit. It's just supposed to be you and me. You… and… me," he paused for emphasis, walking over and shoving his finger into the soft tissue of her chest.

"But God…"

"God-shmod," he suddenly reached up to rub the tension knots out of his neck. "Do you love me, Sarah?" his tone dropped, his voice noticeably softening.

"Yes." She looked up into his face.

"Do you think that I love you and the kids?"

"Justice," she began to whimper, exhausted by their fighting.

"Do you?" he asked again, unwilling to give up.

"Yes, you love us all," she conceded, grabbing a tissue off the table to blow her nose.

"Then why is it so hard for you to believe that what I did was done for our family? I don't want to raise our children in poverty, Sarah. I want them to sleep in their own house, and go to school with new clothes and proper fitting shoes. I don't want to see my kids wearing someone else's hand me downs all the time. Do you?"

"This is all about clothes?"

"No." He grabbed his usual chair and joined his wife at the table. "It's about me being able to provide for my family without having to rely on charity."

"I have to go." Sarah slowly rose from her seat. "I can't just not show up for my appointment with the Bishop."

"Don't go." Justice reached across the table, desperately grasping at his wife's left hand. "I'm asking you one last time not to go."

Slowly pulling away, Sarah's fingers slipped out of her husband's grasp. "I have to go," she whispered, bending to pick up her purse.

"Then you go," he muttered, rising up from the table and blindly stumbling down the back hall.

Chapter Thirteen

"Mama always said life was like a box of chocolates.
You never know what you're gonna get."

—*Forrest Gump, 1994*

Toes tapping under his desk, Wally struggled to wrap up his cold call, secretly hoping the woman would just tell him to take a hike and hang up the phone.

"But that's my problem, young man," she slowly explained for the second time. "I want to make a decision, but my daughter wouldn't be very happy if I did. Maybe you want to call back when she's home."

"Maybe I will. Have a nice day, ma'am," he quickly disconnected the trunk line and ran off to the men's washroom.

He'd waited as long as humanly possible, and now if he didn't get his pants down in the next five seconds, Wally was convinced his bowels would explode and he'd shit all over his tighty-whitties.

"Freeman, Walter Freeman," the receptionist's voice called

out over the building's overhead intercom. "Please come to reception. Freeman, to reception," she concluded her quick little announcement.

Gritting his teeth in preparation for what he knew would be anything but pleasant; Wally forced himself to bear down. "Ohhhh God," he couldn't help but moan, the pain of passing his first stool excruciating, to say the least. Light beads of sweat forming on his upper lip. He quickly unrolled three or four wraps of toilet paper. Clenching the bleached tissue between his fingers, he forced himself to push a second time, closing his eyes while praying his throat didn't open and release a scream.

No one had ever warned Wally about the morning after. Every time he'd been lucky enough to stumble onto a little gay porn, the movie always ended with the two guys blowing their loads in total and complete satisfaction. There was never a disclaimer about torn rectums, blood spotting, and diarrhea from the self-inflicted sperm enemas. This was a secret obviously kept just between the boys.

"Walter Freeman, please come to reception," the voice continued overhead. "Walter Freeman, you're wanted at reception."

Rising up from his seat, he gingerly dabbed himself clean, stomach relieved after holding his bowels for the duration of his phone call.

"Wally, you in there?" a man's voice boomed from the other side of the bathroom stall.

"Yeah, what's the rush?"

"You better get out here as soon as you can. Looks like your little trainee was just caught with his hands in the cookie jar."

Wally was zipping up his pants as he ran from the stall. He took a quick second to glance at his reflection in the bathroom mirror. There was no doubt in his mind; he looked scared.

"We're done," the doctor announced, walking up behind Tony, as he stood motionless in the middle of the waiting room. "I think we set some kind of record; twenty patients in just under four hours."

"And no complaints," Tony added.

"Well," the doctor shifted his heavy medical bag from his right hand to his left, "I guess I better be going."

"Let me help you," Tony offered, reaching over to relieve his heavy load. "I have to get moving, too. Plans, you know." He shrugged his shoulders, unwilling to speak Karen's name in case it somehow jinxed their first date. As they walked out together, Tony suddenly stopped dead on the front stairs. "Marcus, can I ask you a personal question?"

"Of course, son. Go ahead."

"Can you honestly tell me how you knew you'd found the right woman? What kind of signals should I be looking for so I know I'm not wasting my time?"

"I'm a divorced man," he chuckled at the obvious irony of the situation. "I really don't think you want my advice."

"But you were in love once," Tony argued, "and you know I'm closer to thirty-one than I am to thirty, and I'm still alone. I don't have time to play any more games, Marcus. How am I going to know when I've met Mrs. Right?"

Jaded after too many years of marital discord, Marcus turned to face his young protégé with a sympathetic smile. "I can't tell you when you've found the right girl, Tony. I don't know when you should hold on, but I sure as the hell can tell you when it's over."

"When's that?"

"Well," the doctor leaned forward to extract his bag from Tony's hand, "when all you can think about is finding a good place to bury the body, then you definitely know that it's over."

Both men chuckled to themselves, turning to walk off in opposite directions.

Tony couldn't remember the last time he'd been in a movie theater. Thinking back, it had to be at least seven or eight years. He'd never intentionally boycotted the industry; he just found that after the release of his first porno, the magic was gone.

Paying to watch the little woman pretend to be in love, while the big strong man rushed off to kill the bad guys had somehow lost its appeal. When Tony looked up at the screen, all he could think of were unflattering camera angles, actors lobbying for better quality lube, and the extremely low industry pay. Movies were no longer an escape; they were a constant reminder of his past. And because of his experience in front of the camera, Tony couldn't believe that he was about to suggest a movie date.

From her upstairs window, Karen watched as Tony twisted sideways to extract his wide shoulders from the back seat of the taxicab. Once again, she was fascinated by his enormous size. If he had wanted to, a man like that could easily crush a woman to death in the circle of his own arms. But then, if given the chance, what a way to die.

"Mr. Destiny is knocking at your door," her roommate teased, still lounging in her housecoat.

"Come on in," Karen flung open the door and greeted Tony with a smile. "I was hoping you wouldn't forget about me."

"Why would I forget?" He suddenly stopped dead in his tracks, eyes locking on Alicia's form as she lounged on the couch in a silky pajama top.

"That's my roommate, Alicia. She was just getting up to throw on some clothes," Karen joked in an attempt to make everyone a little more comfortable.

"Hi there, Tony." She stretched out her legs, taking the time to make sure each of the muscles in her calves were properly released.

"Hello Alicia," he answered back, promptly turning his back on the girl and effectively tuning out her little show.

"I'm ready," Karen announced, slinging her purse over her shoulder and tying her jacket around her waist.

He swung open the door, and graciously stepped aside to allow Karen passage. "Since we really know very little about each other, I thought a movie might be a good idea."

"Why?" she asked, signaling for him to follow her down the back stairs.

"Well, for starters, we wouldn't have to worry about making a lot of small talk."

"True," she agreed, flashing a small passkey across an infrared scanner. "But if we sit together through a movie without talking, we won't be in any better condition for our second date. Will we?"

He liked her. He barely knew the woman, but he liked her. "Alright missy, if you don't want to go to the movies, what else do you suggest?"

Pulling open the first of two security doors on their descent to the underground parking garage, Karen tried to come up with a better idea. "To be honest, I don't really know. We could go eat. That gives us something to do while were making a whole bunch of the inane small talk you're not so fond of."

"That'll work," Tony wholeheartedly agreed. "You have a place in mind?"

"Not really. Do you?"

"Maybe," he smiled a naughty little grin.

Half an hour later, as Karen slowly sipped her glass of ice-cold draft, she took a moment to appraise her dinner date. Although the plastic bib adorning only the top portion of his chest seemed to emphasize his massive build, Tony seemed quite at home in the middle of the seafood restaurant.

"I can't remember the last time I ever ate a whole lobster," Karen nervously giggled. "Please stop me if it looks like I'm going to eat its liver or something else really gross. Alright?"

Smiling and nodding, Tony leaned back just as the waitress swooped in and dropped their steaming plates down on the table.

"If you need any extra butter or napkins, just help yourself," she pointed to a corner table laden with supplies. "I'll swing back around with more beers."

Picking up his lobster fork and shell crackers, Tony raised them in a mock attack. "Are you ready?"

"Ready," Karen copied his lead.

Unbelievably, she managed to finish two whole lobsters, while Tony triumphantly topped her with a grand total of four. Downing three beers each, a shared Caesar salad and a side pot of Boston baked beans, their appetites were absolutely sated. It was the best meal Karen had eaten in years, and she made a point of letting Tony know.

"I can't thank you enough. When we were driving here, I recognized the neighborhood and I'd resigned myself to heading off to some old pizza joint. But all-you-can-eat lobster," she raved. "How did you ever find this place?"

As he stretched his arms wide to emphasize his size, Tony gave a mock scowl. "Take another look at me. I know every good all-you-can-eat joint in this city."

"I hear you. But look, if you're ever craving a low cal, no carb, totally organic salad, I'm your gal."

"I'll keep that in mind," Tony smiled, amused with her sharp sense of humor.

"How about a walk?" Karen suggested. "I wouldn't mind burning off a little of that butter before it permanently settles on my hips."

Tony nodded his agreement, and accompanied Karen around the corner and right into the middle of the arts district.

"Sometimes, when I'm feeling a little bored with my routine,

I come down here and grab a little bit of culture," she explained, catching Tony's furrowed brow as he watched an artist spray paint a model's body in the front window of an art gallery.

"Culture?" he teased. "Is that what we're calling it these days?"

"Come on." She suddenly slinked her fingers into the palm of his right hand. "I wanna show you my favorite little shop."

Tony sucked in his breath and let himself be dragged along, enjoying the simple pleasure of their adolescent handholding.

"Miss Karen," a woman beckoned the minute she spotted her face.

"Don't let me open my wallet," she quickly rose up on her tiptoes and whispered in Tony's ear. Gently pulling free of his grasp, she stepped forward, warmly embracing the elderly shopkeeper.

As the women visited, Tony took a moment to evaluate the wares. Everywhere he turned, hanging from the rafters and clinging to the walls were replicas of angels. Ceramic, glass, pottery, wood, and even feathered.

"Tony, come here," Karen beckoned. "Miss Matilda Weatherburn is going to show us her newest creation."

Squeezing into the woman's back room, they stood silently while she unveiled a three-foot hand-carved statue.

"It's beautiful," Karen blushed, her reaction somewhat confusing.

"The lines are perfect," Matilda stressed, running her weathered hand down the backside of the naked angel, her breasts and genitalia discretely covered by ornately carved wings.

"Pine?" Karen recovered her composure and leaned in for a closer look.

"White oak, a hardwood with a beautifully opalescent color. Don't you agree?" She suddenly turned her attention to Tony.

"It's really, beautiful," he vigorously nodded his head. "I've never seen anything like this before. Who's the artist?"

"I am," Matilda announced. "But it's a joint collaboration. Karen posed for me."

"Mattie, that was supposed to be our little secret."

She turned to brush the young woman's face, and leaned forward to whisper in her ear. "I thought if you brought him here to see it, he must be pretty special to you."

Karen stepped back and looked at Tony, his attention still riveted to the breathtaking lines of the sculpture.

Chapter Fourteen

"Badges? We ain't got no badges!
We don't need no badges!
I don't have to show you any stinking badges!"

—*The Treasure of the Sierra Madre, 1948*

"We've never had anything like this before in the entire history of our company, and I can't believe I have to deal with this right now!" Wally's boss angrily shook his head.

Wally knew that anything he said would probably come out wrong and zipping his lip was more than likely his best bet. Especially until he understood exactly what was going on. Unfortunately, his trainee and boyfriend Billy Grant didn't feel the same way.

"Listen, it's not my fault that you guys can't afford to pay a decent base," Billy stood his ground. "How can you expect anyone to live on two hundred and fifty bucks a week? That's total bullshit!" he attempted to argue his case.

"You're a trainee," the boss leaned across his desk and shouted directly at Billy's face. "That's not supposed to be a living wage. It's just set to cover some basic expenses while you learn the ropes."

"It's still bullshit," he grumbled a second time.

"Enough with the base," the regional manager stood up from his chair. "Let's get to the bottom of these cash deposits. Someone wanna explain that?" He looked from Billy back to Wally. "Or should I just call the cops and let them sort it out?"

"I'm not sure what you're talking about, sir," Wally finally relented. "I haven't been in the field a lot lately. Actually, truth be told, I haven't taken an appointment in over six weeks. I've been trai..."

"Yes, we know. You've been training," the manager jumped in to finish Wally's sentence. "But wasn't it you who signed these contracts?" He threw a pile of papers down on the conference room table. "Aren't those your signatures, Mr. Freeman?"

"I never signed them," he stood his ground, stomach beginning to turn as the severity of the situation finally hit home.

Grabbing a piece of paper from his personal folder, Wally's sales supervisor began scanning a list of totals. "According to our preliminary findings, our accounting department is short eleven thousand dollars in cash deposits, and," he anxiously began cracking his knuckles, "we haven't even had a chance to finish our investigation."

Taking a second to glance over his shoulder at Billy, Wally was shocked to see him calmly sitting back in his chair, acting as if the entire scenario was doing little more than cutting into his spa time.

"I'm sorry, sir." Wally turned his attention back to his superiors. "But I did not sign those contracts or collect any cash deposits. I didn't..."

"That's enough." His boss held up his hand. "We know it wasn't you, Freeman."

"How?" Billy suddenly snapped back to attention.

"Well, for starters, I personally interviewed three of the clients who signed those contracts, and when I showed them Wally's business card, they didn't recognize his face."

Vindicated at last, Wally sucked in a giant breath of air, collapsing back into his chair.

"But they recognized you, Mr. Grant," he turned his attention back to Billy. "You booked those appointments in Walter Freeman's name, made the sales, and then pocketed the cash. Isn't that right?"

"I'm not saying another word without a lawyer."

"Do we look like cops?" The regional manager turned to his sales manager and began to howl with laughter. "I sure as hell hope I wear a better suit than any of those flatfooted buggers. Tell me I do, Ted. Cuz I'll be pissed to think my wife is buying me crap off the rack down at JC Penney's."

"What do you want?" Billy suddenly jumped to his feet, obviously unnerved by the light-hearted banter.

"Eleven thousand dollars," Ted glared across the table, "and any other additional deposits we find missing. You're going to pay back every penny, or you *will* be needing a lawyer. Understand?"

"I don't got it," Billy began fidgeting with the edge of the table. "I kinda spent it."

"Oh shit," Wally muttered aloud without even realizing he'd opened his mouth.

"Listen up, Grant," the sales manager summed up their position. "We're giving you three minutes to clear out any of your belongings, and thirty days to payback our deposits. If you screw up on either, we're gonna call the cops and let them take care of the situation. Are we clear on this?"

"Whatever," Billy responded by rolling his eyes.

"Now, get out of here."

"Freeman, you grab a box from the storage room and help this kid get packed. And you watch him. I don't want him stealing any phone books on his way out the door."

"Eat me," Billy mumbled under his breath as he turned and strutted out of the room.

Wally grabbed the first cardboard box he could find and rushed back toward the bullpen.

"Fucking assholes," Billy continued to curse. "Look what they did. They took bolt cutters to my lock." He flung the severed shackle into the trash. "What'd they think I was doing, hiding some cash in the company filing cabinets?"

"Let's just pack up your stuff," Wally tried to reason with his boyfriend. "The sooner you get out of here, the better."

"For who? For you?"

Wally ignored Billy, quickly stuffing his papers and training manuals into the cardboard box.

"What's the matter, Wally? Afraid that someone might find out you're one big fucking… HOMO?" he shouted at the top of his lungs.

"What are you doing?" Wally hissed, roughly shoving the box into Billy's chest.

"Oh, fuck you and you're little suburban housewife. I hope you rot behind your white picket fence."

Wally stood motionless, absolutely stunned that his Billy would spew such hurtful venom. "Why did you do it?" he finally managed to ask. "If you needed money that bad I would…"

"You'd what? Sell one of your kids? You ain't got no fucking money."

Trudging over to his desk, Wally pulled out his chair and dropped down into the seat, catching a glimpse of another salesman peeking around the corner.

"Look Billy, I don't care what you think about me, but you better take their threats seriously. If you don't pay back the deposits, they'll come after you. I know they will."

"Let 'em," he laughed, changing his mind and tossing his box of personal belongings down into the garbage. "They try and pull any *Law and Order* shit on my ass, I'll go public with a case for sexual discrimination. I'll let everyone know they fired me and then set me up as a fall guy after finding out I was gay."

"But that's a boldfaced lie."

"Prove it," he dared Wally. "You know I have the balls to stand up in court and let everybody know that you and I were lovers. And then, I'd testify in front of everybody that when the bosses found and approached you. Then, you agreed to frame me in a bid to keep your homosexuality under wraps."

"Billy."

"Don't you *Billy* me," he warned. "I think this would all make great copy for the early morning news. Don't you? Oh, and what about your little Annette?" he put his hands on his hips and began wiggling his hips. "How do you think she'd take the news?" he giggled, mocking a woman's high-pitched laugh.

"Get your ass out of here," a voice boomed from somewhere deep within the group of salesmen standing guard at the bullpen's main door.

"Piss off," Billy turned and hissed. "This has nothing to do with any of you. It's been me and Wally."

Wally hung his head, so embarrassed by the afternoon's events that he couldn't even face his co-workers.

"Freeman, this guy still your friend?" one of the men in the group demanded as he slowly stepped forward.

Painfully raising his head, Wally reluctantly took the opportunity to step back and take a slow look at Billy Grant. He was very good looking; there was no denying that. But underneath the well-sculpted muscles and perfectly capped teeth, he was just ordinary; another guy who hadn't amounted to anything substantial and who went home every night to an empty bed. Within the blink of any eye, Billy's stock was beginning to plummet.

Slowly rising up from his chair, Wally finally summoned the courage to face his peers. "No guys, he's not my friend. And the way I see it, his three minutes have just run out."

———————————————

Focusing on the pages of his newspaper, Justice struggled to make his way through the front-page headlines. As he attempted to sound out the words, he forced himself onward—line... by painful line.

He had left school as a youngster to help his mom after she broke her back, while she was laid up in a cast. Somehow, Justice managed to get lost in the shuffle. Between his siblings and his cousins, there were so many Mallory kids attending the same Catholic school, the nuns somehow failed to notice that he never returned after Christmas break. When he began to work full time in a lumberyard by the age of twelve, Justice's paycheck suddenly became a valued part of the household income. If he quit his job and went back to school, it would have been a hardship borne by the entire family. After a very brief discussion with his parents, his education was put on hold.

Everyone agreed that's he'd return one day—the family just needed his financial help for a few more months until his father got his expected raise. Justice agreed, not that his opinion actually carried any weight. When the raise came, so did the hospital bills, and it was decided that Justice would take another year off. Two years turned into five, and before he realized it, he was an adult moving out of his parent's three-bedroom apartment.

He never blamed his family for his lack of formal education.

They did the best they could with what little they had. Raising five children on a laborer's salary had been a daily struggle, and Justice knew that if it hadn't been for the church's food hampers, many a night they'd have gone to bed hungry. He lived a childhood of *just enough*. There was just enough food to keep the belly quiet, but not enough ever to feel fully satisfied. They had just enough hand-me-downs to be clothed, but never enough to feel completely warm. And there was just enough attention to be accounted for, but never enough attention to really know that you were loved.

When Justice began seeing Sarah and she agreed to marry him after only two short months of dating, he vowed they would never live a life of *just enough*. His children would never be measured by their contribution to the family coffers and everyone would most definitely graduate from high school, even if he had to sell a kidney to pay for their education. Finally, Justice vowed that none of his children would be forced to order *the same* in a restaurant, just because they weren't educated enough to read the menu.

Raising his head to check the clock, he debated whether he should start making some kind of supper. Living without the luxury of a microwave oven or the extra cash for take-out foot, Justice knew that feeding a family took a little planning.

He still made a decent pot of hamburger soup. Experience had taught him that a frozen lump of ground beef could be slowly pan-fried until it thawed and crumbled into bite-sized pieces. Dropping the meat into a pot of boiling water with a couple handfuls of raw macaroni and a half bag of frozen vegetables, he only needed to add two cans of tomato soup before filling the bowls of his waiting children.

"We're home," Sarah announced, stumbling through the door with a bag of groceries and all three kids in tow.

"I see that," Justice replied, still unsure of his wife's mood.

"Why don't you kids go to your room and play a game. Give Mommy and Daddy a chance to talk."

"Snack," they all chanted in unison, clamoring to dig their fingers into the box of crackers their mother has purchased at the store.

"You heard your mother," Justice barked as each of the children turned and quickly high-tailed it down the back hall.

Finally alone in the tiny kitchen, Justice watched Sarah dart back and forth between the pantry and her kitchen cupboards.

"I just picked up what we needed," she explained without being asked. "They gave me two rain checks. One for toilet paper, the other for elbow macaroni. Funny how they only run out of the stuff when it's on sale," she mused.

"How was your appointment?" He cut right to the chase.

"It was fine. The Bishop promised to pray for us all."

"Why?" Tony felt the familiar anger begin to rise. "Does he think we maybe need a little special dispensation for all our sins?"

"I didn't tell him," Sarah admitted before bending under the sink to stow the empty grocery bags.

Roughly folding his paper in half, Justice stood up and stuffed it deep into the trash. "What exactly didn't you tell him, Sarah? Did you leave out the part that I won't accept any charity from his church, or that maybe I'm thinking of sending Justice Junior to public school? Or maybe you didn't tell him that I went out and got myself a vasectomy? Is that what you didn't tell him, Sarah?"

"What do you want from me?" she cried. "You've just damned yourself to hell and you expect me to wanna celebrate. What's the matter with you, Justice?"

"I don't think it's me." He dropped his shoulders and released a huge breath of air. "I think it's you, Sarah. Your heart is so full of God, and church, and prayers, that you don't have any room left in it for your husband."

With his van parked in front of his house, Wally carefully debated his options. He could go inside and pretend nothing happened, crossing his fingers that no one from work called up to check on him. Or, he could come clean with his wife, explaining in limited detail how his trainee got caught falsifying contracts. Neither choice seemed viable.

"Wally," Annette suddenly pounded on the driver's window. "What are you doing? Is something wrong?"

Jumping out of the van, he landed on the concrete clutching his briefcase to his chest. "Well, things got a little crazy today at work, and to be honest, I was just trying to get my head on straight."

"Come on inside," Annette coaxed her husband, still holding the two bags of trash. "I have a bottle of red wine I've been saving since New Year's Eve, and I think tonight's the night we pop the cork. Don't you?"

Wally silently nodded, setting down his briefcase to relieve his wife of her burden. "I'll be right inside," he promised, moving off toward the plastic garbage cans.

Annette picked up her husband's briefcase and rushed inside the house. It'd been so long since he'd been home for supper that she'd stopped setting him a plate.

"Scooch over," she motioned to her oldest. "Daddy's home and he's going to want to eat."

As the kids each dragged their chairs over to make room for their father, Annette quickly put down a clean plate and grabbed the salad bowl, intent on fluffing it up with a few extra greens.

"I smell meatballs and mushroom gravy," he flashed his best fatherly smile. "You leave any for your pops?"

"No," Colin chirped, throwing a paper dinner napkin over the bowl of steaming meatballs. "We ate it all," he laughed, amused by his own joke.

"Maybe I should just go for a drive and buy myself a pizza then?"

"No," the children all howled in unison.

"Well, what am I going to eat then?"

"Meatballs," Colin roared, ripping off the paper cover.

By the time the whole family had finished their supper, the mood had become almost festive. Monica never once complained about the grease in her food, Colin and his sister Tammy managed not to knock over each other's milk, and Wally actually seemed interested in what his children had to say. Annette wanted to wrap the moment in plastic wrap and save it forever.

"Want me to help clear?" he offered.

"No, I'm fine," Annette pecked her husband on the cheek. "Why don't you run upstairs and change out of your suit. I'll get the kids settled, and then open that bottle of wine that I squirreled away."

Happy to have someone else take control for a little while, Wally accepted his wife's direction and headed up the stairs. By the time he returned to the main floor, the kids had disappeared and Annette was just finishing up in the kitchen.

"Grab a seat on the couch, I'll bring down the wine as soon as I turn on the dishwasher," she gently coaxed him.

Dropping down onto the lumpy cushions, Wally slowly scanned the room, suddenly compelled to take stock of his situation. He did own his own home, although mortgaged right to the hilt. He had a loving wife, three kids, and he was gainfully employed. Not bad for thirty-two.

"Here we go," Annette suddenly interrupted his train of thought. "Let's have a glass and you can tell me all about your day." Wally was still debating just how much he would share when his wife handed him a large glass of red wine and snuggled in at his hip. She said, "I can't remember the last time we did this. Can you?"

"It's been ages," he agreed, throwing his left arm around her shoulders to pull her in even closer.

"So baby, what happened at work today? Did you get some bad news?"

Downing half his glass of wine, Wally just opened his heart and plunged right in. "Remember my trainee, William Grant? I mean Billy," he used the familiar nickname to jar his wife's memory?"

"Yes."

"Well, he was booking appointments in my name, selling pre-arranged funeral packages, and collecting deposits in cash."

"That sounds dangerous. Did he know enough to fill out the contracts properly? They always looked pretty complicated to me."

"The contracts are the least of my problems," he shook his head. "Turns out Billy was keeping the cash and not even bothering to turn in the agreements. Management was only tipped off when one client called in to cancel. You know, they still have that forty-eight hour cancellation clause."

Annette just shook her head, scrambling to understand Billy's justification.

"If the one guy hadn't called in," Wally mused, "who knows how long he might have gotten away with his scam."

"They're not holding you responsible, are they?" she shifted her position to look her husband right in the face. "Cuz you didn't have anything to do with this, did you?"

"I didn't even know he was booking appointments."

"So now what?" Annette reached out to set her glass on the coffee table. "Do you need to call a lawyer? Is there going to be any kind of lawsuit? You're not on probation are you?" She continued to barrage him with a litany of questions.

Reaching for the bottle, Wally slowly refilled his glass. "No, no, and no," he answered in a succession of monosyllabic replies. "The company knows it was all Billy's doing. But they are going to come after him for the deposits."

Lifting up her glass, Annette threw back a large gulp before continuing, "How much were the deposits?"

"Eleven grand."

"Holy shit!" she exclaimed. "He scammed eleven thousand dollars in two months?"

"Give or take," Wally nodded. "And they haven't totally finished with their investigation yet."

"So, now what?"

"Well, for the time being, they're discontinuing the trainee program."

"You're back in sales?"

"Basically."

"We'll be fine," she patted his leg.

"Billy is really mad. He lost it today at the office. I think he kinda blames me." Wally shrugged his shoulders. "So I want you and the kids to be extra careful for awhile. Fishing a business card out of his jogging pants, Wally reluctantly handed it to his wife. "This is Billy's picture. If he shows up at the house, I don't want you to open the door. Do you understand?"

"He's not going to show up here, is he?"

"I doubt it," Wally sincerely hoped. "But if he does, just send him packing and then call the cops. He's not the man I thought he was, and I don't want him around my children for one second. You never know what he might be capable of."

"You're scaring me," Annette admitted.

"I don't wanna scare you or the kids, but before he was thrown out of the office, Billy starting yelling about going to the media with the fact that he was gay."

"He's gay?" Annette repeated, pulling the picture up to her face to re-examine his photograph. "He's so handsome. Are you sure?"

"Anyone can be gay," Wally corrected his wife. "You can't tell just by looking at their picture, you know."

"I know, but look at him." She flashed her husband the business card. "He coulda had any woman he wanted."

"As I was saying," Wally reiterated, "I don't want you talking to any reporters either. The company wants to keep a lid on any possible sexual harassment suit," he lied, hoping her company loyalty might help guarantee her silence.

"I promise," she nodded, still hypnotized by Billy's photograph.

"Could you tell?"

"Tell what?" Wally reached for the television remote.

"That he was gay. Did you pick up on any of his vibes?"

"Annette, for Christ's sake, it's not like the man had some special odor or secret tattoo. How was I supposed to know he was gay?"

"I don't know," she nervously giggled. "Maybe it was something in the way he carried himself, maybe something to do with his clothes."

"Well, I couldn't tell." Wally flipped on the television, running up and down the list of channels.

"Well, I would have known." Annette sipped her wine. "Women have an extra sense. We know these kinds of things."

"So you tell me," Wally leaned forward to top off his own glass.

Chapter Fifteen

"The stuff that dreams are made of."

—The Maltese Falcon, 1941

While he still lounged in his bathtub, Freddy reached over the edge and scrambled to grab his watch. He'd purposely risen an hour before his usual wake-up just to allow himself the luxury of this bath. Satisfied that his skin was softened and his hair follicles pliant, his picked up his Mach III razor and began to shave.

Starting with his ankles, Freddy pulled the razor upwards in small six-inch strokes, forced to repeatedly stop and rinse the hair from the blades. Right leg completed, he moved over to the left, mindful of the healing scab from his last shave. By the time he'd finished both legs, ankle to thigh, the razor was completely dull.

Popping out the old cartridge, Freddy quickly replaced the disposable blades with a sparkling new set, intent on finishing his job. Shaving his chest was always a tricky feat. He would have loved if he could just wax it, but who could afford it on a student's budget?

Luckily, he only had to deal with a small patch of hair, situated mid-chest between his pecs.

His armpits, however, always proved to be difficult, the concave shape forcing him to bear down with the razor to capture the spiky hairs. This was not a task he could complete when pressed for time. Rushing usually led to very painful results, especially when shaving the coarse hairs on his groin.

As Freddy rinsed his body and evaluated his work, he happily noticed only one nick on his right ankle, a wound that would probably stop bleeding the minute he stepped out of the bath and allowed his skin to dry.

Smooth as a baby's bum, Freddy's young skin glistened as he rose from the water and immediately began smoothing lotion over his chest. Massaging the aloe-based gel into his freshly shaven skin, he found himself aroused by the movement, his heart pounding as he slowly bent down to rub his calves.

Quickly tiding up his mess by rinsing the hair from the bottom of his tub, Freddy left the bathroom and walked toward his bedroom closet. Pulling down a beautifully wrapped box, he gingerly opened the package, mindful not to destroy the gold foil ribbon.

"Oh, it's perfect," he cooed, lifting the sheer pink teddy from beneath the wrapped tissue. Gently laying it on the bed, he slowly wiggled his fingers upward between the material's inner lining, gently lifting the fabric carefully up and over his head.

Spinning to flutter the lace trim, the young man danced around his room, ecstatic with the sensation of the teddy as it brushed his freshly shaven thighs. He was beautiful—how could he not be—modeling two hundred-dollar lingerie.

Stopping for only a moment to choose a delicate pair of white lace panties to accent the teddy, Freddy slowly pulled them on, disappointed that even though his penis was flaccid, it still created a discernible bulge in his underwear.

Finally ready to pose in front of the mirror, Freddy slowly turned and appraised his own silhouette.

Not good enough!

He'd never be happy as long as he was plagued with his birth body. He needed to continue with his transformation, but that was a one-hundred-thousand-dollar operation. Transgender surgery was very expensive, and any reputable surgeon wouldn't even consider operating on a patient until they were at least twenty-one years of age and had lived as a woman for at least twelve months. Never mind the months of hormone therapy required to prepare the body for the surgical transformation.

That was, unless you were able to find yourself an *in*.

Ten years ago, Lucy Nally had decided her son was going to attend a reputable school and receive a top-notch education. So immediately after his grade nine graduation, his mother had introduced him to the world of university prep classes. By the time Freddy entered his senior year of high school, he'd fallen right in line with his mother's way of thinking. As per Lucy's plan, he would attend a well-respected medical school, but during his education, Freddy would focus his energies on acquainting himself with some of the best doctors in the business. He'd find a surgeon to operate on him, and he didn't care if he had to offer himself up as a human guinea pig to guarantee the success.

Freddy had known since he was a prepubescent boy that something was off in his world. In retrospect, he couldn't actually remember a time when everything felt right. Society's image of what was acceptable clothing did not appeal to him. The toys he was offered, the games he was expected to play, nothing was of interest. Then when puberty hit, any lingering doubts were immediately washed away.

Freddy did not want to have sex with girls, because he was attracted to boys. Unfortunately, any teenage boys who in turn were attracted to him were drawn to what they mistook as his same-sex tendencies.

More than once, Freddy physically had to spurn their homosexual advances. He simply wasn't gay. He didn't want to be a male having sex with another male. Freddy desperately just wanted to be female, a young girl who was able to have sex with boys. The yearnings in his heart were simple, it was his body that was so complicated and in need of repair.

After pulling off his teddy and dropping it back into the designer box, Freddy threw the ribbon inside and slapped the cardboard lid shut. He needed to quit spending all his money on these extravagances, forced to run around campus in a wild attempt to locate copies of used textbooks to make up the deficit. If he was going to continue with his taste in clothing, he needed a part-time job. And although most professors adamantly spoke out against it, Freddy didn't care. His ultimate goal wasn't to earn one of their coveted little degrees. He was there to make contacts, and disappointingly, he'd yet to meet anyone of substance.

Dr. Clifford's after-hours surgeries were becoming harder and harder to handle. Medically, the procedures were routine. However, emotionally, they were beginning to tax him beyond his limits. Every single hospital in the free world had strict policies regarding doctors operating on family or close friends, guidelines put in place for good reason. However, when he performed surgery behind closed doors without a hospital's board of ethics governing his actions, anything was possible.

Busily patting dry his instruments with the blue cotton toweling, Marcus was unaware that Dr. Martin Hood was walking up behind his back.

"I feel that I should be doing more than just thanking you." Martin stood back and watched his friend and ex-colleague finish with his clean up. "Do you know, I remember a time, not that many years ago, when we had a bevy of attractive young nurses who were more than happy to clean up in our wake."

"That was a lifetime ago." Marcus never even cracked a smile as he reached for his medical bag.

"I know, but sometimes I just like to take a walk down memory lane. Can you blame me?" the elderly doctor chuckled. "To many of the interns, we were even regarded as Gods. Now..."

"Now I'm the pariah of the medical community. How things have changed," Marcus continued with his duties.

"I made us a quick little breakfast. Hope you have time to eat."

"Sure, but first I want to look in on Olga one last time. Do you mind?"

"Not at all." Martin excused himself and went back to check on the French toast.

Slowly making his way back down the hall, Marcus took one last deep breath and entered Olga's room.

Happy to see that she was peacefully sleeping, he walked around her bed and checked the monitors, still surprised at all the ICU equipment Martin had been able to purchase for cash. It appeared that if you had the cash to spend, you could walk away with top of the line equipment.

"You're doing very well, Olga," he spoke to the unconscious patient, an old habit from his clinical treatment days. "The surgery was a big success and we were able to remove nearly all of your protrusions. When you wake up, you're going to be just as beautiful as you were before," he outright lied.

"Everything fine?" Martin whispered from the door. "I was starting to worry that maybe there was a problem here."

"Everything looks fine." Marcus nodded back at his old friend. "I just wish she'd open her eyes before I leave."

"Don't worry." Martin stepped forward to pat his wife's hand. "She's a sleeper, can't seem to get enough these days. She'll wake up when she'd damn good and ready."

Following his friend back down the hall toward the kitchen, Marcus joined Martin at this breakfast nook.

"It's so nice to have company for a meal. Please, sit down and enjoy."

Pulling up his heavily padded stool, Marcus couldn't help but take stock of the spread. A basket of mixed pastries, yogurt with fresh raspberries, French toast sprinkled with powdered sugar, and a large crystal bowl of stewed fruit filled the counter top.

"This is quite the spread, doctor. I didn't know you normally ate so well."

"Alright, you caught me." Martin smiled. "I knew you'd probably be spending the night to help monitor Olga's recovery, so I ordered in a few extra groceries."

Not exactly dying of hunger, Marcus realized that anything less than a full plate of food would probably offend his host. "Well, are we waiting for other guests, or can I dig in?" he teased.

"Help yourself." Martin grinned, spooning a small portion of yogurt into his own fruit bowl

By the time both men finished their plates and emptied the carafe of coffee, it was nearly ten in the morning.

"I really should be heading down to the clinic. You want me to stop by later?"

Shaking his head, Martin rose and began clearing their dishes. "Olga's recovery from these surgeries is usually fairly routine. If I have any problems, I'll just ring you at your office. You've done enough. Just head back to your clinic."

"Alright then." Marcus stood to shake his friend's outstretched hand. "You know where to reach me if you need anything."

"Oh yes," a thought came to Martin as he walked his guest

to the front door. "I meant to ask you how your assistant, Tony, is doing. I really enjoy his company. He's quite an interesting young man."

"That's actually an unfortunate story, when you think about it." Marcus stopped dead in his tracks. "If that boy would have been raised by any other blue collar family, I predict he'd be a world class physician by now. A natural diagnostician, if you ask me. But instead, he grew up on the back streets just north of the Italian ghetto, and spent his teens just fighting to stay alive. Truly, he's a doctoral thesis on nature versus nurture, don't you think?"

"It could very well be. But I'll pass. Feel free to tackle it yourself." Martin reached forward to open the front door.

As Marcus turned and walked out to his car, Martin slowly closed the door, locking and then carefully activating the perimeter security.

———

Scanning the job board down at the student union building, Freddy picked a focal point and began systematically reading all the postings one after another. Side to side, he worked his way across the entire wall. After a few minutes, he finally found a couple that piqued his interest, so he quickly scribbled the information down on a scrap of paper.

"Hey Freddy," a guy called out from across the hall. "When's the last time you checked your e-mail, buddy? I've been trying to reach you for a couple of days."

"Sorry." He turned to apologize. "I've been a little busy. What's the emergency?"

"Remember when you said you might be interested in taking on a roommate if you found just the right person?"

"Yeah?"

"Well, I got the right person. So let's go." He grabbed Freddy's arm.

"Where?"

"A little meet and greet. Now hoof it, or you might miss out."

Heading down the stairs to the coffee shop, Freddy allowed himself to be steered in the direction of a corner table.

"Freddy Nally," his classmate announced, "I'd like you to meet Callie Brent."

"Nice to meet you." He quickly recovered his manners and thrust out his hand.

The girl who rose from behind the table was drop dead gorgeous. Five foot two, maybe three; she was the prettiest little blonde he'd seen in a very long time. From her wavy ringlets down to her glowing smile, she was absolutely perfect, and within five seconds, Freddy was truly enamored with her.

"Hi Freddy, nice to meet you," she giggled, obviously nervous about the impromptu interview. "I hear you might be thinking about renting out your spare room if you find just the right tenant. So tell me, what kind of person are you looking for?"

Ready to jump across the table and grab Callie in a giant bear hug, Freddy realized it was probably out of the question, so he chose to make polite conversation instead. "Well, I'm looking for someone who's not to hung-up on themselves, kind of a free spirit."

"What else?" Callie grinned ear to ear.

"Someone my own age—not some thirty year old that I have nothing in common with."

"And?" She continued to spur him on.

"Hey," Freddy's classmate interrupted. "Why don't you guys grab fresh coffees and hash out the details."

Laughing, they both walked over to the counter and ordered mugs of hot chocolate, continuing the casual interview.

"Well, you've just described me to a tee," Callie gushed.

Freddy nodded, silently patting himself on the back for his ability to read people. "Why don't you stop by and have a look around my apartment. This all may be for nothing if you hate the look of my place."

"Doubt it," she grinned, "but if we need to do any redecorating, we'll do it together. Okay?"

"Okay." He reached for a scrap of paper. "Here's my address and phone number. I'll be home anytime after my last class. So if you wanna drop by after five, I'll be glad to give you the guided tour."

"I feel like I've know you for years," Callie smiled, rising to her feet to retrieve her knapsack from underneath her chair. "I'll be down by six, I promise. See you later, Freddy." She departed with the cutest of waves.

Watching her almost skip out of the coffee shop, Freddy made a mental note to blow off his last class and rush home to do a little housecleaning. He desperately wanted to make a good impression, and a sink full of dirty dishes wasn't a step in the right direction.

Forcing himself to attend his first afternoon class, Freddy was still unable to focus on the professor's lecture. Uninterested in the topic, he bent down and quietly pulled out his notes from the job board, reviewing the handwritten page of information.

Lab assistant — Veterinarian sciences. Sure, he'd possibly be working with doctors, but not the right kind. He crossed it out.

Data organizer — Medical research. The right department, but he wasn't interested in burying himself in a hundred pounds of clinical data.

Continuing to scan his own notes, it wasn't until halfway down the page that Freddy finally took notice of something he'd written.

Student needed / good computer skills — Department of plastic surgery.

It was a match made in heaven. The pay? Who cared? He'd

volunteer his time for free to get his foot in that door. Circling the information in red, Freddy couldn't wait to get out of class and check on the posting. Screw his last class; he was ready to blow off the remainder of the afternoon.

Chapter Sixteen

"I'm king of the world!"

—*Titanic, 1997*

It had taken two days of repeated messages before Freddy had finally been able to connect with the head of the plastic surgery department. Dr. Chew was an extremely busy man, and it wasn't until Friday morning that he'd been able to work Freddy into his hectic schedule.

"Double, double." Freddy announced to the counter girl, digging down in his pocket to extract a couple of singles. "And could you double cup that?" he suddenly remembered to ask, not interested in burning his hand as he made his way back across the campus.

Coffee being poured, Freddy took the opportunity to glance one last time at his tattered copy of the campus map. Following his notations, he was able to pinpoint Dr. Chew's office, a location well hidden and almost impossible to find without specific directions.

"Cinnamon sprinkles?" someone whispered right behind his head.

"Callie." Freddy instantly spun on his heels to face her newest friend. "I thought that was you," he grinned from ear to ear.

"What ya doing?"

"I have an appointment with Dr. Chew in plastic surgery."

"Why?" she asked, not one to wax philosophic.

"Part-time job, I'm hoping. Maybe a few bucks, a little extra credit. Who knows what'll come of it." Freddy picked up his large paper cup.

"Well, I talked to my parents, and although they're not crazy about me having a guy as a roommate, they've agreed to pay my rent."

"That's great." He leaned over and lightly bussed Callie on the cheek. "I was starting to have my doubts when you never called."

"I know. It's good news though, isn't it?"

"Well, I hate to run, sweetie, but I have to make this appointment. Not a good idea to keep the doctor waiting on our first meeting."

"Good luck." Callie smiled, gently squeezing Freddy's left hand before he turned to leave.

He made his way across the campus, threading back and forth through the halls of higher learning, finally finding himself at what he hoped was the right door. Nervously turning the knob, he took one last deep breath before stepping inside.

"Can I help you?" a lady reluctantly pulled her eyes off a computer screen.

"My name is Frederick Nally. I have a ten fifteen with Dr. Chew."

Pulling down an alternate screen, the woman leaned forward and ran her finger down the glass, searching for just the right block on the doctor's timetable.

"You're here to help out with the research project... and... you're the first year student from..."

"Medical Sciences," Freddy politely finished her sentence. "I'm here to apply for the job."

"Well, take a seat. Did you bring a resume?"

Pulling his papers out of his knapsack, he anxiously handed the secretary his information. "Has Dr. Chew interviewed a lot of students?"

"Well, we posted the job Monday morning, and at last count, we had over twenty-five applicants."

"Oh." he sank down into a waiting chair. "I guess I'm not the only one interested in this job."

Without warning, a grey haired oriental man entered through the same door Freddy had used, and silently walked up to the secretary's desk to retrieve his messages.

"Good morning, sir," the woman politely addressed him. "Your ten fifteen appointment is here to see you."

"Send him in," he answered, never raising his head as he moved straight through the front office and disappeared behind a second door.

"Follow me." The lady stood up, escorting Freddy into Dr. Chew's private office.

"Thank you." The doctor nodded at his secretary, casually motioning for Freddy to take a seat as he accepted the folder. Scanning the enclosed information, the doctor suddenly lifted his chin to appraise the young man occupying his guest chair. "You're first year? Medical Sciences?"

"Yes, sir. Hopefully premed."

"Hopefully?" He repeated in a questioning tone. "You don't have any confidence in your abilities?"

"I don't believe confidence is enough, sir. Sometimes outside factors seem to play a hand in our destiny without any warning."

Closing the folder, the doctor suddenly stood up from behind his desk, twisting his hips to face his credenza. Within a minute, he was brandishing a silver tray boasting two sparkling tumblers of orange juice, mindful to set the drinks in the middle of his desk. "Try to avoid caffeine. It's extremely detrimental to the human body. More than most people realize," he cautiously warned. "I'm preparing to co-author a paper for a student on the long term effects of accidental caffeine poisoning from over the counter nicotine patches."

Nodding, Freddy extended his arm and accepted the glass, not sure if he was supposed to take a sip or wait for the doctor's lead.

"Go ahead, drink. If I know you students, it'll be the first substantial dose of vitamins that's crossed your lips this morning."

He was right, and Freddy took the opportunity to tip his glass, a little surprised by the volume of pulp draining down the back of his throat. "Thank you, sir." He leaned in to set his empty glass back down on the tray.

"More?"

"Sure. I mean, yes please." Freddy quickly recovered his manners. Settled with his second glass, the young student sat back and waited for the doctor to begin his interview, suddenly quiet comfortable and no longer in any rush to leave.

"I assume that you, like most of the kids of your generation, are quite adept where computers are concerned. Is that a correct assumption?"

"Yes sir, I can hold my own with most of the computer geeks," he smiled.

"Well, sorry to disappoint you," the doctor rose from his chair, "but your computer skills will be wasted on this job."

Freddy didn't know how to respond. He was sure the posting had mentioned computer experience.

"And before you quote the job posting, let me add that it was mistake. It was supposed to read no computer experience necessary, interview skills a must."

"Oh, I see." He shrugged his shoulders.

"Well, Mr. Nally, are you still interested in continuing our meeting?"

"Yes sir, I am." He sat up straight in his chair. "Besides, if I was in love with my computer, I'd have applied to the faculty of computer sciences."

"That's fair," the doctor smiled. "Now I want you to take a piece of paper, and interview my secretary. I assume you don't know her on a personal level."

Freddy shook his head.

"Good. I'll give you five minutes, then I'm going to call you back and we'll compare notes. Are you ready?"

"I think so." He dug into his knapsack for a pad of paper.

Watching Julia finish her make up for the party only seemed to escalate Serena's bad mood. "Damn it," she whined. "I really feel like the poor little maid, watching the princess get ready for the ball."

"I don't know about *the ball*, but I'm pretty sure there'll be at least a *couple balls* hanging around," Julia teased. "How's my eyeliner?"

"Good," Serena nodded, still pissed that she wasn't well enough to make their director's party. "I feel pretty good. Maybe I should just get dressed and come with you? I don't want to disappoint Manny."

"You don't wanna disappoint Manny? Then don't let him see you with your tits all infected. By the way, are you rubbing on that cream from the doctor?"

"Yeah. Every two hours like he told me."

"Good, cuz Tony said the antibiotics aren't enough. You gotta use that tube of special cream, too."

Waltzing right up to the bathroom mirror, Serena quickly

unbuttoned her blouse and completely exposed herself. Leaning in as close as physically possible, she began inspecting her nipples. "They're not oozing anymore," she happily reported, unfortunately wincing the minute her fingertips grazed the swollen tissue of her left breast.

"You're still not going," Julia called out in a singsong kind of voice.

"Fine." She tromped out of the bathroom and began rummaging through the refrigerator. "What am I supposed to do all night while you're off doing tequila shots with Johnny Long Dong?"

Julia finished with a final coat of mascara before closing up her make-up drawer. "I left you a couple rocks on my dresser, but spread it out. It's the only thing in the house, and I don't want you climbing the walls before I get back. Got it?"

"I hear ya," Serena nodded, already making plans for her escape. "And in case I forgot to tell you, that was real nice of you to pay for my clinic visit and medication. I promise to pay you back as soon as I finish my next job."

"I know," Julia smiled. "You'll be working again in another week. I'll tell Manny that your flu is almost gone, and he can count on you for his next flick."

"Have a blast," Serena called out as Julia left in a flash of hairspray and tightly laced leather."

Not hungry, nothing to watch on satellite, Serena decided to do a little dope and maybe grab a nap. "Two rocks." Serena starred down at the dust-covered dresser. What in the hell was she supposed to do with an entire night and just two small rocks?

As she reached out with her right hand, she purposely passed over the crack cocaine and grabbed straight for the cordless phone. Serena knew Manny was programmed into Julia's speed dial; she'd seen her call him enough times. Sucking in one last deep breath for courage, she moved her thumb and pressed down the fourth button.

"Hello Manny." Serena pasted on her biggest smile, even though he'd be unable to see her face.

"Who's this?" a guy on the other end demanded, obviously too busy to bother with idle chitchat.

"It's Serena. I'm a friend of Julia's. We both just starred in the last porno you directed. You know, the one with the squirt bottle," she hoped to cue up his memory.

"Oh yeah, I heard Manny was trying out some new ass. But you're talking to Sigmund. I'm Manny's older brother. Whatcha want?" his German accent suddenly breaking through.

"Well, it's Friday night, and I'm sitting around with nothing to do."

"Aren't you going to the party in the Sunset Motel? The one Manny set up with the California buyers."

"No, I was too sick. But now I'm suddenly feeling better. Know of any other parties that I can attend?"

Sigmund brushed off the girl hanging on his arm, picking up his double shot of vodka as he moved away from the edge of the vacant dance floor. "You're that sexy little blonde," he attempted to conjure up her face from his brother's latest video.

"That's me, Sugar." She smiled, picking up a rock and carrying it over to the living room.

"Well, I do work on other projects, a few films all on my own. Without Manny," he reiterated so there would be no confusion. "We have different tastes, so sometimes, Manny and I work independently."

"Kind of like me and Julia." She pressed the speaker button on her phone. "We're friends, but we have different tastes; so sometimes we work independently, too."

Sigmund broke out into a hearty laugh. "I think we're on the same wavelength, my little Serena. I'm actually filming tonight. A special flick called *Scat Cat*. You interested in taking a starring role?"

"Scat Cat," she repeated, trying out the title. "This has nothing to do with animals, does it?" She suddenly demanded, not the least bit interested in being fucked by a horny German shepherd.

"No animals, just scat," he laughed, amused by her ignorance.

"How much?" she asked, taking the opportunity to light up her rock and inhale a lung full of smoke.

"Starring role, a thousand bucks. You wanna support from the sidelines, two hundred and fifty."

"Well, then I wanna be the star, of course."

Sigmund flicked open his pen and scratched Serena's address down on the palm of his hand, quickly scribbling a five-pointed star beside her name.

Following Dr. Chew through the recovery ward, Freddy couldn't help feeling like an impostor. Dressed in a white lab coat, complete with stainless steel note board, he actually could have passed for a resident doctor.

"You are here to extract information, not to render any sort of opinion, medical or otherwise. Clear?"

"Clear?" Freddy repeated.

"This first patient is a young woman in her early twenties. She is suffering from a severe case of Symmastia."

"Symmastia?"

"Breadloafing, uni-boob?" the doctor tried, hopping the slang term might actually trigger his student's memory banks.

"I've never even heard…"

Quickly flipping open the woman's chart, the doctor leaned over and showed Freddy a post-op photograph of the woman's chest, six months after her breast augmentation.

"That's awful," Freddy gasped. "Both her breasts are all joined together, like one giant boob with two nipples," he muttered in disgust.

Taking a moment to allow his student to process the information, Dr. Chew extracted his pen and began making notations. "This is not uncommon in women who undergo sub-muscular breast augmentation by untrained plastic surgeons."

"What did they do wrong?"

"During surgery, the muscle attached to the sternum and running horizontally between the two breasts is accidentally cut. Right after surgery, the operation may even appear to be a success, but as time passes, the patient's condition worsens." He knowingly shook his head. "Within a few days, the pressure of post-operative swelling forces the implants to move, and since the muscle that would normally hold the implants apart, away from the cleavage area has been severed, the implants migrate toward the center." Dr. Chew quickly scribbled a quick diagram of the patient's sternum and ribcage. "As a result of the pressure, the tissue can lift from the sternum and allow the implants to move into the center." He quickly drew arrows to give a sense of direction.

Freddy couldn't help but suck in his breath, unable to formulate any response.

"This movement causes the appearance of one large implant across the chest, hence the term, Breadloafing."

"Can you fix it?" Freddy finally spit out, shocked that any woman would be expected to live the remainder of her life in this horrible condition.

"That is why she is here under my care," Dr. Chew smiled. "Her first name is Lydia, and she has agreed to be interviewed for my case histories. The patient is waiting." He held out his hand.

"Now?" Freddy shook his head in amazement. "You want me to march in there and just start asking that woman a raft of personal questions."

"No," the doctor shook his head. "I want you to ask her these questions." He handed Freddy a three-page questionnaire. And remember, no opinions. You are there to interview the patient and take notes. Nothing more," he warned for the hundredth time.

"Can I ask you one more question, sir?"

"Sure," the doctor closed up his own papers to face his student. "What's your concern Mr. Nally?"

"Why have a first year student with no medical experience handle such an important interview. Don't you think a second or third year student with a better understanding of anatomy would do a much more competent job?"

"No, I actually tried third years last semester and the results were disastrous," he sadly reported. "Too much knowledge can sometimes be a curse. You will sit with the patient and record her responses in layman technology on a one to one basis. You will not be influenced by your education. You will not have any personal expectations of her existing condition or her expected recovery. You are clear of all prejudice. You, Mr. Nally, are exactly what I need."

"I appreciate your confidence, Dr. Chew. I just hope I won't let you down."

"Follow me." The doctor took off down the hall. "I will introduce you to Lydia before I leave for rounds."

Freddy obediently followed; not exactly sure what he was getting himself into, but willing to give the doctor's program a chance.

Having completed the formal introductions, Dr. Chew excused himself and left the room, praying that his instincts wouldn't fail him. He usually had a sixth sense about people, and this young man appeared to very sensitive. His intelligence was a given, accepted into the program at the tender age of eighteen. The doctor was obviously gambling on his people skills. Either way, he'd know within a couple of days. Two or three interviews and it would be obvious if he had a malleable product, someone he could mold to enhance his paper. He didn't have time for any further mistakes. He just prayed that he'd chosen the right student.

Chapter
Seventeen

"I am big! It's the pictures that got small."

—*Sunset Boulevard, 1950*

Serena didn't recognize a soul at the video shoot. Fairly new to the industry herself, she'd only met a handful of actors. Still, she would have felt much more comfortable if somebody's face had been familiar.

"Hey everybody," Sigmund shouted from the side door of the Laundromat. "Come round back, we're setting up inside here."

Slowly falling in line, Serena trudged along with the assembled group toward the rear entrance past all the drawn blinds.

"You said two hundred." Sigmund continued to haggle with what appeared to be the Laundromat's owner. "You trying to shaft me now? Cuz I know a thousand other places that'll be more than willing to shut down for a night."

"You calling me a liar?" the huge hulk of a man took another step toward the director. "I remember three hundred, so either pay me or pack up all your fucking shit and get the hell out of here!" he ranted.

Throwing his chin back and rolling his eyes at the ceiling, Sigmund had to fight every urge to grab the man and just squeeze until white brain material squirted out his ears.

"Three hundred?" the owner held out his hand.

Reminding himself that he was in the United States of America and he couldn't handle his problems the old way, Sigmund pulled out his bankroll and peeled off three C-notes. "You can do all your own cleaning," he yelled. "We're just filming and leaving."

"Whatever." The man waved his hand back over his shoulder.

"Alright people." Sigmund turned back to his actors. "We've got this place for the next four hours. The janitor will be in around two a.m. to clean up, and I wanna be long gone before that bitch gets a look at this place," he chuckled to himself, the laughter somehow evolving into a deep-throated snort.

"I got the poly," one of his grips called out while the other began pulling out camera gear. "Where we setting up?"

Dropping his eyes down toward the tiled floor, Sigmund slowly shuffled around in a circle until he was able to locate the recessed floor drain. "Here, right here." He stomped his foot. "Roll out the poly nice and wide. I promised that fat bastard that we wouldn't get any on the washers and dryers."

Everyone nodded as if they all knew what he was referring to.

"Okay kiddies," Sigmund shouted. "Let's strip so papa can see what we're working with."

Everyone instantly obeyed and began shedding their clothes, Serena included.

"Are we gonna get a chance to *clean up*?" Serena whispered to one of the other girls, feeling her confidence surge since remembering her own douche bottle.

"Are you fucking mad?" the chick laughed in Serena's face. "This is scat, we ain't cleaning fuck all beforehand.

Scat, scat, Serena continued to chant the word over and over in her head. It meant nothing to her, so she was totally unprepared for what came next.

"Let's warm up with a little finger painting. You," Sigmund pointed to a young chubby kid pacing back and forth by the coin-operated soap dispensers. "You dump me a load in the middle of that polythene, and you two," he pointed toward Serena and another girl, "you pick it up and rub it all over his body."

Serena suddenly froze, her legs instantly glued to the floor.

"And be careful girls." Sigmund stopped to light a cigarette. "I just want it on your hands. We don't have time for a whole bunch of hose downs, so just smear it all over his cock, and get your asses out of there."

Not even able to speak, Serena just stared wildly as the naked kid walked across the polythene-covered floor and squatted down on his haunches.

Without any further warning, he closed his eyes and began to defecate right in the middle of the polythene. Pushing and groaning, the kid looked as if he'd been holding his bowels all day, waiting hours for the director to cue his dump.

"Look, it's a coiler," one of the guys laughed, standing off to the side, casually fumbling with his cock as he worked to maintain his own erection.

As the kid let out one final moan, Serena noticed the mobile camera move in for a close up, panning directly onto the pile of fresh, human feces.

"Girls," shouted Sigmund, "time to make your move. And," he held up his hands to momentarily stop the action, "I want you two down on your hands and knees crawling in toward the shit. Act like it's chocolate and you can't wait to get a whiff."

Unconsciously backing up, Serena only realized she was out of room when her naked backside bumped into a wall mounted folding table.

"What's with you?" Sigmund yelled, quickly stepping around the polythene as he moved up toward his star. "You heard my directions," he yelled in her face, "now get down there and earn your thousand bucks!"

"I can't. I can't do... that." She began to cry. "I didn't... didn't know what... what scat was." Her wails began to fill the room.

"Listen bitch," he shoved her naked body toward an empty corner. "You make porn, this is just a different kind of porn. So what's your fucking problem?"

"It's shit," she tried to dry her eyes with the back of her had. "I can't rub that over his body. I'll puke!"

Sigmund stepped back for a second, suddenly conferring with one of his cameramen. "Alright," he smiled, confident he'd come up with a workable compromise. "Hit your knees, spread the shit, but when you think you're ready to puke, just give me a signal."

"What?"

"We're gonna film it. Could be a nice touch. So you ready now?"

"No!" she answered, some of her old spunk finally beginning to surface in her voice.

———————

By the time Callie and her ex-roommate had finished hauling up the last of her boxes, Freddy had finally figured out why he was suddenly so excited about the prospect of his new roommate. It was the personal bonding. He could almost feel what couldn't be seen. The closeness between the two girls was so obvious, giggling at their own private jokes, snickering at a shared memory. No wonder they were having such a difficult time parting ways.

"You'll love living with your boyfriend." Callie turned to comfort her old friend, tears welling in both their eyes.

"I do love him, but living with a *guy*," she stressed, "I don't wanna live with a *guy*, I wanna live with you."

Laughing through her tears, Callie reached out for another hug. "You *can* teach him to give a decent pedicure, and he already promised me not to leave the toilet seat up. And who knows, with enough practice, maybe he'll even start to eat baked feta on his pizzas."

"But who's gonna loan me when I run out of tampons?" she mumbled into Callie's neck.

"You'll be fine," Callie said as they stayed locked in their embrace.

Freddy silently slipped out of the kitchen and retreated to his room, intent on giving the girls some measure of privacy while he took the time to sort through his interview notes.

It was going to be a struggle to manage a full class load and his job with Dr. Chew, but in his mind, any sacrifice would definitely be worth it. Dr. Chew was one of the city's most respected plastic surgeons, and finally, Freddy felt like his first semester of university might actually be worth something.

"She's gone," Callie announced, dropping down onto Freddy's bed in a fit of tears.

"Oh sweetie, she'll be back, I promise." He reached out to stroke her hair, gently tucking a stray lock behind her left ear.

"I'll just miss having someone who really understands me. She knew me, knew all the secrets in my head." Callie sniveled, left arm flailing in an attempt to reach the tissue box.

"Well, we're roommates now. Maybe we should share a secret. Would that make you feel better?"

Interest piqued; Callie forced herself to wiggle upright as she delicately blew her nose. "Yeah, that might work. But you first," she giggled, wiping the remaining tears from her cheeks.

"A secret," Freddy mumbled aloud, so many to choose from, so little time. "Alright, but these secrets are for life. Promise?"

"Promise."

"Well, I do love the grad gown you have hanging in your closet," Freddy quickly blurted out.

"And?"

"And I wish you'd let me try it on," he quickly pulled up his hands to cover both his eyes.

Confused, Callie sat in silence. "I don't get it. What's your secret?"

"Didn't you hear me?" he dropped his hands, face turning a bright shade of red. "I said I loved your gown, and I wanna try it on."

"Ohhhhh." Callie finally clued in to the situation. "You wanna *try on* my dress. I get it," she giggled. "How come?"

"It's just a thing I've had since being a little kid. I love beautiful clothes, and unfortunately, most of the beautiful ones are women's."

Jumping off the bed, Callie ran to her room and returned with the dress, quickly peeling off the drycleaners plastic, she happily thrust it toward Freddy's chest. "Well, try it on."

The waist was much too snug, and even with the addition of a padded bra, the bust's extra material puckered in unflattering dents. Still, Freddy felt beautifully at peace, twirling circles in the middle of his room. "I can't imagine what it would be like to actually wear this in public. You must have felt like... like a princess," he stammered, looking for something better than that old cliché.

"It was a special night," she admitted. "I even lost my virginity in that dress."

"No way," Freddy gasped, hands rushing up to cover both his cheeks. "You have to tell me. You have to, you have to," he chanted over and over.

"Well, it really wasn't planned, but..."

———————

Gently pulling out his one c.c. needle as he released her tie off, Sigmund rose to his feet just as Serena's head began to bob. "That's good smack, ain't it, baby?" he gently stroked her chin. "We'll just give you a few more minutes to pull it together and then we're gonna film your big scene. Okay?"

"Okay," Serena managed to mumble through her haze.

She had absolutely no intention of filming some shit scene, but she had been interested in Sigmund's dope. So when he offered her a hit to think things over, it suddenly didn't seem like such a bad idea. And he was right about two things. The shit would wash off, and he would be sending her home with a thousand bucks cash.

"All right, you little fuckers, enough pissing around," the director shouted. "Our little star is back on track, but we're gonna have a little change in plans. You two," he pointed at the guys smoking a joint by the rinse tubs. "You two help her over on the poly, and lay her beside the pile. You," he pointed to the other girl.

"Candy. My name's Candy."

"All right, *Candy*," he stressed the pronunciation. "I want you to pick up that pile and drop it on Serena's belly. Then you lie down on top of her and begin wiggling around, kind of sliding back and forth. You know, like smearing a dab of butter between two pieces of bread," he motioned by rubbing his palms together. "You get what I mean, baby?"

"Yes," Candy nodded, almost tripping over the curled edge of the polythene.

"Alright, let's get ready to roll," Sigmund barked. "We've just got a little over three hours left, and I want at least two more set ups."

———————

They were both still sitting on the bed laughing and crying, when Freddy noticed that the clock was beginning to near midnight. "Holy shit, I still have to type out a list of answers for Dr. Chew. I can't believe we've been yammering for so long."

"I'm so glad I found you." Callie leaned across the bed and hugged her roommate. "Today could have been the worst night of my life, but you rescued me. You're my knight in shining armor... no, I mean crimson satin," she corrected herself.

Standing up to say their goodnights, Freddy had a hard time letting go, afraid that if Callie left his presence, the magic would somehow disappear and the spell would be broken.

"I want you to promise me something." Callie turned to grab Freddy's hand. "I want you to promise that come tomorrow morning, you won't be all weird or anything. Promise me?"

"That's just what I was thinking," he gushed.

"So, do you promise?"

"I swear. Now go to bed and get some sleep. I have to run out and meet Dr. Chew first thing, but as soon as I'm back, we'll have some breakfast and start unpacking the rest of your stuff."

Callie rubbed her eyes and nodded her head, following her new roommate's instructions.

With the apartment quiet, Freddy began setting up his workstation at the kitchen table, complete with a bowl of munchies and a bottle of water. His Saturdays were usually relegated to grocery shopping, homework, and housecleaning—he would now have to budget his time to include Dr. Chew. His first interview report was due early, and no matter what, he wouldn't let the doctor down. He was more than willing to stay up all night if necessary. Freddy believed that job would open doors for him, and he'd given the interview his best effort, attempting to balance sympathy with clinical objectivity.

"Your name," he had muttered, recording the proper spelling

of Lydia's first and last, followed by her hospital ID number, copied directly off her plastic wristband.

"You look so young," she'd immediately blurted out after Freddy finished Part A of the questionnaire. "Are you in high school or med school?"

"First year, medical sciences," he reassured the young woman. "How old are you?"

"I'm twenty-three, but I feel like I'm a hundred and ten."

Continuing down the form, Freddy noticed he only had a couple questions that were more general, before they became a hell of a lot more personal.

"You ever seen anything like this before?" Lydia whispered, turning her head to see if anyone else was listening to their conversation.

"No," he reluctantly shook his head. "I'm kinda new, so I don't have a lot of experience to draw from."

"But you're a guy," she argued. "So be honest. Would you date a woman who looked like me?"

Dr. Chew's words rang over and over inside Freddy's head. *Render no opinion, just record the information.*

"How about we just finish this questionnaire so you can get some rest?"

"Fine," Lydia moaned, turning away to shield her eyes. "I think I know your answer anyway."

Freddy knew exactly what she was referring to, but pretended not to hear her comments. "So, Part B... Was this your first experience with plastic surgery?"

Struggling to sit up straight in her bed while she wiped an errant tear, Lydia very carefully adjusted the pillows piled up around her neck. "I had my nose done for my sixteenth birthday. My mom had been saving up from the grocery money since I was twelve. And I paid for these veneers the summer of grade eleven." She pulled back her gums to show off her teeth. "But otherwise, I'm pretty much natural, well... until this." She slowly pointed toward her chest. "Did you know that he is gonna be the third doctor who's gonna try and fix me?"

"No." Freddy began flipping through his pages, searching for the appropriate blank.

"Yeah, Dr. Chew is my last hope. I'm pretty much out of cash."

"Hold on," he flipped over his questionnaire and scanned down the page. "Here it is. Can you tell me how you've managed to pay for your plastic surgeries?"

"Which ones?"

"I think they mean them all. But let's start with the original implants. How did you pay for them?"

"I saved up the cash," Lydia proudly announced. "I worked doubles every weekend, and picked up all the overtime I could handle."

Freddy rushed to scribble down her answers.

"But after the first one, when things started fucking up... oops, I probably shouldn't use that word in here, should I?"

"It's alright," he smirked, not even bothering to lift his head.

"Well, before I went in for my first repair job, I had to cash in a bond I'd bought when I'd dated this accountant. Then for my second repair, I had to split it up between two credit cards."

"Wow," Freddy couldn't help but remark. "This has been really tough on you."

"You have no idea." Lydia twirled her fingers in her lap. "For this surgery, my last," she emphasized, "I had to sell my car."

Skipping to his next question, Freddy read it aloud before lifting his head to gauge the patient's reaction. "Can you tell me how the surgery that brought you here has affected your life? For example, your career, your relationships, your sense of self-worth?"

"You talking about the first one, or the repair jobs?"

Dropping his head down toward his papers, Freddy frantically searched for any corroborating explanations. "I think they mean your original surgery," he mistakenly answered, interpreting the form incorrectly.

"Well," she sighed, "I can tell you what it was supposed to do for me."

Freddy just nodded his consent.

"It was supposed to get me off the main floor and into the private dining lounge; that's what it was supposed to do."

"And," he encouraged her.

"And instead I lost my job."

"Cause of all the other surgeries?"

"No, cuz I look ridiculous in the uniform. I don't have any cleavage," Lydia angrily threw her hands in the air. "My chest look like someone stuffed a garden hose down the middle of my boobs and pumped me full of water. You tell me who's gonna hire a cocktail waitress with no cleavage? Cuz let me tell you, honey, business men don't tip waitresses with their blouses buttoned right up to their neck."

"Do you think you'll ever have anymore plastic surgery in the years to come?"

"You talking about after the repair, aren't you?" Lydia confirmed.

"Yes, after the repair." Freddy squeezed the notation in beside the typed question.

"I don't know; I'm only twenty-three. How in the hell am I going to know how I'll look when I'm all old and wrinkled at forty?"

"Just a couple more," he'd promised, turning to the last page of the form. "How many of your close family and friends have had plastic surgery in the last five years?"

Taking a moment to tally her list mentally, Lydia came up with six, maybe seven; if she was willing to count an old acquaintance that she no longer spoke to.

The remaining steps had been somewhat routine; concluding with Lydia's signature enabling Dr. Chew to publish any and all of the answers, providing her identity was strictly protected.

Freddy had risen to shake her hand, wish her the best of luck, and quickly remove himself from her room, petrified that he might never find the courage to interview another patient.

Chapter Eighteen

"Snap out of it!"

—*Moonstruck, 1987*

He knew he should probably head down to the office and make cold calls, but Wally just couldn't work up the energy to make the trip. When he chose to stay home instead and work on the house, he decided it was as good a time as any to prep the backyard for the coming winter. Before long, the leaves would have to be raked and garden pots stowed in the shed. All the kid's plastic outdoor toys could be collected and the Christmas lights strung around the eaves. Actually, not a bad way to spend a Saturday if you enjoyed working outside with kids playing at your feet.

"Daddy, can we make pumpkins?" Colin begged, toting a handful of orange garbage bags pre-painted with triangle shaped eyes and gape-toothed smiles.

Quickly scanning the yard, Wally bent down and reluctantly

shook his head. "Sorry Colin, but we just don't have enough leaves yet. Maybe next weekend."

Suddenly spotting the neighbor's cat precariously balancing on the edge of the joint fence, his son dropped the bags where he stood and ran off to attempt capturing the animal with his bare hands.

"Be careful." Wally yelled after his son. "She'll scratch your eyes out if you get hold of her tail."

"I finally found them." Annette happily announced, poking her head out of the metal storage shed. "Come help me."

Carrying out the boxes for his wife, Wally stood back as she dove down into the collection of fall decorations. "Look at the wreath," she excitedly clamored. "Even the berries are still red. I'm sure glad I spent the money on that can of lacquer. Now I won't have to strip it all down and start over."

Bending to pick up his rake and grab a pair of pruning shears, Wally silently plodded off toward the front yard. Pruning back the summer's growth never one of his favorite tasks.

"You need some bags?" his wife interrupted his train of thought as he's just knelt down beside the hedge and began trimming the clumps of shriveled berries.

"No, I'll just let them drop and then rake 'em into a pile later."

"So, what do you think?" she trotted up the front steps to hang her favorite decoration. "I always admire a home with a beautiful wreath. Don't you? It just somehow exudes warmth."

"Looks good," Wally agreed, amazed at his wife's natural craftsmanship when it came to making something beautiful out of leftover ribbons and dried up old twigs.

"Well, I'm going to take the kids in and make brunch," she smiled. "I'm sure little Tammy needs to use the potty, and I really don't want any accidents today."

"I'll be in as soon as I finish this side," he waved his pruning shears toward the unruly hedge.

With Annette and the kids finally sequestered inside the house, Wally figured it was safe to pull out the gas powered hedge trimmer. When he returned from the attached garage, he yanked on the cord and sent the motor whirling, finally able to reach right across the maze of tangled branches.

"Wally," a voice shouted. "Hey Wally," it repeated for a second time.

As he continued with his trimming, he nearly had a heart attack when a hand clamped down on his right shoulder.

"Fuck." He yanked his fingers off the trimmer's handle, the emergency kill switch automatically extinguishing the blades. "What the hell?" he continued to curse. "I could have cut your hand off."

"Well, maybe I deserve it," Billy chuckled.

He stared at his ex-boyfriend as if looking at the face of a stranger, Wally stood speechless, only ten steps from the house's front door.

"I thought you'd be in the office today, but when I drove by, I didn't see your van. I decided to swing by your house." He shrugged his shoulders. "Hope you don't mind."

"Of course I mind," Wally barked, recovered from the shock of Billy's unexpected appearance. "What the hell do you want from me?"

"I just wanted to say that I'm sorry."

"Good." Wally turned his back and yanked the cord on the trimmer.

"But I have something else to say," Billy shouted at the top of his lungs, fighting to compete with the roar of the gas motor.

Once again pulling his fingers back, Wally allowed the trimmer to die. "This is not the time or the place," he hissed. "So I suggest you get the hell away from here before Annette comes outside to see what's going on."

"Meet me later?"

"No."

"Well, I'm not leaving until you agree to meet me," Billy announced, crossing his arms as if preparing to wait him out.

"We have nothing to talk about. You almost got me fired, you know that?"

"Well, don't be such a baby, Wally. I was the one who did get fired, not you. And I'm the one who's stuck paying back the eleven grand."

"You're the one who took it." Wally's voice jumped an octave, a common occurrence during moments of extreme stress.

"Please, I really need to talk to you," Billy begged. "I wanna apologize. Come on." He stepped toward Wally as if moving in for an embrace.

"Don't!" Wally barked. "My kids could be watching."

"Then name a time and place, or I'm just going to keep coming back."

Wally felt like a rabbit in a cage, running in circles with no place to go. "Well," he conceded, "I was going to swing by the office this afternoon. We can meet at your apartment instead. I'll be there at two."

"I was thinking more of a nice seafood restaurant, something with…"

Wally glared straight into Billy's eyes. "I'll be at your apartment at two o'clock. If you're not there, so be it. But don't you ever come back here again!" he warned.

Billy leaned around Wally and casually waved at the patio window, smiling as if he'd just spotted the face of a friend.

"Who are you…?" Wally spun around and caught Colin's face peeking out from behind the living room sheers.

"See you at two," Billy conceded, turning and slinking off down the sidewalk.

"Who was that?" Annette's voice suddenly called out from the front step.

Wally's first instinct was to lie—a story about a Jehovah Witness already formulating on the tip of his tongue. "That was Billy Grant from work. He wants to have a meeting with me this afternoon."

"That was Billy?" Annette rushed down the steps in her stocking feet. "Which way did he go?"

"I don't know, and I don't care," Wally barked, bending down to pick up his assortment of tools.

"What did you tell him?" She searched her husband's face.

"I told him to get the hell off my property."

"Are you going to meet him?"

"I haven't decided yet."

"I think we should talk about this," Annette firmly announced.

Wally agreed, hoping that his wife's bravado was still intact after they'd spoken.

While the children occupied themselves with their coloring books, Sarah began working on her lesson plan for Sunday school. With Justice working a ten-hour shift down at Jupiter Greenhouse, she thankfully had the remainder of the day to herself. Quickly remembering to check on any holidays that might coincide with her duties as Sunday school teacher, she immediately noticed the pagan holiday of Halloween, garishly marked on her grocery store calendar.

"Halloween," she whispered to herself, turning to dig into the Sunday school mail passed down from the church's secretary. Sorting through the papers, she finally found the exact information she'd been looking for, leaning back in her kitchen chair, she prepared to digest the information.

Dear Sunday School Teachers:

Before the time of enlightenment, a heathen festival full of superstitious beliefs and occult ceremonies developed in honor of the lord of death and his followers of the damned. On the night of October 31ˢᵗ, this lord of death allegedly summoned all the condemned souls and allowed a select few to return to earth and take temporary residence amongst the living.

Because of this association, Halloween is thought to be a night for attempting to work evil charms and inflicting all types of spells. In the best interest of our congregations, we strongly suggest that you explain this fact to your Sunday school students and substitute a Halloween party with a Fall Celebration.

Blindly grabbing for her teacup, Sarah brought it up to her lips, sipping the brewed liquid without even a momentary glance away from the pages.

Halloween costumes shall be replaced by children wearing light colored clothing adorned with loving signs of natures such as; leaves, flowers, grains, and mature fruits and vegetables. Each student attending the celebration should receive a basket of treats relevant to your community (excluding any commercial candy decorated with Halloween logos).

Under no circumstances will the children of our congregation be encouraged to roam the streets of our

*community and beg for treats from family, friends, or
neighbors.*

Respectfully.
G.L. Grier
Administrational Services

It was almost too much information to comprehend in one
sitting, so after boiling herself yet another cup of tea, Sarah picked
up the papers and attempted to read through them a second time.
This time round, she carefully underlined any words she did not
recognize in pencil, taking the time to individually look each and
every one up in her own pocket dictionary.

"What are you doing, Mommy?" her daughter suddenly asked
from the far side of the kitchen table.

"Mommy's doing God's work," she flatly answered—her child
was no stranger to such a reply.

"When you're done working for God, can you color with us?"

"My work will never be done, sweetie, but Mommy will take a
break and go color with you. Want to go right now?"

"Yes, please," her daughter grinned, reaching for her mother's
hand.

By the time Grandma Freeman had picked up all three kids and
successfully strapped them into her car, Wally was already having
second thoughts about his plan.

"If you're not over by nine a.m. tomorrow," Wally's mother
informed them, "the children will be accompanying me to
church."

"We'll be there." He leaned forward to hug his mother before she readied herself to leave, wondering how she'd feel about her first-born son if he finally revealed the truth.

"I'm dressed," Annette announced, having thrown on a clean pair of jeans and a hooded grey sweatshirt.

"What about the oven?" Wally motioned toward the red light glowing on the control panel.

"Oh shit, the ham." Annette turned and rushed back into the kitchen. "How long are we going to be gone, cuz it'll probably be fine until three or four."

"Just shut it off," he sighed. "I don't want to have to worry about the house burning down while I'm gone. Do you?"

Annette reached across the burners and clicked off the heat, nervously moving to her husband's side. "I'm ready."

"Then let's go." He turned, grabbing the van keys off the kitchen counter.

Ten minutes later, Wally pulled into a parking lot and quickly located a visitor parking space before turning the engine off in the family van.

"I don't really know what would be the right way to do this, Annette. All I know is that I owe you the truth. So," he sucked in a huge breath, "I'm just going to lay it all on the line. I had a homosexual affair with my trainee, Billy Grant, and I think he might be planning to blackmail me to raise the deposit money he stole."

Annette had been taught in high school biology that all respiratory functions were controlled by involuntary muscles, and no matter how traumatic an event, the body would continue to breathe, as long as the muscles were intact. But suddenly, she wasn't so sure and was actually afraid she might be destined to make medical history.

"I can't believe that I cheated on you, Annette. I love you. I don't want to lose you, or my children."

"I don't understand," she was finally able to mutter, no tears, no hysterical shouting. "How could you have an affair… with another man? You're… you're not gay."

It was Wally's turn to evaluate his own breathing, his throat tightening as if wrapped round and round with spools of nylon rope. "I love you," he repeated, the absurdity of the situation starting to grate on Annette's nerves.

"Are you trying to tell me you're a fag? A guy who likes to have sex with other men? Cuz I really… Wally… I, I don't understand what you're trying to tell me."

He reached across the bucket seat, and Wally pulled his wife into his arms, surprised by her willingness to be touched. She never fought him, yet she never responded to his embrace. It was like hugging a rubber mannequin. Anatomically correct, yet absolutely lifeless.

"Are you leaving me?" Annette finally began sobbing into her husband's chest.

"No baby, I love you," he tried to soothe her.

"But," she suddenly jolted upright in her seat. "You had an affair with Billy? What does that mean exactly?" she pulled a wad of tissue out of her jean pocket. "Cuz to me, that just sounds like you're a homosexual."

As he squeezed the steering wheel with both his hands, Wally struggled to find some common ground. "I'm not gay, I'm married, to you!" he emphatically pointed out.

"But…?"

"I just had some urges. Urges like… in college," he suddenly jumped on an idea. "You hear stories about kids playing around, trying things out. But it doesn't really affect them long term. That's what happened to me," he swore. "I just acted on some stupid urges."

"You never went to college," Annette sniffled.

"Exactly, that's why I had to get it out of my system. And I'm done, it's gone."

Staring straight forward through the pitted windshield, Annette struggled to understand her husband's way of thinking. She could have handled bankruptcy, even cancer, but finding out that her husband had a homosexual affair... well, that was kind of uncharted waters. "Do you like having sex with women?" she slowly pulled away.

"I love it." He spun in his seat, throwing his hands in the air. "You know I do."

She didn't know anything right now.

Checking his watch, Wally really hated to push his wife, afraid she might actually buckle under the pressure, but he did have a two o'clock deadline to keep. "I don't want to hide anything else from you." He reached out to hold her hand. "So I'm going up to Billy's apartment to see what he wants. Do you wanna come with me?"

Did she wanna go with him? It was kinda like asking James Dean if he was going to bother switching gears. "I... I... I don't know," she stuttered, a bad habit she'd finally conquered back in seventh grade.

"Well, I'm going in. Billy lives on the second floor, apartment number twelve if you change your mind." He patted his wife's shoulder. "I shouldn't be long."

Annette sat motionless, frozen behind a wall of pain and confusion.

He suddenly decided to pull out his keys before opening the driver's door. Wally stopped for a second to evaluate his wife's condition. "Are you going to be alright?"

She nodded, words literally evading her.

"Billy, open the door," Wally called out; after ringing the apartment's buzzer at least four or five times with no answer.

"You made it." The door suddenly swung open.

"Why are you in a housecoat?"

"Sorry, I was just in the shower. But come on in." Billy stepped away from the door, purposely allowing his robe to fall open. "You want a drink? I have a really nice merlot?"

"No." Wally stood his ground, not even willing to take a seat on the heavily cushioned couch.

"Relax, no one's going to attack you. Sit down, you're making me uncomfortable."

"Well," Wally began to shout. "You make me uncomfortable, too. What was with you dropping by my house this morning? You want us both to go down for your cheating and lying?"

"Just shut up and remember who you're talking to, Freeman."

"Who?" Wally called him on his last statement. "Who am I talking to? You're not my co-worker any more, or my boyfriend. So who am I talking to?"

Billy didn't like the way the *new* Wally was acting. He needed to get control of the situation fast, and if a showdown wasn't going to work, he always had other options. "Ever since our last night in your van, my lower back has been killing me. Would you please rub it a few times, just enough to take out the tension?" he begged in his most seductive voice.

Wally never moved an inch.

This time, Billy allowed his robe to totally slide off his shoulders, and then he walked straight to where Wally was standing—only wearing a tight set of cotton briefs. "Don't you like me anymore? Cuz I still like you." He slowly picked up Wally's right palm and began pulling it over toward his own cock.

"Don't." Wally roughly yanked back his hand, unaware of the door slowly opening behind his back. "Don't you ever touch me again!"

"You heard him," Annette echoed her husband's sentiment. "Quit touching him, you fucking pervert!"

"Pervert?" Billy began to laugh. "It takes two, baby." He walked over to a side table and poured himself a large glass of red wine.

"I know what you did to my husband, and we're..." she reached for Wally's hand, "we're here to tell you to leave us alone."

"Came clean did we, hey Wally? Decided to play *confessional* with the little missus?"

"She's my wife," he answered. "I had to tell her."

"True." Billy slowly pulled on his robe before dropping down into his antique wingback. "I'm just wondering what exactly you *had to tell*? Did you mention that you're a bottom, and you like it best when I'm rough? Oh, maybe you left out the part where you love to shove you cock up my tight little ass instead of inside her stretched out old pussy?"

Before Annette could be bullied into returning an insult, Wally stepped forward to her rescue. "Shut up, you asshole! You know damn well that I didn't hurt my wife with a replay of all the gory and disgusting details, because I obviously have more class than you. But for the record, she knows we engaged in homosexual sex, and that's enough."

"You surprise me, Freeman." Billy set his glass down on one of two matching end tables. "I didn't know you're balls were quite... that big. And I do know your balls."

"So." Wally swallowed hard, struggling not to notice the growing bulge between Billy's legs. "Why exactly did you stop by my house? What did you want to talk to me about?"

Rising to top up his glass, Billy suddenly diverted from his original plan and walked straight up to Annette's face. "Let me give you a little advice, honey. Just cuz you've got a ring on his finger, doesn't mean you've got a ring in his nose. He wandered once, sweetie. Chances are, he's gonna jump the fence again!"

"That's enough." Wally forcefully spun his wife around to face the door. "We're leaving, and if you ever come by my house again, I'm gonna call the cops!"

Annette was too shocked to even attempt translating her thoughts into words

Unfortunately, Billy still had enough words left in his arsenal for everyone. "By the way, *Annette*," his tongue played with her name. "What makes you so damn sure that I'm your husband's only lover?"

———————

Never one to waste, Sarah slowly picked out the seams holding last year's fairy wings to the back of her daughter's white cotton dress. It had taken her over an hour to remove the stuffed pantyhose spider legs she'd previously attached to her son's sweatshirt, so she knew the last fifteen minutes she'd spent with the seam-ripper was just the beginning.

"Spiderman legs," her son happily announced the minute he picked up the first section of stuffed pantyhose. "Me Spiderman." He began waving it wildly around the living room.

"No honey." Sarah jumped up from her chair. "Give that to Mommy, that's not for playing." She took the leg away, to her son's disappointment. "Go color with your sister, alright?"

She was so deeply immersed in her project, Sarah almost jumped out of her skin when her husband unexpectedly swung open the apartment door.

"Don't you keep this locked when I'm gone?" Justice opened their line of communication with an accusation. "Anybody could just walk in here and take one of the kids."

"Sorry, I was just carrying up some boxes from the storeroom," she explained. "I must have left it unlocked by accident."

"Well, please be more careful." He turned to lock the deadbolt behind his own back. "What are you doing?" he asked, setting his lunch cooler down by the boot tray.

"Daddy, Daddy." The kids came running from their bedroom. "You have anything left?"

For reasons Justice couldn't understand, his kids just loved to snack on any leftovers from his lunch pail. Soggy sandwiches flattened by his thermos, beaten up apples, crushed cookies; they were all treasures in his kid's eyes. "Sarah?" he turned to his wife, not willing to feed the kids if their lunch was just a few moments away.

"Go ahead." Sarah smiled at her children. "But all the wrappers come back to the kitchen," she warned, not the least bit interested in finding tiny balls of plastic wrap hidden between the folds of their beds. "You're home early." She quickly glanced at the living room clock before putting down her seam ripper. "Was there a problem?"

"It's pouring rain." He gave his coat a quick shake before hanging it up in the closet. "Haven't you been outside today?"

"No, not yet. I kept meaning to take the kids to the park, but I got so tied up with my lesson plans for church tomorrow, that I lost track of time."

"Well, it's too late now. It came down in buckets, so the ground is all soaked."

"They've been happy." She quickly stuffed the remaining Halloween costumes back into the green garbage bag.

"I'm working tomorrow," Justice announced, poking his head in the refrigerator to see if anything tickled his fancy.

"What about church? You missed service last week, too?"

"Not an option."

Cleaning up her papers, Sarah found herself wondering whether it would be a good time to bring up the church's new policy on trick or treating.

"Sarah, I was wondering if you were interested in looking at a new place with me?" Justice casually questioned, knowing she'd been dreaming about moving into a three-bedroom apartment every since their third child was born.

"You found one we can afford?"

"I put the word out at work, and one of the hor... ti... culturists," he took his time pronouncing the word, "said he had a house for rent."

"Where?"

"Millbrook, only ten minutes from here. And he's even willing to look at some kind of purchase contract. I can't remember the name of it, but it's a kind of a lease where you don't have to put up a lot of cash."

"Oh Justice, God hasn't forsaken us. He's ready to reward our faith."

Unconsciously grinding his rear molars, Justice bent over to wash his hands in the kitchen sink, a habit Sarah usually abhorred.

"When can we see it?"

"I said I'd check with you first; see if you were interested. He did give me the key, just in case you were curious." Justice slowly fished it out of his back pocket.

"Kids," Sarah yelled out at the top of her lungs. "Get your coats. We're going for a truck ride."

As Justice circled around the neighborhood, Sarah scanned the houses looking to match the correct address.

"There it is," she squealed, already in love with the idea.

"He said the basement had a lot of water damage, so it's been stripped, but I could build it out again as soon as we'd saved enough for lumber and supplies."

"But there's three bedrooms on the main floor, right? That's what you said, three bedrooms," she began jabbering like a jaybird.

"That's what I said." Justice leaned forward, turning his head to flash his wife a great big smile.

"Can we have a dog?" the kids began to clamor, caught up in the excitement of moving to a house with a yard.

"Let's look around before we start buying a pet," he announced, slamming the truck into park before reaching over to unbuckle his kids.

"It smells funny," Sarah was the first to announce.

"Well, it's been locked up like a drum for weeks," Justice explained, attempting to pull the owner's key out of the open front door.

"There's no appliances," she added with disappointment. "How are we going to afford to buy a fridge and a stove?"

"No problem, he said it'll come with five appliances."

"Five?" his wife stopped opening the cupboards to do the math.

"Fridge, stove, washer and dryer, and," he stopped for emphasis, "a dishwasher."

Sarah was amazed at their good fortune. "The rooms are so big. Why would anybody want to move out of this house?"

"I don't know, but I don't think we should look a gift horse in the mouth, do you?"

Sarah just grinned, leaning down to hug her children as they all ran up into her arms.

"I just wanna check the basement. If I don't find any water after a rain like today, then I think we're good to go."

"Praise the lord," Sarah chanted aloud. "Praise the lord in all his glory and thank him for his blessings."

"Amen," Justice yelled up from the depths of the basement. "She's as dry as a preacher's liquor cabinet!"

Chapter Nineteen

"A woman's heart is a deep ocean of secrets."

—*Titanic, 1997*

"Hello, Mother Freeman," Annette cleared her throat. "I was wondering if you'd mind keeping the children until a little later in the day."

"Not at all, dear. Is there a problem?"

"Oh no." Annette curled up the fingers on her left hand, viciously pressing the nails down into the tender flesh of her own palm. "Wally had to run out with the van, and I'm… I'm… We'll pick them up before supper. Okay?"

"That's fine with me, dear. You know how I feel about my grandbabies. It seems like we never have enough time together."

Repeatedly dabbing at her dripping nose instead of taking a chance and blowing it, Annette fought to hang onto her composure. "Thank you," she forced out the words, three seconds from hanging up the phone.

"Hey, I just had an idea," her mother-in-law announced. "I was going to make a really nice pot roast, you know, the one Wally likes with the baby red potatoes. Well, how 'bout I bring it round about five, and we can all sit down and have ourselves a nice family dinner?"

"I really don't feel well." Annette blew her nose, no longer concerned with disguising the noise.

"You know, dear, come to think of it, you're not sounding like yourself. Maybe I should keep the kids another night?"

"Tomorrow's Monday and there's school."

"But if you're sick?"

"Listen," she unintentionally adopted a firmer tone. "Either Wally or I will be round to pick the kids up before supper. Please have them ready."

"I will, you don't have to tell me twice."

"Sorry, but I'm going to hang up now," Annette almost cried.

"Please call me if you need anything all, alright, dear?"

"I will, I will," she promised, desperate to get off the phone.

"Bye sweetie."

"Bye." Annette pressed the end button, finally able to disconnect from the torturous call.

"Was that my mom?" Wally inquired.

"Yes," she answered, turning to set the phone back into its charger. "She's agreed to keep the kids until later this afternoon."

"I'm so wiped," he moaned. "I think I'm going to lie down on our bed and have a nap. I… I didn't really sleep well… you know, on the loveseat and all. Really wish I'd have bought you that bigger couch," he weakly attempted a stab a humor.

"I didn't sleep either." Annette tried to massage the puncture marks out of her left palm.

"Then you should go lay down, too," Wally conceded. "I'll stretch out in Monica's bed. It's long enough."

"It's a day bed," she stated the obvious. "Monica's just about outgrown it herself."

Wally was stumped and much too exhausted to spar verbally with his wife. "So what now?" he threw his hands in the air. "Should we draw up a schedule, maybe ink a line down the middle of our bed? What do we do?"

"I don't know," Annette cried, surprised that she was still able to drudge up actual tears. "I don't have a fucking clue what we're supposed to do?"

In all the years they'd been married, Wally had never heard his wife curse as much as he had in the last twenty-four hours. It was unsettling, to say the least.

"I'm going to lie down. You can do whatever you want." Annette turned and stomped up the bedroom stairs.

Karen sat alone at her kitchen table, repeatedly attempting to sink the floating Cheerios with the tip of her spoon.

"Any left?" Alicia asked, picking up the box and giving it a good shake before her roommate even answered.

"Oh, I took it all." Karen finally snapped out of her trance. "But I think there are a couple of other boxes in the cupboard."

"Piss on it, I'll just eat this." Alicia grabbed a piece of dried pizza out of an open box.

Karen said, "One of these days, you're..."

"I know," she interrupted. "One of these days I'm gonna bite into a cockroach and not even know it. So what's up with you?" she plopped down into one of the swivel chairs.

"Nothing."

"Nothing, my ass. Look, I have to meet someone right away,

about this thing, so you're going to have to spill it out a little quicker. No time for games," Alicia bluntly summed up her morning plans.

"It's been five days and he hasn't called."

"I assume we're talking about your little steroid puppy," she continued to chew.

"Tony, Tony DeMarco," Karen corrected her friend.

"Yeah, so?"

"Well, I really liked him, and I thought we had something kinda special going on. I was sure he'd call."

Standing up to grab yet another chunk of the leftover pizza, Alicia changed her mind and this time hopped up on the kitchen counter. "So?"

"So, I really wanted him to call and I can't figure out why he didn't?"

"Maybe you give bad head?"

"Piss off." Karen grabbed her bowl, no longer interested in being teased.

"Well fuck, I don't know why he didn't call you." Alicia jumped up off the counter and threw her half-eaten slice back in the box. "He's not married, is he?"

"No, he said he was single."

"Oh, I know what you mean. A man's never lied to me before, either."

Tossing her remaining breakfast down the sink, Karen quickly rinsed the bowl before loading it into the dishwasher. "I didn't get the sense he was a bull-shitter. He just didn't seem like the type. It's kinda like…" she struggled for an explanation. "It's like he doesn't need to impress anyone, so he doesn't have to lie."

"That's profound." Alicia bent over the counter and quickly squiggled Tony's last name on a corner of the cardboard box. "So what you gonna do now? Stop by the local church and maybe light a few candles?"

"I'm going to do absolutely nothing. Today, I'm staying at home, I'm going to finish my laundry, and suck up at least eight hours of really bad television. And you? What's on your agenda?"

"I gotta work a little later."

"But I thought you were on nights. What happened?"

"Long story. Let's just say that my supervisor is going to have to get his kicks looking down some other bitch's blouse."

"What?" Karen spun on her heels. "You actually went to management and reported this guy? I'm shocked. I thought you'd of just taken a pair of scissors and stabbed him a couple hundred times in each eye."

"Interesting, but I wasn't in the mood," she flashed Karen the finger. "So I made a little deal instead. I get days, he gets suspended, and nobody has to bleed."

"You're good."

"Well, I better blow. Don't wanna be late now that I'm the poster girl for women's rights and all."

"You go girl," Karen laughed, suddenly feeling a little better. "Are you going to be home for supper?"

"What you making?" Alicia called out from her bedroom.

"It's bad manners to ask someone what they're cooking before you decide whether or not you want to accept their invitation."

"I know. What you making?"

"Sweet 'n sour meatballs and wild rice."

"White rice."

"Wild rice," Karen argued back. "You know this isn't a negotiation, don't you?"

"White rice and I promise not to borrow anymore of your underwear when you're not home."

"Eeewww," Karen moaned as a shiver ran down her spine.

While lying on his side in his daughter's bed with his knees bent at a forty-five degree angle, Wally couldn't help but wonder what the future was going to hold. Would Annette leave him, or maybe just throw him out of his own house? And work... how long would they keep him on staff now that everybody knew about him and Billy? Shit, he was probably the laughing stock of the entire sales floor.

Two months ago, everything had been fine. He'd had a decent job and he was bringing home a decent wage. Then, the sales manager had tapped him to help work the kinks out of their mentoring program. It had sounded great. A thirty percent increase in his base salary, and no more stupid cold calls. God, how he hated cold calls.

"Hello Mrs. Smith, this is Walter Freeman calling from Eternity Funeral Homes. I don't want to alarm you, but did you know that the average family pays anywhere from thirty-five to fifty-five percent more when there's no prearranged funeral package in place at the time of a loss?"

He shook his head, disgusted with the company's mandatory script. If Wally had been allowed to format an opening bit, it would have come out a little different.

"Hello Mrs. Smith, this is Wally calling. You and I both know you've got one foot in the grave, so how about I stop by with some casket brochures, and you pick out your favorite box?"

Well, at least it wouldn't all be bullshit.

"Never mention the words *death* or *money* when selling a prearranged funeral package," his manager had continually harped. "Those two words will turn your client off."

He figured it was kind of like ordering a condom salesman not to mention the words *cum* or *disease.*

Right now, Wally would sell his soul to win the lottery and be able to run away. Of course, he'd leave Annette with plenty of money to raise the kids while he was gone—he wasn't a total schmuck. It was just that he suddenly felt totally useless. He'd failed, miserably, and hanging around to face the disappointment in everyone's eyes was an inconceivable punishment.

Lying alone on their marriage bed, Annette found herself unconsciously occupying only her side. After years of practice, she automatically respected Wally's space, mindful not to roll on his pillow or hog his half of the blankets. It was another symbol of marital programming she'd subjected herself to for no apparent reason.

"A hot meal and a clean house will be appreciated by your husband," her mother had actually lectured on their wedding day. "Don't underestimate the power of a cheerful greeting when he walks in the door. No man wants to come home to a whining housewife and disobedient children. Home should be a destination he rushes to after a hard day's work. Not a place he avoids at all costs."

Her mother should have known what worked and what didn't. She eventually managed to alienate away every single one of five husbands for the past twenty years.

"And don't forget to please him," her mother had winked, as if passing on a pearl of wisdom. "A man won't look across the fence if he likes the view in his own back yard. And between you and me, fifteen minutes of *intimate time* a couple times a week ain't a lot to pay for children, and a nice home. Now is it, honey?"

Annette wondered just how much she'd actually paid. Wally obviously had taken her youth, that was just a given. But what about her confidence? Would she ever be able to look herself in the mirror again and believe she was a desirable woman? Her husband had chosen to have sex with a man instead of making love with her. What was she supposed to think of herself?

Sitting up in bed, Karen shook her head, disgusted with the mental picture beginning to formulate in her mind.

She wasn't a prude—she understood homosexual sex—she just couldn't believe it. Why would a grown man want to stick his penis in another man's bum hole? Didn't it hurt? What about all the poop up inside? Did they just poke around among the turds?

"The sheets," she suddenly gasped, all the little pieces of the puzzle suddenly falling into place. Her husband had been leaving brown stains on their bedding for weeks. He had blamed it on diarrhea, but she now knew different. It was the after-effects of sex; it was sperm and junk running out of his bum hole. It had dripped down all over the sheets of their marriage bed.

Jumping up to her feet, Annette stood back and stared at their covers. Maybe they'd had sex in *her bed*, maybe they'd been rolling round naked right on *her comforter*. She couldn't tell, and there was only one way to be sure. She jumped up and began ripping off each layer of bedding.

Running to her linen closet, Annette dug deep into the back, finally pulling out a set of pumpkin colored sheets bought on a whim from a neighbor's garage sale. Still wrapped in their original packaging, she deemed them safe, quickly carrying them over to her mattress.

Now, would washing everything in hot soapy water really be enough to sterilize her bedding, or would she be reduced to lighting a giant bonfire in the middle of the backyard? At this point, Annette couldn't be sure.

Walking away from her disheveled bed, she found herself unconsciously wandering into the master bathroom.

"Uh... Billy gave me the cologne," she chanted, mocking her husband's speech patterns. "Billy gave me the cologne, cuz I was letting him stick his cock in my ass," Annette added as an afterthought. What other reason would anyone have to buy a colleague four hundred dollars worth of aftershave? It was such bullshit and she'd believed it all.

"What makes you so sure I'm your husband's only lover?" she asked the mirror, Billy's parting words still ringing over and over in her ears.

Annette felt her world began to spin, the life draining right out of her legs. As she dropped down to the cold tile floor, she found some small measure of comfort lying horizontal, eyes blinking as she fought to remain consciousness.

"Again?" she suddenly groaned, noticing that the caulking was pulling away from the shower door. She'd just re-caulked the joint less than a month before. How in the hell was she supposed to get a good seal if she still had a quarter inch space between the molded shower stall and the bathroom tiles?

Carefully reaching out, Annette slowly began to pick at the rubbery caulking. With a little effort, she was able to pull it all off, leaving a huge pile of irregularly shaped white pieces in the middle of her bathroom floor.

"That was stupid," she muttered, suddenly realizing that she didn't have any more caulking in the house to reseal it. Well, she'd put up a note, and everyone would just have to take a bath. Life was full of disappointments and everybody might as well get used to it.

Chapter Twenty

"Today, I consider myself the luckiest
man on the face of the earth."

—*The Pride of the Yankees, 1942*

"
B ut we can't afford to pay rent on our apartment and pay
the rent on your house," Justice reminded the man. "And
if we don't give at least one month's notice, they're just gonna keep
our damage deposit. We need that money. That'll pay to hook up
all the utilities in your house. We can't do it without our damage
deposit, and if..."

"I hear you," Murray agreed, Jupiter's *in-house* horticulturist.
"Why don't you come with me?" he motioned for Justice to follow
him back into his private greenhouse. "Never been in here, have ya?"
he flicked on a massive array of overhead fans.

"No, I work more with all the border shrubbery and fruit trees
down in delivery."

"Well, let me show you what I do," he smiled, "it might actually be of interest. See these marigolds?" he pointed to a plastic tray of sprouting seedlings.

"Yes," Justice answered, instinctively tucking his hands in his pockets not to damage any of the works in progress.

"We're trying to cross breed them to grow at least twenty-eight to thirty-two inches in height, with blooms of four to five inches in width. Then we're going to attempt a grafting project with a domestic willow. It's the most likely to accept such a graft."

"Why?"

"Why not?" Murray laughed, slapping Justice on the back. "Jupiter will be the first greenhouse in the state to offer the marigold as a prunable shrub. I admit it's a little crazy, but..." he continued to move down the rows, "but you never know what'll happen."

Walking through another set of hermitically sealed doors, Justice began to feel the dampness invading his cotton shirt and clinging to the muscles on his back.

"So what'd your wife think, you know, of the house?"

Stopping to wipe his brow, Justice tried to find the words to express Sarah's excitement. "She's thrilled. She wants to move this weekend. But..."

"But you have to give notice," Murray repeated. "Maybe we can do something about your situation."

"How's that?"

"I know a guy looking for a little two bedroom, and he'd probably be ready to take over your place immediately. I'll call him tonight and see if he's interested."

Concentration suddenly focused on a small grouping of plants, Justice couldn't stop himself from wandering over for a closer selection. "Is this what I think it is?" he laughed, timidly reaching out his right hand to brush the tender young leaves.

"Yep, good old Cannabis seeds. I brought 'em over myself from

Mexico, during my fourth year of University. That line is almost like family," he joked. "Been with me longer than my wife."

Stepping aside, Justice carefully watched as Murray moved forward and began misting the two-foot plants.

"Almost ready for transplanting," he thought aloud. "Better get 'er moved before the stalks weaken in these piddly little six inch pots."

"Aren't you worried about… your boss seeing the plants?" Justice couldn't help but ask.

"I am the boss," Murray casually reminded him. "Sure, I don't actually own the greenhouse, but on site, I'm the top dog. Who's going to fire me? They had a hard enough time hiring someone with a degree for what little they pay."

Shrugging his shoulders in silent agreement, Justice quickly decided that it was probably a good idea to change the topic. "I still have your key." He pulled it out of his jeans.

"Well, let's negotiate then. You know the rent, I know you got a wife and three kids, so everything's out on the table. You interested in taking the house?"

"I'm more than interested, but I have to tell you, I'm a little worried about my super. He's always warned us about subletting. He's really against the idea, you know, wanting to pick his own tenants."

Setting down his misting bottle and leading Justice back through to the main potting floor; Murray took a few minutes to collect his thoughts. "You know, this rental is becoming one big fucking headache. My old lady is threatening to leave me if I put another ad in the paper for a *house to rent*. So, I think I'm about to make a corporate decision," he announced with an air of authority. "I'm gonna give you and your family the house right now, first month free." He slapped the young man firmly on his back.

Unsure if he actually understood the offer, Justice waited, hoping the Murray would explain it all a little further.

"You go home and tell your wife she can start moving her shit this weekend. That way you don't have to rush and you won't lose your damage deposit. Me, well I don't have to worry about finding anybody to rent the house. It's a win-win situation. And," he waved his finger as if warning a small child, "I know where you work. You're not going to fuck around on the rent, are you?"

Thrusting out his hand to seal the deal, Justice found himself anxiously rocking back on his own heels. He couldn't wait to get to a phone and deliver the great news. "I'm gonna call Sarah right away," he bragged. "She's gonna flip out when I tell her about our deal."

"Okay, you take it easy, man." Murray nodded his head, anxious to get back to his transplanting.

With her laptop already loaded, Karen was ready to jump in her car and head off to work when she spotted the note and small package sitting in the middle of the kitchen table. She snatched up the paper and quickly began deciphering Alicia's sloppy handwriting.

> *Dear Karen,*
>
> *Wasn't quite sure how to explain, so I chickened out and just left you a note.*
>
> *Watch the DVD—it'll clear everything up.*
>
> *Sorry babe, but sometimes it's just better to know. Hope you agree.*
>
> *Love, A.*

"A DVD?" Karen muttered; ripping open the plastic bag that Alicia had obviously wrapped around the rental. Reduced to spinning the black plastic case in her hands, she carefully inspected all edges of the box for any hint of the contents. No title or genre, nothing to offer any sort of explanation. Glancing at her watch, she quickly decided to skip her stop at the drycleaners and just pop in the disc. At least she'd get a hint of the big mystery before leaving for her office.

As the movie began to run, Karen began reading the opening credits aloud, a little put off by the low quality of the filmmaking.

"Starbrite productions presents, HIGH SCHOOL HOTTIES! Starring," she snickered at the gimmicky yellow sunbursts flashing across the screen, "TONY THE TOOL."

It suddenly wasn't so funny anymore.

Bending down to snatch the remote off the coffee table, Karen turned up the volume before taking a seat on the arm of the couch.

"Oh, Mr. Gibson," a young blonde girl strutted around what looked to be a working automotive garage. "I just don't understand why you won't let any of us girls take auto shop?"

"Yeah," another brunette echoed her friend's opinion. "I'm good with my hands."

When Tony DeMarco, aka, *Tony the Tool* strolled into the frame, Karen almost fell off her perch. This man looked much younger, with a huge mop of curly black hair, but it was definitely *her Tony.*

"You're going to have to prove it," he growled, his voice sounding unnaturally deep, possibly an audio defect due to the quality of the amateur video.

"We will," the girls wholeheartedly agreed, kneeling down on the padded moving blanket someone had thoughtfully spread over the concrete floor.

Frantically depressing the stop button, Karen threw down

the remote and raced out of the room, stumbling straight to her bathroom as the first waves of nausea washed over her. Her turn to kneel, she finally gave up and pulled down the lid on the toilet, confident that the moment had passed.

"That's the way to please me," Tony's voice echoed from the living room, the DVD player automatically releasing the disc from its temporary pause.

Forcing herself to stand, Karen awkwardly stumbled back into the living room and slapped the power button on the television, immediately distinguishing the picture. With another quick swipe, she reached down and ejected the movie from her machine, now sorry that she'd ever spent the extra money on a second DVD player for the living room.

Shaking her head in disbelief, Karen abruptly returned the disc back into its case before securely wrapping and stuffing the movie down into her purse. Minutes later, she drove as if on a personal mission, making a direct beeline for Alicia's work.

"Karen, what are you doing here?" her roommate demanded the minute she appeared on the lounge floor.

"Where did you get this?"

"Patty, I'm taking my lunch," Alicia announced to a passing waitress

"But it's only a quarter to ten?"

"I'm hungry now," Alicia barked, quickly ushering Karen out the back of the building and straight toward a solitary picnic table.

"Where did you get this?" Karen slammed the plastic bag down on the wooden slats.

"From the rental store on the corner of Peek Street. They carry a lot of old stuff from the eighties and nineties. You know, vintage porn." But that wasn't the information Karen was looking for and Alicia knew it.

"How did you find this?" she shouted for the second time.

"I just googled his name. Came up with a bunch of hits for different guys named Tony DeMarco, but when I saw a few pics from a body building competition, I knew that I'd found your Tony.

"But that still doesn't explain the connection to that." Karen pointed an accusing finger down at the plastic bag.

"Right, but when I dug a little deeper, I found that he actually had a record. Your Tony DeMarco was nabbed for indecent exposure back in the late nineties. He was caught with his pants down." Alicia rolled her eyes at the obvious pun. "Arrested when an unlicensed porn shoot was caught filming in one of the city's parks."

"I see." Karen covered her face in shame, absolutely crushed that she'd fallen for such a despicable human being.

"Starbrite Productions was named in the original arrest, so making the trip to the video store was kind of a logical next step. I'm so sorry, sweetie." Alicia threw her arms around her friend. "I just thought..."

"You thought I'd want to know," Karen sniveled, finishing her roommate's sentence.

"Cuz I'd wanna know," Alicia answered in response.

Slowly pulling away, Karen turned to her purse and retrieved a battered tissue, not sure if she wanted to blow her nose or wipe her eyes. "How could I have been so blind? He admitted to me that he worked in some kind of underground clinic doing God knows what for some quack, and then... and then this," she pointed to the DVD. "No wonder he spends so much time working out at the gym, trying to look so buff."

"I don't know if it matters, or if you really wanna know, but the kid at the video store had some more information."

"What kind of information." Karen wiped the tear escaping the corner of her eye.

"Well, this kid considered himself quite a little aficionado of porn, and after Starbrite Productions folded, he couldn't ever remember seeing *Tony the Tool* star in any other movies."

Pushing the DVD out of her reach, Karen turned to deal with her friend. "I know I'm not acting like it, but I am grateful that you did all this. It's probably much better to find out now, than after dating the guy for a couple of months."

Not satisfied, Alicia continued to justify her actions. "It's not that making a couple pornos automatically condemns a man to death, it's just that you," she flapped her arms at her side. "I know you, Karen, and you couldn't have handled it."

"Could you have handled it?"

"I don't know," Alicia honestly admitted. "I've never met any porn stars before—well, not that I know of—but maybe, for a little while. I'm not saying I'd wanna take him home to the parents, you know, but if the connection was real, maybe…" she flapped her arms for the second time.

"I gotta get to the office." Karen stood up from the table. "I've been working at home since Thursday, and I have to download all my client files."

"Are you fine?"

Brushing off her slacks, she turned to look Alicia straight in the eyes. "I'm not, but I will be," she forced a weak smile. "Thanks for all the legwork."

"It's the internet, baby. We all cruise on the super highway and nothing's really private anymore."

"Will you take care of that?" Karen motioned toward the movie, too disgusted to lift up the plastic bag.

"Sure, no problem."

Back in her car, Karen blew her nose twice before slamming the gearshift into reverse. This had to be one of the worst days of her life, and all she could think about was how much she had liked the guy.

"I can't believe it," Sarah continued to mumble, "I just can't believe everything's working out so well."

"I know." Justice nodded his head, forgetting that his wife was unable to see him on the other end of the telephone. "I've already loaded a few empty boxes in my truck, but most of 'em are really dirty, so I'm only picking up the clean ones."

"I can check at the grocery store, too. Sometimes they have extra fruit crates near the back by the bulk storage bins. Oh Justice," she gushed, "this is the beginning of something really wonderful. I can feel it. Our life is finally taking a turn for the better."

"I can feel it too, Sarah," he agreed.

"Oh, what about a lease? Didn't your Mr. Murray have something for us to fill out?"

"Not Mr. Murray, just Murray," he reminded his wife. "He's not that kind of guy, he's really down to earth. Murray's a lot like you and me, baby—his handshake is his word. And I trust him."

"That's good, and I'm glad you two have hit it off so well." Sarah leaned over the stove to stir the boiling pot of macaroni. "But I'm gonna need some kind of lease or rental agreement to take down to the utility company. They aren't going to transfer our power and water just on my say so. I know this for sure, we need some kind of written agreement."

"Oh Sarah," he groaned. "You know I hate all that paperwork."

"I do, but just ask him for the papers and bring them home. Don't even try to read anything in front of Murray's face. Tell him your wife handles all the papers and you'll bring 'em back the next morning after I've filled them all out. That'll work." Sarah set the spoon down on the edge of the countertop. "Besides," she reasoned, "lots of wives handle stuff like that. He won't think nothing of it."

"I'll check on it, I promise."

"Oh sweetie, I can't wait to tell the kids. But..." She suddenly fell silent. "Maybe I should wait 'til supper and we can tell them together?"

"No, you go ahead," he laughed. "That'll give you a good couple of hours to calm them both down before I get home and have to deal with the puppy dog issue."

"You big chicken," Sarah teased, so very grateful to be back in the good books with her husband. "How about burgers and home fries for supper?" she asked, knowing full well that it was one of her husband's favorite meals.

"You don't have to do that. I know Monday is usually leftover soup day and that's fine by me," he reassured his wife.

Sarah turned her face toward the macaroni pot and silently shook her head. "Let's just leave it at as a surprise. I'll have supper on the table by six."

"I love you, baby," he ended the call, slowly hanging up the receiver.

"Hope that was your wife," Murray walked up beside him, "cuz I'd hate to think that you needed the extra bedroom for your girlfriend."

"That was my Sarah," he quickly confirmed. "And actually, I'm really glad to run into you again."

"What you need?"

"Sarah reminded me to get a copy of the rental agreement from you and bring it home."

"We don't need to bother with contracts. Contracts are for enemies who plan on taking each other to court," Murray rationalized.

"No, no, no... that's not the reason," Justice began to mutter. "It's the utilities, the power, and water, and gas. She said we need a lease to get them moved, is all," he nervously tried to explain.

Murray scratched the back of his head as if stalling, finally he put his hands on his hips and began to slowly lay it out. "See, after the flood, when the insurance company came by, they didn't wanna give me much money cuz the house was a rental, not my principal address. You following me?" he stopped to make sure Justice understood.

"Yes, I do"

"So, anyway, I had to eventually tell a little white lie and sign an affidavit, saying that I was separated from my wife and was living in the house at the time of the flood, before they'd even consider paying me what I deserve. It was bullshit, man!"

"Oh, I see. But what now? How is Sarah supposed to move the power from our apartment to your house without some kind of a lease?"

"Well." Murray picked a few seed pockets off the twill of his shirt. "Utilities in a three bedroom usually run a hundred and fifty in summer and two hundred and fifty in the winter. Of course, it matters how many are squatting in the house, and I believe you when you say it's only going to be your wife and your kids, so..." he quickly dropped his hands and looked Justice straight in the eye. "I'm willing to make you another deal."

"What's the deal?"

"I'll keep the utilities in my name for the first five or six months until all the hassles blow over with the insurance company, and you can just pay me a flat fee of two hundred dollars extra a month. Tack it onto your rent. And hey," he included as an afterthought. "I'll throw in free cable."

"We don't watch television. Sarah doesn't like what she's seen on TV."

"Whatever." Murray brushed off Justice's last comment. "It's a hell of a deal. Look, you and your wife are going to save a whole whack of hook-up fees. And hell, maybe I'll even hire you to do a little renovating while you're still living there. So, you still interested?"

"I am." Justice once again thrust out his hand. He liked doing business with Murray. He really was a man's man.

———————

After reluctantly accepting two handfuls of messages from the company's receptionist, Karen stumbled through the glut of front-end staffers and made her way toward the back wall of offices. As she quickly unlocked her door, and silently moved inside, she was absolutely stunned to realize that her private space had been violated.

"Who did this?" Karen demanded, running out toward the first person she saw walking down the hall. "Who was in my office today?"

"I don't know, Miss Taylor. I work in payroll. Maybe..." the girl stammered, scanning the room for anyone else who might be able to help.

"Did you see who went in there?" Karen demanded from a fellow accountant.

"Karen, what are you talking about? Did somebody break into your office?"

Waiving him off as if dismissing a bug, Karen marched straight to the office manager and demanded five minutes of his time.

"You have an emergency, Miss Taylor?"

"Someone's been in my office in the last five days, messing around with my stuff, and I demand to know who let them in?"

"Are we talking about a theft?" he sat up in his chair, suddenly worried that all hell was about to break loose on his watch.

"No," she barked, angrily re-crossing her legs. "I'm talking about a violation of my private space, a space that you vowed to keep secure."

"I think we should have a look," the manager announced, standing up from behind his desk to lead their investigation.

Throwing open her door, Karen quickly stepped inside and made just enough room for her manager, mindful to close the door the second they'd both cross the threshold.

"You want me to use my authority to apprehend the *Balloon Man?*" he began to suppress a threatening snicker.

"This is my private space," she sternly reminded him. "No one, and I mean no one, is supposed to enter it during my absence unless there's an emergency. Well, what exactly was the emergency?" she demanded, throwing her hands into the air and inadvertently sending one of the helium inflated hearts bouncing off a side wall.

"I'm sure reception will be forthcoming with photocopies of the delivery slips for the last five days. That in turn will tell us who sent you the balloons, as for who opened your office; I'd have to throw the blame on me."

"You?"

"It's company policy, Miss Taylor.

"What policy?" Karen demanded.

"Check your 2004 Collective Bargaining Agreement. Section 14, Subsection 6. *Should any deliveries of a personal nature arrive for a company employee during their absence; all said deliveries shall be stowed in the employee's personal working space. Should the deliveries be of a perishable nature, the employee will be notified as soon as possible regarding the nature of the delivery. If unable to reach the said employee, the Office Manager will make the appropriate arrangements for the disposal of the perishable items. Any costs for disposal will be passed along to the employee.*"

"You actually took the time to memorize that?"

"I've memorized the entire handbook. Why?" He bristled at the question.

"No reason. Thank you for your time." Karen shook her head, signaling that their exchange was suddenly over.

"Can I ask you one question?"

"Can I stop you?" she sarcastically snapped.

"Why the stuffed lobster?" he picked the plush red toy up off the corner of her desk.

Chapter
Twenty-One

"Honey, you're too sweet for rock 'n roll."

—*Almost Famous, 2000*

"Wake up. This is housekeeping," the voice continued to reverberate in Serena's brain.

"What?" she barely managed to moan.

"I said this is housekeeping. Come on, lady. I need to clean your room," the chambermaid attempted to rouse the sleeping guest.

"Go... away," Serena pleaded, slowly turning her face toward the smoke stained pillowcase, consumed by yet another wave of dry heaves.

"You got twenty minutes left. You gotta be out of your room by one p.m.," she warned, before slamming the hotel room door.

"Fuck you," Serena whispered between gasps.

"For Christ sakes." Another young girl limped by the bed. "I still can't find my other boot."

Barely conscious of her own surroundings, Serena repeatedly

blinked her eyes, attempting to focus on the form moving back and forth through her line of sight.

"Hey, is it under your side of the bed?" the stranger demanded, her level of agitation rising by the second.

"What?"

"I asked if it was under the bed. What's the matter, bitch? You done gone deaf?"

For reasons beyond her comprehension, Serena had absolutely no control of any limb. She just seemed to be one throbbing ball of hurt.

"Help me," she begged, not sure whether anyone was still in the room.

"I ain't holding nothing, so how the fuck am I supposed to help you? Get off your ass and get to work!"

Mouth still open, Serena continued to struggle for breath, afraid to bring her teeth down lest her gooey lips become glued together from lack of moisture.

"I'm going down to the strip, grab a couple *nooners*, then pick up some rock. Wanna come?"

Starting to panic at the thought of being abandoned, Serena arched her back and let out a guttural scream.

"What the fuck you doing?" the girl marched up to the bed and shouted down into Serena's face. After no reply, she opted for a little gentler approach. "When's the last time you fixed?"

"I... I..."

"You're too sick and you're freaking me out. I'm fucking off." She was finally able to yank her boot out from under a corner table. "Listen, call your pimp, and tell him you need a fix, bad! He'll probably send somebody by to shoot you up," she reasoned, snatching the phone off the nightstand and roughly setting it down beside Serena's right hand. "You're no good to nobody laid up in here."

"I'm not a hoo... ker."

"Whatever," was the last word Serena heard before the girl slammed the door.

She knew that she was in rough shape, she just didn't know why. It might be the after-affects of a really bad trip? Maybe dirty heroin, cut with Drano? She couldn't remember.

Wriggling her fingers, the only part of her body she was strong enough to maneuver, Serena was suddenly aware of the dampness. She had no idea if it was cum, blood, or anything in between. All she knew is that she stunk. The more she focused, the more she became aware of her surroundings and they were anything but pleasant.

It was funny how she could be shivering uncontrollably one second, and burning up the next. Getting a drink of water quickly became all she could think of. Still too disorientated to decipher any of the fragmented memories from the recent past, Serena started to worry about her immediate future.

"Help me," she began to whimper, praying that anyone would hear her pleas. But the reality of the situation was that Serena was totally alone, and this wasn't the kind of place where screams from a guest's room were considered a sign for concern.

Her only hope was the telephone sitting next to her hand, and it took absolutely all of her strength just to lift the handset. She should have dialed 911, but with her limited strength, Serena focused on one number... Julia's home line.

"Answer," Serena muttered, the word distorted by the fumbling motions of her swollen lips.

As the unanswered telephone continued to ring at Julia's house, Serena painfully rolled over in her bed and debated her next move. She felt like she'd just been gang banged by the entire first string of the Dallas Cowboys. She barely had the energy to pick up the phone and dial it again, but it was her one and only hope. There was absolutely no way in hell she was up for anything else, no matter what the pay. Manny would just have to find himself some other star, cuz she was definitely down for repairs.

"Julia," Serena continued to cry out for help, her bottom lip cracking deep enough to release a large droplet of blood.

"Fuck me!" Julia finally barked from the warmth of her own bed, lifting up the ringing phone and instantly slamming the receiver back down into the cradle.

This time when the shivers hit, they knocked Serena right back into unconsciousness, and when she was finally able to poke through the fog, she found her legs twitching, struggling to free themselves from the binding sheets.

Forcing herself to focus all her energies on the task at hand, Serena desperately clawed at the bottom sheet with her right hand, fighting to drag the phone just a couple of inches closer. It had been within her reach before she'd passed out, but her spasms had obviously bounced the handset across the mattress.

Fingers finally reaching the cord, she was now able to pull it back within reach for dialing. Fighting to stay awake, Serena slowly punched in the number, eyes burning as she forced them to pierce though the descending fog.

"What do you want?" Julia ripped her handset off the cradle, not the least bit interested in any attempt at civility.

"Help... me," was all Serena was able to croak.

"Who's this?"

"Meeeee..."

"I'm not in the mood." Julia shook her head, looking around the bedroom for her smokes before preparing to disconnect her phone.

"Serrr... en..." was all the young girl mumbled before passing out once again, her weakened heart now dangerously palpitating within the sunken walls of her chest.

Stopping dead in her tracks, Julia scrambled to make sense of the situation. "Serena?" she called out. "Is that you, Serena?" she yelled again, a bad feeling beginning to build in the pit of her stomach.

Serena's body now jerked with convulsions—she dangerously teetered on the edge of deep shock.

Pulling the phone away from her ear, Julia quickly read the hotel's name on her call display. "The Crystal Place?" she mouthed in disbelief. That had to be one of the worst places in town. Why was Serena calling from there? What could have gone so wrong in the last three days that she ended up in a hole like that?"

Yanking off her nightshirt with one quick swoop of her hand, Julia bolted toward her closet and grabbed the first hoodie and pair of jeans she could reach. Forgoing any of the usual subtleties such as underwear or a hairbrush, she just shoved her feet into an old pair of sneakers and pivoted on her toes, scanning the room for any signs of her purse.

"Where's my fucking wallet?" she swore, bending down to grab the smokes tucked behind her beside-lamp. Quickly stuffing them into her pocket, Julia only stopped one last time to retrieve an old switchblade, and carefully slipped it into the rear pocket of her jeans as she snatched her purse off the kitchen table.

Julia burst out of her apartment building's main door. She knew better than to even try to hail a cab on the front sidewalk. She'd at least need to make her way around the corner to the entrance of the grocery store where she'd probably fair a little better.

"Hey, Taxi," she waved, her heart pounding wildly in her chest, the sudden burst of cardiovascular exercise a shock to her entire system.

"Where to?" the driver continued to chew on his granola bar as she slid into the back seat.

"The Crystal Palace," Julia admitted with a reluctant sigh. "I don't have the exact address, but I could..." she stalled, reaching down into her purse to dig out her phone.

Shifting his car into drive, the cabbie pulled onto the street. "Don't bother calling, I know where to go," he shrugged, sneaking a quick glance to appraise his fare. "You don't look like the type," he simply stated.

Julia knew exactly what her driver had implied, and in some strange way, it was almost a compliment. "I don't work there," she thankfully confirmed. "I'm just picking up a friend."

"Want me to wait outside for ya?"

Julia evaluated her situation. If Serena was in as rough a shape as she sounded, she probably wouldn't be able to walk. She'd need help carrying her out, and experience told her that none of the staff at the Crystal Place would likely give a shit.

"Here we are," the cabbie announced, putting his car into park before turning back to collect his fare. "Twelve bucks, lady."

"Here's thirty." she handed the man a twenty and a crumpled ten. "Will you help me, I think my friend might be sick and I won't be able to carry her alone."

She'd already tipped him eighteen bucks on a twelve-dollar fare. "Why not." He stuffed the money into his breast pocket before turning back around to pull the keys out of his ignition.

Marching up to the front desk with her driver in tow, Julia slapped a twenty-dollar bill on the counter. She didn't even bother to speak until she had the desk clerk's full attention. "You've got a girl up in one of your rooms who's really sick. She passed out when she was talking to me on the phone. If you don't help me find her, I'll just call 911 on my cell and wait for the cops to start busting down your doors. What's it gonna be?"

––––––––––––

Finally sequestered behind the privacy of her own office walls, Karen began the task of cleaning out her personal space, anxious to strip away all reminders of Tony DeMarco. One by one, she stabbed at the helium balloons, releasing the pressurized gas before dropping the tattered foil down into her trash.

When finished with the balloons, she snatched the six red carnations out of the small glass vase and abruptly snapped the stems in half, unceremoniously dropping them on top of the balloon wreckage.

Left with only the ten-inch stuffed lobster and an unopened card, Karen walked over to her chair and slowly sat down. She should just throw the remainder in the trash, but for reasons she couldn't comprehend, something wouldn't allow it.

"Miss Taylor?" the receptionist's voice suddenly boomed over the telephone's speaker system.

"Yes," she answered, abruptly stowing the lobster and card in a side drawer.

"I've located the delivery slips for the last seven days, as per the office manager's request. Would you like me to send them up to your office?"

"Hold them," Karen announced, realizing that a little walk might help to clear her head.

Returning with the slips, a fresh cup of coffee, and her company mail, Karen reminded herself that she'd actually started the day hoping to get a little work done. She needed to download her client files if she planned to be paid anytime in the near future, that was a given. As for the staff meeting that afternoon, the jury was still out.

"Hey there Karen," a man's voice called out from her doorway. "Heard you had a little meltdown this morning. What's the matter, gorgeous? Got your very own private stalker?"

"What's the matter, Leroy? Tired of playing with yourself so you thought you'd come over to my office and hassle me for awhile?"

Her next-door neighbor, a forty-five-year-old divorced man, spent a good chunk of every week trying to convince Karen that they were a match made in heaven. According to him, since they were both chartered accountants with *similar interests*, (she'd yet to figure out what he meant by that,) they *owed it* to each other to explore their options.

"Old boyfriend can't take the hint?" he continued to tease, somehow deluding himself into thinking that any contact with Karen was better than no contact at all.

"Is there actually something you need?"

"Not really, but if you're free—which I assume you are, since you just spent an hour popping balloons—how about a little pasta for lunch?"

"No, thank you." She shook her head, suddenly dying to be left alone.

"How about a drink after work?" Leroy continued to plow ahead. "I could take you somewhere nice."

"You don't know anywhere nice."

Quickly running out of suggestions, Leroy began to sweat, his ten-dollar cologne permeating his polyester shirt and wafting through the recycled air.

"Can you please close my door." She lifted the cover on her laptop, signaling their weekly exchange was now abruptly over.

Leroy accepted his defeat and began backing out, her doorknob clenched tightly between the fingers of his right hand. "If you change…"

"I'll buzz you," she nodded, not bothering to lift her eyes.

"Just press 313." Leroy slipped in his office number before reluctantly turning to leave.

She stood up and took four large steps toward her door. Karen clinched her jaw in irritation before spinning the lock, determined to stop anyone else from snooping around in her business. "Oh, piss on it." She finally relented after returning to her desk seconds before ripping open the envelope holding Tony's card.

Karen. Some people have it and some people don't. Money can't buy it, and experience can't teach it. You, my dear, you are one of the lucky few who were born with it. And trust me when I say, you'll have it 'til the day you die. Hope you're willing to share a little with me. Tony.

By far the strangest card Karen had ever received, it somehow still managed to leave her feeling cheated.

She'd finally met a man who she felt intellectually and physically drawn to, and then without warning, he turned out to be some kind of social deviant, a guy who stuffed his private parts down the throats of eighteen-year-old co-eds for kicks. Once again, she'd proven to be the worst judge of character.

Unwilling to leave the card behind to fuel the office gossip, Karen shoved it down into the folds of her computer case, even managing to make room for the toy lobster.

Chapter
Twenty-Two

"Hello, gorgeous."

—*Funny Girl, 1968*

Finding Serena wasn't going to be easy by any stretch of the imagination. Probably not a registered guest at The Crystal Palace, she could have been lying unconscious in just about any of the thirty-six occupied rooms.

"Serena, where are you?" Julia desperately called out, knocking on doors at random, as she ran up and down the hallways of the second floor.

Room by room, the desk clerk followed behind, rapping his knuckles on the doors while simultaneously calling out to announce his presence. If no one answered back, he forced his pass key into the lock and walked on inside. So far, he'd caught six couples in the middle of various sex acts, a crack party, and two drunks passed out on the floor. They were just half way through the building.

"I can't stand around here forever," the cabbie complained,

checking his watch to see just how much time he'd blown for an eighteen-dollar tip.

"Only five more minutes," Julia promised, turning to hit the stairs up to the next floor.

"Hey lady," the desk clerk rushed back into the hall. "I think I found your friend."

Congregated around the bedside, all three held their noses to block the stench.

"What's that stink?" the driver demanded, turning to run back into the hallway and grab a fresh gulp of air. "Smells like someone died in there," he yelled back over his shoulder.

"Serena," Julia called out. "Are you awake, baby?" Not sure if they were already too late, Julia slowly reached toward her neck, fingers shaking as she intuitively fumbled toward the carotid artery.

"Hee... llp," the word managed to escape from the girl's mouth, the movement ripping open a dried blood clot and releasing fresh droplets from her bottom lip.

"We have to wrap her up," Julia began to bark a succession of orders. "Find some clean blankets," she shouted before running off toward the bathroom.

"Think I should call an ambulance?" the desk clerk looked over at the cab driver, neither wanting to be associated with all the hassles of a dead body.

"I don't know," the cabbie shook his head. "Ask her," he nodded toward Julia as she suddenly appeared with two dampened towels.

Wiping the encrusted vomit off Serena's upper chest and both sides of her neck, Julia took a second to look around the room. "Grab that comforter," she ordered. "We're going to peel these disgusting sheets off her body, and then rewrap her in that thing. Everybody understand?"

Both men nodded as Serena continued to moan, passing in and out of consciousness.

"Oh baby." Julia shook her head and swallowed hard. She'd never seen anything like this, and she hadn't exactly lived a sheltered life.

"What's that?" the clerk pointed down to Serena's naked chest.

"I think its pus." Julia gagged, wiping the large glob of milky fluid off the right side of her one breast.

"She's rotting from the inside out, that's the problem." The cabbie stepped back, hoping the air was a little fresher closer to the door. "There's pus everywhere." He pointed down toward Serena's crotch while simultaneously averting his eyes and retching.

"That's it." Julia threw down the towels in disgust. "Let's just take her now."

Throwing the comforter down on the floor, all three held their breath and moved in, lifting her lifeless body off the sagging mattress. Serena only groaned, but almost slipping out of their hands when they were forced to peel a corner of the soiled cotton from her back and lower buttocks.

The three somehow managed to negotiate two flights of stairs, and made it down to the cab, stuffing Serena's body into the back seat without causing too much of a commotion.

"I'm sorry," the desk clerk offered, not sure what else to say as he stood back and watched Julia crawl in beside Serena, gently lifting her neck in an attempt to clear her air way.

"Where to?" the driver demanded, taking a second to wipe off his hands on a dry roll of paper towels.

"The Changeroom," Julia sighed. "Do you know the address?"

He nodded yes, fondly remembering the days when he used to ferry little old ladies back and forth to the grocery store.

Bathrooms and living room already cleaned, Freddy moved on toward the bedrooms. He planned to do his roommate's first, especially since he assumed it would take considerable time. Lifting up his pail of warm water, Freddy grabbed his towel, and headed into Callie's domain.

"Oh, come on," he groaned, trudging over to her dressing table to survey the damage. Everywhere he looked, the surface was littered with bottles, tubes, or little cakes of shiny powders. The girl's room looked like the make-up counter from some department store had exploded. Yet somehow, Callie never left the house looking like a painted clown. She applied everything with a light touch, and that in itself really impressed Freddy.

Straightening up the bottles of perfume before plucking out the small blonde hairs that had inadvertently fallen amongst the collection of eye shadows, he suddenly noticed that one fingertip on his right hand had somehow become coated with a bluish powder.

Rubbing his thumb against the fingertip, he brought them both up to his nose, surprised to find the dry powder had the slightest fragrance. Heart beating a little faster than normal, Freddy raised his hand and swiped his finger across his right eyelid, taking another second to wipe his thumb across his left.

The effect was startling, the navy shadow instantly drawing his attention to the oval shape of his own eyes. Without any further thought, Freddy slid into Callie's padded make-up chair. Tucking his legs under her dressing table, he began to experiment.

The sand colored foundation was definitely the wrong tone for his skin, but the smoothing effect was noticeably different. Having watched other girls apply their make-up on numerous occasions, he was no stranger to a triangle sponge or stainless steel eyelash curlers.

"What ya doing?" his roommate suddenly chirped from over his shoulder.

"Oh, I was just playing around." He scrambled to grab a handful of tissue.

"You're kinda cute," Callie announced, standing back with her hands balanced on her hips.

"Really?"

"Well, kinda," she teased before walking up to where Freddy sat. "But you've made some mistakes." She handed him a clear bottle of make-up remover. "Take it all off and we'll start again."

"Are you sure?"

"Whatever possessed you to use green eyeliner and blue mascara? Are you color blind?"

Freddy just grinned, wetting his tissue and rubbing it vigorously back and forth over his face. "You don't mind that I was playing around with your stuff?"

"No, I don't mind. But do me a favor and always close the lids." Callie reached over to her tube of mascara and tightened the wand. "A good tube of midnight blue can run you anywhere from twenty to thirty bucks. Not something to piss around with," she warned.

As Freddy sat back and patiently waited, Callie began to work her magic.

"Are we talking to our mother these days?" she casually inquired.

"Sure, why?"

"Well, she's left three messages about fall break, and between you and me, I don't think she's going to let it drop. And..." she stopped speaking to carefully line his upper eyelid. "And she keeps leaving some girl's number and address for you. I wrote it down."

"Don't bother, I have it already."

"So who's Jennifer?"

Watching Callie slowly map out the location of his cheekbones with the elongated end of a make-up brush, Freddy debated coming clean.

"See what I'm doing?" she broke into a teaching tone. "If you use the positions of your eyes and nose as base points, it's pretty basic make-up artistry to know where to apply the blusher."

"I see." He watched in amazement as Callie slowly accentuated the curves of his face with soft strokes from her brush.

"So, tell me. Who is Jennifer?"

"She's my ex-girlfriend from high school. You surprised?"

"No. Should I be?"

"Well," Freddy waved his arms over the assorted make up. "If most people saw us right now, they'd think I was gay."

"Are you?" she leaned back against her dresser.

"No, I'm not. But I…" he didn't have a clue how to fill in the blanks.

"I'm not a psych major, but give me a little credit." Callie reached over to slap him in the arm.

"Okay," he finally confessed. "I wanna be a girl!"

Nodding her head in agreement, Callie reached for a tube of concealer, lightly dabbing small dots underneath Freddy's bottom eyelids. "I can see that. I love being a girl, and I wouldn't want to be stuck as a man for anything."

"But you were born female."

"True. So what are you gonna do about it?"

"I want surgery," he simply stated, carefully watching Callie for her reaction. "I want to have gender reassignment surgery as soon as possible."

"Open your eyes wide and look at the ceiling," she ordered, reaching for her mascara brush. "Does your family know?"

"No fucking way. They'd freak. My mom would end up in a loony bin," he laughed. "She nearly lost her mind when I broke up with Jen, warning me that I might never find another girl who loved me for who I really am."

"Sounds like she already knows." Callie moved to the other eye.

"Maybe. I don't know," Freddy moaned. "Mom's one of the

reasons I picked a school so many hours from home. I needed a little
privacy, if you know what I mean?"

"I do. So who's your idol? Who do you wanna look like after
surgery?"

"Jennifer Aniston," he answered without thinking. "She's the
most beautiful woman I've ever seen."

"Yeah, she's hot, but she's getting pretty old. I think you should
pick someone younger."

Freddy debated it for a second. "No, I think I'm gonna stick with
Jennifer Aniston. She's a classic beauty, not a super inflated version
of some Barbie doll."

"Can you really pick who you wanna look like?"

"A little, I guess. I don't really know all the details about
the surgery. I'm just kind of in the middle of investigating my
options."

"I'll help," Callie offered. "I think it would be kinda cool to
research it."

Freddy's mouth turned up in a large grin.

"What do you think?" Callie stepped away her dresser, allowing
Freddy his first look at the total transformation.

"Oh, my God," he gushed. "I love it."

Standing back, Callie was a little surprised herself. "You're going
to make a beautiful woman someday."

"Someday," Freddy vowed.

Quickly scrolling down through her contact list, Julia frantically
searched her cell phone for the number to the Changeroom. She
needed Tony's help, and if he wasn't at work, she didn't know what
she was going to do.

"Tony, is that you?" she demanded the minute a man's voice answered the line.

"This is Tony, who's this?"

"Oh Tony," she almost broke down in tears. "It's Julia calling. I really need your help."

"Julia?" he repeated, not instantly recognizing her voice. .

"Julia, you know, from porn," she summed up their association in the simplest of terms.

"Oh, right. Julia. What's the matter? What's your problem?" he demanded.

"Remember that girl Serena I brought in with the infected nipples?"

"The bad piercings?"

"Yeah. Well, she's really sick now. I think she might die!"

This time the cabbie couldn't help but react, pressing down on the gas as he sped through his second red light.

"What's the matter with her? Is she having trouble breathing?"

"We're here." The cab driver slammed his car into park.

"We're at your front door." Julia dropped her phone into her purse and reached over to grab the door handle.

Before they'd even had a chance to pull the girl from the back seat, Tony and Dr. Clifford were at their sides.

"Move away!" the doctor barked. "Let me see the patient," he sharply ordered from his position at the driver's door.

Obeying his instructions, Julia and the driver backed unto the streets, oblivious to the cars whizzing by behind their backs.

"Carry her in," the doctor ordered, turning to run back inside the Changeroom's door.

Preparing to follow, Julia suddenly felt a hand clamp down on her left arm.

"I don't wanna be an ass, but I gotta work. I got kids." The driver shrugged his shoulders.

Reaching back inside the cab, Julia was once again assaulted with the terrible smell; her senses had obviously become accustomed to the stench during their ride. "Here, it's everything I have." She handed the drive another forty bucks from the bottom of her purse. "If it's not enough, I..."

"It's fine," he shoved the money down into his jeans. "You better go inside and take care of your friend. I hope she's fine."

Julia turned and ran down the basement stairs.

"Over here," Tony yelled out the minute she burst through the door.

Everyone in the waiting room fell absolutely silent, debating the identity of the woman as she raced past them, following the path of the lifeless body of the girl.

"Is she alright?" Julia raced up to Serena's side.

"Sit down," the doctor ordered.

"Over there," Tony pointed to an empty chair. "Don't move, or I'll have to take you out."

Obeying, Julia dropped into the chair, eyes wild as she watched the doctor begin assessing his patient.

"She's covered in feces," he announced, picking up her left hand and inspecting the dried material to confirm his suspicions.

"Has she been shooting any *Cleveland Steamers*?" Tony spun his neck toward Julia.

"I don't know," she cried. "On Friday night I went to a party, and when I got home, Serena was gone. This is the first I've seen of her in three days."

"Who brought her home?" he continued to interrogate Julia.

"Nobody. She called me from the Crystal Palace. I went down and got her."

Shaking his head in disgust, Tony turned back to the doctor. "She'd probably hooked up with some guys shooting scat films. Sounds like they dumped her at the Palace when they were done with her."

"Let's get some fluid into her." The doctor raised his face to look at Tony. "I'm also gonna need a massive dose of penicillin, and a broad spectrum antibiotic. What do we have left in the storage room?" he questioned, aware they were running dangerously low and in dire need of a restock.

"I don't know about the antibiotic, but I'll check for penicillin. What you prefer?"

"Bring whatever we have. We have to get her started on something right now. She's got septicemia." He shook his head.

"What's that?" Julia called out from her perch, dying to rush forward but afraid of being ejected from the room.

"Your friend had cellulitis of her nipples when you first brought her in a few days ago. That's an acute infection of the skin and deeper tissues. Now," he carefully peeled the remaining blanket from Serena's body. "She's gone septic. That's an overwhelming infection where destructive bacteria moves directly into the blood stream."

"I don't get it."

Reluctantly motioning Julia over, the doctor began a crash lesson in pre-med. "See this abscess?" He pointed to a large formation of pus localized around the left nipple.

"Yes."

"Well, just try and imagine what it's like when some of this pus and bacteria starts running up and down the length of your body through your veins."

"She going to die?"

Ignoring the questions, Dr. Clifford continued with this diagnosis. "The bacteria, which we'll call the invading organisms, are now attacking her entire body. We're not treating an infection localized in her nipples anymore, we treating her entire respiratory and pulmonary system."

"Doctor, is she going to die?" Julia repeated.

"I'm not sure," the doctor admitted, relieved to see Tony appear with a handful of vials.

"Well, we've got the post-op cocktail you keep on hand for all the *trannys* after their female to male surgeries. It's got antibiotics and penicillin, doesn't it?"

"Yes, but it's also laced with testosterone," the doctor shook his head, quickly realizing that he didn't have any other choice.

"Well." Tony looked down at Serena and then back up at the doctor. "It's your call, Doc."

Grabbing a syringe off a nearby tray, Dr. Clifford plucked a bottle from Tony's hand and began filling his needle. "It's the best we've got."

As the doctor began to administer the medication, Tony started the clean up. Double gloved, he slowly lifted Serena's legs into the stirrups, preparing to flush her vagina and rectum out with warm, soapy water in an attempt to remove any lingering feces. The second procedure would be sterile saline solution in preparation for the antibiotics.

"Can I help you?" Julia offered, swallowing hard to settle her stomach.

"Gloves," he nodded his head toward the cardboard box.

Returning to Tony's side, she bit down on her lower lip as he slowly inserted a rubber tipped hose into Serena's inflamed vaginal cavity. "Slowly squeeze the bag," he instructed Julia. "We need to flush out as much as possible. No use letting anymore of this crap be absorbed into her bloodstream."

As Tony washed the oyster-sized gobs of pus and flecks of human feces from Serena's orifices, the doctor struggled to stabilize her vitals. "She's going into defib," he suddenly yelled out, signaling for Tony to pull up the second-hand crash cart parked in the far corner of the exam room, underneath the peach colored bed sheet.

"Paddles." Tony tried to hand the doctor the defibrillators as he simultaneously reached over the control panel to flip on the power switch.

Full attention still glued to the sound of Serena's returning heartbeat, the doctor slowly straightened his back and waved off the cart.

"Did she die?" Julia shrieked.

"Not yet," he whispered, satisfied that her heart had momentarily regulated itself. "But I'm afraid it's just a matter of time."

Chapter
Twenty-Three

"Nobody puts Baby in a corner."

—*Dirty Dancing, 1987*

"I don't know about you," Callie said as she plopped down onto her bed, "but I'm starving. I'm so hungry that my stomach thinks my throat's been slit."

"What?" Freddy began to laugh. "Where'd you come up with something like that?"

"My dad. He's got a whole shit load of them. You should hear some of his stuff. He'd crack you up."

"I would like to meet your parents someday."

"You will, I promise. But now, what about some chow? I'm dying," she fell back on her bed clutching her stomach as if writhing in pain.

"Sure, alright. Let's order then. I got ten bucks."

"I don't wanna order," she slowly pulled herself erect. "Let's go out."

"Like this?" Freddy turned to face the mirror.

"Why not, but first we need to make a few other adjustments." Yanking open two of her dresser drawers, Callie pulled out a pink bra, a tank top, and a pair of grey sweatpants. "Take off your tee-shirt."

Freddy nervously obeyed, preparing to yank the cotton shirt over his head when Callie came flying up to his side. "Stop!" she freaked. "If you wanna be a girl, you've gotta start acting like a girl. Watch me," she ordered. "First, scrunch up the material from your bottom hemline to the top of your neckline."

Freddy watched, carefully preparing to follow suit.

"Then, when your hands are full, slowly lift it over your face, making sure to stretch the neck wide enough so that no material never touches your make up."

"What about my hair?" Freddy stopped in mid-removal.

"It's okay to touch your hair. That's why it's always make-up first, and then clothes, and hair last. Trust me, the order is important, but don't worry cuz I'll explain that more later." She waved her own tee shirt in her hand. "Now, you do it."

Freddy stretched the neckline as far as possible and slowly pulled it up over his head, unfortunately hooking his chin in the process and nearly dislocating his neck when he gave the material a last jerk over his head.

"Well, well, Princess Grace. I think we'll have to work a little more on that move later. But, let's just keep going for now." She handed him the pink under-wire bra. "Put this on, too."

Heart pounding, Freddy delicately fingered the lace trim, amazed at the firmness of the under wire cups.

"That's a front closure, just like the one I'm wearing," she pointed down to her own white bra. "So open it up, wrap it around your body, and then bring the cups together in the front of your chest.

You'll see how the little metal S-shape slides through the cloth clasp."

"I did it," he proudly announced, grinning at his teacher.

"Now we need some shape." Callie began scanning her room for some workable filler material. She knew better than to try bulky socks or wads of tissue. She was looking for just the right consistency when she suddenly thought of the circular shaped face sponges her mother had included in her bath basket. "Hold tight," she ran to the bathroom, ripping open the cellophane to retrieve the white sponges.

"What are those?"

"Your boobies," Callie giggled, carefully positioning them in each of Freddy's cups. "Now, pull the tank top over your face, kind of the reverse of what I taught you for taking it off. Bunch and stretch," she reminded him about the material.

Spinning to admire his newfound shape, Freddy couldn't help but react to the reflection greeting him from the mirror. "I'm so curvy," he gushed, running his hands up and down over his artificial breasts.

"Now the bottoms," she motioned toward Freddy's jeans. "Take yours off and put these on."

Following instructions, he unbuttoned his pants and allowed the loose denim to fall down to his ankles. "I'm telling you, I'm gonna look stupid," he warned his roommate, slowly pulling the sweatpants up and over his thighs.

"Roll the band down like mine." Callie pointed to her own waist. "See how it sits. Just on my hips, not up by my waist. You don't wanna look like a geek, do you?"

"The waist isn't my problem." Freddy pointed to the bulge in the front of his pants. "This is."

Hands on her hips, Callie surveyed the damage. "That is a

problem," she wholeheartedly agreed. "Can't you... tuck it in or something?"

"Tuck it where?" Freddy laughed. "Maybe up my ass?"

"Hang on, I've got an idea."

"What's that?" Freddy demanded as Callie waved an *itty-bitty* pair of black briefs in front of his face.

"Control top—meet—boy bulge." She held them up to measure against his waist.

"There's no way."

"Trust me," she argued. "If I can get into them, so can you. Now off to the bathroom, and don't come out until they're on," she ordered, taking the opportunity to change her own clothes.

It took a good ten minutes, but when Freddy returned, the sweatpants hung perfectly.

"You look great," Callie encouraged him. "Where'd you... where'd it go." She cautiously leaned in for a closer look.

"Kinda pulled toward the back," he nervously explained. "Let's just say that I'm not sure how comfortable it's going to be when I sit."

"Then we'll stand." Callie grabbed her purse and steered Freddy toward the door.

"What about my hair, you said the hair was always last?"

Opening her bag, Callie squeezed a glob of scented gel into the center of her left palm, dropping the tube on the counter before turning toward Freddy. "Alright sweetie, today you're going punk," she announced, vigorously rubbing her palms together before running them over Freddy's entire head.

"I like wisps."

"Then wisps it is." Callie smiled, pulling small pieces of hair down toward the center of Freddy's face, effectively framing his mouth and eyes with a soft feminine look.

"Do I look like a girl?"

"Let's go. We'll see what they have to say." Callie pointed to the apartment's main door.

————

It took Tony at least fifteen minutes to clear everyone out of the waiting room, but in the end, after all the complaining, the patients eventually followed his instructions and quietly left. But then, who really was going to argue with a man of his stature.

"This is exactly why I don't bother making friends." Julia stared down into her cup of coffee. "They either die, or move away, or just piss you off so much that you don't wanna be anywhere near them."

Tony took another sip from his mug, allowing Julia the time she needed to vent her frustrations.

"You were right to get out when you did. I don't know why I didn't do the same."

"You could still leave now," he gently reminded her.

"And do what?" Julia snickered. "I never graduated, and I've never even worked with computers. You know, the last real job I had was running the shirt press down at the fifty-nine minute cleaners. How pitiful is that?"

"That's bad," Tony agreed, standing up to refill his cup. "You could always waitress, or maybe sell clothes, or shoes?"

"Maybe, but do you think I'd make enough to live? My rent is seven hundred a month plus utilities. And even then, it's in a shit neighborhood."

"I don't know the exact answer, but you're running out of time. You know it, and so do I." Tony sadly shook his head.

"I know, and it's really changing, too," Julia began to think aloud. "Did you know that the films we used to make are considered soft porn now? Since you left, it's a whole new ball game, my boy."

"Really, I thought fucking was fucking. How much can it change in ten years?" He returned to his seat.

"Well, for starters, there's Viagra now. I can't remember exactly when, but around '98 or '99, it became pretty common for all the guys to use the stuff. It's not really like having sex anymore; it's more like being beat with a giant *supercock*."

"Thought you like 'em hard?" he teased.

"Honey, that ain't hard, that's assault with a blunt object. These guys have no feeling, no sensation; they just pound away on you 'til you're raw and bleeding. You ever try to blow a guy who's taken Viagra?

"No, I can't say I have."

"Well, it's like having a battering ram shoved down your throat for a couple of hours. I'm really starting to hate it. Every time I see one of those red-faced, dopey looking fuckers, I know he's running around with a case of Redi-wood!"

"I guess I haven't been keeping up lately, I didn't realize the industry was so different," Tony admitted, having poured all his spare time and energy into the field of medicine.

"It's not only their cocks, it's everything," Julia vented. "Remember how anal used to be kink? Something a few chicks specialized in; maybe one or two who liked a little pain? Well, now it's commonplace. If you don't do full anal, rimming and penetration, you don't work. It's that fucking simple."

Shaking his head, Tony scrambled for the right words. "Even before I finally worked up the nerve to quit, I could tell it wasn't a business I wanted to be a part of anymore. It wasn't about making movies where sexy people enjoyed each other's bodies, it was…?"

"It was punishing," Julia interrupted. "It's all becoming about endurance. How many cocks can she take in her ass at the same time? How many guys can blow their load down her throat before she pukes? It's getting really sick. I can't do a shoot straight anymore. It's just too damn painful."

"The last movie I saw was at my buddy's stag," Tony admitted. "In that DVD, a guy was dropping gobs of his own spit down into this chick's twat while roughly yanking apart the folds with his own fingers. I'll tell you Julia, that turned me off right then and there. There's absolutely no pleasure in that—it's strictly degradation. What'd he think that chick was; a spittoon?"

"I know; the lines are getting all blurred. Used to be a pretty basic division between normal porn, and kink. Now," she laughed, "it's anybody's game."

"I wonder why?" Tony mused.

"Simple." She rose to refill her cup. "It's the fuckin' internet. Back in the '60s and '70s, a director was still a little bit of an artist. But now, any fucking moron with a camera can make a porno. All he has to do is get a chick stoned, rape her with a cob of corn, and in an hour, you'll see it for sale on some xxx website. That's the shit I have to compete with."

"You know, I can't think of a single person who has anything good to say about the internet," Tony thought aloud. "It's like all it did was bring a bunch of backroom slime off the streets into our own living rooms. What's so good about that?"

"Tony," Dr. Clifford called out from the examination room. "I'm finished. You can both come back inside.

"You wanna hear something really sick?" Karen admitted as she quickly set her mug down into the sink.

"What?"

"I don't even know where Serena's from. If she dies, I don't have a fucking clue who to call."

Throwing his arm around Julia's shoulder, Tony gently supported her as they both made their way back into the examination room.

"Pepperoni for sure," Callie agreed, "and mushrooms. I gotta have mushrooms."

Taking a minute to evaluate their choices, Freddy nodded his head in agreement. "And it better be a large, I'm famished," he whispered in Callie's ear.

"Large," she passed the message on to the guy working behind the till.

"Is that to stay or go?"

"To go," Freddy finally spoke up; barely loud enough to be heard over the restaurants clatter.

"Can't believe you two girls are going to eat a whole large pizza by yourselves. Maybe you need some help?" he winked. "I'm off in," he spun around to look at the clock, "ten minutes. I'll buy a case of beer and meet you both by the bridge."

"Sounds good," Callie giggled.

"But we... we don't know your name," Freddy nervously interrupted.

"Marshall, just like Eminem," he proudly informed them.

"Marshall?" Callie repeated for clarification.

"Ya you know. Marshall Mathers, aka Slim Shady, aka Eminem."

Freddy yanked on Callie's arm, pulling her a good three feet back from the front counter. "This guy's a freak. I'm not going anywhere with him, and neither are you!"

"I know," she attempted to quiet him. "Just watch and learn." Stepping back to the counter, Callie smiled up at Marshall. "My friend just reminded me that all we have is ten dollars, so we're gonna walk across the street and have a couple burgers instead."

Glancing over his shoulder to make sure his shift manager wasn't watching; Marshall quickly changed the price without changing the size of the order. "That's nine fifty, please."

"Keep the change." Callie flashed him a brilliant smile as she dropped two five-dollar bills down on the freshly wiped counter.

Pizza tucked underneath Freddy's arm, Callie waved a cute little good-bye to Marshall before they both rushed through the door and took off running.

"Mental note: we don't go back," Freddy verbally posted the reminder.

"I agree, but let's enjoy our victory. We're eating supper for half price and…"

"And?" Freddy pushed.

"And he thought we were both girls."

"I know," he chuckled to himself, "that was pretty sweet. I can't believe that a little eye shadow and fake boobs could fool that guy."

"Come on, you're gorgeous. I bet you could fool anybody."

"Maybe, but right now I'm starving and our big box of *half off* is getting cold."

Agreeing, Callie took the lead and they both high-tailed it back to the privacy of their own apartment.

———

Waiting until both Karen and Tony had reached their positions beside the examination table, Dr. Clifford began his explanation. "I finished debriding all the tissue from the patient's nipple sites. However, from experience, I believe the atrophic scarring will be substantial."

"Atrophic," Tony quietly repeated under his own breath. He knew that the sunken recesses and pitting of the skin due to the infected fat and tissue the doctor had been forced to remove would leave Serena's breasts looking horribly deformed.

"Then she's going to live?" Julia blurted out, shocked to hear the doctor talk about long term scarring.

"I didn't say that," he gently corrected her. "But I had to do what I could for the patient in case she turned the corner and her fever broke."

"Is the cocktail helping?" Tony asked, stepping up to evaluate the remaining fluid hanging in her drip bag.

"It's only been an hour, so it's actually too soon to tell. But it's safe to say that I don't think it's doing any harm."

"That's good." Tony turned toward Julia, nodding his head to show her the doctor had taken positive steps.

"I must say that I think you need to call 911, and take her to the county emergency room. They're better equipped, and will be able to properly treat her septicemia." The doctor turned away, deciding it was once again time to change into another pair of sterile gloves.

"That's not a bad idea," Tony agreed with the doctor. "Doesn't matter if she has insurance or not, they'll still take her. They have to."

Stepping around the bed, Julia picked up Serena's arm and began rubbing the back of her hand. "I don't know what to do with you, baby. I've been to county, they're just gonna treat you like a piece of garbage cluttering up their emergency room floor."

Tony and Marcus exchanged knowing glances, neither bothering to waste their breath in arguing with what they both knew to be the truth.

"The doctor says you might die," she continued to explain to the unconscious patient. "But I think you're gonna be strong and fight like hell to live. So now, I have to try and decide what's best for you."

"I know a nurse down at county," the doctor interrupted. "If I make a call, she might be able to make sure Serena gets a little extra care. Maybe," he announced without meeting Julia's eyes, "they'll have room for her tonight in a ward. Get her out of the emergency room so she can properly rest and recover."

"Nope, I don't think that's the answer." She gently set the patient's hand back down on the examination table. "I've been saving some cash for a little nip and tuck, and I think I'd rather spend it down here at the Changeroom. I don't think I could live with myself if I just threw her to the wolves down at county."

"Well, if you're sure," the doctor looked across the table at Tony, "then we'll need to run for some more supplies."

Checking his watch, Tony realized it was almost six in the evening. He'd have to move if he was going to be able to buy anything tonight. "I have about sixty dollars on me," he tallied in his head.

"I spent everything I had on the cab and the hotel clerk," Julia announced. "But if Tony can take me home, I can dig out my stash."

"That'll take too long." Tony shook his head. "I gotta get to my guy before seven or we're gonna have to wait until morning, and that might be too late."

"I don't have much in my wallet," the doctor shrugged, but you can check the emergency box in my desk. I think there's at least a hundred dollars left from the last time we bought supplies."

"Too bad I threw everyone out of the waiting room. I bet there was at least three or four hundred dollars sitting back there."

"Go clean out my wallet and my petty cash," the doctor ordered. "I'll take a moment to make a list. And Julia," he turned toward the young woman. "I'm going to need your help, so I want you to change out of those dirty clothes and into a clean set of scrubs. You'll find everything you need in the back storage room. Just follow Tony, he'll show you what I mean."

As Julia changed and Tony collected all the available cash, Dr. Clifford seriously began evaluating his patient.

She was in a lot more pain than he had initially realized, so when Serena had regained consciousness while he was debriding her wounds, the doctor relented and gave her a shot of morphine. He didn't normally ever allow opiates the clinic, there was too high a risk for break-ins should drug-seeking criminals become aware that it was on-site. But since he found himself forced to deal with more and more traumas, it was slowly becoming a necessity.

Should Serena somehow make it through the next twelve hours, he'd need to start a procedure that was a little more evasive than just a topical debriding. The patient's nipples were showing preliminary signs of necrosis. Left untreated, they would no doubt develop into gangrene, and if that happened, she'd have no choice but be subjected to a double mastectomy. That was a surgical procedure he was absolutely *not* equipped to deal with, under any circumstances.

This wouldn't be like lopping off a toe or a baby finger. Dr. Clifford would be performing major surgery in the walk-in clinic's examination room, which was an impossible feat. Forget the fact that he had no anesthesia machine, who was going to assist him? Tony was learning fast, but he was far from being a surgical nurse.

No, the only option was to remove the girl's nipples and hope for the best before things really escalated out of control. Hopefully, Tony would be able to find his black market supplier before the guy went underground for his night job. Serena's life possibly depended on their success.

Chapter
Twenty-Four

"Get your stinking paws off me,
you damned dirty ape."

—*Planet of the Apes, 1968*

I t started innocently. He had his arm draped over her side, his
fingers casually brushing the curves of her breasts. Yet within
a few minutes, Annette knew that Wally had something else in
mind.

Lying motionless, she hoped he'd either assume she was fast
asleep or at the very least, not interested in sex.

"Annette, are you awake?" Wally suddenly raised his head and
whispered into her right ear.

"Yes," she answered, as she kept her body still. "Why aren't you
sleeping?'

"Well," he stalled, obviously struggling to choose just the right
words. "I was wondering if you'd be interested in… well, you know,
in maybe making love?"

Her heart skipped a beat, and Annette swallowed hard; it was her turn to word her response carefully. Just earlier that evening, once the kids had all been tucked into bed, Wally and Annette sat down and discussed the realities of whether or not they should continue their marriage. It was a heated discussion, fraught with tears and accusations, but in the end, they decided their family was worth another try. Wally swore it would never happen again—a single blip in his life—which he contributed to his strict upbringing and lack of experimentation in his teenage years.

Annette swore she wouldn't dwell on his sexual identity; she felt confident that her husband was a heterosexual and wouldn't be looking to replace Billy with another male lover. Both were skeptical of the other, but they were determined to try to salvage their marriage.

"Sure, I guess we could," Annette relented. "But remember, you promised to use a condom for the next six months until all the follow-up test results are clear."

Flipping over to his right side, Wally dug into his nightstand and retrieved a row of prophylactics, strung together in groups of five. "I bought them at the pharmacy today. They have spermacide, and they're ribbed for pleasure. Sounds like fun," he attempted to lighten the mood.

Forcing herself to remain silent, Annette turned over just in time to watch her husband quickly tear open a corner of the first package and expertly roll the latex sheath down over his erect shaft.

"Do you want me to play with you?" he asked, referring to their time-honored foreplay technique where Wally manually stimulated Annette's clitoris and vaginal lips with the fingertips of his right hand.

"No, just hold me," she scooted across the bed and snuggled into his chest.

As soon as he felt her body cuddle up to his left side, Wally's arm dropped and circled around her back, slowly beginning to massage his wife's buttocks. "That feels nice, right baby?"

"Yes," she admitted, enjoying the simple skin-to-skin contact.

"Why don't you play with me," he encouraged her, gently guiding her left hand down toward his cock.

"I don't…" Annette suddenly found her fingers pressed around her husband's shaft, his entire palm clamped down over hers to ensure a firm stroke.

"That's good," he moaned. "Now up and down, and don't forget the head."

Yanking her hand out from underneath her husband's grip, Annette flipped her hips and instantly rolled away.

"What's the matter, baby?" Wally quickly followed his wife over to her side of the bed. "I thought it was going well."

"I'm not into it, maybe tomorrow." She wiped the tears from her eyes; silently praying her husband would take the hint and leave her alone.

"Why are you crying?" He slowly pulled her over onto her back.

"You really wanna know?"

Sitting up to flick on his bedside lamp, Wally peeled the condom off his shrinking penis, quickly rolling it into three before wrapping it in a tissue and dropping it down into his trash.

"That's the problem." Annette pointed at her husband's genitals. "You're so experienced now, you… you handled that rubber like you'd been dealing with them all your life." Her voice cracked into a sob.

Staring down at his own cock, Wally was actually speechless.

"It's like I don't know you anymore," his wife admitted between the tears. "And you never used… used to talk so much when we were making love. You're talking all the time now," she broke down into full-blown sobs.

"Oh baby," he turned to throw his arms around her shoulders.

"Quit calling me Baby! My name's Annette." She jumped out of the bed and raced off toward the bathroom.

Bewildered, Wally sat alone among the crumpled sheets, reliving every single minute as he tried to figure out exactly what he'd done wrong.

Locked in the bathroom, Annette sat on the toilet seat and continued to cry, wondering if she'd ever be able to enjoy her husband's touch again.

———

By Thursday morning, Sarah had been packing for almost two solid days and was finally nearing the end of their belongings. Boxes were piled in the hallway and in every corner of the living room; their apartment was starting to look more like a storage unit than a home.

"Mommy, I can't find no socks." Her daughter appeared for the second time in the middle of the kitchen. "Do I gotta wear socks?"

"Yes, you do. Remember what happened last time you went barefoot in your runners?"

"Bwisters." Mary shook her head. "I don't want no bwisters."

"Then find some socks." Sarah gently turned her around and propelled her back toward the kid's bedroom.

"Sarah," Justice began to yell the minute his foot crossed the apartment's threshold. "I got the word," he popped his head into the kitchen.

"What word?"

"The utilities are all hooked up. Murray says we can move in whenever we're ready. That's the word," he ran over and picked up his wife, actually swinging her in a full circle.

"Justice Mallory, you put me down," she ordered, secretly loving every second of their embrace.

"Let's go have another look. We can take a tape measure and write her all up."

"What exactly would we be measuring for?" Sarah teased. "What we got is what we got. We don't need a measuring tape to see if it's going to fit or not."

"Alright, then let's just go. Ya wanna?"

"Sure, but let's at least make it worthwhile. Why don't we load up the kitchen table and all the boxes here on the lino?"

"Maybe we should take the kids, too?"

"Very funny." Sarah swatted her husband. "And how come you're not working today?"

"I have to work Saturday instead."

"What day?" Sarah spun back around to face her husband.

"Saturday, not Sunday," he repeated for a second time.

"Good, cuz the priest is coming down Sunday to bless the house."

Peeling back the plastic wrap on a plate of oatmeal cookies, Justice popped two in his mouth and quickly chewed the snack. "Shouldn't we wait 'til we're completely done moving before we start inviting company?"

"We are not spending a single night in that house until it's blessed." Sarah shook her finger in her husband's direction. "You know that."

"I know, just thought you'd wanna wait until you could fix him a proper dinner after service before you invited him down is all."

"I'll invite him back as soon as we're settled."

Justice shrugged his shoulders, and decided he could better spend his energies loading the truck instead of debating the priest's visiting schedule. "You get the kids ready, honey, and I'll have everything loaded in twenty minutes."

As they pulled up in front of the house with his family's first load of belongings, it occurred to Justice that he was finally home.

There would be no more flights of stairs, no more noisy neighbors banging on the walls. He was about to move his family out of their cramped little apartment and into their very own house. Grass, and trees, and a fenced yard for the kids to play in were nothing short of a dream come true.

"Stay in the yard," Sarah yelled as the children jumped out of the truck and led the charge toward the house's front door.

Standing alone on the sidewalk, Justice looked up one side of the street and then down the other. It all looked so normal, so *family like*. This was exactly what his wife and kids deserved, and for the first time, it was something that Justice had been able to provide all by himself.

"Daddy, hurry up," everyone yelled from the front step. "You have the key."

"No, I don't," he teased, pulling out the front pockets in his denim jeans.

"Justice," Sarah warned. "I've got an arm full of boxes. Please open that door."

Fishing the house key out of his back pocket, he unlocked the main door and stood aside to allow his family entry.

"Help me open up the windows," Sarah called out from the kitchen. "The place is really stuffy and I want to air it out."

Room by room, they opened the windows, pleasantly surprised to see that Murray had left behind nearly all the window blinds.

"Daddy, there's three bedrooms," the kids announced in unison. "One for you and mommy, and two for us, right?"

"That's right. So what's the problem?"

"We just wanna know; who gets their own room?"

Justice motioned all three of his children over to the vacant living room.

"All right Mathew." Justice turned his attention to his eldest son. "You tell me who you think should have their own bedroom and why."

"Me, cuz I'm the oldest."

"Fair enough," he nodded. "Now how about you Mark. Who do you think should have the private room?"

"Me, cuz Mathew says I snore the most and it keeps him wake at night."

As he dropped down to his knees, Justice coaxed his daughter out from behind her mother's back. "Mary, do you want to have your own bedroom?"

"I'll sleep with Mommy," she volunteered, forever sneaking into her parent's bed whenever she woke up in the middle of the night.

"Mary is going to have her own room." Sarah stepped forward to deliver the bad news. "You boys are going to share the other."

"Why?" their little voices rang out in unison.

"Cuz she's a girl, and cuz your mother said so." Justice looked down at both his sons, challenging them to argue his point.

Silence.

"Let's unload the boxes before lunch."

"Lunch?" Mathew's eyes began to sparkle."

"Picnic lunch," his father sweetened the pot. "But nobody touches anything until all the boxes are loaded into the house.

The next sound Justice heard was the slamming of the front door as his sons scrambled on the back of the truck and began unloading their mother's kitchen supplies.

The telephone rang at least ten times before Annette's mother finally answered the call.

"Mom, I almost hung up. What took you so long?"

"Dear, I don't think you want me to describe my bowel movements, now do you?" she actually waited for a reply.

"No," Annette laughed. "So tell me, how you been feeling, Mom? Your back still holding up?"

"I'm pretty good, considering."

"Considering what?" Annette knowingly walked into the trap.

"Ever since Carlos left, I've been spending so much time getting my house back into shape—I just knew my back was probably going to act up. It's hard moving furniture all by my lonesome," she moaned as if mentally reliving the physical strain.

"Sounds like you could use a hand, Mom."

"Well, my neighbor in the duplex popped over a couple of times when he saw me struggling with my patio table."

"Mom," Annette warned.

"I didn't ask him, he just offered. Besides," she began organizing a list of excuses. "I get the feeling that man sometimes needs a little break from his old ball and chain."

"Promise me you won't make any trouble, please?" Annette begged, mindful of her mother's reputation back in the old neighborhood where all the married women ended up treating her like a social leper.

"So, how is Wally? Still training them new salesmen?"

"No," Annette cleared her throat. "He's back in sales full-time."

"And the children?"

"They're good, Mom."

"Well then, sounds like everything is going really well."

"Mom, can I drive up for the weekend, maybe spend a couple days? Just you and me alone, without the kids?"

Annette's mother pulled up a chair, and plopped down by the wall phone, determined to hold her seat until she got down to the bottom of the problem. "Alright, what's the matter, Annette?"

"Mom, I'm just wiped and I thought a weekend away might be the break I needed."

"Blah, blah, blah," her mother mumbled on the line.

"Mom, stop that!" she barked. "You know I'm not ten years old anymore."

"Well, then stop lying like a child and tell me the goddamn truth!"

Her own mother had to be one of the most abrasive women Annette had ever known. She had the tact of a barroom drunk, and the morals of an alley cat. But Vivian Robinson could smell bullshit a mile off.

"Wally and I are going through a rough patch and need a break, is all."

"Let me get this straight." Her mother took a moment to evaluate exactly what she'd heard. "You're going to pack a suitcase, leave all three children at home in your husband's care, and then drive three hours to spend the weekend at my house? Do I have it right, dear?"

"In a nut shell."

"What'd he do?"

"What'd who do?" Annette answered her mother's question with another question.

"Your husband obviously did something terribly wrong if he's willing to stay home all weekend without any transportation and babysit the kids so you can gallivant across the countryside."

"No Mom, it's not like that," she instantly argued back. "I haven't even mentioned this to Wally yet."

"Oh Mary, mother of Jesus," Vivian began to curse. "Who's your husband having sex with?"

"Mom?"

"Well, you all but admitted to me that he's been screwing around."

"How?" Annette demanded, her patience beginning to wear thin.

"Well, no woman in her right mind plans a trip and decides to leave her kids at home with her husband without even bothering to ask him," Vivian lectured in one long breath.

"Oh really," she groaned, knowing full that her mother was just getting wound up.

"But you already know, my dear, that your husband wouldn't dare say no to you cuz he's got a lot to be sorry for. You could do just about anything right now and he'd never deny you. And trust me Annette, there's only one time when a woman's got that kind of power. That's when she'd caught her man *fucking around!*"

"Oh Mom," Annette began to sob. "I just don't know what to do."

———————

"Freeman," the sales manager barked from the end of the hallway. "Come here. I need to talk to you for a minute."

That was it. The game was finally over. Strangely, Wally felt a giant flood of relief. They would fire him; he knew that. He'd just hold his head high, pack up his belongings, and get the hell out of the office. He wouldn't have to listen to all the whispers behind his back, and then he could look for a job where nobody knew anything about his past. This was actually a blessing in disguise, and by the time he reached his manager's office, Wally was actually sporting the smallest semblance of a smile.

"Freeman, grab a chair. I have something a little sensitive to talk to you about," his sales manager motioned before standing up to close his own door.

"I know what you're going to do, sir, and just let me say that I've enjoyed working here, but…"

"Freeman," he broke into Wally's train of thought. "I've got two files here that I know are goldmines, but…" he searched for the politically correct terminology. "None of the guys want 'em cuz the couples are… same sex," he finally found the courage to blurt it out. "They're not cold call leads, these potential clients actually phoned us direct, looking for a rep to help them pick a package. Don't get a lot of those," he chuckled knowingly.

"No, we don't," Wally agreed, his palms beginning to sweat as he wrung his hands in his lap.

"Well Freeman, you and I both know your numbers could use a serious hike up, so I… well… I kinda thought of you."

Not sure whether to be flattered or insulted, Wally chose silence and let his boss continue with his explanation.

"Now, I'm not insinuating anything, but I thought you might be a little more willing to deal with these people, being that you're…"

"Being that I'm what?"

"Don't make me say it, Freeman." The man shook his head, disgusted with the entire conversation.

"I'm not gay." Wally stood up from his seat, challenging his boss to argue the point.

Linking his fingers together before setting them down on the files in question, the sales manager opted for the truth. "Relax, I personally don't give a shit if you're a pillow biter, or not. This is strictly business."

Not sure if he actually believed the man, Wally still relented and returned to his seat.

"Did you know that my sales numbers are directly affected by your weekly sales? Your numbers go south, and so do mine. So you see, Freeman, when I say I don't care what you do in your spare time, I really mean it. What I care about are your weekly totals. So tell me," he leaned as far across his desk as possible, "how do they look?"

"Like shit," Wally grinned, finally feeling like he was communicating with his boss.

"Well then, I think you and I should consider pointing your sales talents in another direction. You see these?" he thumped his hands down on the small stack of files. "These are what we in management call *sign-ups*."

Wally leaned in; his curiosity piqued.

"A sign-up file doesn't need a salesman to show up at their house and deliver a well rehearsed pitch. A sign-up just needs a warm body to show up with a catalogue and take the order. And here's a little footnote for ya. Sign-ups usually spend anywhere from double to triple of the industry norm."

"I'd heard that," Wally admitted. "But word in the bullpen was that all of those kinds of files were filtered back to the main office so the company didn't have to pay any commissions on the sales."

"That's bullshit! The truth is, the files are passed out at the discretion of management, and the commissions are all payable."

Unsure if they were bargaining on a couple of files, or setting down the guidelines for a long-term arrangement, Wally was careful to word his reply. "I think you know that I can keep a secret, so any arrangements we come to will be held in the strictest of confidence. However, other than my *supposed* sexual orientation, why'd ya pick me?"

"You're hungry, Freeman. You need to earn a shitload of cash, and you need to earn it fast. You're a loner, nobody's really interested in hanging with you anymore, and obviously nobody's interested in being your partner. And," he threw in the final point, "most of the sign-ups are a little eccentric. I believe you can fill out the contracts without judging or offending any of them. Am I right?"

"Absolutely," Wally smiled. "Now, how about we look over a few of those files?"

———————

At the curb in front of the prospective customer's house, Wally plucked the client file off the passenger seat and quickly scanned the contents. "Burt and Colin, Burt and Colin," he repeated the names until they rolled smoothly off his tongue. "Domestic partners, both professionals, no dependents." He continued to run his fingers down the page. His boss was right; they did look good on paper. He cracked open his briefcase, and quickly riffled through his packages to make sure he had the right brochures and matching contracts. Satisfied, he decided it was time to introduce himself.

"Good afternoon," a tall black man said as he answered the front door.

"Good afternoon. My name is Walter Freeman." He thrust out his hand.

"From the funeral home?"

"Yes," he smiled.

"Well then, come on in. Colin and I have been waiting for you."

Settled in what Wally assumed to be their formal living room, he found himself quickly appraising the value of their furnishings. Impressed by what he saw, he instantly opted for the premium package brochures, carefully tucking the others out of the clients' line of sight.

"I... I mean we," Burt suddenly corrected himself, "have decided that besides a will, we needed to plan our internments."

"That's very thoughtful," Wally congratulated the couple. "You'd be surprised how many couples in our age group never have the vision to take care of such important details such as their inevitable internments when they're still in good health, a firm mind, and a financially stable position."

"I told him not to wait 'til one of us was sick." Colin lovingly nudged his partner.

"I believe," Wally delved into a time-honored sales script, "that for a select minority such as yourselves, money is not the issue. Am I correct?"

"We're financially secure." Burt nodded before taking a second to pat Colin's right knee.

"Well then," he picked a brochure out of his briefcase, "I believe you should make your own decisions and have all of your last wishes carried out to *your* specifications. Is that not what both you gentlemen had in mind when you called our office?"

"That's exactly right," they both nodded in agreement.

"Life is funny." Wally took a second to run off on his own tangent. "We don't always get to do exactly what we want in life, but maybe, after our deaths, we can ensure our internment is handled with dignity and in a manner that we feel is appropriate."

"Can I ask you a personal question?" Burt politely interrupted.

"Sure."

"Are you gay?"

Wally glanced down at his left hand, his vision focused on the wedding ring securely banded around his ring finger. "Why do you ask?"

"You just seem to understand us. It's as if you know what it's like to be gay and to be forced to live in the straight man's society," Colin offered as an explanation.

Wally pulled out the blank contracts and set a dual set on the cherry wood coffee table. "I'm married with three children." He lifted his left hand and spun the palm to flash his wedding ring.

"Sorry," Colin quickly apologized. "I didn't mean to insinuate anything."

"Don't worry," Wally lifted his head and smiled. "I'm not the least bit offended."

Chapter
Twenty-Five

"One morning I shot an elephant in my pajamas.
How he got in my pajamas, I don't know."

—*Animal Crackers, 1930*

I t had been years since Tony had been inside Julia's place, but surprisingly, with minimal effort, he had been able to walk straight up and knock on the right door.

"I can't believe you haven't moved," he'd teased. "You must really love this old neighborhood."

"Nah, I think I'm just too damn lazy to look for a better place."

Julia's stability was actually a testament to her longevity in the porn industry. Twelve years in front of the camera was nearing an industry record, but even *she* knew her days were numbered. Changing her look and reinventing her image just wasn't cutting it anymore. She was twenty-eight years old, and when you worked for flesh peddlers, that made you at least ten years past your prime.

"Do you wanna a beer?" Julia had offered the second Tony settled himself inside her apartment.

"No, but if you have any kind of juice, that would be great."

She made her way toward the fridge, and bent down to scan the shelves, quite confident she'd seen a stray juice box hiding somewhere in the back.

"How's Serena been sleeping since you got her home?" Tony pulled out a list of questions directly from Dr. Clifford's own hand.

"Not bad." She set down the box minus the straw. "She's always begging for another shot, but once she quiets down, she usually rests for three or four hours straight."

Tony scribbled down the information, raising his head to see Julia spark up a fresh joint. "The doctor wanted me to remind you that you can't mix any street drugs with what he's prescribing. It could be lethal."

Slowly pulling the joint away from her lips, Julia made the motion to offer it to her guest who quickly declined with a small wave of his hand. "I've been following the doc's orders as best I can. It's just that sometimes, Serena gets really pissed and won't let me change her dressings."

"Well, just do the best you can. Fighting with her isn't going to accomplish much of anything. She asking a lot of questions yet?"

"Not really, but I know for a fact that she doesn't remember being at your clinic. As far as Serena's concerned, she called me from the hotel and I brought her straight here. She's was too sick to remember anything in between."

"The doctor says that's normal," he reported. "Serena may never recover any of the memories from her two-day stay at the clinic."

"What about the weekend she was out running around town? The scat film, will she remember any of that?"

"I don't know," he admitted, grabbing a clean knife off the drain board to slice open his box of juice. "At this stage, I'm not sure she'd wanna remember."

"Julia?" a voice called out from the bedroom. "Julia, are you there?"

Quickly making their way down the hall, Tony immediately noticed upon entering the bedroom that Julia had indeed covered the bedroom mirror and removed the bedside phone as per the doctor's instructions.

"Who are you?" Serena demanded, her voice slurred from the pain medication.

"That's Tony from the Changeroom. Remember him?" Julia stepped forward to buffer her nervousness. "Tony's been helping me take care of you."

"I remember," she muttered, closing her eyes to gather up her remaining strength.

"Dr. Clifford sent me with some more antibiotics for your infection. And he wanted to know if I could check your dressings?" he tried to sound as professional as possible considering the situation.

Serena slowly opened her eyes, searching Julia's face for a sign.

"He's cool, let the man have a look."

With Julia's recommendation still hanging in the air, Tony pulled a pair of rubber gloves out of his brown paper bag and prepared for the examination. "Can you help me, Julia?"

"What ya need?"

"Pull back the sheet, and slowly start peeling off the dressing, alright?"

"Can do," Julia answered, her nursing skills having improved tenfold since her unexpected apprenticeship under the doctor's private tutelage.

"I'm gonna give you a shot, Serena," Tony warned. "This will help you deal with any discomfort."

Smiling, she took two breaths and waited for the buzz, welcoming the express ticket to *La La Land*.

As Serena drifted in and out of consciousness, Tony and Julia carefully peeled back the bandages, gingerly exposing her chest to daylight.

"It's really starting to pucker," Tony tenderly touched one line of sutures. The doc warned me that might happen as the swelling recedes."

"It looks like hell," Julia winced.

Tony quickly raised his face and shot her a look.

"Sorry," she apologized, motioning that her lips were now zippered shut.

"I have to take her temperature," he explained, carefully slipping a battery-operated thermometer deep into Serena's ear canal. "He wants to make sure she's still not septic."

Pulling out the thermometer, he discarded the disposable cap before taking a second to read the display panel and record the information.

"How's it look?"

"She's still running a bit of a low grade, but I think that's normal considering everything her body's been through."

"What about her privates?"

"Next stop," Tony announced, continuing to peel the remaining blankets off Serena's body. Leaning in for a closer look, he suddenly stood up and walked over to the wall, switching on the overhead lighting to illuminate the situation better.

"Something wrong?" Julia rushed up to his side.

"Looks like she's still leaking pus." He bent down a second time and gently removed the sanitary napkin. "This isn't good."

"But you said she might leak for a few days."

"It's Friday morning. She should be done by now."

Watching Tony inspect the soiled pad, Julia suddenly felt her emotions stir. He was a good man, a caring man—a man she could possibly learn to love.

"You got a sandwich bag or something else I can drop this in?"

"I got a bread bag," she offered. "You gonna take it with you?"

"Yeah, the doctor wants to see if there's any blood or anything else of concern."

Flying off to the kitchen, Julia was only gone a minute before she returned with an empty bread bag full of dried crumbs.

"Let's bandage her up." Tony quickly shook the crumbs into the garbage before dropping in the soiled pad.

Carefully redressing Serena's wounds, Julia stopped what she was doing to look up into Tony's eyes. "What am I gonna tell her when she wants to see what's under the bandages?"

Tony shook his head side to side. He knew that answer wasn't written anywhere on his page of instructions.

He wanted to bring flowers or chocolates, but they seemed a little contrite, so instead Wally opted for a nice bottle of pink Zinfandel. Taping his company envelope to the glass neck, he snuck into the house and set it down on the kitchen counter, sneaking back out of the room before Annette even noticed he had been in the house.

"And remember to put the forks on the left," she called out to her daughter Monica. Daddy promised to be home for supper, and I want the table to look… what the hell?" she broke her own train of thought.

"Surprise," Wally called out, rushing into the kitchen to hug his wife.

"You just about scared me to death." Annette nervously tightened her ponytail.

"Open the envelope," Wally said, excitedly danced around the room, only pausing long enough to pull down two long stemmed wineglasses from the cupboard above the sink.

"What is it, Mommy?" Monica instantly picked up on the excitement.

"I don't know, honey."

"And you won't 'til you open it," Wally grinned, handing his wife a freshly poured glass of wine.

Ripping open the sealed envelope, Annette plucked the check out of the tattered paper, her eyes instantly locking on the number. "Five hundred dollars?" she looked toward her husband for an explanation.

"It's the weekly bonus!"

"I don't get it."

"Neither have I before. I'm the company's top salesman for the week. My numbers were the highest." Wally did a little victory dance in the middle of the kitchen floor.

Shaking her head, Annette struggled to digest the information. "You were the company's top salesman for the week?"

"Yeah, and if I keep my numbers up, my sales manager figures I might even make top three for the month. What ya think of them apples?" he teased. "That's a thousand dollar bonus."

"I'm so proud of you, Wally," Annette began to cry. "I knew you could do it, I always knew you had the ability."

"What are you gonna buy Mommy?"

"Its Daddy's money," Annette handed the money over to her husband.

"No, it's yours. Buy something for the house. Maybe… bedding, or dishes, or something," he suddenly pointed to the pile of unmatched stoneware sitting untouched on the edge of the counter.

"Five-hundred dollars is a lot of money to spend on dishes or sheets." Annette finally recovered her composure.

"Well," Wally laughed, "then I suggest you take a couple hours

on Saturday and do a little shopping. I'm sure you have a running
list of things we need."

Pulling the bread bag out of his pocket, Tony slowly handed the
doctor the package.

"Was she feverish, sweating, and signs of heart palpitations?" he
quizzed his assistant while extracting the sanitary napkin.

"No, but the incision is puckering really bad. I'm afraid that the
sutures are even gonna pull at her chest muscles. Do you remember
that guy who'd shot himself in the leg, sewed it up himself, and then
finally came to see us a week after the fact?"

"I do," the doctor continued to examine the sanitary napkin.

"Well, it was worse than that."

"Worse?" Dr. Clifford emptied his hands. "I did the best I could
under the circumstances. I used the finest suture silk I had, and
I…"

"You saved her life," Tony reminded his boss. "She'll just have
to go for plastic surgery to fix it up."

Without speaking, the doctor turned his attention once more
to the sample of Serena's discharge. "How long had she worn this
pad?"

"Just an hour or so. Not that long," he reluctantly reported. "You
know, Julia's really not that bad at nursing. She's got the natural
touch, kind of like you spotted in me. Maybe one day we could
afford to bring her on in here?"

"Maybe," the doctor mumbled, shaking his head as he tossed
the soiled napkin down into his trash. "Right now, I think we better
worry about the other patients we've got sitting in our waiting room.
Bills to pay you know," he nodded his head, signaling Tony that he
was ready for his next patient.

Tony nodded back, having already agreed to stay open late for one week to make up for the lost revenue when Serena lay fighting for her life in the back of their clinic.

Leading a young kid and his mother into the examination room, Tony quickly settled the woman on the table and parked her son on the empty stool.

"How long ago since your mom was beaten?" Tony quickly appraised the woman's bruises before turning to face her son.

"Two days, I think," the kid looked up at the ceiling as if the answers were written on the water-stained tiles. "I was at my dad's, and when I came home, she already looked like this."

"When did you get home?"

"Today, after school. Even though my dad was 'posed to have me for a couple more days, he got called out of town and dropped me back at my mom's."

"Good evening," Dr. Clifford entered the room, plucking the woman's form off the edge of the examination table. "How are you today, ma'am?"

"She can't hear you," her son quickly explained.

"Is your mother deaf," he turned and smiled at the woman.

"Not before he beat her. I think he did something to her ears this time."

Biting his own tongue, the doctor began his examination, his worst suspicions immediately confirmed after an initial inner ear exam.

"Step-father or boyfriend?" Tony inquired, not that it had any bearing on the outcome of the woman's medical examination.

"Boyfriend. They ain't married," the kid flatly reported. "Is she gonna be okay?"

Grabbing a pad of paper, the doctor quickly scribbled out his diagnosis, revealing the page to his patient.

As she sobbed her response, the doctor turned back to the young boy to announce his findings. "Both your mother's ear drums were burst during the attack. I assume your mother's boyfriend probably hit her like this," he cupped his hand and slowly brought them up to the boy's ear as if simulating a blow to the side of his head.

"How long before she's better?" he timidly asked, watching Tony cross the room and silently hand his mother a box of tissue.

"Son, this is permanent," the doctor shook his head. "Your mother is going to be deaf for the rest of her life."

"Come with me," Tony motioned the boy back into the waiting room. "The doctor wants to spend a little time alone with your mother."

"But she can't hear nothing," he argued through the tears.

"The doctor can write more notes, they'll be able to communicate."

As he ushered the boy out of the examination room, Tony did not envy the doctor's next step. He knew Dr. Clifford was going to try to convince the woman to let him call the police and charge her boyfriend with assault. He also knew the woman would probably say no and just head back home to her abuser.

Chapter Twenty-Six

"Made it, Ma. Top of the World!"

—White Heat, 1949

"Someone's at the door," Wally moaned, the doorbell jarring him out of the first peaceful sleep he'd had in weeks.

"Who is it?" Annette woke, rubbing her eyes as she struggled to read the clock radio without her contacts.

"I'll get it." He staggered from the bed, his head a little fuzzy from the wine.

"Bathrobe," Annette called out, her limited vision still enabling her to see her husband's naked body crossing their bedroom floor.

"Oh yeah," he laughed, running his fingers through his hair.

They'd all celebrated Wally's accomplishment together, kids included. And once the children were safely tucked in their beds, the parents had retreated upstairs to the privacy of their bedroom. It might have taken a second bottle of wine, but Annette had finally been able to make love to her husband. It wasn't a nine or ten on the good old *sex o' meter*, but it definitely was a step in the right direction.

Lying in bed as her husband rushed off to answer the ringing door; Annette finally felt the first thread of tissue begin to mend over her broken heart. It would be slow, but she was patient, and this morning she finally believed the old adage that time could heal all wounds.

"Annette, you come on down here," a woman's voice yelled from the bottom of the stairs.

"Mom, is that you?" She jumped from between the sheets to wrap herself in a terry cloth robe.

"It's nearly nine o'clock in the morning, child. Tell me I didn't wake you?" She furrowed her brow at Annette's disheveled appearance.

"It's Saturday, Mom," was the best defense she could muster on such short notice.

"Where are my grandchildren?" she set down her bags and marched right through the house.

"Nice to see you too, Vivian," Wally called out after his mother-in-law. "I'll just take your bags upstairs," he laughed, knowing she couldn't hear a word he was saying.

"I'm so sorry," Annette began to apologize in a whisper. "I forgot to tell you that she might swing by this weekend. With everything that's happened, I guess…"

"Don't worry." He leaned over and kissed her warmly on the lips. "We'll manage just fine. But *you* can tell the kids that grandma is sleeping in their room."

"Punishment accepted," Annette grumbled, forcing herself to follow her mother up the stairs.

"He's sure acting all lovey-dovey," Vivian rolled her eyes. "If I didn't know any better, I'd say that you two kissed and made up."

"What? You have spies in my house, Mom? Cuz you always seem to be one step ahead of me."

"And don't ever forget it," she warned. "I've got twenty more years experience where men are concerned, and you might as well benefit from my wisdom."

"How about I make us all some breakfast, and you can go wake your grandchildren," Annette suggested.

"They're still sleeping, too? What kind of schedule do you have them on?"

"It was Friday night, Mom. Wally and I let them watch a video until eleven. It was kinda a treat."

"Good-mannered and well-behaved children are a treat. Cranky and overtired little brats are not."

Annette nodded her head, seriously debating whether it was too early for a shot of whiskey with her coffee. By the time Annette had fried up a batch of blueberry pancakes, Vivian had the entire house in an uproar.

"Grandma says I gotta cut my hair," Colin wailed as he ran straight for his mother's legs. "Don't give her the scissors, she said she's gonna cut it really, really short," he continued to shout at the top of his lungs.

"Colin, listen to me," Annette dropped down to her knees. "Grandma's only teasing you. She wouldn't cut your hair without my permission, would you, Grandma?" Annette stood up the minute her mother walked into the kitchen.

"For Christ sakes, Annette, he looks like a little girl. I thought it was Tammy when they were all lying in their beds."

"Coffee ladies," Wally attempted to change the topic. "It smells really good."

"Go call your sisters for breakfast," Annette shooed her son out of the room, grabbing three clean cups from inside the dishwasher.

"Breakfast is great. I can't remember the last time we had pancakes with real blueberries." Wally winked at his wife.

"I used to make waffles on weekends for the kids. That was my specialty," Vivian leaned over and wiped Tammy's mouth. "You remember my waffles, Annette?'

"Vaguely," she muttered, rising up to clear the table.

"Well, you were the youngest, and remembering has never been your strong suit."

"So, what you ladies up to today?" Wally carried his plate to the counter, silently wondering if he needed to stop by Athlete's World and buy himself a black and white referee's shirt.

"Well, I was planning to do a little shopping, remember?" Annette looked to Wally for support.

"Sounds good." Vivian grabbed the carafe of coffee to refill her cup.

"And I'll keep the kids," Wally announced. "That way, you two can enjoy yourselves without having to drag them all around the mall. Sound good?"

"Thanks." Annette smiled at her husband.

"Yes, thank you," Vivian mimicked her daughter. "That would really be great."

Pulling out of the driveway, Annette silently started to count down from ten, wondering just how long it would take her mother to bring up Wally's affair.

"He doesn't look too sorry to me," Vivian pasted on a smile and waved at Wally as he stood on the front step surrounded by his children.

She'd only made it to the number four.

"Does he know that I know?"

"No Mother; and it's going to stay that way. Alright?"

"I don't understand you, Annette. You know a leopard doesn't change its spots. How can you trust him?"

"Mother, he's babysitting the kids, what kind of trouble do you possibly think he's going to get into at home?"

"I'm not talking about this afternoon. I'm talking about Monday, Tuesday, whenever he's out of your sight. What makes you so sure he's not going to hit on the next short skirt he sees?"

"Oh, just a feeling, Mom." Annette couldn't help but chuckle. "I'm pretty confident that Wally won't be hitting on any other women."

"Well, as long as you feel confident." Vivian shook her head.

"I don't think Sarah's gonna take very kindly to a television in her house," Justice reluctantly shook his head. "But I appreciate your offer, Murray."

"You know, we get some bad weather up here, possible tornados, and such."

"Sure, lived here all my life," Justice agreed.

"Well, think of it as an early warning system. You should keep it around to watch for weather reports whenever it looks like a storm is going to break. Kind of like an extra safety feature for you and your family."

"I don't know." Justice continued to shake his head, definitely tempted, but not brave enough to endure his wife's wrath.

"Well, take it home, and if it's really a problem, you can always bring it back to work."

"Sounds good." Justice stepped forward to shake his landlord's hand before loading the nineteen-inch set in the back of his truck. "You know, I think I'll run her over to the house on my break and plug it in. Maybe if I have 'er all set up before Sarah comes over, she'll realize it's not all that bad."

Scooting over to the house during the lunch hour, Justice

carefully followed Murray's instructions, heading straight to the basement to find the electrical panel.

"Follow the thick white cord," Murray had told him. "Wherever it pops through the floor boards—that will be the room that's set up for cable. If you have any problems, don't call the cable company, be sure to call me. You understand?"

Justice understood. Everything would be handled through his landlord, and that was just fine by him.

"There you are." He finally located the panel. Swinging open the metal door to locate the white cable, Justice nearly jumped out of his skin when a rolled-up catalogue escaped its hiding place and fluttered to the floor. Picking up the high gloss paper, he couldn't help but flip through the pictures.

"Holy cow," he swore, or came as close to cursing as he usually dared. "This is some nice stuff." Justice continued to flip through the pages. The best Arctic Cat had to offer was beautifully photographed and laid out for prospective buyers. Page after page of snowmobiles, four-wheeled quads, and the newest in utility vehicles graced every page. It was a collection of overpriced dreams, as far as Justice was concerned; still, he didn't have the heart to chuck it in the garbage. Instead, rolling it back up into its original condition, Justice tucked the catalogue in his back pocket and continued with his mission.

"Alrighty, let's see," he muttered before turning on the set.

The first channel had four women sitting around a table in a fancy restaurant, sipping big tall drinks. There were two blondes, a red head, and a brunette, all acting like they were awfully rich with fancy clothes and fancy hair dos. Continuing to watch the scene play out, Justice found himself paying attention to their conversation, drawn by their laughter. That was until he realized that they were talking about the desired length of a man's penis.

Stepping forward to change channels, the show cut to break,

taking a moment to advertise the DVD version of *Sex in the City* for sale in stores right now.

"Sarah ain't gonna like this," Justice muttered. Not even bothering to change the station, he just flicked off the power and began wandering around the house. They'd been so lucky to stumble across this place, almost as if it really had been a gift from God. His family deserved a good home in a good neighborhood, and until he met Murray, Justice wasn't sure it was ever going to come true.

"Hey there, hello," a voice called out from his front room.

"Hello," Justice hollered back, totally surprised that some stranger had wandered unannounced into his house.

"Hi," the young girl smiled. "You Earl?"

"No, my name is Justice."

"Justice, that's kinda different. You out for *justice*?" She began to laugh, fashioning her fingers into pretend guns, and firing imaginary bullets from her hips.

"Can I help you?" he asked, his patience suddenly running a little thin.

"I's looking for Earl, you know where he's at?"

"I never met no Earl." Justice leaned past the girl to see if she had any back up waiting for her outside on the walk.

"Well, that bites," she nervously began to chew her nails. "You in the same business as Earl?"

"I work in a greenhouse."

That seemed to be just the answer she was looking for. "So, you take it on trade, too?" She dropped her jacket on the floor and began eyeballing the empty rooms.

"Well, I like cash better, but I've worked for trade before."

"When you moving in for real?"

"My wife and kids will all be here this weekend."

"Kids, that's cool. I gots me two, but they're with my ma." She began unzipping her jeans.

"What ya doing?" Justice took two steps back.

"Oh, you're one of those," she laughed. "Alright, I'll slow it down." She began to wiggle her hips. "But if you want a show, I want an eight ball. Deal?"

Justice had absolutely no idea what the girl was talking about. For all he knew, she was speaking in a foreign language.

"You pay for deliveries?" she asked, gyrating to some unheard music.

"I do my own deliveries."

"That's cool, but if you ever need someone to mule for ya, I'm up for it."

"Mule? We use trucks."

"Trucks," she stopped dancing long enough to appraise the man. "How big was your last delivery?"

"Bulk or pots?"

"Pot. How much pot?"

"I didn't count exactly," Justice crossed his arms at his chest. "But we had a three-ton cube van and the floor was full."

"Holy fuck," her face flushed and her eyes began to twinkle. "I heard they were sending down some heavies, but I never thought I'd get to meet any in person."

"I think you better leave," Justice opened his arms and waved as if ushering a stray calf through a gate.

"What about our deal? Ain't you holding anything?"

"All I brought was my TV," Justice pointed to the living room. "Ain't nothing else in the house."

"Thanks for fucking wasting my time," she buttoned up her jeans and angrily snatched her jacket up off the floor. "When did you say you'd be all moved in?"

"By Monday, before I go back to work at the greenhouse."

"Fine, I'll come back round on the weekend," she turned and stomped out the front door.

Once again standing alone in his house, Justice made a mental note to remind Sarah to keep the front door always locked. You just couldn't tell by looking at people. But he had a funny feeling that if his visitor was friends with the previous renters, they were probably a little on the wild side, too.

She looked to be probably no more than fifteen or sixteen years old, she had that look in her eyes that Justice remembered from his younger days. Back home when he was growing up, he learned real fast that there were two kinds of girls in the world—the ones he wanted to walk to the dance, and the ones he wanted to walk home.

When you walked a girl to a dance, you held her hand, brought her punch, and hoped to be lucky enough to hold her close for one or two slow dances before her parents took her home.

But when you walked a girl home, you'd get to hold her tight around the waist, maybe share one of her daddy's beers, and if you were lucky, spend an hour or two kissing in the dark behind their barn.

The girl who strolled into his house was definitely the kind you walked home after the dance. He could tell this wasn't her first trip *behind the barn* and it didn't take a genius to see it in her eyes. He just wasn't sure what she was willing to trade it for. He'd ask Murray; maybe he would have some information about that Earl character that had lived there before. Either way, he was glad to be alone. It gave him a chance to check the rest of the deadbolts and window locks.

Satisfied that they'd probably hold up, Justice locked up the house and began pacing off the back yard. The lot was fifty by one-hundred-fifty, with a lot of open space. He was good at estimating size and everybody down at the greenhouse knew it. No matter what the crews were loading, whether it was the bulk mulch, or a fresh load of potting soil, they called him over to help estimate the yardage. He was a walking weigh scale and more than one guy had won cash, betting on his estimates.

Justice Mallory was a hell of a worker. He put as much into his job as he put into his family. He saw this house as his reward for a life of hard work, sacrifice, and devotion. He was sure that his life would be perfect from now on.

Chapter
Twenty-Seven

"The stuff that dreams are made of."

—The Maltese Falcon, 1941

It was Sunday morning, and after an especially exhaustive week of treating his clinic's patients, the doctor was ready for a little rest and relaxation.

"Sausage will work," he decided, digging into the back of his freezer to retrieve a generous portion of pork links. Quickly unwrapping it, Marcus dropped the frozen lump down into his Teflon pan. "Nice and slow," he continued to murmur, setting the stove on medium before covering the heavy skillet with its clear glass lid.

"Anybody home?" a voice surprised him from the back hall.

"Elizabeth, is that you?" The doctor covered his eyes and purposely stumbled toward the apartment's door.

"No, it's not Elizabeth Taylor. Try again," the woman's voice encouraged.

"Umh, let me see. Is it Anne Margaret?"

"No." She shrugged off her coat and rushed up into his arms. "It's Teresa Caroline Lutz," she purred in a heavy Italian accent.

"Welcome home, honey." Marcus bent down to kiss his girlfriend's lips. "I really missed you this time."

"That's nice. But... does that mean you never really missed me the time before?" she winked, her face still turned upward in hopes of a second kiss.

"Come on in, you must be wiped right out." He ushered her into the warmth of his kitchen. "I didn't expect you until tonight."

"Early bus," Teresa offered, taking a second to peek under the fry pan's lid before sliding into a kitchen chair.

"How's your mother doing? Is it still her angina?"

"Yes, but she's also developed further complications from her diabetes. They're talking about amputating the big toe on her left foot. It's just awful, you wouldn't believe the infection that's set in since my last visit."

"I probably would," he muttered under his breath, slowly flipping over the lump of soggy bacon. "I've had my own little week from hell down here. You wouldn't believe the patient that came through my doors."

"What was it?"

"Another so-called *actress* from the porn business. But this one was in really bad shape."

"Beat up?" Teresa gratefully accepted the cup of coffee from Marcus's hands.

"No, more like a walking glob of pus. She'd been filming one of those disgusting movies where the men and women defecate on each other. The poor girl was infected inside and out. I actually broke the cardinal rule and kept her overnight."

"Really?"

"She was kind of a friend of a friend of Tony's. I couldn't just throw her out on the street. She'd have died. Anyway, she's doing much better, and though she'll be disfigured, she'll probably live... for now."

Taking a second to add a small teaspoon of sugar to her steaming cup, Teresa slowly rose to add a splash of cream. "Mother won't be coming home from the long-term care center. Her cardiologist confirmed it." Teresa nervously raised the coffee mug up to her lips.

"I'm sorry, honey. I didn't realize your mother's condition had deteriorated so quickly."

"Well, that's not all of it." Teresa nervously shifted in her chair. "Mom signed over the restaurant to me, as well as the house. I just knew she had a reason for calling me down. Then, she asked that I move back home as soon as possible to run the family business. And I was wondering, my dear... I know it's a big decision and all, but will you consider moving home with me?" she was finally able to blurt out.

"But the Changeroom, Teresa. I just can't close the doors. Where would all those people go?"

"Where did they go before the Changeroom? Something else would open up; I guarantee it. Honey," she rose from her seat to wrap her arms around his waist, "we all like to think we're irreplaceable, but in truth, life always goes on without us. Don't you think it's time to start thinking about yourself for a change, Marcus? Maybe it's time to think about retirement?"

"Retire?" he chuckled. "I'm still a month behind on my payments to the linen company. How am I even supposed to fathom retiring?"

"The restaurant, it'll provide plenty of income for us both. We'll have a house, and hours of yard work to keep us both busy."

"That's *your* inheritance, Teresa. Your mother gave that to you. She didn't want you blowing it on some washed-up old boyfriend."

"Yes," she pulled back from their embrace. "My washed-up old boyfriend, the retired doctor. Isn't he just an uneducated bum?" "My professional reputation isn't worth spit. You know that." "But that's the beauty of it," she argued with renewed vigor. "It's a brand new city, and we could start fresh. No one will ever have heard of you, or the Changeroom. I'm sure you could find work in one of the hospitals or nursing homes. And," she pointed an accusing finger at his chest. "You'd finally get out of that goddamn basement you've been forced to call a clinic!"

Marcus stepped around his girlfriend to shut off the frying bacon, his appetite suddenly gone.

Rinsing the plastic washbowl with boiling water, Julia wiped it out and returned it to its new home underneath her bathroom sink. Old bandages discarded in the trash, she decided to check on Serena one last time before taking a breather.

"How ya doing, sweetie?" Julia smoothed the covers around the girl's waist.

"I'm tired," she moaned, the pain medication beginning to filter through her bloodstream.

"When you wake up, you're going to eat some soup, right?"

"Sure," Serena mumbled, her eyes fluttering one last time before closing for a prolonged nap.

Turning to leave, Julia bent down and plucked another small shred of bologna off the bedroom carpet, obviously having missed the piece during her last clean up. Serena was becoming a handful, refusing to eat, begging for more and more drugs to counteract her pain. Julia wasn't sure how much longer she'd be able to wet nurse the girl. She had obligations, too.

The rent and utilities still needed to be paid. Magic fairies weren't going to appear with wads of cash to take care of her bills, and now with a good chunk of her nest egg blown on Serena's care, she didn't have any back up for a rainy day.

Deciding to grab a fresh beer, Julia lit a smoke and dropped down into the couch. There was absolutely no way in hell Serena was going to be able to work for a long time, if ever. What fucking hope did she have of ever getting paid back? Unless... her brain began to whirl with the stirrings of a plan.

Picking the cordless phone off her coffee table, Julia pressed Manny's number on the speed dial, dragging heavily on her smoke while she waited for him to answer.

"Go for Manny?" he barked after only two rings.

"Manny, its Julia calling. You know, Julia Meyers, from your movies?"

"Hey, I was looking for you last Saturday. We shot a quick one—I coulda really used your ass for a couple of hours." He stopped to drag on whatever he was smoking. "And let me tell you something else. I'm getting really fucking sick and tired of them cock-sucking, underage, bitch whores, trying to play like they know porn. What happened to all the pros in this business?" he ranted in an angry tirade. "If I get one more little snot nosed, split tail, who doesn't know how to swallow without fucking gagging, I swear, I'll shove my boot right down her throat. Some of them damn girls; they've just got no fuckin' class!" he continued to rant.

Class, Julia fought back the urge to laugh. That was kinda like the pot calling the kettle black. Listening to Manny scream and yell about chicks with no class was about the funniest thing she'd heard in weeks. "I hear ya," Julia agreed. "Speaking of pros, you been in this business a long time, haven't ya, Manny."

"I'm an original, babe," he smugly chortled over the phone.

"Well, can you tell me who's big into kink right now?"

"Kink?" he howled. "Fuckin' everybody!"

"Well then, let's narrow this down. Who's filming scat here in town?"

"Scat, I really hate that shit," Manny snickered at his own pun.

"So, do you know?"

"Fuck yeah, I know," he barked, suddenly offended that Julia would question his connections.

"I'm sorry, Manny, but we both know you're the only guy who's really got his finger on the pulse of this city. You know what's happening in every backroom studio in town," she heavily stroked his ego. "I've been around a long time, too, and I know that you were the only guy worth calling. You know everybody."

"Fuckin' right I do." He took a second to swallow a couple mouthfuls of his drink. "Well, let's see," he stopped to think. "Scat is really a specialty shoot. Lots of guys won't touch it cuz the clean up's a bitch. Nobody wants to deal with the mess, and the bitches, the ones that'll film that shit, they're the bottom of the barrel. Trust me on that, girl, cuz I know exactly what swims around in the bottom of that barrel."

Just talking with Manny for an extended period was starting to make her stomach churn. She was grateful for his willingness to share information, but Julia also knew that Manny's information wouldn't come without a price. Might as well make it good, she reasoned, grabbing a pen and paper to make a few notes.

"So, if a girl wanted to star in scat, who'd she call?"

"Fuck man, is that your bag now?"

"Hell no, but I got a girl who's begging to get into it and I owe her a favor, you know. So can you help me out?"

"Sure, some day when I got a guy that nobody wants to work

with, you'll help me out, too," he added, the terms now laid down in stone.

"Rolly, down in little Italy, he's done some of that. And old man Leung, but you don't wanna mess with the Triad, so forget them," he mumbled. "And... and I hear there's a crew working out of the diner on Bay Street. Word is... *any pussy will work.* So there you go," he summed it up. "That's what I know."

"Thanks Manny, I appreciate the help."

"No problem, kid," he muttered, fully aware that he'd purposely left his brother Sigmund's name off the list.

"That's everybody?" She drew a line under the word Bay Street.

"Just watch yourself." He took a second to flash her a warning. "Guys who film that brand of kink don't have much respect for life in general, and if they don't like the way you look at them, they'd probably be just as happy to turn it into a snuff. Ya hear me, Julia?"

"I hear ya," she answered, waiting on the line until Manny hung up his phone.

——————

As he sat at a small wooden desk crammed in the corner of his living room, Marcus continued to sort through a pile of personal mail that had accumulated during the workweek.

"More coffee?" Teresa hovered near his chair. "There's still one last cup left in the pot."

"Nah, I'm fine," he smiled back.

"Marcus, I think we need to talk about this. I don't want to fight, but pretending that we don't have any decisions to make won't make our problems go away."

"It's just the clinic," he rose up and began to pace the small room. "It's all I have. It's my job, it's my life, it's…"

"What about me, I'm a part of your life too, aren't I?"

Stopping to rub his neck, Marcus opted for another coffee, gathering his thoughts in the kitchen before returning to make his point in the living room. "I was married for twenty-one years before my wife decided that I wasn't good enough for her, or my own children." He gently lowered himself back into his chair.

Teresa took a deep breath, remaining silent and allowing him a chance to say his piece.

"The people I treat—the uninsured, the indigent, and yes, the criminal—well… they need me. I can't abandon them."

"I need you, too."

"No." He walked over and sat down beside her. "You might want me for my company, but you don't *need* me."

"I love you, Dr. Marcus Clifford. Your kindness, your love of your fellow man, everything about you is precious to me. And since you're taking your sweet time about it, I wanted to know if you'd marry me too?"

With his next breath stuck in his throat, the whir of his ceiling fan was the only sound in the room. "You want to marry me?" He suddenly found his voice.

"For a long time, my dear, but since you haven't gotten around to asking, and we're not getting any younger, I decided to take the initiative myself."

He felt compelled to stand for no other reason than to jump-start his heart. Marcus began once more to pace the room. "You don't need to marry me, Teresa. The world is full of eligible bachelors who'd kill to meet a caring and beautiful woman as great as you."

"I'm confused," she screwed up her face in a desperate attempt to understand his point. "Is that a yes, or is that a no?"

"Yes, I wanna marry you," he smiled the saddest smile. "But no,

Teresa, I won't. You can do so much better than me. I wouldn't be doing you any service by walking you down that aisle."

"Marcus, for Pete's sake, listen to yourself. You're pushing me away because you're not good enough for me? That's has to be one of the biggest bullshit excuses I think I've ever heard. If you don't want to marry me, then say so. I think I deserve a straight answer. Don't you?"

The mood in the living room instantly shifted from playful teasing, to heartfelt honestly.

"I won't be moving with you," he stated in one simple sentence. "My life is here at the Changeroom, and I really think it would be best if you started over without me."

Teresa stood up, grabbed her purse and suitcase, and walked out of Marcus's front door.

Chapter
Twenty-Eight

"A boy's best friend is his mother."

—*Psycho, 1960*

S tanding guard in front of the microwave, Freddy waited for
his bowl of instant macaroni and powdered cheese to finish
cooking before settling back down at his computer. With Callie
still out on her date, he found himself spending the evening alone,
surfing the Internet. He knew he had a ton of research to do, along
with at least twenty anatomy diagrams to memorize—he just wasn't
in the mood for any academic work.

Blowing the steam off his macaroni, he sat down and typed in
the word *tranny* into the search engine. The screen was instantly
flooded with sites all linking him straight to a collection of
pornography. He found it wasn't as easy to research a sex change
on the Internet as he'd originally thought it would be. The moment
he clicked on any field containing the word sex, he was instantly
linked to a hundred different sites, all selling various mediums of

porn. Whether you preferred live video, the written word, or just a naughty screen saver of naked pictures, it was all there for your perusal.

It had taken a lot of experimentation over the last month, but Freddy had finally found a measly three or four reputable links, printing off page after page of practical information. Hidden under his bed in a three-ring binder, he stored the print outs—only taking them out late at night when no one was around to look over his shoulder.

After weeks of study, Freddy had been disappointed to learn that there was no magical cure. Gender reassignment surgery was a very long process, with multiple medical procedures, all required to change the body from male to female. He'd also learned that male to female transformations were forty percent more popular than female to male. But that made perfect sense, since what woman in her right mind would want to be a man?

At this stage, his bank account still appeared to be his biggest obstacle—well, that and the fact that he didn't really have his family's support. It was all so depressing. He'd been waiting to hit the consensual age of eighteen for what seemed like a lifetime, and it just wasn't Freddy's nature to sit back and wait a minute longer. He'd almost given up for another night—ready to shut down his laptop—when he stumbled on something interesting.

"What's this?" he muttered, setting down his half-eaten bowl of macaroni. Inadvertently linking up to a new medical site, Freddy had stumbled on a *Cross the Border* Mexican clinic, offering a complete sex changes for only ten thousand dollars US. No step-by-step surgeries, all the procedures were combined into a single operation. It sounded like a dream, and wriggling on the edge of his chair, Freddy could barely contain his excitement. He snatched up his pen, and began taking notes, recording the doctor's name, complete with phone number and mailing address for the clinic.

All he needed was a referral from a local doctor, twenty-five percent down to hold a date, and the remaining payment due on the day of surgery. Freddy has just stumbled onto a site for *Medical Tourism*, and he couldn't have been more elated.

"Ten thousand!" He stood up from the kitchen table, wandering around in circles as he pondered his dilemma. "Where in the hell am I going to get ten thousand bucks?"

Slumping back into his seat, Freddy reluctantly added the site to his list of favorites before exiting the screen and logging off his computer. After a quick paper tally of his finances, he realized he had a little over eleven hundred dollars in his savings and checking combined. Ten percent didn't even warrant a phone call.

"I'm home," Callie announced, slamming the apartment door behind her back.

"I thought you'd end up spending the night at your boyfriend's place," Freddy threw over his shoulder.

"Nah, he was kinda in a funny mood, so I blew him off and just came home. And what'd you have for supper?"

"Mac and cheese."

"Any left?" Callie began snooping around the kitchen counter.

"How can you be hungry? Didn't you go out for supper?"

"Dim sum. I hate it, Neil knows it, and he doesn't give a shit. I'll tell you, if I was paying, we'd have gone for mushroom and onion burgers with a pile of fresh cut fries smothered in chipotle sauce."

Mouth watering, Freddy looked down at the drying pasta sticking to the side of his cereal bowl. "This bites, let's make grilled cheese."

Snuggled together on the couch, sharing a large plate of fried white bread filled with gooey processed cheese, they took turns exercising their vetoes on the cable line up.

"How about a movie?" Freddy suggested.

Callie sighed, not the least bit interested in running out to the video store. "Let's just talk. How about playing truth or dare with me?"

"With only two people? Don't we need a group?"

"Hell no." She set the plate down on the floor. "Two will work just fine. Who goes first?"

"Me." Freddy got up from underneath the afghan. "Truth or dare?"

"Truth," Callie giggled.

"Here goes, little girl. Have you ever dreamed about having sex with another woman, and if you could, who would it be?"

"Not fair, that's a two-parter."

"Come on," he urged, "it's your game, you trying to quit before we even get started?"

"Fine." She rolled her eyes. "I think my Spanish teacher in grade twelve was really hot. She was on some kind of teacher exchange program, straight from Italy, and she was absolutely beautiful. There, you happy?" She blushed under the weight of her own confession.

"No biggie." Freddy shrugged his shoulders. "Everybody, at one time or another, has a same-sex fantasy. It's actually basic psych 101."

"Satisfied?"

"Sure, your turn," Freddy yielded the floor.

"Truth or dare?"

"Truth," he nervously smiled.

Callie took a second to dip her hand over the edge of the couch to retrieve the last bite of sandwich. "Okay, I got it," she announced with a mouth full of toast. "Did you ever have sex with your girlfriend Jennifer, and…" she paused for effect, "why did you really break up with her?"

He knew this moment would be coming—he just didn't realize

he'd have to deal with it so soon. "Maybe I should take a dare," he teased—ducking his head the second a pillow came flying across the couch.

"Come on," Callie urged.

"Jen and I were best friends all through junior school. She was a great person, and we had a lot of fun together growing up in the same neighborhood. Then," he began picking crumbs off the knitted blanket, "when we hit high school, everybody started pairing off and dating. I didn't really like anybody else, and I guess she always did have a bit of a crush on me, so…" he threw his hands in the air, "we became a couple, too."

"So?" she urged Freddy on.

"So of course we had sex, that's part of dating, isn't it?"

Callie nodded; the story was not half as exciting as she had hoped it would be.

"So, last spring before the end of grade twelve, I told Jen my plans to go to University and she freaked. She thought we'd both go away together, maybe try art school, get an apartment, you know," he twirled his hands in the air. "She thought we'd move away together and play house in the big city."

"Art school? I didn't know you liked art."

"I don't," Freddy laughed, "but then, Jen really didn't know me all that well."

"So that's why you broke up; cuz you came here to University?"

"Not really," he slowly shook his head. "We broke up cuz she caught me blowing Darin Winger at a bush party one night."

"Oh," Callie sat with her mouth open. "That's really not what I expected to hear you say."

"Well, it's the truth." He leaned back into the couch, waiting for his roommate's eventual signs of disapproval.

"The first time I blew a guy, I almost choked to death," Callie confided. "Nobody told me not to do it with a cold. I couldn't breathe through my nose at all," she snickered. "You should have seen me, sputtering, and coughing like I'd swallowed a bug or something disgusting."

Freddy threw his body across the couch and hugged her with all his might.

"What's the matter?" Callie sat motionless, wondering just what she'd said to bring her roommate almost to tears.

"You're so precious." He sat back and stroked her face. "You don't judge, you just accept."

"So, I guess *that's* why your girlfriend Jennifer broke up with you. Cuz of that Darin guy?"

"You could say that," Freddy began to roar, the initial fear of Callie's rejection turning into a fit of uncontrollable laughter. "I guess she knew it was over when... when..."

"When he came in your mouth," Callie began to giggle. "Cuz I know—as a girlfriend—that would've probably clued me in."

After a chorus of giggles that left them both in tears, Freddy and Callie found themselves once again padding around the kitchen, this time looking for something carbonated to quench their thirst.

"Does your mom know about you and that Darin guy?"

"Hell no," Freddy barked, spitting a fine spray of orange soda toward the sink. "That would just about crumble her nice little world. Mom's biggest concern is whether Dad should repaint the deck, or lay artificial turf. Something like that would be just beyond her scope of comprehension."

"You weren't afraid Jen would spill the beans?"

"I was at first, but then when I realized all the secrets I was holding for her, well, let's just say that I think she knows better."

While Freddy downed the remainder of the can of cola, Callie carried the fry pan from the stove toward the sink. "If you ever go ahead with your dream of surgery, your mom's gonna have to be told. Don't you think?"

"You don't know her," he trudged back to the living room couch. "I'm her pride and joy. I'm going to become a doctor and make the family proud. You know the routine? Take care of your mama in her old age?"

Fidgeting with the dishcloth lying on the counter, Callie never answered; she just waited for Freddy to finish his train of thought.

"I don't think there's a way to prepare your family for the fact that you were born with the wrong parts. No matter what I say or what I do, Mom's going to blame herself, and worse yet, she's going to blame Dad."

"But…"

"But nothing," he cut her off. "My mother is a very strong willed, family-orientated woman. She'd see me as a personal failure. I can't talk to her about this. I'm just going to have to show up one day and reveal the new me," he pulled at his shirt's hem and attempted to curtsey.

"She'll die of shock."

"No, she won't. She loves me; she'll come around. Mom just can't be part of my life while I'm making decisions. She'd confuse me. You just don't know what being around her is like."

"And if she doesn't accept you?"

Freddy had never considered that fact. His mother had always loved and supported him, even if her love could sometimes be a little stifling. He'd never taken a moment to imagine what it would feel like to be cast out of his own family. His parents wouldn't do that to him, and it didn't matter if he lopped off his penis and dressed up as a girl. He was their child, born of their union, and they'd always love him, no matter what sex he chose to be. He was sure of it.

Karen had arrived ten minutes early, using the extra time to check the weight room, the juice bar, and the massage tables for any sign of Tony before retreating to the women's locker room.

"I absolutely abhor working out at night," one of girls began to complain. "It's such a meat market. Just look around." She flicked her wrist toward the other women primping and preening by the mirrors. "This isn't a workout; this is a fucking bar without booze. Might as well just grab a seat and see what we can pick up."

"Enough already," Karen snapped. "I thought it might be a good idea to break our routine and try something different. What are you, fifty? You need to get home and make supper for your old man?"

"Sorry," her friend apologized.

Karen waved her off, slamming the metal locker before dropping down to lace up her running shoes.

"What the hell's the matter with you?" Both girls circled her position.

"Yeah, you drag us out here on a Sunday night, and now you're biting our heads off like we've done something to piss you off."

Deciding to come clean, Karen stood up and leaned against the bank of lockers. "I met a guy here at the gym, and we went out. But he turned out to be a total schmuck, and I'm a little stressed about running into him during the day."

"I figured," Sandy nodded. "Why in the hell would you drag us down here at eight o'clock on a Sunday night if you weren't all fucked up?"

"She's not fucked up," Jolene argued in her defense. "She's just coming off a bad relationship, so give the girl a damn break."

"Relationship! Give *me* a fucking break," Sandy was quick to argue back. "You need to date at least three times, have sex once, and know his middle name before you can call it a relationship."

Karen looked around the room at her friends. "Can everybody

just shut up?" she laughed. "We only went out once, but I really liked him. I even took him to see my statue."

"Whooohoo," both her friends teased.

"Not *the* statue?" Jolene was the first to start, gracefully flapping her arms as if attempting to fly.

"Why didn't you tell us?" Sandy brought her palms together as if in prayer, bowing her head and slowly backing away from Karen's position.

"Quit it!" Karen picked up a stray sock and leveled it at the first body she could reach. "Tony was just someone I really wanted to get to know."

"*Holy fuck, man.*" Sandy rushed up to her friend's side. "You're not talking about *the Tony,* from here at the gym, are you?"

Karen just nodded, dropping down to the wooden bench securely bolted to the locker room floor. "Yes, Tony DeMarco, the guy from the Changeroom."

"Holy shit." Jolene slid in beside her. "I didn't know you were going out with him. How did it happen? Did he ask you, or did you… or forget it. Of course he asked you, you'd never have the balls," she continued to ramble until Sarah noticed the tear in Karen's eye and quickly stepped forward to stop the interrogation.

"What happened, why did he turn out to be such a butt hole?"

Karen wanted to confide in her friends, she just didn't want her date with Tony to become some kind of legendary joke. Like the time Sandy found herself in bed with her date's father after she got really drunk and had been seen necking with him at some neighborhood Christmas party.

Sandy shot Jolene a quick look, letting her know without a single word that it was time to close her mouth. "Hey Karen, why don't we try working out at another gym for awhile? I hear the women's Y has a killer Pilates program. Maybe we should try a couple of classes? What ya think?"

"I'm not running from here," Karen confirmed. "I didn't do anything wrong, and I won't be chased out of my own gym."

"That's right," Jolene chirped up, "It's a free country, you can work out wherever, and whenever, you damn well please. Don't let Tony make you think different, cuz if he says anything, I'll kick him so hard, he'll cough up his own nuts."

"Slow down, Rambo." Karen wiped her eyes. "He doesn't even know how I feel yet."

"Okay," Sandy announced, hands on her hips. "That's about all the bullshit my brain can take for one night. Spill the details, now."

"Tony used to be *Tony the Tool*, as in pornography."

"No way," Jolene spun around to see if anyone was eavesdropping on their conversation. "Your Tony starred in adult films, like pornos?"

"Not *like* pornos," Karen nervously leaned back on the bench and pointed her toes up toward her shins, aggressively stretching her calf muscles. "They *are* pornos. The real thing." She relaxed her calves and let out a huge rush of air.

"Holy fuck. How'd ya find out? Did he tell you?" It was Sandy's turn to take over the questioning.

"No, he didn't say anything. Alicia found a copy of an old movie."

Sandy and Jolene just exchanged knowing glances; neither very impressed with their friend's latest roommate.

"I think you should confront him," Sandy announced, suddenly riding her high horse. "I always wondered what *those* kind of people think when they're filming that shit. Doesn't it ever occur to them that maybe, a couple years down the road, their parents, or even their kids might get hold of a copy?"

"Yeah, I always wondered about that, too." Jolene jumped up on her matching high horse. "They just lay back and have sex while some pervert runs around the bed and films them. I just don't think there's enough booze in the world to get me drunk enough to where I'd even consider doing that kind of shit. Don't those people have any respect for their own bodies? What about disease? Don't tell me everyone's in top notch condition?"

Karen had her answer. If there had been any lingering questions about whether Tony DeMarco could fit into her world, her two oldest friends had just stepped up with the answer.

"I can't wait to run into him." Jolene took a second to check her hair in the wall mirror. "I just might have to remind good old Tony that people like *him* aren't welcome around people like *us*. What if your kids were here, Sandy? Would you want him skulking around the gym with your daughters hanging out at the juice bar?"

Karen never said a word; she just bent down and quietly started to unlace her sneakers, the motivation to work out suddenly gone

Chapter
Twenty-Nine

*"Well, here's another nice mess
you've gotten me into!"*

— *Sons of the Desert, 1933*

"I promise that she'll be out for at least another three or four hours," Julia said as she quickly checked the charge on her phone. "And as soon as she wakes, you call me."

"I've never babysat no growd up before," her neighbor complained, eyes still scanning the front room. "You sure she not gonna wake up screaming and call the cops?"

"No ma'am," Julia patiently tried to comfort the older woman. "She's not being held here against her will, she's just recovering from surgery, that's why she's so drugged up."

"So you say." The lady stood up and walked around the room. "What if I'm hungry?"

"Help yourself to the fridge. Not much to choose from, but I'm sure you'll find something to eat." She smiled at the three-hundred-pound woman. "I'll be back as soon as I can. Just tell Serena that you're my friend, and you're house-sitting, alright?"

"I don't care. For forty bucks, I'll tell her you ran off to join the god-damn circus," she chuckled, both her chins giggling from the effort.

"Okay, this will work." Julia reached for her purse.

"Never been invited in for coffee before," her neighbor felt the sudden urge to state the obvious. "You always running back and forth like you're too damn busy for any of us."

Stopping dead in her tracks, Julia realized the issue would have to be dealt with right here and now. "Well, you were already living here before I moved in, right?"

"Right?"

"Well then, when I moved in, why didn't you come over with a pie or something and welcome me into your neighborhood?"

The woman was speechless.

Julia held her ground, knowing full well that if anyone had knocked on her door with some kind of sweets, she'd have either ignored them, or told them to take a flying leap.

"Yous right, I shoulda came calling. I'm sorry. Maybe next week, you can stop by for coffee and we can get to know each other a little better. You know," she shrugged her shoulders, "like good neighbors."

"Like good neighbors." Julia nodded her head as her hand pushed open the front door.

"See ya soon," the lady called out, already turning and making her way toward Julia's refrigerator.

Briskly walking down the street, Julia sucked in two quick breaths of air, trying to focus on the job at hand. She was preparing to head down to the Bay Street Diner to see some guys about filming scat. The only problem; she didn't have a clue who she was looking for, so she'd have to be patient and lay down a little bait.

Seated in the back of the taxicab, Julia stretched her neck to catch a quick glimpse of herself in the cabby's rear-view mirror. She looked consumed, like a woman on a mission, but she didn't look like she'd be desperate enough to film porn covered in human feces.

She yanked open her bag, and dug around, evaluating the contents. Any kind of makeover would have to be quick, but Julia was an old pro. By the time she stepped out of the cab, she looked like a woman in need of a hit, a job, and a strong cup of coffee—not necessarily in that particular order.

"Hey doll," one of the waitresses smiled over her coffee pot and plate of scrambled eggs. "Just grab a seat and I'll be right over."

Hopping up on the red vinyl, Julia quickly dug for her cigarettes, tensing the muscles in her lower forearm so the cigarette shook wildly at the end of her fingertips.

"Coffee, doll?"

"Yeah." She grabbed the cup, wrapping both hands around the warmth, the minute the waitress pulled back the glass pot.

"How about some soup? You look like you haven't eaten in a week."

Julia nodded, pleased that the black eyeliner rubbed underneath her eyes and in the hollows of her cheeks was having the desired effect. "How much is the soup?" she asked, pulling out the rumpled five-dollar bill she'd previously plucked from her own wallet.

"Soup and coffee is three and a quarter. And don't worry, I'll load you up with crackers and plenty of refills," the waitress winked.

Julia allowed herself only a hint of a smile, not wanting to appear too anxious to talk.

"Tomato and rice," the waitress announced, setting down her steaming bowl. "And I brought you a roll with butter, on the house," she winked.

Accepting the gift, Julia ploughed straight into the food, forcing herself to devour the soup as if no other sustenance had crossed her lips in days.

"Slow down, honey. You'll make yourself sick."

Raising her head, Julia took her time, consciously stumbling over her own words as if searching for the courage to speak. "Umh, I mean, umh..."

"Spit it out, doll." The waitress reached across the counter and patted her arm. "You're not gonna shock me cuz I'm way too old, and I've heard it all at least a thousand times."

"I'm looking, well, I'm..." she dropped her head and began shredding the paper napkin. "I need a job," she admitted in a rush of breath.

"No shit. So tell me, doll, what can you do? You ever bus tables, maybe run a commercial dishwasher?"

Julia just shook her head.

"Well, you got strong ankles? Maybe you wanna learn to waitress?"

"Actually," she whispered, just loud enough so the woman would know she was speaking, "I can make movies."

"You can make what?"

"Movies," she repeated, her answer mumbled as she spoke through the fingers rushing up to cover her mouth.

Shaking her head, the lady bent over and slowly refilled Julia's cup, genuinely disappointed that she'd even bothered to befriend another one of *those* girls. "I think you're looking for Boyd. He's in the back booth, wearing the purple shirt."

Setting her five-dollar bill on the counter, Julia lifted her face and looked the woman straight in the eye. "Thank you," she smiled, "and keep the change."

"Don't thank me." she wearily stuffed the bill into the folds of her apron. "It ain't nothing to thank me about." She spun on her heels and wearily made her way down the counter.

Downing her coffee, Julia set down the cup and slowly slid off her stool. Nervously making her way across the diner's floor, she walked straight up to the guy's table and stood quietly, waiting for anybody to acknowledge her presence.

"Refill," one of the men pushed his cup toward the edge of the table, not bothering to lift his eyes and see who was visiting his table.

"I don't think she's the waitress," the man in the purple shirt announced.

"No, I'm not," she whispered.

"Well, if you're not the waitress, what do you want?"

"I'm Julia, and I was wondering if you know anything about making adult films?"

After first smiling up at Julia, and then back across the booth at his fellow diner, the man suddenly slid to the end of the seat and exited his booth. "I'm Boyd," he stuck out his hand. "That's Pete. Wanna take a seat?"

Julia slid into the booth, and moved as close to the wall as humanly possible. Not sure if she was just method acting the part of the strung out junkie, or actually picking up on some wicked vibes, but she suddenly found herself genuinely afraid of her new acquaintances.

So, you're looking for work?" Boyd asked, throwing his arm around the back of the seat.

"Yeah, I haven't done it for awhile, but I really need some cash." She chose her words carefully, allowing the desperation to permeate her voice.

"Why kind of movies you make?" Bert demanded, signaling for the waitress to bring over fresh coffee.

Careful, Julia silently warned herself. *Let them know you've been around, but don't come off as if you know too many people in the business.* "Umh, nothing special. I never really starred in anything, but sometimes I'd get bit parts playing the extra for a two-on-one scene."

"I got it," Boyd took control of the conversation. "You've always been the chick with her ass to the camera. Nobody's ever put your name on a cover, and you wanna have a little glory. Am I right?"

"You'd put my name on the cover?" she asked, forcing her eyes wide open as if suddenly realizing her dream.

"Let's just slow down here," Pete leaned forward across the table. "We're not filming anything 'til later in the week, and I'm not even sure we need another chick. Hell, I've got numbers for a hundred women who wanna spread it for me. Why should I hire you?"

"I'll work real hard, and I need the money," she picked up a packet of sugar and drained the contents down her throat.

"I bet you will," Boyd began gently rubbing her left shoulder. "So," he pushed his cup toward Julia, encouraging her to wash down the granules, "Anything you won't do?"

She shook her head, acting as if she didn't really know what he was alluding to.

"We have been looking for a special star." It was Pete's turn to make the pitch. "A girl who isn't afraid to try something new, something real *avant-garde*."

Avant-garde, my ass, Julia's mind raced back to Serena's condition.

"I don't know no French," she muttered, "but I'm up for new things. And…" she stalled, making sure she had both their attention before continuing, "I really need a little pick me up, so if I promise to make whatever kind of movie you want, do you think you could front me a couple of bucks?"

In the fifty minutes between classes, Freddy ran across campus and quickly made his way straight to Dr. Chew's office.

"Freddy," the doctor smiled, happy to see his young protégé the minute he crossed through the main door. "I've been tabulating some of your results, and I've come across an odd occurrence."

"What occurrence?" Freddy bent down to move a stack of medical journals before pulling up the nearest chair.

"Well, even though it's not your peer group, you seem to gain the most insight and file the most comprehensive interview papers when dealing with twenty-something females. Care to explain?"

"I don't know, maybe they remind me of my sister, or maybe…"

"That's enough." Dr. Chew held up his hand. "I asked you to explain, not to lie. If you're unwilling to tell me the truth, then I think it's just best if we part ways."

Once again flabbergasted by the doctor's insight, Freddy struggled with his ability to come clean.

"You know, Freddy, I've been a doctor for a lot longer than you've even been born. I doubt you could say anything that would surprise me."

Why did people always think that he was worried about surprising them? He actually didn't give a damn what anyone thought of him, he just wanted to find the quickest and most efficient way to realize his dream.

"Sometimes during our teen years, we find our body experiencing changes that are not only unexpected, but sometimes unwelcome."

"Dr. Chew," Freddy interrupted, not the least bit interested in hearing another long-winded version of *the boy who woke up gay*. "I'm not a homosexual. I do not have homosexual tendencies, and I do not only relate with women because I have trouble relating to boys my own age."

"I'm glad to hear that, Freddy." The doctor smiled.

"I relate better with women because I really am a woman. Somehow, during my development, I got a penis instead of a vagina. It was an anatomical mistake, because emotionally and mentally, I am one hundred percent female."

Standing up from behind his desk, the doctor stepped past Freddy's chair and closed his office door. "How long have you felt this way?"

"Since I can remember," he admitted. "I even hated my toys. I wanted my sister's dolls. Mom bought me Star Wars action figures to compensate, but they just weren't the same. You see; I loved to change the doll's clothes and brush their hair. And even though actions figures come with bendable legs and a hundred little interchangeable parts, they just aren't the same."

"Do you mind if I ask you a few questions?" The doctor politely established some ground rules.

"Go ahead, I trust you," he admitted.

"Well, what kind of sexual urges did you experience during your early pubescent years?"

"I wanted to be with boys, but not in a homosexual manner. I wanted to be a girl with long silky blonde hair and round little breasts. I wanted the boys to want me because I was cute, not because they were gay and wanted to suck my cock."

"I'm going to make a few notes, Freddy. I hope that doesn't bother you."

"Go ahead," he crossed his legs.

"Presently, are you a virgin?"

"No, I've had sex quite a few times."

"Hetero?"

"Well, actually, both," he reluctantly admitted, knowing that it went against his original declarations. "But you gotta understand. I was dying to know what it felt like to touch a guy."

"Have you ever been totally fulfilled in a sexual relationship?"

"I've had orgasms, if that's what you mean?"

"No," the doctor attempted to clarify his point. "What I meant was, have you ever been in a sexual relationship, whether it be for a night, or for a month, where you felt totally fulfilled? Satisfied that all your sexual desires were being met."

"Not even close," Freddy admitted.

"What was missing?"

"Me. I had the wrong body. I didn't have the right parts."

After collecting his thoughts for a moment, the doctor continued, "If you had different parts, do you believe you would be satisfied?"

"With different parts, I believe I would have different partners, therefore yes, I think I would be satisfied."

"You've given this a lot of thought, haven't you, Freddy?"

"Dr. Chew, this is all I think about, night and day."

"Have you ever attempted a public outing, dressed as a female?"

"Just once," Freddy smiled to himself, wondering if the pizza guy was still sitting under the bridge with his warm case of beer.

"Why only once? If this has been something you've dreamed off since childhood, why wouldn't you attempt to pass as a female on more than one occasion?"

"See, that's where I differ with all you professionals in the medical field." He crossed his arms and assumed defensive posture. "I don't need a trial run to see if I like being a woman. I am a woman!" He raised his voice. "Nobody seems to understand that point. I don't know how to explain it, but somewhere, somehow, the universe messed up and I got a penis instead of a vagina. It's that simple, I just need to find someone to fix my problem."

"Then I take it you are interested in a sex change?"

Rising from his chair, Freddy walked over toward the doctor and yanked up his tee shirt. "See the right nipple on my chest?"

Leaning in, the doctor did a quick inspection. "Elongated, somewhat deformed. Birth defect?"

"No," he yanked down the shirt and returned to his chair. "When I was little, I used to lay in bed at night and yank on my nipple, trying to stretch out my breast so I'd look like my sister. The bigger her chest grew, the more I resented her. By the time she'd passed through puberty, I could barely stand to talk to her because of my pure jealousy."

Dr. Chew set down his pen, folded his hand on his desk, and looked hard at Freddy. "How have your parents reacted to your sexual dilemma?"

"To my knowledge, it's never been discussed."

"Really? I find that a little hard to believe. I must tell you that even though you have not been privy to any discussions, chances are, your parents would have picked up on your sexual confusion and spoken of it."

"Maybe, but if that was true, my mom would have confronted me. She wouldn't have been able to keep it a secret all these years. She's just not wired that way."

Fiercely debating his options, Dr. Chew silently decided on the straightforward approach, confident that Freddy was adult enough to handle the decision. "A colleague of mine and I are working on developing a psychological profile for sexually confused teens. It's taking a lot more of our time than we originally budgeted, since most young men and women your age are unwilling to participate in such a frank decision."

"Gee, I can't see why?" Freddy snickered.

"Well, I'd like to use you and your past as our primary source, for our study. Your identity would be protected of course."

"Of course," he repeated.

"So, are you interested?"

"Maybe, but first I have a couple questions for you."

"Go ahead," the doctor encouraged.

"Have you ever heard of Cross Border sex change operations?"

Every drop of color drained from the doctor's face.

"I'll take that as a yes. So for my full and complete co-operation in your study, I'd like you to type me a written referral."

"Freddy, I don't think that's a good…"

"And," he interrupted the doctor; "I also want you to help me find a job on campus where I can raise ten thousand dollars as fast as humanly possible."

Chapter Thirty

"Oh Jerry, don't let's ask for the
moon. We have the stars."

—*Now, Voyager, 1942*

Adjusting the choke for the third time, Justice leaned in, pulled the starter cable with all his might, and hoped for the best.

"Why won't it run, Dad? Does it need more gas?" His son Mark poked his head out from behind a clump of willow trees. "Cuz I can bring you the jug."

"Nah, it ain't the gas." He stood up and shook his head. "I don't know, son. She just don't seem to wanna start. I've checked the sparkplugs, the gas and oil, and of course, the starter and the choke. Can't see what the problem is, though."

Mark just stood motionless, watching his dad's every move, confident that the mower would soon run under his father's expert hands.

"Where's Mathew? Thought he was supposed to be helping you pick up branches after school."

"Gots another nosebleed. Mom said he had to lie down 'til after supper."

"Nosebleed, huh?" Justice flipped the cutting table over to have a peek underneath at the blades.

"Yeah, it was running pretty good this time," Mark excitedly reported. "Got it all over his good school clothes, too."

"You know, when I was a kid, I used to get in all kinds of fights at school, and when I got home," Justice admitted, "I'd just tell my mother they were nosebleeds from running too hard. You think that's maybe what your brother Mathew's doing?"

"Don't think so."

"Well, did you see him all day, and at every recess?"

"No, I was playing ball behind the school at noon hour, and Mathew wasn't. Don't know where he was at noon, probably talking to them girls."

Things were starting to add up in Justice's mind. His eldest son, Mathew, was ten years old, and he was starting to realize that girls were good for more than just teasing. He probably got into a little scuffle with the boys over one pretty face or another. It would pass, Mathew just needed to remember that he went to school to learn, not to sneak kisses in the boot room.

"What's that?" Mark knelt down, pointing his fingers at the gnarled mess.

"Holy cow." Justice bent down to take a closer look. "It's damn barb wire." He shook his head. "Someone wrapped her clean round the blades. That's why I couldn't start it." He continued to mutter, tromping off toward the garage.

With the overhead door barely attached to its tracks, and only a handful of second hand tools to decorate the bench, Justice's detached garage would have appeared vacant. However, after filling the ten by twelve-foot concrete floor with the empty moving boxes and all the broken furniture Mathew had hauled up from the house's basement, it had started to look like it belonged to a family.

"What ya looking for, Dad?" Mark was right on his heels, following him through the garage's side door.

"Pliers. Gonna have to cut all the wire off before I can even think of getting 'er to run."

"Can I help?"

"Go in the house. Tell your mother I need a paper bag for the pieces."

As Mark ran off toward the back door, Justice grabbed what he needed and prepared to unwrap the wire.

"Dad, Dad," Mark screamed from the back door. "Mom says you better come inside now. Mathew's not right, and she needs your help."

Dropping his tools right on the grass, he ran straight for the back door, almost bowling Mark over as he moved like lightning through the house.

"It's Mathew." Sarah came out of the boy's bedroom, blood drops adorning both her sleeves and the front of her shirt. "I can't stop it, Justice. He just keeps bleeding and bleeding. I don't know what to do."

"Let me look." He marched past his wife, caught off guard the minute he saw the huge puddle surrounding the boy's head.

"Mathew, are you awake?"

"Dad, I don't feel so well," he began to whimper, turning his face, and exposing one of the few unsoiled areas on his pillow.

"What should we do?" Sarah demanded from the doorway, both her younger children clinging to her hips. "I've tried ice, I've tried cold compresses, I... I just don't know," she threw her hands up in the air. "It's like a leaky faucet, it just won't quit running."

"Mathew," Justice gently sat on the edge of his son's bed, amazed at the copper smell rising up from the pooled blood. "Son, were you in a fight today at school?"

Rolling his head back toward his father, Mathew weakly coughed in an attempt to clear his airway, his plugged nose was forcing the blood to trickle down the back of his throat.

"I'm not going to be mad, but I need the truth, son. Did you get popped in the face today at school?"

He whispered, "No," and closed his eyes, focusing all his attention on his breathing.

"I don't know what to do," Sarah cried, her limited list of home remedies totally exhausted.

Rising up to his feet, Justice yanked the wallet out of his jeans and checked the inside pocket, knowing that it'd be almost empty. He'd paid Murray his rent, and although they hadn't paid any utility deposits, just the extra gasoline from the move alone had eaten up all the spare cash.

"We'll just watch him for another hour and see if it stops. If it doesn't, then we'll have to take him in."

"Take him where?" Sarah repeated, knowing that health insurance was a luxury they just hadn't been able to afford.

"Just watch him good." Justice stomped out of the house.

Mary toddled off to find her toys as Sarah rushed to the bathroom to grab a handful of clean towels. Left alone, standing at his brother's door, Mark struggled to make sense of the situation. He was only nine, but as far as he understood, his dad had decided not to take his brother to the doctor because he didn't have any money in his wallet.

This memory would stay with the young boy for the rest of his life.

Tromping around the clinic, Tony continued to stash boxes as if throwing bulk freight on the back of a delivery truck.

"Not to be a nag," the doctor gently interrupted, "but you know that some of those contents are breakable."

Stopping mid-throw, Tony reluctantly turned and set the last box down on the floor. "Sorry, I really didn't mean to trash the place. I guess I'm kinda in a shitty mood is all."

"I've been noticing. Let's have a coffee together. I need to put my feet up, and I think you might need to talk."

Following like an obedient child, Tony grabbed his favorite chair beside the coffee pot and waited for the doctor to take a seat.

"Teresa's left me," Marcus announced, his revelation catching his friend off guard.

"Why?" Tony sat up and straightened his back. "I thought you guys were actually going to get married and buy a nice little house somewhere off in suburbia."

"I guess it just wasn't meant to be." Dr. Clifford pulled up a chair and sat down at the table. "She wanted me to move home with her, run the family restaurant, and live happily ever after in her parents' old house."

"Doesn't sound that bad," Tony shrugged, "a pretty comfy retirement, if you ask me."

"But I'm not ready to retire."

Tony leaned back, the chair creaking as the front legs slowly lifted up off the concrete floor. "So what you planning to do then? Work here until you drop dead of old age?"

"I don't know, but I'm just not ready to pull down my shingle and close up shop. So many people in this community would suffer without us."

"They'd make do."

"Funny, that's what Teresa said."

"Well, it's true. People have been dirt poor for generations before us, and they'll still be eking out a living a long time after we're all dead and buried. We're just here to do what we can, while we're able to do it."

"You sure have changed from the pessimistic little snot who used to come in for AIDS tests and penicillin shots."

"I'm getting old too," Tony admitted with a sigh. "And you know, if I found the right girl who wanted to settle down and play house with me, I don't think I'd be so quick to throw it all away."

Filling two mugs with coffee, Marcus passed a cup to Tony before returning to his chair. "You know, I haven't been quite as successful in my life as I thought I would be. Hell, at one time, I actually believed I might win the Nobel Prize for medicine. But, things don't always pan out the way we hope. So I've been forced to adjust my dream."

"What does that mean?"

"Well, I believe that to do something positive with my life, I now have to give all my energies to the Changeroom. I know this next statement is going to sound a little cold, but Teresa can replace me in a couple of months. She's quite the catch, you know, especially now with the restaurant and owning her own home. Husbands are a dime a dozen, but our clinic," he opened his arms to encompass the entire room, "we're unique, and I think that my calling in life is right here in this stinky old basement."

"That's depressing," Tony smirked. "You telling me that we're doomed to treat junkies, wife beaters, and hookers for the rest of our lives?"

"And gang bangers, and street people, and the indigent. Never forget the indigent, my dear boy."

His turn to share, Tony set his cup down on the table, not the least bit interested in drinking the freshly brewed coffee. "I don't mind the thought of working here for the rest of my life. I can actually live with the shitty money, and the really long hours, but what scares me is the thought of doing it all alone. What's the point of sacrificing everything for this clinic, if you still go home to an empty place, night after night?"

"You're at that age," the doctor nodded. "Usually hits women in their early thirties, but men, it hits a little later. You have a case of the *nesting instinct*. You wanna settle down and spread your seed."

"Maybe," he answered, knowing damn well that the doctor was absolutely right. "But the way things are looking, nobody's going to be interested in settling down with a guy like me."

"What about that girl you dated? What was her name?"

"Karen Taylor. She's an accountant downtown."

"An accountant. Where'd you meet her?"

"At the gym. She actually approached me," Tony smiled to himself, neglecting to mention that her original mission was only to verify a few lines of gossip.

"You like her?"

"I do, I mean, I did, but I haven't heard from her in two weeks."

"Oh well, you're young, you'll meet someone else. Look at you, Boy, you're in your prime. Women must throw themselves at your feet."

"The only women falling at my feet were paid to be there," he joked with the doctor, both aware of the fact that he was referring to his old days in the adult film business.

"So, you giving up on this Karen?"

"I don't know. I'm not gonna hassle the woman. If she doesn't want to see me, what am I gonna do?"

The doctor nodded; he was fully aware that his assistant wasn't the type a man to force himself on any woman, no matter how much he liked her. "Why don't you call her one more time, and this time, leave a message that it'll be your last unless you hear a reply. That way, if she's playing any kind of game, she'll realize that it's time for her to make a move."

"She's not the kind of woman to play games."

"Then maybe she's away on business," Marcus offered, unable to offer any other explanation without having even met the girl.

"You know," Tony looked around the room. "Maybe this is it for both of us? Maybe you're right, our destiny is here at the clinic? Not everybody gets married and lives happily after, you know?"

"Lord, how I know."

"Well, then I guess we better stop dwelling on our personal lives and get back to work. Besides, if Karen doesn't want anything to do with me, I know a few other women who might."

The doctor smiled, fully aware that Tony didn't mean a single word he just said, since he was still totally hung on up on that Karen girl since their first, and only date.

"Anyone there?" A voice rang out through the clinic's halls.

"I thought you locked up?" The doctor turned to set down his cup.

"So did I." Tony jumped to his feet to intercept the intruder.

"Hi, I'm Freddy McNally, and I need a referral letter from the doctor. Can he see me now?"

"Can you see him now?" Tony turned toward Dr. Clifford as he stepped out of the lunchroom.

"Let's see what you got," the doctor held out his hand as Freddy nervously handed over his papers.

"Referral letters are thirty bucks, and that includes your exam. But if there's blood work too, that'll be another forty," Tony quoted from memory. "The doctor will..."

"This is a doctor's referral for sexual reassignment surgery," Dr. Clifford interrupted, turning over the printed web-page form, in an attempt to validate its authenticity. "You know what you're thinking of doing here, young man?"

"Yes," Freddy rolled his eyes, praying that he wouldn't have to listen to a repeat of Dr. Chew's lecture.

"I've never heard of this clinic… in Mexico." He slowly handed Tony the paper, never taking his eyes off the patient. "All your form is asking for is the name of the contact that you'll be reporting to upon your return—a doctor for follow-ups."

"So will you sign it?"

"How'd you find out about this place?" Tony demanded.

"I'm a research assistant for Dr. Chew, down at the University."

"Tranh Chew, the plastic surgeon?" Dr. Clifford took the paper back from Tony's hands.

"Yep, that's him. He's working on publishing a paper on plastic surgery blunders and co-authoring another on sexual confusion in teens. I work out of his office right on campus, interviewing his surgical candidates for him."

"So," Tony couldn't help but interrupt, "why didn't he sign your referral?"

"Conflict of interest, he's my boss," Freddy lied. "But he sent me here. Said he knew the doctor, and he'd make a good follow-up contact after a surgery like mine."

"I'm flattered," Dr. Clifford handed back the paper. "It's true, I have worked with many post-op patients after their sexual reassignment surgeries, but Dr. Chew is a leading practitioner in the field. I didn't think he even knew about the existence of my clinic."

"That's how I found out about you, down at the University."

"Alright, young man," the doctor conceded. "I'll start with your paperwork, and Tony can take you upfront to open a file."

"Thanks, Doc," Freddy grinned; thrilled that he had taken the initiative to copy down the Changeroom's address off one of the University's bathroom walls.

Slowly chewing his supper, Justice sat at the head of the table and watched his children pick at their plates.

"What's the matter, Mark?" Sarah encouraged. "You always loved my breaded chops with homemade apple sauce."

"I do, Mom, but I just ain't hungry."

"Well, eat it anyway," his father barked. "Your mother didn't go to all this trouble so you could push the food around in little circles. So eat something." He stabbed at his own plate, sending the a few cooked peas flying across the dinner table.

"Mathew," Sarah instantly jumped to her feet when she saw her oldest son enter the room, turning to rush around the table to his side. "What are you doing, baby?"

"It's supper," he bravely announced, taking a second to steady himself on the back of his sister's chair.

"Well then, have a seat." Justice gave him a wink and a grin, leaning over to pull out his son's chair.

"Your shirt's on inside out." His younger brother reached over and pulled at the shoulder seam. "You look like you got dressed in the dark."

"That's enough," Sarah reminded Mark, dampening a paper napkin in the kitchen sink to dab carefully at the dried blood still caked around her son's ears and lower neck.

"I tried to wash, Mom, but…"

"That's fine," she soothed, dropping the napkins in the trash before retaking her seat at the table.

"How's your head feeling, boy?"

"It kinda hurts, but I can live with it."

"After you have some food in your belly, then I'll give you one of my headache tablets," his mother promised, usually reluctant to medicate any of her children. "And I want you to tell me the minute it starts bleeding again, even if it's just a bit."

Mark suddenly dropped his fork and looked around the table. "He's gonna start bleeding all over again?"

"No," Justice reached for the butter dish. "What your ma means is if it *should* start up again, then your brother should tell us right away. Understand?" He looked toward both his boys.

They nodded, appetites gradually returning bit by bit.

"I just don't understand what could have brought that on," Sarah thought aloud, reaching across the table to spoon a healthy portion of peas onto her daughter's plate. "You swear to God you weren't in a fight today?"

"I swear, Mom. I haven't been in a fight for at least a week."

"Probably just comes with growing up is all," Justice laid his knife and fork across his empty plate. "When I was a kid, I grew so much in one summer that my ma had to sew bands of cloth round the bottoms of my pants. It was unbelievable, it didn't matter what I ate, or how much I slept, I just kept growing like a weed for two or three months straight."

Shaking her head, Sarah felt like she had to speak her mind. "No, this is different, honey. This isn't about growing, or anything of the such. This is nosebleeds, and they don't have nothing to do with hitting puberty."

"Puberty, puberty," Mark began to tease his older brother. "You're going to be in puberty," he began to sing.

"Enough!" the single command settled the entire family as Justice stood up and excused himself from the table.

"Are you going back outside, Dad?" Mathew asked, quickly shoving two giant mouthfuls of mashed potatoes down his throat. "I wanna help," he announced, quickly downing the remainder of his milk.

"I think you'd best rest," his mother quickly jumped into the conversation.

"I'll just watch," he promised. "I don't wanna sit in my room no more. Please let me go outside," he begged with all his heart. "I can't look at that blood no more. It just looks like a big red puddle of death."

Sarah almost stopped breathing, never having heard her son speak in such heathen terms. "I... I... I can't believe you talked like that, Mathew Michael Mallory."

His mother had just used his full name, and that was never a good sign. "I'm sorry, Mom." He tried to cover his tracks. "I didn't mean to say anything to get you all worked up."

"It's all my fault." Sarah bowed her head. "I've been so busy packing up the apartment, and then getting everything settled here in the house, that I haven't been keeping up with your religious instruction. It's really my fault," she continued to blame herself.

Justice never said a word. He had just finished lacing his boots, and was turning to grab his work gloves, when he noticed that his daughter was pointing across the table at her older brother.

"Oh Mathew," Sarah cried, jumping up and running round the chairs. "It's starting again and it's worse than ever."

Head back against his chair, he pinched his nose and closed his eyes, suddenly struck with the thought that he actually might drown in his own blood.

"Honey, help me carry him into his bed," Sarah called out.

Sliding his left arm under her son's knees and his right behind the middle of his back, Justice easily lifted his boy out of the kitchen chair.

"Take him to our bed," Sarah announced. "I haven't had the chance to change his sheets, and I don't want you laying him down in that mess."

Justice never spoke a word; he just followed his wife's instruction and carried his son to the master bedroom. Right behind his back, Sarah appeared with an armful of fresh towels and a basin of water.

"Tell Mark to put all the food on the counter, and clear the table. I'll be out to finish up as soon as I can." Sarah fought to take control of the situation, her fingers shaking as she wiped the small river of blood escaping Mathew's left nostril.

"Mom," Mathew began to cry. "Is God punishing me for something I did wrong?"

Sarah was speechless—mortified to think that one of her children was actually capable of inviting God's wrath.

Chapter
Thirty-One

"Here's looking at you, kid."

—*Casablanca, 1942*

Forcing her eyelids to stay open, Serena lay back in the bed and repeatedly blinked, fighting to focus on the three television sets... no... make that one television set, resting on top of Julia's dresser.

Her vision was definitely blurred, but at least she was alive. She knew it because she was in pain, and ever since she was a little girl, her grandmother had convinced her there was no pain in heaven.

"How are you?" a huge form loomed over the foot of Serena's bed. "Julia?"

"No child, my name's Martha. I'm here while Julia ran out."

"Ran where?" Serena found herself irritated at being left alone with this total stranger.

"I don't know." She moved closer toward Serena's head, "but I'm supposed to call her on her phone the minute you wake up."

"Well, call her then," Julia moaned, suddenly dying to scratch underneath the bandaging wrapped around her entire chest.

Martha turned to leave the room, and disappeared from Serena's line of sight, as she lay motionless in the babysitter's wake, reduced to taking stock of her limited surroundings.

"She wants to talk to you," her caregiver quickly waddled back up to the side of the bed.

Accepting the cordless handset, Serena slowly cleared her throat before attempting to speak. "Hello Julia," she said.

"Hey girl, I'm surprised you're up," Julia whispered into the phone, continually checking over her shoulder to see if anyone was listening.

"Hey girl, I'm surprised you left me with this Amazon," she sarcastically snapped back in return.

"Sorry, but I had to run out. You usually sleep for at least three or four hours."

"Well, I'm awake now. I suppose this giant doesn't know how to give me a shot, does she?"

"Doubt it," Julia apologized again. "But I'll be home within an hour. I'm sure you can hold on that long."

Listening to Julia make further excuses regarding her unavoidable absence, Serena decided that if you couldn't go to the mountain, you should bring the mountain to Mohammad. "I'll see you in an hour." She pressed the end button.

"Uh hello, Bertha," she called out from her prone position.

"Martha," the hulking figure corrected her from the doorway. "My name is Martha, and I'd really appreciate it if you called me by my right name."

"So, you wouldn't happen to be a nurse, would you, Martha?"

"Hell no, I hate hospitals and needles. They give me the willies."

"This is fucking great," Serena cursed under her breath. "Well, can you at least help me sit up?"

Walking over to the girl's bed, Martha stopped just short of touching her.

"Come closer," Serena beckoned. "You gotta help me support my back when I sit up, cuz I can't really support my... own weight," she groaned, gritting her teeth through the pain.

"Where you going?"

"To the can. Where in the hell do you think I'm going?"

"Alright," Martha nodded, wiping the potato chip crumbs onto her pant legs before moving in closer.

"Be careful, my tits are on fire."

Carefully working in unison, they managed to get Serena's feet on the floor with both hands planted firmly on the edge of the bed.

"Okay, I'm ready to stand," she started to take a succession of deep breaths. "On three. One, two... three!"

Martha bent her knees and carefully lifted, slowly pulling the young girl up to a standing position.

"Oh fuck," Serena hissed, her breath coming in sharp little gasps as she fought to handle the bursts of pain coursing through her entire body. "You gonna have to help me to the john. I can't do it alone."

"I won't drop you," Martha promised, slinking her right arm around Serena's waist as they slowly began to shuffle across the bedroom floor.

Martha positioned Serena's body at the base of the toilet, and then hiked up her nightgown, before carefully bracing herself to act as a lever to lower the girl down onto the seat.

"Holy fuck," Serena continued to cuss, only allowing herself a deep breath after her naked bottom had finally made contact with the acrylic seat.

Martha stood motionless as if waiting for further instructions.

"A little privacy please."

Backing out, she gently closed the door behind her back.

When she was finally alone, Serena slowly raised her hands to rub her face. Everything fucking hurt, from her neck all the way down to her knees. Bandages swaddled her entire upper chest, and every time she peed, it was like pushing out goddamn razor blades. "Holy fuck," she groaned, tears running down her face as she allowed intermittent squirts of urine to be released from her body.

"Are you fine?" Martha's voice called out from the other side of the door, a little concerned that she might not get her whole forty bucks if her charge passed out on the bathroom floor.

"Back off! I'll call you when I'm ready, alright?"

"Alright," she conceded, stepping away from the bathroom and relegating herself to straightening the crumpled bed.

Realizing that her bladder was finally empty, Serena took a cleansing breath and wiped her forehead, surprised by the cold sweat that had broken out all over her face.

"Hey, lady," she began to yell, aware that not only was she unable to wipe herself, but she'd never be able to stand up from her sitting position.

"You want me in?" Martha called out, unsure whether she was supposed to enter the bathroom, or just stay outside where she was.

"Please… come in," Serena begged through clench teeth. "I can't get up, and even if I do, I'm gonna be dripping piss all over the floor."

Shaking her head, Martha knew it was time to take charge of the situation. Opening the unlocked door, she immediately stepped inside and switched into *mother mode*.

"Careful," Serena begged as her helper lifted her up off the toilet, gently patting her bottom with a wad of toilet tissue.

"I wanna look in the mirror," she announced, having not seen her own reflection for countless days.

Sidestepping out of her patient's line of vision, Martha slowly turned, still hanging on to Serena as she appraised her face in the mirror.

"I look like I've been beat with the ugly stick. Twice," she added for effect.

"Don't look permanent, you'll heal up. I've taken a few beatin's in my days, and I still look the same."

Serena couldn't help but smirk.

"Well, I always looked this way," Martha shrugged, the stab at humor not lost on her charge.

"Can you help me take off some of these bandages? I'm itching to death under all this wrapping."

Swinging open the medicine chest, Martha scanned the contents and found a small pair of manicure scissors. "Now hold still," she ordered, unbuttoning the girl's nightgown before carefully cutting through the preliminary layer of dressing.

"Don't slice me."

"I won't if you stay still. But are you sure we should be doing this? I'm just supposed to watch you, not changing none of them bandages."

"Just help me... please?" she honestly begged, her tone taking on the desperation of woman in severe pain.

Martha got down to business, adjusting the angle of her scissors as she took on more and more layers of the dressing.

"I feel dizzy. I need to sit," Serena began to wobble on her feet, the room spinning in circles before her eyes.

Slamming the toilet lid down with her right foot, Martha gently guided Serena back to a seated position. "We better get you back to bed, you look like hell."

Arguing with her eyes, Serena finally found the strength to put her objections into words. "Let's just finish this first."

Without taking the time to argue, Martha leaned down and continued with her job. Once she was down to the final layer of gauze and padding, she began to worry that she'd revealed something that was supposed to stay covered.

"Done?"

"Uh, what exactly happened to you?"

"I don't remember, but I know I had a bad infection. Julia kept pumping me full of antibiotics and pain killers."

"I think we should just put this stuff back and wait until your friend comes home," Martha lifted up a discarded swatch of cotton bandaging.

"Like fuck! Now help me back on my feet."

Once again positioned in front of the mirror, Serena began to take stock of her chest. "Take off the rest," she suddenly demanded, lifting her right arm to touch the uneven surface of her left breast.

"Okay," Martha walked around the back, sliding the hospital nightgown off her shoulders before slowly cutting through the last layer of gauze.

As the wrappings fell down to the floor, all Serena was left with were two circles of cotton padding stuck over each breast.

"I think they're stuck, maybe if we slowly…" Martha mused.

Shooing her hands away, Serena slowly began peeling off the first pad. Wincing as the dried blood from her incision adhered to the cotton padding, she closed her eyes and gathered her strength, removing the remaining pad with one swift yank of her hand.

Martha never said a word; her shock clearly evident as she quickly clamped her fingers over her own mouth, stifling any comment that might be waiting to escape her lips.

"What happened to me?" Serena whispered, shuffling a step closer toward the mirror. "I've been butchered!"

"What did happen to you, girl?" Martha couldn't hold back her shock any longer. "It looks like somebody bit out chunks of your tits."

Both her nipples had been surgically removed, as well as large areas of tissue to compensate for the spreading infection after her home piercings had been severally contaminated with human feces. Pulled together with rows of surgical sutures, the puckered black thread gave her a Frankenstein-like appearance.

"Please get me back to bed," Serena pleaded in a little girl's voice, her fingers trembling as she worked to pull up the cotton fabric of her nightgown.

Martha shook her head and swallowed hard. "Let me." She walked over and finished with the buttons. "We'll get you back to bed so you can rest."

At that moment, Serena quit speaking. But then there wasn't much to say when your future shriveled up and died right in front of your very eyes.

———————

Opening her purse and digging out the small travel size bottle of Tylenol, Sarah downed two tablets with a large glass of water. Not usually prone to headaches, especially of this caliber, she swallowed her third dose that day.

"I just checked on Mathew," Justice reported from the bathroom door. "He's sleeping, and I don't see any fresh blood anywhere."

"Good," Sarah smiled, dropping the pill bottle discreetly back into her purse. "I guess we should think about moving him to his bed. The sheets must be dry by now. I'll go check the dryer."

Tenderly grabbing at his wife's arm as she turned to rush out of the bathroom, Justice pulled her firmly into his embrace. "Slow down for a second, you've been running like a jack rabbit all night."

Releasing a deep sigh, she allowed herself to mould to her husband's form, grateful for his strength at a time when she felt completely drained.

"Mommy," Mary whimpered from behind her father's back. "Mathew's in your bed, and..."

"Come to Mommy," Sarah untangled herself from her husband's embrace and swooped down to pick up her daughter. "You're gonna have to sleep in your own bed tonight, baby."

"But Matty's in your bed. Me wanna, too."

"Come with me," Justice stretched out his arms. "Mommy's got to check the clothes dryer, and you need to go to sleep."

Mary leaned away from her mother and almost fell into her father's arms. "Rock me," she smiled, cuddling into the warmth of his chest.

"I'll check on the bedding, you tuck her back into bed," Sarah smiled, pecking her baby on the cheek before heading off toward the basement stairs.

As she began to fold blankets on the homemade table Justice had set up for her near the washer and dryer, Sarah was suddenly consumed by a wave of nausea. Slamming her hands down onto the tabletop to steady her stance, she opened her mouth and gulped a giant lung full of air.

"Honey, I'm just running out to put the mower away and lock up the garage. I'll be right back in the house," he yelled from the top of the stairs.

Remaining motionless and praying the nausea would pass, Sarah finally relented and turned around to lean her lower back against the edge of the table. She was exhausted. Justice was right; she had been running most of the night.

Eventually, she forced herself to turn back to her chores, slowly working on finishing her laundry. She only had two more blankets and the load would be folded. But why in the world was she just about dead on her feet? The last time she'd been this worn out she..."

"Sarah, are you still downstairs?"

"Yes," she yelled up, heart pounding as the revelation began to take hold.

"You coming up?"

"Right away," she threw everything into her basket, planning to finish her load upstairs.

"I tucked Mathew in his bed," Justice began pulling the blood stained sheets off their mattress. "He's so exhausted, he didn't budge an inch."

"I'm thinking of keeping him home from school tomorrow. I don't want to take a chance his nose will get bumped on the playground or in gym class."

"Good idea," Justice agreed, rolling the soiled bedding into a giant ball. "Want some help?"

"No," she shooed him away. "I'll make the bed, you just check on the kids one last time, and make sure all the outside doors are locked."

Nodding in agreement, Justice began his patrol, checking every door and window to make sure it was locked. The idea that his family was sleeping at ground level in a new neighborhood still felt a little disturbing, to say the least.

He loved the house, but he felt so exposed. Everywhere he turned, there was a window opening them up to all the prying eyes of their neighborhood. They were never alone. Anyone standing out on the street could watch their comings and goings without them even knowing it. It was unsettling, and Justice was struggling to come to grip with it. Just another problem he didn't need to burden his wife with.

"You prefer bologna or meatloaf sandwiches?" Sarah appeared at his side.

"Don't need neither." He moved to the sink to rinse his thermos. "We're having a barbeque at lunch tomorrow. A thousand man-hours down at Jupiter without a work related injury. Everybody's pretty happy about it. They're talking giving out bonuses come Christmas, if the profits continue to rise."

"A bonus," Sarah mused. That would sure come in handy if her premonition turned out to be correct.

"I don't know how much, but they're talking about a percentage of our monthly salary. I don't know, maybe five percent."

As she pulled the used sandwich bags and empty juice box from her husband's lunch kit, Sarah debated about sharing her suspicions with her husband. "You back on normal shifts for the rest of the week?"

"If you're worried about the weekend, I'm pretty sure I'll be off on Sunday."

"It would be nice to attend service as a family."

"You know," Justice prepared for his morning coffee by pre-filling his thermos with sugar and powdered cream. "They pay time and a half for weekend workers."

"Justice Mallory, don't even start up that conversation with me. I will not sell the souls of my family for a fat pay check come the end of the month."

"I not talking about selling our souls; I just thought I'd mention it, is all."

"Well, consider it mentioned," Sarah turned back toward the sink.

"Guess you're right," he conceded. "Look around here. The five of us are managing just fine."

Sarah felt the pain return, this time pulsing right through her temples. "Yeah, the five of us," she muttered, wondering just how she'd tell her husband their number might soon rise to six.

Chapter Thirty-Two

*"Tell 'em to go out there with all they got
and win just one for the Gipper."*

—Knute Rockne, All American, 1940

S ince she was still messed up from a little unexpected partying with her new friends; Boyd, and his brother Pete, Julia sat back on the couch and attempted to make sense of her surroundings. The basement wasn't familiar, nor were any of the guys filing down the stairs, but what the hell, she felt great.

"He wants me to film everything freehand? What the fuck's the matter with you guys?" The cameraman turned on his heel and marched over to where Boyd was relaxing in a tattered old recliner. "Look, no matter what, I'm still gonna need the rest of my equipment, and if you don't get someone to bring it over to me, you can fucking film this piece of shit yourself."

Nudging Pete firmly in the ribs, Boyd passed off his joint before slowly rising from his seat. "Look asshole, we're gonna shoot this garbage right here, and right now. If you want your five hundred bucks, then you'll wing it! You walk out on me, and I'll let every director in town know that you left me high and dry, five minutes before we started shooting. You want that rep following your ass around town?"

"Fine," the cameraman angrily conceded. "But I don't wanna hear jack shit about shaking or bad lighting. Cuz once we start rolling, I won't have a free hand to adjust bugger all. You get it?"

"Got it." Boyd turned to Pete and signaled him to start moving.

Forcing herself to rise up from her position on the couch, Julia stumbled over toward the action, afraid that she might have stayed at the party just a little too long. "I better be going, I got a date tonight," she tried to sound as casual as possible. "Don't want him to start without me."

"Ah, don't rush out, babe, cuz I've just got to take care of this little thing, and then I thought we could sit around and make some more plans," Boyd attempted to convince Julia to stay.

Turning her wrist to check her watch, Julia noticed that it was nearly eight o'clock, four hours since she'd left Serena in Martha's care. "I appreciate the smoke, and the beers, but I gotta roll. You be sure to call me in the next couple of days if you wanna make that special movie you've been planning."

Grabbing her roughly by the shoulders, Boyd pulled her firmly toward his body and forced his lips down onto hers. Surprised, yet not repulsed enough to pry herself free, Julia allowed him free rein over her mouth.

"I'll be calling your sweet little ass, you can bet on it." He suddenly reached around without provocation and filled his right hand with a generous portion of her butt cheek.

"And my friend Serena, what should I tell her?" Julia pushed just a little bit harder, spurred on by the drug-induced haze numbing her inhibitions.

"Tell her thanks for the offer, but I don't film scat. Can't stand the stuff. But maybe I can hook her up though. It's just really hard to say right now. I'll have to make some calls, see who's got the word out for *dumpers*." By this, he referred to the men and women capable of holding their bowels, then defecating on command. "Once I find out who's hiring, then I'll surely be able to get your girl connected."

"Thanks," Julia smiled, aware that directors routinely passed women back and forth when they'd over exposed them in their own markets, and if they wanted a fresh piece of ass for their latest project.

Unfortunately, these moves were rarely lateral. Once you'd been overexposed in soft porn, you had no choice but to move on to hard core. Done with hard core, you were forced to move into light fetish. Fetish brought you to heavy kink, and after kink, the only thing left was snuff… or the retirement home. And as the old saying went: *everything ends badly, or else it wouldn't end.*

As she began to move up toward the first floor, Julia had to step back the minute a man's dark form began his descent into the basement, two leashed German Shepherds eagerly trotting behind.

"I see we're ready to roll," Boyd clapped his hands together.

With the help of the wooden banister, Julia managed to pull herself up the stairs just as the camera's flash mount illuminated the basement floor. Struggling to reach the top stair, she stopped, turning back to take one last look. Both dogs were anxious to hit their mark—barking wildly, running circles around the two naked women who crouched on hands and knees in the center of the concrete floor.

Grateful to be back out on the street, Julia trudged a two blocks before eventually finding her way out of the low-income row housing.

Once she was finally hailed a cab, she relayed her address to the driver, settled back in the seat, and began taking stock of her afternoon.

She hadn't found out exactly who had filmed Serena's last flick, but she made another valuable contact in the world of fetish-porn. She wasn't interested in turning that contact into a starring role, but it never hurt to be friendly with the people who bankrolled the camera. A girl never knew when she was going to need a favor; the more friendly faces in the world, the better chance you had of getting whatever she needed.

Suddenly worried that Serena's babysitter might have abandoned her post, Julia asked the cabbie to step on it, desperately needing to get home and check on her patient.

———————

"That's it. I've checked everywhere in the van, and there's just no other bag. I don't know where she could have left it, but trust me Annette; it's not hiding anywhere under the seats."

"Mom," she turned her attention back to the telephone. "Wally just came inside from checking the van, and you never left it there. Maybe you can phone the bus company; they might be holding it in their lost and found."

"I don't think somebody is going to walk up to the bus driver and just turn in a fifty dollar sweater. Do you?"

Annette would have been more than happy to pay the fifty dollars just to have her mother hang up the phone. "Well then, what would you like me to do from this end?"

"There's nothing you can do," Vivian sighed. "I guess that trip just cost me an extra fifty bucks for nothing."

"We'll keep our eyes open, we promise." Annette strummed her fingers on the kitchen counter.

"You call me if it turns up, alright?"

"I will, and thanks for coming up to visit us, Mom. We really enjoyed your stay." She forced a smile, dying just to put her feet up, and not bother with anymore search and rescue missions.

"Supper's in the oven." Annette was finally able to hang up the phone and call out to her husband. "I kept it warm. You ready to eat or you wanna grab a shower first?"

"I'll eat first. I'm starving."

Handing Wally his plate, Annette joined him at the table, anxiously waiting for details of his day's events.

"It wasn't as hard as I thought," he mumbled, taking big bites of his meatloaf and mashed potatoes. "Remember, I told you that they were loaded, and really old?"

"I do."

"Well, let's just say it was an understatement. That couple each has one foot in the grave, and the other balancing on the edge, if you know what I mean."

"Walter," she scolded.

"Anyway," he picked up a raw carrot and snapped it in half. "They both wanted top of the line funerals. We're talking the full fleet of family cars, premium caskets, and a hot meal served after the funeral. A hot meal," he repeated. "Nobody pays those kinds of prices anymore for a hot meal—maybe for cold cuts, with a nice fruit platter—but not a hot meal." He continued to shake his head. "Let me tell you, Annette, they never spared any expense."

"How much did you make?"

"Well, I'm thinking it was at least a thousand dollar night."

"You've got to be kidding," she gushed.

"I'm not," Wally jumped up from his chair to grab the file from his briefcase. "Here, look at their numbers."

Annette studied the contracts while her husband wolfed downed the remainder of his supper. "And you know what's even better? They've got a shitload of rich old friends."

Rushing up to her husband's side, Annette threw her arms around his shoulders, hugging him tightly before branding him with a searing kiss. "I love you, Wally."

"I love you too, Annette," he instantly replied. "But as much as I'd love to sit here and scarf down another plate of food, I have to finish a mountain of paperwork before I hand in these contracts tomorrow morning. I don't want any mistakes. You understand, don't you?"

She did, and picking up his empty plate, she actually encouraged him to run off and sequester himself behind the closed door of his den. "I'll be upstairs waiting for you when you're done. Take your time, I'll just watch television."

Wally nodded, happy that he'd finally become the kind of husband and provider that his family truly deserved.

Angrily jamming his gearshift in and out of first gear, Billy Grant sat across the street in his older sub-compact and just stared at Wally's house. The stupid little bitch-of-a-wife never even bothered to close the curtains after dark; their entire *joke of a life* was splayed out for everyone in the neighborhood to gawk at.

God, how Billy hated that woman. She actually had the gall to walk into his apartment and look him straight in the eye, daring to stake claim to a man who didn't even want to sleep next to her tired old ass. What gave her the right?

Wally Freeman belonged to him, and he wasn't ready to let go. Nobody, especially not some frump-ass housewife, was going to steal his boyfriend. Billy had dragged that guy, kicking and screaming, out of the closet. He sure as hell wasn't going to sit back and watch Annette Freeman throw him back inside and lock the door. He was better than…"

"What," Billy barked into his ringing cell phone, incensed by the intrusion.

"Billy," a man's voice almost purred on the line. "Where you been hiding, my boy?"

"Here and there." He nervously began peeking out the foggy windows of his car. "Where you calling from?"

"Wondering if I'm in town?"

"No... it's just the static," he lied. "I was wondering why we're having such a bad connection, is all."

"Listen up," the man's tone instantly reverted to business. "You missed your last payment, and I don't think you want me to send someone down to collect in person. Do you?"

"No, oh no, I really don't," he nervously stammered.

"So then, you little cum wad, you better bend over and pull my cash out of your ass."

"My last job didn't pan out like I thought. So I've had to use my payment cash just to survive."

"You won't need to worry about surviving if you don't make your payments," the older male barked. "If you were backed into a corner, why didn't you call us? Other arrangements could have been made."

Other arrangements. The term sounded so accommodating, yet...

"Now we have ourselves a little problem, Billy my boy. You owe me last week's payment, and this week's payment is already due tomorrow. What you going to do to keep your ass crack vertical, and walking the streets?"

"I have an idea, actually." He turned to stare at Wally's front door, "I was working on it when you called."

"What kind of idea? It ain't gonna land your ass back in jail, is it?"

"I'm never going back," Billy hissed into the phone. "I'd rather die than spend another night locked up with all those homophobic *faggo* motherfuckers."

"Faggos," he chuckled. "That's a new one for me. What in the hell is a faggo?"

"It's a fucking jerk who beats your ass by day, and then fucks it raw all night."

"Thanks for the vocabulary lesson. Now let's get back on topic. What's the plan, Billy boy?"

"I've made contact with a nice little middle-class wasp. His family is pretty typical; ya know, wife and a couple kids. And with just a little more work, I'm sure I'll be ready to turn him out."

"How much more work?"

"Not much. He's totally frustrated with his life. It's been years since I met a guy walking on ice that thin. If I don't rescue him, I bet you he ends up on the front page of the newspaper with a revolver shoved halfway down his throat."

"Billy, you ain't actually still believing that you're rescuing those little pukes, are you?"

"I am," he argued. "They're so repressed. They're as rigid as a pew in a church. If I don't save them, they'll live that way for the rest of their wasted, little lives."

"Fine by me, Florence Nightingale. You can run around and save whoever the hell you want, but in the mean time, you've still got weekly payments you're indebted to keep. So unless you wanna be the one swallowing the fucking revolver, I suggest you make good tomorrow. And I don't care how."

Billy hung up, feeling more focused than ever, but before activating the next step in his plan, he would need to hustle up a few bucks.

After parking two blocks from the local gay stroll, he changed in the car. He pulled off his tee shirt, and unceremoniously threw it in the back seat before shoving his arms back into his leather jacket.

A final check of his pockets to make sure he was loaded down with condoms, and Billy was off to work.

He hated working the streets, having to compete with the sixteen-year old twinkies, but the payoffs were immediate, and could be very rewarding in a relatively short period. If you had an eye, and could pick your tricks, a thousand dollar night wasn't an unreasonable goal. Unfortunately, ten different men pile driving his ass inside of six to eight hours, could easily lead to a torn rectum—a painful side effect that Billy was anxious to avoid. He'd just have to make sure to pick up a few blowjobs in between. The money wasn't as good, but it'd give his body a chance to rest.

"Hey Billy," a guy yelled from across the alley. "You wanna do a double?"

"Not tonight," he answered back. At half the money for double the time, it wasn't exactly a profitable venture.

Walking straight to his favorite spot, he leaned back against the wall, pulling up his right leg and bending it at the knee. "Come and get it boys," he threw out at no one in particular. Within five minutes, two vehicles had started cruising him, circling the block as they either worked up the courage to pull over, or took a couple extra minutes to make a few bullshit excuses on their phones.

The first red pickup to pull over was a total waste of his time. Farm plates, it was driven by some tired old farmhand looking for a ten-dollar blowjob, so without delay, Billy quickly turned his back and pretended not to notice. Within a minute, the guy got the hint and moved on, just as a decked-out mustang rounded the corner.

Billy could smell trouble for a mile, three young guys cruising the block, looking for laughs was never a good scene. With a two four of beer, maybe a baseball bat in the backseat, they could corner a hustler in a vacant alley and really mess him up long-term.

With adrenaline beginning to course through his veins, Billy finally spotted his savior in the form of a black four-door sedan.

"Hey," he yelled out toward the car as it made its second lap around the block.

Slowing down to a crawl, the passenger window suddenly lowered and a deep male voice boomed out from the car's interior. "You getting in or what?"

That was all the invitation Billy needed, and without another moment's delay, he grabbed the handle and swung open the door. "Looking for a party?"

The man never answered, he just waited for Billy to drop down into the seat before tromping down on the gas and speeding off into the night.

Chapter
Thirty-Three

"We'll always have Paris."

—*Casablanca, 1942*

"Miss Taylor, hello. Excuse me, Miss Taylor," the receptionist buzzed her for the third time in a row. "You still have two calls holding on lines three and four."

"Thank you," Karen shouted up from underneath the desk. She quickly grabbed the remaining papers that had somehow managed to flutter to the back corners when she'd dropped her file, and finally crawled out and made her way back into her chair.

"Karen Taylor," she announced after punching the first available number.

"Yo bitch; it's just me, Alicia. What took you so long? I must have been holding for a good ten minutes."

"Sorry, but can you hold? I gotta check who's on the other line."

"Karen, that's why..."

Without waiting for her roommate to finish her sentence, Karen answered the second line

"Karen Taylor, may I help you?"

"Hello Karen, it's just me... uh, Tony DeMarco," the caller nervously cleared his throat. "I'm sorry I haven't called before this, but things have been extremely busy down at the clinic."

Karen sat speechless, totally unprepared for his call, and absolutely unsure how to reply.

Continuing to fill the silence, Tony fell back on his *Plan B*. "I hope the stuff I dropped off wasn't too forward, but I just wanted you to know that I had a really great time and I was thinking of you."

"I got it all." Karen couldn't help herself, a smile threatened to spread across her entire face. "You shouldn't have spent that much money. You barely know me"

"True," Tony nodded on his end of the phone. "But what I know, I really liked. So, before I keep you any longer, can I take you out again?"

This was going to be harder than she had ever imagined. "I'm really not in a good place to be dating right now."

"What does that mean exactly? A good place?"

"Well, work's so busy; I've got to play catch-up just to stay in line with the status quo."

Tony didn't have a clue what Karen what saying, but his guts told him she was in the process of blowing him off.

"Okay, that's fine," he started to wrap up the call. "I'll let you get back to work. Your roommate said you were really busy anyway."

"Tony," Karen unconsciously bit her bottom lip. "I really liked you, but I just have to be honest. I don't think I'd be able to handle your history... you know, of pornographic movies."

Tony's next breath caught in his throat. "I gotta go," he reached over to hang up the phone.

"Tony, Tony," Karen continued call out. "Please don't hang up."

Slowly pulling the receiver back to his ear, he sat motionless, not sure about what he was waiting for. Neither spoke, both sitting uncomfortably on opposite ends of the line.

"I won't bother you again," he mumbled in a very low voice.

"You're not bothering me," Karen ran her fingers through her hair, once again at a loss for words.

"I'm sorry," he offered, not exactly sure which sin he was apologizing for.

"I kept the lobster," Karen blurted out, as if holding onto the token of their first date actually proved something.

"We've got patients. I really have to go now."

She didn't want to let him go, but knew that like a neighborhood stray, she'd never be allowed to keep him.

"And Karen," Tony summed up his call. "That was over ten years ago. I can't take it back, but if it's any consolation, I really do regret it."

Before she could answer him, the phone went dead in her hand.

"Miss Taylor," the receptionist's voice buzzed through the minute she'd hung up her phone. "I have a message from line four. You're to call an Alicia, ASAP. You have the number."

Karen punched at her phone, not even aware that tears were running down her face until they landed in circular splatters on her desk pad.

"Karen, I'm so sorry," Alicia instantly began to apologize. "He called here looking for you, and I tried to warn you, but that tight-ass receptionist kept putting me on hold. Next time she asks if it's business or pleasure, I'm gonna tell her it's none of her fucking business."

"That's okay," she sniveled into the phone. "I had to talk to him one of these days."

"Maybe, but that's the kind of shit you didn't need at work."

"He said he was sorry, and that he really regretted it. He sounded so hurt," Karen took a second to grab a tissue and wipe her eyes. "Do you think I made a mistake?"

"Let me ask you something. You tell your little work-out bitches about Tony?"

"Yes," she sighed.

"So what exactly what did little Miss Sandy and her shadow Jolene have to say? What was their advice for you when dealing with *Tony the Tool?*"

Taking a second to wipe her nose, Karen quickly looked up at the ceiling and searched for some hidden ounce of strength. "They thought he was scum—they're probably going to flip him off the next time they see him down at the gym, and... well, you know the rest."

"So then how in the hell is he going to fit into your life? If those two aerobic airheads can't stand the thought of him, what exactly did you plan to tell your parents when they asked you about your new boyfriend?'

"It's not like they'd need a resume," she argued back. "Nobody's going to demand to know everything he's done for the past ten years."

"Hold on, lady," Alicia suddenly threw her donut down on the counter. "Why are you arguing with me? I didn't tell you that he had to go. You're the one who made that decision yourself."

"I know, but he's better than those movies. That was a long time ago."

"You had one date. One supper. How in the hell do you know what this guy is really like?"

"I just know," Karen whispered. "I think I might have made a mistake."

"Oh, fuck me. Are you telling me that you're planning on calling him back?"

"I don't have his number," Karen revealed, suddenly hit with the revelation.

"So now what? You just going to hang out at the gym until you accidentally run into him again?"

"No, I have a better idea." Karen suddenly felt inspired with a plan. "I know where he works. I can just stop by and see him at the Changeroom."

"This I gotta see," Alicia snorted into the phone. "You have any idea what kind of place that is?"

"Some kind of medical clinic for poor people. Right?"

"Right," Alicia began to laugh. "Don't move. I'll pick you up in an hour, and we'll drive over together."

"Thanks."

"Yeah, whatever. You can thank me later if you still feel like it."

Karen hung up the phone and flopped back in her chair, wondering just what she was planning to do when she finally saw Tony again… face to face.

Readying Olga for her bath, Dr. Martin Hood took his time with the preparations. His daily routine had become little more than caring for his wife's medical and personal needs. There was absolutely no point in rushing; tomorrow would be the same as today, no different from the day before.

"Let's get you undressed," he smiled down at his invalid wife, her right eye wandering in a completely different direction than her left.

"It's time for a sponge bath, and then maybe a haircut." He gently pushed a strand of graying hair away from her eyes.

"Cuuutt," she repeated, fond of the last syllable from any sentence.

"Yes, I think a haircut would be a great idea, my dear. We don't want knots in the back of your head, do we?"

Reaching around to unbutton Olga's nightgown, Martin's right hand suddenly encountered an unexpected area of dampness.

"What's going on?" he muttered, pulling back his hand to inspect the fluid now coating his fingers.

"Onnnn," sputtered the syllable from Olga's mouth as Martin gently pulled his wife into a sitting position on the edge of her bed.

"Oh, no," Martin sighed, every drop of color draining from his face. "Hold on, sweetie." He laid her back down. "I have to make a call." He rushed over to the cordless phone, and dialed the Changeroom, praying that Marcus was available to take his call.

"Is something the matter, Martin?" Marcus demanded after leaving a patient to take the call.

"It's Olga. She's experienced a large amount of cranial bleeding. From a quick examination, I'd also guess that there's a small amount of spinal fluid mixed in with the blood."

"Cranial bleeding?" Dr. Clifford repeated. "From what? Did she fall, or are we still talking about the leaking sutures from her last procedure."

"I know you're such a busy man, so I never called. But there's been a new development as of late."

"Tell me," Marcus pulled one leg up and settled on the edge of his desk.

"It seems that due to excessive swelling, the plates in Olga's skull have begun to shift. Now, you and I both know that normally an adult skull is one hundred percent fused. However, Olga's has been separating, and the plates have been shifting."

"Mother of mercy," Marcus cursed. "What in the world was going to be next?"

"I'm afraid the shifting plates are not only pushing up and out through the skin covering her skull, but they're possibly nicking or severing her spinal cord."

Looking down at the frayed edge of his lab coat, Marcus wondered just what Martin proposed to do.

"I was wondering; could you possibly spare a little time to come down and properly exam Olga with me? It's kind of a two-person job at this stage of the game."

"Of course I'll come," he nodded. "Let me finish with my last patient, and I'll be right down. You need me to bring anything?"

"No, I'm afraid there's not a lot we can do."

"Well, just hold on a little longer. I'll be down as soon as possible."

Martin disconnected the phone and returned to his wife. Her eyes aimlessly wandered the room as her brain scrambled to control even the simplest of her bodily functions.

As they careened up and down the back alleys toward Tony's location, Karen sat quietly, squeezed into the small bucket seat of Alicia's car. "I don't have a clue what I'm going to say."

"Don't look at me," Alicia laughed. "I'm just the tour guide on this little safari, just here to make sure none of the lions take a bite out of your ass."

Having found an empty meter to park the car, both girls quickly ran down the steps toward the Changeroom's front door, anxious to get off the street and out of the public's line of sight.

"What if he yells at me? What if he tells me to go to hell and get out of his office?"

Swinging open the door, Alicia stopped just long enough to smirk. "Look around, my dear. I don't think they've ever thrown anybody out of this place."

Karen had heard all the stories circulating around the gym, but nothing would have prepared her for the clinic's smell. It wasn't pure; it was kind of a mixture. A combination of blood, sweat, some kind of cleaning fluid, and the pungent stench of body odor, all hung together like a cloud over the waiting area.

"I don't know." Karen stood in the doorway, her courage dissipating with every breath.

"Get your ass in here," Alicia turned around to grab her friend's wrist, yanking her over the threshold and into the middle of the room.

"Now what?" Karen whispered.

"I don't see him, do you?"

Karen just shook her head, secretly relieved that he was nowhere in sight.

"We'll wait," Alicia motioned to two chairs.

As they sat in a corner and watched the room continue to fill behind them, Tony suddenly appeared from the back, arms cradling a sleeping three or four-year-old boy.

"My baby," a man stood up and rushed to the child's side. "How many stitches?"

"Just five, but if you keep letting your kids play in that abandoned lot with all the broken glass, next time the doctor might not be able to sew him back together."

The man nodded, gratefully accepting the bundle. "Don't know how you do it, man. I can't stand needles and blood."

"You get used to it, it's the job..." Tony stopped in mid-sentence, his eyes locking with Karen's.

"Well, I better get home," the man turned and walked toward the door. "Tell the doctor thanks."

Tony nodded, his eyes still locked on Karen's position.

Forcefully nudging her roommate in the ribs, Alicia almost pushed Karen off her chair, encouraging her to stand up and speak to Tony, face to face.

"What are you doing here?" his eyes darted back and forth between both women. "Is somebody hurt?"

"No," Karen began to blush, suddenly feeling extremely stupid for showing up unannounced at his workplace. "I... I..."

"She wants to talk to you," Alicia leaned forward and announced.

"What about?"

"I don't know. Maybe she wants to sell you a couple magazine subscriptions," Alicia smirked.

"We have magazines," he shook his head.

Good thing he's cute, Alicia thought to herself, *cuz he doesn't seem to be all that bright.*

Building up her courage, Karen finally took a few steps toward Tony. "I handled your phone call today really, really badly. I came down here to say I'm sorry for being far too blunt and so very... tactless."

"Blunt is good," he shrugged. "Sometimes beating around the bush just prolongs the inevitable."

Prolonged, inevitable. Maybe the steroid puppy did know a few big words, Alicia laughed to herself.

"True, but I think I was kinda rude," Karen lowered her eyes in embarrassment.

"This isn't good," Tony looked around the room. "Why don't you come with me and we can finish this in the back."

Karen quickly turned back toward Alicia who gave her a sudden nod of approval.

"Alright, I'll follow you," she announced, as if she'd been debating the idea for hours.

Quickly pointing out the coffee machine next to the table and chairs in the lunchroom, Tony excused himself to rush off and move a few more patients through for examination.

"I have to leave," Dr. Clifford informed his assistant, not even bothering to raise his head as he quickly finished up with the last patient on his table.

"But we're full. It's standing room only out there."

"I know," the doctor apologized. "But there's been an unfortunate development with Olga, and Martin called, looking for my help. I have to go to him. You understand, don't you?"

Tony threw his hands up in the air, shaking his head as he searched for just the right words. "Karen Taylor is here. Here, in the clinic."

Marcus patted the patient on the shoulder and stepped over to where Tony was standing. "Who's Karen Taylor?"

"She's the lady I dated, she… she's sitting in our lunchroom."

"Oh boy! What a day for a visit. Well," the doctor began to think aloud. "You're just gonna have to clear out the waiting room, and as soon as everybody's gone, then you two can spend some time alone."

"Some people are gonna to wanna wait. Remember last time? That one guy and his wife sat for four hours."

"It was raining that day. They probably were just looking for a place to squat."

"But it's not even noon. You sure you're not going to be back?"

"I don't know for sure. But having everyone sit around and wait isn't going to do anyone any good. So clear 'em out, and I'll phone you as soon as I know what it's looking like from Martin's house."

Tony nodded in agreement. His stomach began to churn as he realized that the doctor was about to walk out of the clinic and he'd be left behind to explain his absence.

"And one more thing," Marcus added, I have a bottle of Italian red wine in the bottom right drawer of my desk. Help yourself, if you like."

"It's not that kind of visit."

"Well, suit yourself. But just do me a favor and watch your back when clearing the clinic. Nobody's going to be too happy about it."

"And you call me if Martin needs anything delivered."

"I will," Marcus winked before returning to his patient.

Karen finally relaxed a little, reaching over to pour herself a cup of coffee just as Tony reappeared in the doorway.

"There you are," Alicia's voice called out from somewhere behind Tony's back, reluctantly allowing herself to be lead into the lunchroom. "Our buddy here has to do a little patient shuffling, so he's parking me with you for safety."

"Sorry," he smiled at Karen. "But I'll be back in ten minutes. I promise," Tony vowed before taking off back down the clinic's hall.

"Have you had a chance to talk at all?" Alicia instantly demanded.

"No."

"So how's the free coffee?" she reached over and stole Karen's cup.

Getting all the patients to leave the waiting room without being threatened wasn't a simple feat. Most had nowhere else to go, and were not the least bit interested in clearing out without a firm reopening time.

"As soon as the doctor's back," Tony shouted out for the third time. "That's the thing with an emergency. You never really know exactly how long they're going to take. But I promise that as soon as the doctor's back, we'll reopen the doors. You've got my word on it."

That was enough for most as they picked up their belongings and began making their way up the Changeroom's stairs.

"Don't forget this," Tony stepped forward and handed a young man some fresh gauze and white wrapping tape. "You come back first thing tomorrow morning. I want you here at nine," he pointed his finger directly in his face. "That hand is infected and the doctor will have to see you tomorrow morning. You hear me?"

He nodded, accepting the medical supplies and slinking out the clinic's front door.

As he stood at the front entrance of the house, Marcus took a second to check his watch. It had been just under two hours since Martin had placed his original call to the clinic, yet no matter how many times he rang the doorbell, no one answered.

"Martin?" he yelled out, stepping into the marble foyer through the unlocked front door.

The house was eerily quiet; he couldn't even detect the faint sounds of a television playing in another room. He continued to walk down the main hallway, and headed straight for Olga's main floor bedroom.

"Marcus, thank you for coming," Martin stood up from his position on the edge of the bed. "I'm so glad you were able to make it." He threw his arms around his friend in a fierce bear hug.

"Martin, is something the matter?"

"It's time," he said in a choked voice, and wiped his eyes.

The visiting doctor set down his medical bag and stepped around his old friend to examine the patient.

"It was cranial bleeding, just like I thought," Martin walked across the room and dropped down in a wingback chair. "But I was wrong about the spinal fluid. It was actually brain tissue. She's experiencing some form of a…"

"A complex chemical breakdown of her brain tissue," Marcus

finished his dear friend's sentence. "Do you have any idea what's causing the breakdown?"

"Not with my equipment." He motioned toward the heart and lung monitors he'd already purchased. "But it doesn't matter anymore. Does it Olga?" Martin rose to his feet. "It's time for your suffering to end."

Marcus knew exactly what Martin was alluding to. They'd talked about it in great detail, both had agreed that if Olga's condition ever became physically painful, or life threatening, there would be no extraordinary measures taken to keep her alive. She'd already been through far more than most.

"It's time," Martin nodded his head. "And I'm not going to sit back and watch every ounce of fluid drain from her body while her skull erupts like a Hawaiian volcano. For God's sake, the shifting bones of her skull are actually tearing the skin apart. Her brains are leaking out through the fissures. She's dying."

"Then it is time," Marcus solemnly agreed. "Are you sticking with your original injections?"

"Yes, I'm satisfied with my choices." He sat down and picked up his wife's hand. "But I have a favor to ask of you, my dear friend." He turned his face upward and searched Marcus's eyes for an answer.

"Anything, Martin. You know that you just have to ask."

"Well, I'd like you to come back in five or six hours and pronounce. Kind of a safeguard, just to make sure nothing's gone wrong."

"I can do that," he nodded in agreement. "And I think you're right. It would look much better if another doctor pronounced your wife."

"And me," Martin smiled.

"And you what?"

"I want you to pronounce me, too."

"Martin, what in hell are you talking about?"

"I'm going with her." He stood up and handed Marcus an envelope with a handwritten note clipped to the top. "This is my will, a key to my safety deposit box, and the name of my lawyer who drew up the documents in the first place. I'd like you to be my executor, if you wouldn't mind."

"Fuck your will!" He pushed away the sealed manila envelope. "Are you telling me that you're planning to commit suicide?"

"Yes." He gently set the envelope down on a corner dresser. "It's time for Olga to go, and I'd promised her that we'd always go together."

Chapter Thirty-Four

"Hasta la vista, baby."
—*Terminator 2: Judgment Day, 1991*

"Come on, buddy," Billy begged through ragged breaths. "Just shoot already. You're ripping me apart."

The john paid little or no attention to the young man's pleas, continuing to pound away to make sure he got his hundred bucks worth.

Seriously worried about the possibility of tearing his rectum, Billy decided it was high time to take measures into his own hands. Remaining on all fours in the backseat of the sedan, he braced his weight with his left shoulder on the vinyl seat, reaching back past his own cock with the probing fingers of his right hand. Gently starting with a light touch, Billy began massaging the guy's testicles, carefully kneading them into firing mode.

"That's fucking hot," the man cursed, swinging his free arm around to slap Billy's glistening white ass.

Consciously increasing the pressure, Billy's experienced stroking began to encourage the desired effect. Without warning, the scrotum started to pucker, the sac pulling upwards as the testes moved in toward the body.

"I'm gonna cum."

"It's about fucking time," Billy hissed, stepping up the pressure of his massage.

Without warning, he pulled out his cock, whipped off his condom, and shot his entire load all over Billy's bare back.

"What the hell?"

Too spent to answer, the man just collapsed on his side, shoulder embedded in the heavily upholstered back seat.

"Wipe me off," Billy ordered, not impressed that man had covered his lower back with ejaculate.

"With what?" the guy laughed.

"Fine," Billy stretched out his legs and sat back on the seat.

"Hey! You're getting spunk all over my car."

"I told you to wipe it off, but you wouldn't, so... oh, well."

"You're a fucking pig." The man leaned back, sucking in his gut to fasten the button on his suit pants. "You're lucky I already paid you, you know that?"

"Ha. You're lucky I didn't charge you an extra forty bucks for creaming my back."

Neither wasting any more time on the dead-end conversation, the john, and his pick-up both finished dressing before silently returning to the front seat of the car.

Within ten minutes, Billy was back on his corner, a hundred dollars richer, and casually debating whether he should score a little weed to take the edge off his hunger.

"Hey there, stud," a woman called out from a cream-colored Cadillac, her Texas drawl so thick she almost sounded cartoonish.

"Not interested," Billy shook his head, scanning the line of oncoming traffic for new possibilities.

"I can make it worth your while," she teased, waving a fistful of cash from her car window.

Taking a second to turn his attention back to the car, Billy began debating the situation. She could be a cross-dresser, well put together with a respectable day job. But then she could be a pimp, scanning the streets for independents to scoop up and add to her stable of young boys. He just wasn't sure, and not knowing was dangerous territory.

"Come to Mama, little boy." She kept waving her bait.

Irritated with the attention her shouting was beginning to attract, Billy strolled across the street and made his way toward her driver's window.

"Well, ain't you just a sight for sore eyes?" She lowered her sunglasses for a clearer inspection.

"So what you looking for, lady?"

The woman's gaze stripped him bare—her glassy eyes reflected the glittery jewelry adorning her left hand.

"I'm looking for a young thing to make the time pass just a touch quicker."

Billy looked down at the wad of cash now lying across her lap, and then back up at her heavily painted face. She didn't appear to have an Adam's apple, a five o'clock shadow, or any other of the obvious signs of *drag*. As far as he could tell, she was probably a real woman.

"Well darling," Billy consciously changed his tone. "I see you're looking for a little fun. You wanna be a dear and spell out exactly what you're looking for."

"Well, I ain't looking for a man to take me dancing," she laughed, eyes casually checking out the approaching car in her rear-view mirror.

"You like what you see?" Billy opened his arms and turned a slow three hundred and sixty degree circle. "I'm just a flesh and blood young man looking to please a woman just like yourself."

"Sounds awfully good to me." She reached for a small silver flask. "You know, I have a suite at the Plaza. You interested in blowing my lunch hour with me for five hundred bucks?" The woman threw her head back to enjoy a swig.

Billy had just opened his mouth to negotiate the particulars of their deal, when his eyes suddenly spotted every hustler's nightmare tucked discreetly on the floor of the backseat.

"No… I've got plans, so I guess we'll have to try this some other time."

"Ah, that's too bad," she reached down and picked up the cash, slowly counting five hundred dollars out onto her dash.

"I know," he shrugged. "But I can't disappoint my regulars. They're a guy's bread and butter."

"I'll make it a thousand," she tempted Billy.

If he hadn't desperately needed the money, he wouldn't have even been standing at her window. His experience would have made his brain scream, *NO!*

"Can I bring a friend with me?"

"Who you think I am? Wonder Woman?" she snickered, taking the opportunity to gulp down another swig from her flask. "No, I think we'll keep it one on one for right now. Don't you agree?"

Billy didn't agree with anything the woman was saying. She was into heavy-duty bondage, and he could smell it for a mile.

"You know you're on the gay stroll, don't you?" he questioned her.

"I sure do, sugar pie," she casually waved as two angry motorists honked their horns and zoomed around her parked vehicle. "Tell me, stud. Are you a bottom, or a top?"

"Solid top," he answered without a second's delay. "But I'll do bottom for the right price."

"I love bottoms. They're so much fun," she licked her lips.

"My turn," Billy actually took a chance and leaned up against her driver's door. "Why don't you tell me what you're carrying in the back seat?" He nodded toward the leather duffle bag.

"Just a few of my personal things I don't like to travel without."

"Like I said," Billy pulled away, shading his eyes from the afternoon sunshine. "I got plans."

Reaching across her seat, the woman dug down into her purse and pulled out another wad of cash.

"I'm sure we can come to a financial agreement, and as for your regulars," she shook her head side to side. "I'm sure they'll be able to make do for just one afternoon."

"I don't do S and M, but I give good head, and nobody rides me bareback, no matter how much cash they're packing. So you see; you're probably looking at the wrong guy."

"No, I got me the right guy. We just ain't finished negotiating yet."

Hair standing up on the back of his neck, Billy started backing away from the car window when he hit a solid wall of human flesh.

"Where you going, bitch?" a man growled in his ear as a revolver dug into the right side of his ribs.

Billy broke out in a cold sweat, his mind racing as he struggled to get a handle on his situation. "I... I... I was," he stumbled, his mouth as dry as the Sahara Desert.

"We had a date," the looming voice growled. "You trying to run out on me?"

The voice was familiar, but in his agitated state, Billy just couldn't place it.

"Let's go." The man pressed the barrel of his gun even deeper into Billy's side.

Shaking her head in disgust, the woman finally acknowledged that she'd been outplayed.

Turning as if moving in choreographed dance, both men walked off the street, wordlessly blending into the shadows of the back alley.

As the Cadillac pulled back into the main stream of traffic, Billy felt the revolver suddenly disappear from his side.

"You're lucky I showed up when I did, you little shit hole. What the fuck was going through your head? You even know who the hell that was you were trying to hustle out there?"

Billy finally wrangled up the courage to turn his head.

"Yeah, it's me," the man carefully tucked the gun in the rear waistband of his jeans.

"What are you doing here?" Billy demanded, heart still pounding from the close call.

"Saving your ass, you little cocksucker. You were just about to be the evening news."

"So, who was that?" Billy couldn't help but inquire.

"That was Opal, you dumb fuck. And if you'd have crawled into that car, the last thing you would have remembered would have been some humungous dildo, making friends with your spleen."

"That was Opal?" he spun back toward the street, anxious for another glimpse of the city's most notorious Madame. "I thought she'd be different?"

"She's different to all kinds of people."

Billy had been very lucky. Young men had a funny way of disappearing into Opal's world, and when they resurfaced, they were never the same. He'd met a couple of her discards over the last year, and it had been disturbing... to say the least. They'd all been lifeless; the spark extinguished from their eyes. Their only solace seemed to come from the mind-numbing chemicals they ingested on a regular basis. They were the walking dead of the gay stroll, and in an instant, Billy had almost joined their ranks.

"Thanks man. I owe you."

"Yeah, whatever. I only came here for your payments."

Billy dug down into his pocket and pulled out the eight hundred bucks he'd already earned. "Why don't you give me the rest of the afternoon and swing by after supper?"

Shoving the cash deep into his coat, the man nodded his agreement. "Now stick with what you know. Not every car cruising this street is a horny businessman looking for a quick blow. Be a little more careful, or you'll gonna wake up with a giant fist shoved up your ass, and a couple feet of rubber tubing threaded up your dick."

"I hear ya," Billy shuddered. "And I'll see you after supper with the rest."

The older man slapped Billy on the shoulder before turning and heading off back to his own car.

After Alicia waved goodbye and walked out the clinic's door, Tony and Karen were uncomfortably settled into the clinic's lunchroom, an untouched bottle of red wine sitting in the middle of the table.

"I don't know if you want any, but Dr. Clifford said to help ourselves," Tony nervously shrugged, both his hands distractedly fiddling with the corkscrew.

"Guess he thought we might need it," Karen blushed, her own nervousness manifesting itself into embarrassment.

"Should I?'

"Might as well," she nodded, hoping a drink might calm her frazzled nerves.

"Oh, hell," Tony laughed. "I forgot to grab some glasses and I've already locked up the back. How do you feel about drinking out of a cup?"

Karen stood, plucked two ceramic mugs off the drain board and set them down beside the wine. "Pour monsieur."

"I'm really glad you stopped by," Tony said as he handed Karen her wine.

"You didn't look too happy when I first walked in."

"I was really surprised. I kinda thought you'd blown me off on the phone."

As she took a second to savor the taste of the wine, Karen suddenly opted to tell the truth. "I did blow you off, but to be honest, I'm having second thoughts. I don't know what to do, I've… well… I've never run across this before."

His turn to be honest, Tony slowly set his mug down on the table. "I hate the fact that I made those movies when I was a kid. But I can't change that. It's embarrassing, and I was lucky to get out of that life without a drug habit, or worse yet, some incurable disease. Every week, when another *wannabe movie star* walks through our doors, I cringe. They don't have a clue what they're getting themselves into, and it takes everything I have not to pull them aside and shake a little sense into them."

"But maybe if you talked to them."

Tony just shook his head. "I tried at least ten times, and each one basically each told me to mind my own business, in not so many words."

"So, what do we do? About us?"

"It's basically up to you," Tony conceded. "You have to be able to deal with the fact that I had sex on film for money. It's simple. It's either yes or no. There really isn't anything I can do to change the past."

Reflectively chewing the inside of her lip, Karen knew what she wanted to say, but couldn't think of the appropriate words.

"Just spit it out," Tony encouraged her. "We're a little past the bullshit stage."

"I do wanna date you—that is if you still wanna date me—but I'm afraid."

"Of what?"

"Well," she grabbed the cup and gulped down another shot. "I'm afraid that I'm only going to get more attached, and when our relationship progresses to an intimate stage, then…"

"Then what?"

"Well, look at me," Karen suddenly jumped to her feet to pace back and forth. "I'm not a porn star. I can't do those moves. I don't know how, and from what little I've seen, I don't think I even wanna learn. And I don't want to have anal sex!" she suddenly blurted from across the room.

"Neither do I," Tony shifted in his seat. "I wouldn't want anything shoved up my butt either."

"Good," she sighed with relief, a flush of embarrassment coloring her cheeks.

"So what you're trying to tell me is that you might be able to handle my past if you thought you could compete with my sexual exploits?"

"Exactly." Karen dropped back into her chair and took a giant gulp of her wine. "I'm just an accountant. I don't want," she waved her hand frantically over her head, "for you to cum in my hair." She randomly chose an act she'd once seen in a stag film.

Tony wasn't used to anybody being quite this blunt, and although he appreciated her honestly, he wasn't sure how to respond. "You gotta realize. Sex for film and sex in real life are two different things," he tried to explain.

"I know that."

"Sure, you say you do. But I get the feeling you think that I'm all about multiple partners and acrobatic positions."

"Honestly, I don't know what to believe. It's tough from my end."

"You know, sex on film is pretty robotic." Tony struggled to make Karen understand. "You're usually filming in full light with a crew running around your feet. And as for the girl, well, that's a joke."

"But they're so perfect looking," Karen reminded him. "They're willing to do anything you want them to do. They're like giant *Gumby* dolls."

"If you're lucky, you get to meet the chick five minutes before you have sex. If not, you say your hellos walking onto the set. They don't call it acting for nothing."

Karen listened intently, desperately needing to believe everything Tony said.

"It's kind of like a little kid watching Barney the Dinosaur on TV. They might know there's a man inside the purple dinosaur costume, but they sit back and enjoy the program anyway. Well, grown men who watch porn are same way. They know the chick is paid to act like she's having the time of her life; faking orgasms and pretending to like the taste, but the guys watch and enjoy it anyway. It's entertainment."

"One more question?"

"Sure," he leaned back, relieved to surrender the floor.

"Do you have any plans to ever go back and work in the industry?"

"I'd rather be dead broke and live in a cardboard box."

"Okay," Karen happily nodded. "You wanna try that supper thing again?"

"Yes," he grinned, picking up his mug to toast their second date.

Chapter Thirty-Five

"Play it, Sam. Play As Time Goes By."

—*Casablanca, 1942*

Watching the digital numbers on his clock radio change over from 6:59 to 7:00, Marcus forced himself to rise out of bed. Only able to sleep an hour, maybe two, his body was still exhausted, although his mind had been awake and racing since just before dawn. It was time, and he was sure the Martin's plan would be well executed by now, so without another minute's delay; he picked up the phone and dialed.

The operator answered immediately, "911, what is your emergency?"

"This is Dr. Marcus Clifford calling. I'm afraid there might be a problem at my associate's residence. I was wondering if you could please send an officer over to check on him."

"What do you believe is the nature of the emergency, Dr. Clifford?"

"Dr. Martin Hood and I are both physicians. We religiously contact each other on a weekly basis, and I'm afraid to report that Dr. Hood is twenty-four hours late checking in. He is quite elderly and I am concerned."

"Has this ever happened before, doctor?"

"No."

"Does Dr. Hood reside alone?"

"No, he lives with his mentally and physically handicapped wife. She is incapable of making or receiving telephone calls," Marcus continued to read the responses off his best-friend's cue cards.

"I've found a Dr. Hood in our data base. Can you please confirm his home address?

Marcus complied.

"I'm dispatching a car to his residence as we speak. Can I reach you at the number you are calling from, doctor?"

Marcus relayed his personal information and hung up the telephone, checking off another one of his duties.

"Come on," Julia begged, stirring the honey-flavored tea in an attempt to entice Serena to drink. "You ain't had nothing but some water in two days. You can't live off half a glass of fluid."

Serena barely blinked, never mind sitting up to accept the offered cup.

"I'm just gonna leave this here," Julia smiled, setting the tea on the edge of her nightstand. "You drink that and I'll make us something to eat. How about a plate of nachos? No," she suddenly thought aloud. "That might be a little hard on your stomach. How about some chicken noodle soup with crackers? Sounds good to me."

Serena never moved a muscle. As Julia toddled off, her eyes finally began to move around the room. Searching, they scanned every inch of the wall space. She was looking for something, something of value that she could easily pawn or sell. As soon as she found it, she would finally have a reason to sit up and move.

While she waited for the pot to boil, Julia leaned around the corner to peek at her charge. She couldn't believe Serena was giving up now, after everything she'd been through. Julia didn't understand why, and with every passing day, she could feel the girl slipping right through her hands.

"Hello?" a man's voice called out after gently rapping on the front door.

"Tony!" Julia rushed over to open the door.

"Hi there. Got your call, thought I'd stop by, and see how you're both doing."

"Well, we're holding our own. That's about the best I can say."

"You didn't ask for anymore meds, so I just brought you some donuts instead." He lifted up the cardboard box. "Trust me, these are better than antibiotics."

Julia smiled for the first time in days, accepting the box and strolling back into her kitchen to check on the boiling water.

"How's Serena?"

Ripping open the packet of dehydrated chicken broth, Julia motioned toward her bedroom. "She's not really doing that well these last couple of days. I thought it might be withdrawal, but it's more than mood swings. She's so... despondent."

"Despondent?"

"Fuck you, I've been reading a lot." Julia playfully whacked Tony with her wooden spoon. "You know, back in high school, I got some decent grades."

"I believe you."

"Then I found boys," she turned the burner to low, chuckling to herself. "Things were never really the same. Homework was a bitch, and so was my mom, so I basically ditched both and decided to split."

"Julia, if you could turn back the clock, what would you have given to avoid doing porn?"

"Fuck Tony, what's with all the emotional shit? You on some kind of mission to make me cry?"

"No, I'm not here to make you squirm," he smiled. "It's just that my past is really starting to bite me in the ass. Makes me wonder what it might have been like if I'd never sold my dick for cash?"

"I don't think it would have made that much of a difference for me. It's not like making porn has kept me out of the Miss America pageant or anything."

Tony couldn't help but smile. "But maybe you'd have gotten married, had a family, or something like that."

"Nobody's gonna marry me and give me their last name."

"That's what I mean." He sat down at the kitchen table. "If we hadn't made porn, where would our destinies have taken us?"

Prying the metal lid off an old canister, Julia pulled out a pre-rolled joint and began searching the kitchen for a lighter. "Maybe for people like us, it's just best to stick to our own kind. You know, with people in the trade," she sparked up the weed.

Tony debated her last statement, watching Julia fill her lungs to capacity with the bluish smoke.

"Maybe for you, but it never worked for me. I never had any common ground with most of the people I met in the biz."

Julia couldn't help but laugh, remembering one of Tony's first serious girlfriends. Silicone for tits, straw for brains, and a twat big enough to drive a truck through—she was about as superficial as they came.

"Yeah, you're right. Remember *Starr Rising*?"

"I can't believe you have to bring her up," he groaned, accepting the joint from Julia's hand. "She was so..." he sucked the smoke down deep into his lungs, "So..."

"Plastic," Julia roared.

"Enough of my past. How about we check on our little patient before we get too ripped to care," he snuffed out the burning joint.

Reaching out to hold Tony's hand for no other reason than to make contact, Julia led the way into her bedroom. "Serena, you sleeping?"

With her eyes glued shut; she was either fast asleep, or just unwilling to visit with her guest.

"She won't eat, and the only water she's drank has been a couple sips with her pills."

"Dr. Clifford is really busy right now with a personal matter," Tony explained. "But I'll let him know tomorrow."

"You're not working the rest of the day?"

"No," he shook his head, amazed at the lightheaded feeling from just one drag of the joint. "Personal matter, he won't be in until Thursday morning."

Leading the way out of her bedroom, Julia strolled back into the kitchen and switched off the stove. "I don't think there's any point making this right now."

Tony agreed, standing up to help himself to a bottle of water. By the time he downed his first gulp, Julia had already relit the joint.

"Little early for a party, isn't it."

"You got something more pressing?"

Tony accepted yet another toke from his friend's hand.

———————

When Marcus answered his door, two police detectives were standing on the other side.

"May we come in, Dr. Clifford?"

Without speaking, he stepped aside to allow them both passage.

"I'm sorry to report that Dr. Martin Hood and his wife Olga were found deceased at their residence."

Clifford looked down at the floor of his kitchen, instantly recalling the second page of Martin's script.

"How did it happen?"

"It looks like a murder/suicide."

"Please have a seat." He offered both men chairs at his kitchen table, remembering the explicit instructions to *answer their questions, but not to volunteer too much information.*

"Was Dr. Hood experiencing emotional problems as of late?"

"He was a retired physician. His wife was dying, and I think he felt that his world was ending. Did Martin leave a note, an explanation?"

"Actually he did, and that's why we're here, doctor. It seems that Dr. Hood had planned this quite well, going as far as to leave you explicit instructions regarding their burials, and disbursements of his personal assets."

Marcus nodded, already aware of the envelope's existence.

"We're going to need a complete statement detailing your last communication with Dr. Hood."

"Yes," he nodded; giving the impression his total co-operation would be forthcoming.

"You're the owner/operator of the clinic known as the Changeroom? Do we have the correct information?"

"Yes, you do. And for your records, I've known Martin for years. We worked together back at the University before I left to run the family clinic."

"In your opinion, was Dr. Hood capable of administering a lethal injection to his wife before injecting a second lethal dosage to himself?"

Marcus took a deep breath before repeating the memorized answer. "When a man has lost everything he loves, everything he cares about, you have to be prepared for the worst. I believe Martin had reached that point in his life. Olga was his world, and she was dying. He wanted to die with her."

"One more question, doctor?" the police detectives promised. "Were you aware that there is no legal proof of marriage between a Dr. Martin Hood and a Miss Olga Heinz?"

"Yes, I am," he sadly nodded his head. "And I'm sure you're both already aware of Olga's violent assault years back, which ultimately contributed to her debilitating condition?"

Both detectives nodded.

"Well, due to Olga's diminished capacity after her mugging, her consent wasn't a feasible option. So, Martin performed his own intimate version of a marriage ceremony, and although I wasn't present during his vows, I was aware of his binding commitment to Olga's long term care."

"We appreciate your candor, Dr. Clifford," the detectives shook his hand and prepared to depart. "It's a shame it had to end this way."

Locking the door behind them, Marcus had to disagree with the detectives' summation of his dear friend's life.

Martin had enjoyed a brilliant career, dotted with an impressive number of medical achievements. His efforts had been awarded handsomely, and he would forever be remembered in the University's medical archives. Whether he died of natural causes, or by his own hand, these facts would never diminish his accomplishments. Marcus was determined to dwell on these very ideas and vowed to spend the remainder of his days saluting his friend's achievements, not dwelling on his final dying act.

———————

Seated together, shoulder to shoulder on the living room couch, Tony and Julia indulged in yet a second joint. "Where in the hell do you get this shit?" he couldn't help but laugh. "It's fucking me up good and proper."

"Just a little gift from a friend," Julia chuckled, clumsily reaching for Tony's bottle of water.

"Must be a pretty good friend."

"Not as good as you," she smiled, reaching over to pat Tony's leg.

"We've been through hell and back," he laughed. "Remember the time they lost that mini butt plug in Tyrone's ass?"

"Oh, fuck me," Julia moaned. "Guess who they sent in to find it?"

"You had the smallest hands."

"And the strongest stomach."

"You know," Tony reluctantly admitted. "Sometimes I actually miss it. There was nothing to think about," he struggled to explain. "You just showed up, did your scene, then walked out the door and never looked back."

"Well, come back," Julia encouraged. "We're always looking for a hard cock and a fresh face."

"I'm not exactly fresh anymore," Tony argued.

"But I bet you're still hard," Julia slowly moved her hand toward his crotch, pleasantly surprised by its obvious girth.

"Don't do that," he shook his head. "I don't play that game anymore."

"Why not?"

"Cuz I'm in a relationship," he tried to explain without sounding like some inexperienced high school nerd.

"So?" Julia argued, suddenly yearning for a familiar touch. "Do you think we can maybe go back in time for just one day?"

Although her advances were disguised as sexual, Tony knew

that Julia was just craving affection. He'd been there before, and he recognized all the signs.

"Come here, sweetie." He threw his right arm around her shoulder, pulling her tightly into the sculpted muscles of his chest.

Julia resisted at first, uncomfortable with the fact that her face was only inches from the warmth of Tony's neck.

"Sometimes it's just nice to be held," Tony unconsciously began stroking Julia's back. "You know, I can't imagine growing old without someone to hold."

"Me too," an unexpected tear began to run down her cheek. "You know, Tony, I'm running out of time."

"Are you being evicted?" He twisted his neck to try to read his friend.

"No." She cleared her throat to attempt maintaining her self-control. "But I'm staring at the face of thirty, and it won't be long before I can't compete anymore. You know, those eighteen-year-old hard bodies are everywhere in the industry. They're a dime a dozen, and they'll fucking work for crack."

"You're still hot," Tony argued.

"Yeah, I can hold my own now, but what about in another five years? Eventually I'll have to fold up my tent and move on."

"That's true."

"What worries me is that I've been working in porn since grade twelve. Did you know that I actually wore my prom dress in one of my first movies?"

"Baby blue, right?"

"Baby pink, but good guess," Julia chuckled.

"Thirty is young out in the real world; we just happened to have worked in another world is all. You'll make the transition," he promised her. "You're too strong and focused to give up and hit the pipe full-time."

"Are you sure?" Julia reached up and wiped her eyes, "cuz the pipe's looking really good right now."

"It's an option," Tony agreed. "And I bet I can name you at least a dozen people who've chose that route. But you're not the type. I have confidence in you. Look how hard you've been working to help get Serena back on her feet."

"Let's talk about Serena," Julia suddenly pulled away from Tony's embrace. "What do you think she's supposed to do now? No one's gonna hire her to do jack shit. Hell, her tits even scare me whenever I change the bandages."

"I don't know." He threw his hands up behind his neck and slowly stretched the kink out of his back. "But she's really young. Maybe Serena can go back to school or something. Learn to be a secretary, or run computers—something like that."

"It all seems so hopeless." Julia flopped back down onto Tony's chest.

"But we gotta keep trying," he whispered. "If we give up, what's the point of our lives?"

"You must be in love," she snickered down into the fabric of his shirt. "It's the only thing that could explain such a fucking positive attitude."

After the detectives had finally cleared out of Marcus's apartment, he found himself sitting alone at the kitchen table with Martin's last will and testament spread out in front of him.

The contents weren't really that much of a surprise; a large portion of the doctor's estate was already eaten up by his unforeseen retirement and Olga's substantial medical costs. The remainder was allotted to specific individuals, as well as a bequest list for his art collection, and Olga's belongings, still packed into climate-controlled storage units.

As executor, his duties would be quite simple, and with the funds allotted for legal counsel, he'd have no trouble following through with Martin's last requests.

He was a little surprised to find himself listed as a beneficiary, but he was absolutely shocked to find Tony DeMarco's name included in the paperwork.

First thing tomorrow morning, he'd sit his assistant down and let him in on his good fortune. It was going to be a financial windfall for them both, a possible life changing experience.

For the first time since Marcus had opened Martin's will, he realized that he might be about to lose his most trusted employee. How could he realistically expect Tony to come back to work at the clinic with a six-digit bank account? It wasn't that he couldn't now afford to hire a licensed nurse with actual medical credentials; he just didn't want to.

With one stroke of a pen, Martin had unconsciously altered their futures. He had wanted to give them each a hand up toward a more comfortable life, and in doing so; he'd inadvertently transformed their futures.

Rising up from his chair, Marcus quickly glanced at his phone, desperately wanting to call his girlfriend/ex-girlfriend… Teresa. If nothing else, he just wanted to hear her voice. He should call, he reasoned, it was the right thing to do. She had known Martin Hood, and would want to be notified of his death. Dialing, he waited on the line, praying that Teresa would be the one to pick up the phone.

"Hello," a woman finally answered.

"Teresa, it's Marcus calling."

"Marcus," her voice suddenly rose an octave. "I'm so glad you called. I was starting to think I'd never hear from you again."

"I have bad news. Martin and Olga both passed yesterday."

"Together? What was it, a car crash?"

"No," he stopped to look for the right words. "Olga took a serious turn for the worst, and Martin decided to join her."

Teresa's line remained silent; her breathing was the only testament to their connection.

"I did have a chance to talk with Martin the night before. He knew what he was doing," Marcus tried to reassure her, as if it would somehow lessen the blow.

"But he was a doctor," Teresa began to sniffle, as tears began to trickle down the sides of her face. "How could he do that?"

"It's because he was a doctor, Teresa. Martin knew what the future would hold for them both if he were unable to care for Olga. He made the only decision he could live with."

"Live with?" she sarcastically laughed. "His decision killed them both."

"I know," he whispered. "But it was his decision, and no one has the right to judge him but God."

Teresa prayed Marcus was right, unable to fathom the thought of a man as good as Martin Hood burning in hell for all eternity.

Chapter Thirty-Six

"Keep your friends close, but your enemies closer."

—The Godfather Part II, 1974

He'd already downed a large double/double French roast, and was beginning to dance in place, his bladder ready to burst at any second. Nowhere else to run, Billy pressed his crotch up against the nearby shrubbery and released a powerful stream of urine.

"Ohhhh," he moaned, relieved to empty his bladder finally, before he had an accident and pissed his own pants.

"Bye baby," Wally yelled over his shoulder, running out the front door of his house as Annette followed to clean out the flyers someone had stuffed into their mailbox.

"Don't forget to check," she thoughtfully reminded him.

Wally unlocked the doors on the van, threw his briefcase onto the passenger seat, and then walked around the back to peer under the rear wheels. He was much too much too busy to stop and pull crushed pieces of a plastic from under his bumper, never mind having to explain to his youngest daughter Tammy why Daddy had just backed over yet another one of her favorite toys. Satisfied that any potential tragedies had been averted, Wally jumped back into his van and cranked the engine over.

"Don't freak out," Billy whispered from his position in the backseat.

"What the hell?"

"I said don't freak out," he ordered through clenched teeth. "Just put this fucking thing in reverse, and let's get the hell out of here."

Choosing to follow Billy's orders for reasons he couldn't comprehend, Wally pulled out of his neighborhood and headed off toward main thoroughfare. With his fingers nervously fidgeting with the steering wheel, Wally racked his brains, trying to figure out just what his ex-boyfriend was doing hiding out in the back seat of the family van.

"Pull over into there," Billy suddenly sat up and pointed at a drive-thru coffee shop. "I need another shot of java."

As they headed back down the road, side by side in the front bucket seats, both men silently sipped their steaming coffee from paper cups.

"Where are we going?" Wally gingerly set his cup down into holder. "You know I have to get to work, so if you wanna say something, now's the time."

"Busy boy," Billy teased. "Looks like you're doing a lot better since I left our little company."

Cutting across three lanes of traffic, Wally pulled onto a side street and killed his engine.

"What do you want?"

"You," he said, and winked over his cup as he took another sip.

"I'm a married man with a family, and a wife that I love. I'm sorry that I jeopardized it all to have sex with you, but that's in the past now, and I'm not willing to risk it all again."

"So this month we're not gay, but last month we were. Damn Freeman, you're gonna have to get me a copy of your schedule if you want me to keep track of your sexual preferences."

"I don't need you keeping track of anything!"

"Hostile, are we?"

Frustrated with the direction of their conversation, Wally decided to nip it in the bud.

"You obviously want something from me, so lay it out. Why were you hiding in my van?"

"Remember the last time we were together here?" Billy grinned, motioning toward the backseat. "I made you come so hard, your eyes rolled back into your head and you drooled down your own chest. Did you know that, Wally? Did you know that drool actually ran out of your mouth because you were so caught up in your own orgasm that you didn't know what you were doing?"

Sweating under his collar, his breaths coming in shallow gasps, Wally grabbed his cup and began forcing the searing liquid down his throat, welcoming the burn as it took his mind off his growing erection.

"I got a little proposal for you, Wally. It'll bring you the two things you love more than anything in this world."

He never grabbed the bait, remaining resolutely unresponsive.

"Let me explain." Billy turned in his seat, his eyes now burning into Wally's face. "I have connections that will pay really big bucks for a night with you."

Erection deflating, Wally also turned his body inward to make his point.

"You've got *connections* that'll pay money to have sex with me?" He slowly repeated, wanting to be absolutely clear.

"Yes, I do, and you won't believe the kind of bucks these men are willing to pay for fresh young guys."

"Fresh, huh? By fresh, you mean married men like me with everything to lose and only greed as a motivator, right?"

"You won't lose shit. You'll only make handfuls of cash," his eyes lit up with excitement. "Work two or three nights a month; and you'll blow your regular salary out the window."

"Tell me something, Billy. If this is such a good deal, why do ya have to spend time recruiting guys from suburban neighborhoods? Why don't you just take all the work yourself?"

"It's all about variety, Wally. Clients don't wanna look at the same face every time they make a date."

"How much would I make in an average night?" He crossed him arms at his chest. "And don't give me the best case scenario, give me worst. Tell me, what's the least amount I'd take home in a single night."

"Let's see," Billy did a few quick calculations in his head. "One date, no tip… two hundred bucks."

"Only two hundred bucks? That doesn't seem like a shit load of money to me." He snatched his paper coffee cup off the dash.

"Well, that's only one date in the whole night. And that's without any bonus tips. And let me tell you, Wally, you play these guys right, and they'll tip you out at least a hundred or two on each date."

Wally's level of disgust was only matched by his rising level of disbelief. What in the world would give Billy Grant the impression that he'd even consider hiring himself out as a male prostitute? It was almost inconceivable.

"Be honest with me, Billy. Why me? There are a thousand guys walking the streets downtown. I see them every night on the news. They hang out behind the movie theaters and the parking lots, next to the bars. They already live the life, so just recruit them. Why bother working on married business men who don't have a clue what they'd be getting themselves into?"

Billy felt excited by the new Wally. He was showing a side he'd never seen before, and it was very attractive. Maybe he wasn't such *a bottom* after all.

"My clients don't want anything to do with street hustlers. They can spot them for a mile. They want real men from good families—men who aren't carrying diseases or tweaked out on crystal meth. And they're willing to pay damn good money for just the right combination. You understand, don't you, Wally? You can see what I'm offering you here, can't you?"

"One more question, and don't bullshit me, Billy."

"Go ahead, I'll be truthful."

"Why'd you steal the eleven grand?"

Taking a second to evaluate his answer, the sudden realization struck Billy that it was now or never. This next statement might either win Wally over to his side, or scare him off for good. He had once more chance to make his pitch, and it was boiling down to believability.

"I'm gonna lay it on the line," he took a last cleansing breath. "I took the money because I used to be a junkie, and I'd run up some very serious debt. I've been trying to work it off, but my dealer wasn't interested in a payment plan. He just kept pushing me for a lump sum payout."

"So?"

"So I borrowed a few bucks from the funeral home, and I'm making payments on the rest."

Wally sat quietly while he debated Billy's choice of words.

"You still do dope?"

"No, I'm clean now," his ex-boyfriend liberally stretched the truth. "But I've still got some serious debt to deal with."

"The eleven thousand didn't cover it."

"No, that was only about half."

Wally found his mind wandering back to work. He had a twelve-thirty appointment at the guy's office downtown, and he needed to pick up fresh forms at the funeral home before heading out to meet with his client.

"So, will you work with me?" Billy grinned, still confident that he was winning Wally over to his way of thinking.

"Billy, I want to explain something to you," Wally set down his empty cup. "I actually thought for a brief moment in time that you were the answer to my prayers."

"I know, me too, I…"

"Please," Wally held up his hand. "Let me finish."

Billy silently nodded, motioning for him to continue.

"When I first met you, Billy, you were all about excitement, and new adventures. You encouraged me to draw on some really deep-seated homosexual tendencies, and then you exploited them for your own benefit. You made me question my love for my wife, and my children, and most of all, you made me question my own self-worth."

"Like fuck I did. I just showed you there was life out of the closet."

"Yes, you did." Wally slowly nodded his head. "But coming out of the closet isn't everything it's cracked up to be if everything you hold to be important is waiting back inside."

"But you're free. You're liberated now!"

"And what did you try to introduce me to in my new found liberation? A life of drug dependency, promiscuity, crippling loneliness, and a whole parade of deadly diseases? Not much of a trade, if you ask me, Billy. The only positive upside was the wild sex. But I gotta be honest, it's not enough. Cuz when the orgasm is over, and the thrill has passed, there are still another twenty-three and a half hours in the day and you don't offer anything that remotely can fill one second of that time."

"I don't know what the fuck you're babbling about, Freeman," Billy angrily yelled into his face. "I'm offering you the world on a fucking platter, and you're sitting there, whining to me about how many hours there are in a day. You're so fucked up!"

"That might be how *you* see me, but I think I'm actually pretty lucky."

"But what about the cravings, and the yearnings? You've tasted the life; you can't just walk away from it without wanting a good fuck every now and then."

"I thought about that," Wally admitted. "And I think it's a lot like being an alcoholic who has finally started living his life clean and sober. I'll always be tempted, but I'll deal with the cravings by remembering what falling off the wagon is gonna cost me."

"Pretty philosophic," Billy suddenly leaned across the center console and planted an aggressive kiss on Wally's unsuspecting mouth.

"Don't do that," he responded with a powerful shove

"Why? I know you like it."

"I know I do, too. But like I told you a minute ago, I'm not willing to pay the price that it'll ultimately cost me. You're just not worth it. Now get the fuck out of my van, and get the fuck out of my life!"

"Mallory, Justice Mallory," a girl came running down to the potting shed. "You've got an emergency call in the office."

"For me?"

"Yeah, it's your wife. You better hurry."

Justice literally threw his spade against the pile of potting soil and turned to run straight for the main building, quickly leaving the winded secretary in his dust.

"Sarah," he yelled into the receiver. "Is it Mathew? Is he bleeding again?"

"No," she whimpered into the phone. "It's me, Justice," she swallowed hard in an attempt to settle her stomach. "I... I can't quit... throwing up."

"Where's Mary? Is she alright?"

"She fine, but..."

The phone went silent in Justice's hand as he strained to pick up any of the background noises.

"Sarah, are you alright? Sarah, can you hear me?" he shouted at the top of his lungs, every person in the front office now sitting on the edge of their chairs.

"I gotta lie down," she cried. "I'm so dizzy."

"Daddy," a small voice cried out in fear. "Mommy sick."

"Daddy's here, Mary," he shouted. "Daddy's coming home right now."

"Should I call an ambulance?" the accounts manager asked.

"No, I'm going home," he announced, passing the phone to the first woman he could reach. "Keep talking to my daughter, Mary. Tell her I'm on the way and not to be scared," he shouted over his shoulder.

By the time Justice reached his house, Sarah had managed to crawl to the couch and somehow miraculously pulled herself up and onto the cushions.

"Baby, what's the matter?" He ran straight to where she lay and dropped down to his knees. "You look awful."

"Daddy," Mary dropped the telephone and toddled in from the kitchen.

"Hang on," he jumped up again and quickly grabbed the phone. "Hello, this is Justice."

"Is everything all right?" the woman asked. "Are you going to call an ambulance?"

"We'll be fine," he nodded, anxious to get off the phone and back to his wife's side.

"Call if you need anything," she reluctantly disconnected the line.

Hanging up his phone, Justice scooped up his daughter and rushed back to his wife.

"What happened, Sarah?"

"Mommy sick," Mary patted her mother's tummy.

"Oh, I don't know," she moaned, closing her eyes to take a deep calming breath. "I haven't been feeling that great for a couple of days, but when the flu finally hit me, I just couldn't quit throwing up," she took a few seconds to rest.

"Is it just your puking that's scared you?"

"I couldn't stop, Justice, even when all I had was dry heaves, my stomach wouldn't settle down. I thought I was gonna pass out and Mary would be left running around the house... alone. I was so scared," she began to cry.

"It's okay," he leaned forward and gently stroked her cheek. "I'm home now, so why don't you just go to bed and rest. I'll take care of Mary while you have a nap."

"But the bathroom, it's..."

"Just go," Justice ordered. "I'll take care of it."

As Sarah crawled into her bed, Justice settled Mary in front of the television with a bowl of cereal.

"Mommy don't like..." her voice faded off, instantly mesmerized by the dancing cartoon figures.

Taking a second to look around the house, Justice noticed for the first time that Sarah hadn't been keeping things up to snuff for quite a while. The floors were littered with pieces of food, the kids' rooms in total shambles, and the kitchen sink cluttered with dirty dishes. She'd obviously been sick for days by the shape of their home, and he felt like a giant turd for not noticing. He'd just been so busy with the overtime down at Jupiter, and spending his nights whipping the yard into shape, that he hadn't even realized that his wife had been struggling to stay on her feet. Mop and pail in hand, Justice made his way to the bathroom, determined to make it up to her as best he could.

Standing over the kitchen sink, Freddy and Callie both scarfed down a shared order of fish and chips, knocking fingers together every time they met over the huge puddle of ketchup.

"Aren't you supposed to be at work right now?" Callie licked her fingers as she stepped away from the empty Styrofoam container.

"Yeah, but I've had enough of Dr. Chew and all his promises. Remember how he was going to find me a great job where I could make a boat load of cash really fast?"

"Sure."

"Well, he didn't come through with anything."

"Nothing?" she wiped her hands on the dishtowel.

"Well, what would you call a graveyard orderly position for nine eighty-five an hour, with time and a half on weekends and holidays," Freddy rolled his eyes.

"Not bad. Beats flipping burgers."

"Like hell it does. Nine eighty-five? I'll be lucky to save enough up for my surgery by the time I'm forty."

Callie stood to the side, watching her roommate pacing circles around their kitchen, obviously working up his nerve to make some sort of announcement.

"You know, I only enrolled in University to meet up with some doctors who might be able to point me in the right direction. I don't wanna be a doctor," he yelled, "I just want to be operated on by one!"

"So what you going to do?"

"I'm withdrawing this afternoon. I'll get half this semester's tuition back, and I'll be able to keep next semester's in the bank. I'm going for it," he announced, the excitement begin to build. "I'm withdrawing everything I have. After I sell a couple more things, and cash in my birthday bonds, I'll have just enough money."

"You're quitting school? What are you, nuts?"

"Yup, and I'm going for it! Didn't you hear what I said, Callie? I'm going ahead with my surgery."

As she took a second to digest all the information, she found herself in need of a chair.

"What about the referral? Who's going to sign that paper if you're not working for Dr. Chew anymore?"

"Taken care of," Freddy knowingly smiled.

"Hey, where's your computer?" she couldn't help but notice the empty tabletop.

"Sold it. Got five hundred bucks, but I had to throw in my printer and my portable scanner."

"Sit!" she barked, pointing to a kitchen chair. "Now, slow the fuck down and tell me exactly what you're talking about."

Freddy ran off to his bedroom and returned with his *special* binder, laying it open on the table as he began to explain all the details of his plan.

"It sounds so unbelievable," Callie muttered, "but you know what scares me the most, the plane ride home. How are you going to walk onto a commercial flight only seventy-two hours after a complete sex change operation?"

"With my little helpers," Freddy yanked a paper envelope out of the binder's front pocket. "Meet the Vicodin family. Twenty-four little white pills I'd like to think of as my personal saviors."

"Where'd you get them?"

"I stole them from Dr. Chew's office," he carefully tucked the envelope back into his binder. "He won't miss them before I'm gone. He only inventories once a month."

"Are you going down to Mexico," she stabbed her fingers at the papers, "by yourself?"

"You wanna come?"

"Who's gonna pay for my flight?"

"Well, there's your answer," Freddy reluctantly shrugged his shoulders. "I'm going down by myself."

"This is absolutely crazy. You can't fly to another country for bootleg surgery, and then expect to walk on a plane and fly back by yourself."

"I don't have any other choice!" Freddy yelled at the top of his lungs. "If I don't do something soon, I think I'll kill myself."

Callie pulled her eyes away from Freddy's face, forcing herself to begin reviewing the gruesome details of her roommate's proposed surgery.

Chapter Thirty-Seven

> *"I'm as mad as hell, and I'm not*
> *going to take this anymore!"*
>
> —*Network, 1976*

"I s anybody looking for me?" Wally rushed into the office, grabbing his messages before heading back to the bullpen.

"Wally, hold on," the receptionist ran after him.

"I'm kinda in a rush, sweetie. You're gonna have to talk on the run."

"It's about your stuff," she caught up to Wally just as his hand pulled open the empty filing cabinet.

"Where's all my papers?" he angrily demanded, not in the mood for a practical joke when he was already running an hour behind.

"That's what I've been trying to tell you," she grabbed his arm and began dragging him down the hall. "You've been moved into here," she swung open the door, quickly turning back to catch Wally's reaction.

"Why?" he asked, feet suddenly glued to the hallway floor.

"We had a little spare office space, and the sales manager decided that since your numbers were climbing so high, so fast, he'd give you a little reward."

"Holy shit," Wally finally recovered his composure and walked into the dingy six by eight foot room.

"It's dark, but I've ordered you an extra desk lamp, and a better chair. So, do you like it?"

Wally was speechless; the impact of the move was beyond words. He stumbled for a reply, and opted for the physical; turning and throwing his arms around the company's receptionist.

"Oh Wally, I'm so glad you like it. I was the one who decorated it for you," she pointed to the second-hand furniture garnered from the basement storage room. "It's not as fancy as any of the office mangers, but look," she squealed, "you have your own door."

When Wally was finally alone, he sat in his own chair, behind his own desk, and took a quick second to count his blessings. He'd narrowly escaped Billy's clutches, and that solitary thought sent a wave of shivers down his spine. Just the thought of what the future might have held for him and his family if he had actually chosen that life of debauchery had a sobering effect.

He loved Annette, and the future they were building together. She'd given him three of the best children in the world, and it was now his turn to return the favor and build her a solid financial base. No more penny pinching and worrying about mortgage payments, it was time for his wife to reap a few of the rewards. And definitely, no more secret trips to see Dr. Clifford to check for crabs or gonorrhea every time he noticed Billy with an itch.

"Wally," the receptionist buzzed him on his own phone. "Can you swing by my desk? I have a set of keys for you, but I'm covering the switchboard and can't leave."

"Sure." He hung up and made his way straight to the front desk.

"Good job, Freeman," one of the salesmen said and patted him on the back in passing.

"Thanks," Wally smiled, secretly bursting with pride.

Nervously waiting as she finished with her last call, Wally took the opportunity to bend down and check his mail slot.

"Where's Freeman?" the sales manager shouted from his door, oblivious to the fact that other employees in the bullpen might actually be trying to complete their own business calls.

"I'm here," Wally raised his head, tucking his mail under his arm and rushing down the hall. "Wally, grab a seat. I gotta make this quick, but I have a file that needs a little special care.

"First, I'd like to thank you, George, for the private office. I... I just don't know how to show my appreciation without sounding..."

"Faggy?" his sales manager laughed, their camaraderie having progressed to the stage where teasing each other was an acceptable form of communication.

"No, that's not it," Wally snickered. "I just don't want you to get your hopes up and think I'm going to get down on my knees and blow your wrinkled old dick."

George chuckled and shook his head. "Coffee?" he asked.

"No, I'm good." Wally grabbed the nearest chair, still aware of his afternoon appointment. "But seriously, thanks. It really means a lot to me."

"Well, don't get too excited, kid. It used to be a storage room, and if you don't keep up your numbers, that's what it'll be again."

"I won't disappoint you, George."

"I know. Anyway, before I run off to an advertising meeting, I got a call last night from this estate lawyer I know at Bentley and Ashcorp. Seems one of his personal clients died, and his executor needs a funeral planned ASAP for him. Of course, I thought of you."

"Of course," Wally winked. He pulled a pen out of his shirt pocket to make a few quick notes on the back of his mail.

"Don't bother, it's all in here," George said, and handed his top salesman a package. "Drop whatever you're doing and get right over to see a Dr. Marcus Clifford at his medical clinic. The address is right in the file. And don't worry about price, sixty thousand dollars was set aside for their internment."

"Dr. Marcus Clifford?" Wally couldn't help but repeat.

"Yeah. You scared of doctors or something? Cuz I need you to be bring your *A Game* to plan their internments."

"*Their* internments?"

"Yes, we'll be burying both Dr. Martin Hood, and his wife Olga. Dr. Clifford is the executor of this estate, and since they've already passed, you need to get on this A.S.A.P. So you see; time is of the essence here. You're not going down to sell a funeral package; you're actually going down to plan a funeral."

"This is new."

"Yeah, but the commissions are the same, so don't screw this up. We might just be looking at a new market here if word gets around that we did a good job."

"New market?" Wally chuckled. "We sell pre-arranged funeral packages. Hardly anything new about dying." He started thumbing through the collection of papers.

"Trust me, kid, do this file up right, and Bentley and Ashcorp might throw us a shitload of other business. They specialize in estate planning and wills. Treat this file like it's gold, and they'll hopefully return the favor. Got it?"

"Got it," Wally nodded, already deeply immersed in the documentation as he rose to leave his manager's office.

"And make sure to take the updated fall price list. And don't forget the Premium Package brochures," George yelled at Wally's back as he took off down the hallway.

Holding the paper right up in front of his eyes, Wally took one more second to review the manager's notes. "Not exactly the best place to do business," he sarcastically laughed. But this sure beat coming down to the clinic to have a cotton swab shoved up his urethra for another round of STD tests. Reluctantly, he grabbed his briefcase and made his way toward the clinic's front door, cautiously walking down the stained concrete steps.

"Not another fucking salesman," Tony cursed under his breath as soon as he spotted Wally out of the corner of his eye. He'd never understand why the drug companies continued to send reps down into their little shit hole. The doctor barely had enough money for saline and gauze, never mind a sixty-day trial of their newest anti-virals.

"Hello, my name is Walter Freeman and I'm here to see Dr. Clifford."

"The doctor's busy. Thanks for stopping by, but we won't be ordering any supplies through your company," Tony recited his standard line before returning his attention to his files.

"Hey Tony," a man staggered up from the back of the waiting room. "My head's killing me." He pulled away the bloodstained rag to prove his point.

"Sit back down, Jack. I told you you're up next, and I think you've got enough booze in your system to handle the pain for a couple more minutes."

"Tony is it?" Wally moved right up to the front of the intake desk. "Dr. Marcus Clifford is expecting me regarding Dr. Martin

Hood." He thrust out his business card, praying the burly man wouldn't recognize him as one of the clinic's past patrons.

Tony raised his head. Very few of the patients even knew the doctor's full name, never mind his association with Dr. Hood.

"Take a seat. I'll see if the doctor's able to see you."

"Dr. Clifford," Tony called out, only resorting to first names when positive they were alone. "There's someone here from..." he stopped for a second; sorry he'd forgotten to grab the guy's card, "some kind of funeral home. He wants to talk to you about Dr. Hood."

"Oh wow. Is it noon already?"

"You're expecting him?"

"I was expecting somebody."

"What ya want me to do with him? He kind of stands out like a sore thumb in the middle of our waiting room."

"Well, take him to our conference area," Marcus jokingly referred to their windowless lunchroom. "I'll just finish stitching up Jack, and then I'll join him there in fifteen minutes."

"Whatever," Tony shook his head, still bothered by the clandestine circumstances surrounding Martin and Olga's death.

"And Tony, we still on for a drink after work? I have something extremely important I need to talk to you about."

"My schedule's open."

"Okay, so let's try to get out of here at a decent time."

Tony followed his boss's instructions, the knot continuing to grow in the pit of his stomach.

———————

Dumping in the condensed tomato soup, Justice added half a can of water, and half a can of milk, the way he'd seen Sarah heat the soup a hundred times before. Continually stirring the pot for what seemed like an eternity, he finally took a chance and put the spoon to his lips, satisfied that the liquid had reached a sufficient temperature.

"Mary, that's enough TV. Now go wash up for lunch," he called out to his daughter, positioning his wife's soup in the middle of the wooden serving tray with a handful of crackers and a small glass of milk.

Carefully making his way across the living room, Justice slowly opened the bedroom door with his toe. Eyes finally adjusting to dim lighting, he was surprised to see the bedding totally churned into a giant white ball, his wife lying in a fetal position, limbs wrapped tightly around the material.

"Sarah honey, I brought you a little soup. I think it might..."
Justice almost dropped his serving tray.

"Sarah, wake up," he began shouting at his wife.

"Justice," she moaned, instantly reaching up to scratch her face the minute she was conscious.

"Don't do that," he yelled, setting the tray on the floor before reaching across the bed and yanking down her hand. "Sarah, you're bleeding," he exclaimed, shocked that anyone could scratch themselves raw in their sleep.

"I've been so itchy," she said as she struggled to sit up, her strength totally depleted from the nausea.

Without an explanation, Justice reached across the bed and yanked his wife's sweatshirt up, and over her head.

"Justice," she moaned, absentmindedly reaching across her chest to scratch the nape of her neck.

"Oh Sarah, look at you. You're covered in big white blotches," he gasped, unsure for a moment if he should even touch her.

"I feel like I have ants biting me all over." She rubbed her eyes, and then moved her hands to the unseen welts on her scalp.

"You're covered with blisters."

Sarah finally regained enough of her senses to drop her head and inspect her own body.

"Oh no, what's happening to me," her cries filled the room. "I'm infected!"

Gently pulling a clean housedress over his wife's head, Justice wrapped a blanket around Sarah's shoulders, and shouted for Mary to put on her coat and shoes.

"We don't have no money for doctors," she began to cry.

"Yes, we do," he argued, willing to sell his own blood if necessary. "Now let's just get you to the clinic."

"What clinic?"

"It's called the Changeroom. And the price is reasonable for people like us."

Too weak to argue, Sarah stumbled from her bedroom door toward the front step where Justice leaned in and scooped her up, carrying her straight to the pick-up's front seat.

"Mary," she weakly croaked.

"Don't worry, I'll get her. And I'm gonna unlock the back door and leave a note for the boys. So just sit," he yelled over his shoulder.

Sarah couldn't have run off if she wanted to. Mentally and physically exhausted; it took all her energy just to lift her bloodied fingernails toward the freshest patch of blisters now covering her right shoulder.

"Right or left," Freddy held up two separate pairs of jeans.

"I don't know," Callie moaned her indifference, bored with the task of helping him pick out his clothes. "Won't you just be wearing shorts and tank tops in that dry heat?"

"I'd shaved my legs a little while back, and since I've just started growing them out again for the waxing, they look kinda funky."

"Then left," she pointed to the lighter pair. "So how many suitcases are you thinking of taking?"

"I'm thinking only one carry-on," he shrugged his shoulders.

"One carry-on?" Callie shrieked. "Then why in the hell are we dicking around with all these clothes?"

Freddy looked at the piles on his bed and nervously laughed. "It's a weeding down process."

"Like hell it is." She plucked out a few choice articles of clothing and slammed them into her roommate's chest. "There you go. Now you're packed."

"Oh shit," Freddy looked at his watch. "I gotta run to the bank and cash the University's refund check before they close."

"Go ahead, I'll clean this up." She waved her arms as if dismissing a small child.

As he ran out the door, Callie picked up the phone and quickly dialed her parents.

"Don't worry, dear," her mother was quick to reassure her. "Your father should be in the city within half an hour.

"Good." Callie began chewing one of her nails. "And you gave him my new address?"

"He has your address and he's carrying his work phone, so if he gets lost, he can always call either you or me."

"Thanks, Mom."

"You know, dear, your father and I would feel a lot better if you'd let us help you pick out a used car."

"Mom, don't you think it's time that I started doing things for myself. And besides, I wanna be able to prove to Dad that I've got a good eye."

"But you don't know anything about motors and stuff like that."

"True," she conceded the point. "But my roommate, Freddy, is a car buff. He's always puttering around on his car and probably knows more about engines than Dad," she lied right through her teeth.

"We're sure looking forward to meeting your roommate. Will he be there when your father stops by?"

"No, remember I told you that he works for Dr. Chew down at the University?"

"Oh yes, sweetie, I remember now. It's nice to hear he has such a strong work ethic. It wouldn't hurt your generation to take a few hints from a young boy like that."

"Well Mom, I really gotta run."

"Bet you wanna tidy up the apartment, right?"

"Yeah, I do need to put a few clothes away," she glanced back toward Freddy's bed.

"I love you, Callie."

"I love you too, Mom," she hung up the phone, already feeling like a heel for lying to her parents.

Two hours later when Freddy finally walked through the apartment door, Callie instantly noticed his mood had escalated from restless, to agitated. "The airline can't promise me an aisle seat," he grumbled, walking straight toward the refrigerator and grabbing a can of soda.

"Why not?"

"Cuz seats are assigned upon arrival. It's basically first come, first served." Freddy downed half the drink.

"We'll just have to be early."

"Yeah, I guess, cuz the lady at the airline said that most people will choose a window seat before..." Freddy suddenly stopped speaking, his mind replaying Callie's last statement. "We'll have to be early." You talking about the two of us?"

"That's right," she walked over and hugged him. "You can't go alone, that's absolutely crazy. I'm going with you."

"How? You don't have the bucks?"

"My dad just dropped off three-thousand dollars for me, in

cash," she picked the envelope up off the counter and flashed Freddy a quick look at its contents.

"Why would they do that?"

"Cuz I'm buying a car, and they've agreed to pay for half."

"Callie," Freddy shook his head. "You can't do this. It's just not right."

"Yes it is," she argued. "There's no way in hell you can make that trip yourself. The flight home will kill you. You need me. And besides, you don't really have a choice, cuz I've already booked a ticket. They're holding it for me at the airport, and I'll pay for it before we leave."

Without speaking, Freddy's gratitude began to spill from his eyes and run straight down his cheeks. "I was so scared," he admitted through emotional gasps. "I didn't know what I was going to do."

"Well, let me help. First off, I noticed that you haven't made any hotel reservations."

"Since I'm flying in only twelve hours before my appointment, I thought I'd just walk around and see the sights. You know, save a little money."

"That'll work for you, but what about me. I'll be hanging around for three days until we come home. I'm gonna have to book a hotel room, don't you think?"

"I guess," he nodded; suddenly afraid that Callie was walking into something she might not be prepared for. "Sweetie, I think we gotta have a little talk."

"We'll have the next three days to talk all we want. Right now, I gotta finish packing."

Following his roommate into her bedroom, he started digging for excuses.

"I didn't know you had a passport?'

"Sure, mine's still good from last Christmas when Mom and Dad took us to the Bahamas."

"But what about exams? If you miss too much school, you might actually flunk a course. I couldn't handle that, Callie. Your parents are going to be pissed enough without thinking that you've failed a course because of me."

"Freddy," she pulled him down onto her bed. "I'm coming with you, no matter what. Even if I gotta take my own taxicab to the airport and just follow you down to Mexico. I'm still going. Do you understand that?"

"Yeah, I do," he relented.

"And I'm not saying this to make you worry, but what if something did go wrong during surgery and you got really sick? You'll need a friend down there to contact your family and make sure you got the proper care. Right?"

"Nothing's going to go wrong, Callie, and if it does, I'll be lying in the middle of a hospital. What do you think you could do for me that a Mexican doctor can't?"

"You're right," she smiled, suddenly feeling a little foolish.

"But Callie." Freddy reached out to hold her hand. "I gotta admit that I'm really glad you're coming. I didn't want to take my first steps as a woman all by myself."

Chapter Thirty-Eight

*"Carpe diem. Seize the day, boys.
Make your lives extraordinary."*

—Dead Poets Society, 1989

"Fourteen," Callie continued to barter with the street vendor, desperate to buy the hand woven blanket, but determined to see just how far she'd be able to bring him down.

"Twenty-five," he argued. "This good, mi esposa made by hand. Twenty-five really good price."

"Your wife makes those, too?" Freddy pointed to vendor setting up shop directly across the street.

"Fifteen?" Callie hit her top price.

The man nodded, as if he could sense that their negotiations had hit an impasse.

"It's nearly one hundred degrees and it's still morning. What exactly are you going to do with that blanket?"

"But look at the colors," Callie argued back. "It's the exact same green as in my duvet cover. It'll go perfect on the edge of my bed. Don't you think?"

Freddy never answered, he just grabbed her arm and began making a beeline toward the waiting taxicabs.

"What's the rush?" she worked to stuff her first purchase into the wicker shopping tote, adorning her arm.

"How about we check into the hotel, then we can do a little sightseeing? I'm tired of dragging this suitcase around."

Relenting, Callie allowed Freddy to take a direct route to their hotel, a bright pink concrete monstrosity, located on the edge of the main strip.

"This is it," he announced as they both crossed the threshold into their room. "I finally made it. I'm here in Tijuana, and by this time tomorrow night, I'm gonna be a woman," Freddy threw up his arms and spun in a circle.

"Kind of hard to believe," Callie plopped down on one of the two double beds.

"I'd sure like a drink."

"Well, then let's celebrate." She dug in her woven bag for the three-dollar bottle of tequila.

"I can't drink before surgery," Freddy reminded her, cracking open a fresh bottle of water. "Actually," he stopped to look at his watch, "this is gonna be my last bottle."

"So many rules," Callie teased. "Guess it doesn't really matter which country you're in, all hospitals are the same."

"Guess so," Freddy reached down into his bag and pulled out a blood-red scarf. "You know what?" he stepped over to the mirror and slowly wrapped the antique silk around his neck. "My grandmother used to let me play with this scarf, and after she died, I kept it. I brought it along for good luck." He gently rubbed the silk against his cheek. "I guess it's kinda like having family here, without having family here."

"Makes sense." She smiled, watching him once again twirl around the room.

"You know what I'd like to do?"

"What?" Callie began digging in her carry-on for any leftover granola bars.

"I'd like to stop by the hospital and just have a look around. You know, get a feel for the place before I check in tonight."

"Not a bad idea. I'd like to know where the cafeteria and gift shop are. If you're really good, I might even bring you a couple flowers," she teased between bites.

"Well then, let's go," Freddy took a second to adjust his money belt before running out to look for a taxi.

"No way, this can't be it," he continued to argue with the taxi driver. "Hospital, you know, Casa de Salud?"

"Casa de Salud," the cabbie repeated for the tenth time.

"Let's just get out," Callie shot the driver a wicked look. "They'll probably be able to help us inside."

Freddy paid the fare and they both walked inside the building.

"Can I help jous?" a beautiful young woman leaned over the front desk.

"Yes, we're looking for the Casa de Salud."

"I'm supposed to check in for surgery this evening," Freddy interrupted Callie's explanation. "Can you please give us the proper directions?"

"Casa de Salud. Jous are here," she repeated for a second time in less than perfect English.

"But... but I thought it was a Mexican hospital," Freddy muttered in disbelief.

"Si, is hospital," she smiled. "Name?"

"Frederick Joseph Nally," he included his middle name as if worried they might have another Frederick Nally hiding out in a back room.

"Sex change," the woman read. "Ready now?" she motioned for him to follow her into a back room.

"Hold on," Callie clamped her hand down on Freddy's forearm. "We gotta talk about this," she nervously whispered in his ear, consciously steering her roommate toward the building's front door.

Back on the sidewalk, Freddy turned around to take another look at the building.

"It sure doesn't look anything like I imagined it would."

"Let's just go, okay?" Callie begged. "I've got a bad feeling about this."

"The web site said they've performed hundreds of sex changes for men and women all over the world."

"They lied," she began to yell. "You know people will do that to get your money!"

"There were testimonial, and pictures."

"I don't care if the doctor included his fingerprints. This place just isn't right," Callie said. She wanted Freddy to take time to think; he needed to understand just what was going on before he made any rash decisions. "Come on," Callie waved her arms in hopes of flagging down a cab. We gotta get outta here.

"I'm staying," Freddy calmly announced.

"What?"

"I said I'm staying."

"Oh Freddy, you can't," Callie began to cry. "This just isn't right."

"Right?" he started to yell. "I'll tell you what's not right, it's me," he dropped his hand down and viciously grabbed his own crotch. "I'm the one who needs to be fixed, and this... this Casa de Salud... it's gonna fix me."

"No. Please don't go," she resorted to heartfelt begging.

"Callie, go back to the hotel. I'll have a nurse call you as soon as I'm out of surgery."

"I'll just wait."

"You can't wait," he argued. "Besides, surgery is gonna take six to eight hours. Just go back to the hotel. I promise I'll have someone call, alright"

"I can't leave you here."

"Well, you're gonna have to." Then, without standing around for the remainder of the argument, Freddy waved goodbye and disappeared back inside the building.

———————

She had no idea how long the phone had been ringing, or how many times she had slammed down the receiver. This time, she was going to find out exactly who was calling at this ungodly hour, and give them a *fucking* piece of her mind.

"What?"

"Julia?"

"No, it's the fucking Easter bunny," she snarled.

"Well then, get all your eggs in a basket, cuz Peter Rabbit's coming over to pick you up."

"Who is this?" she demanded, tired of the games.

"It's Boyd. 'Member me and my brother Pete, from the other day? We were talking about making movies and shit like that?"

"Boyd, I remember you," Julia struggled to sit up on the couch; simultaneously reaching for her smokes and lighter.

"You still looking for a little work?"

"Always," she took a drag off her cigarette.

"Well, here's what I got. I need a chick for a DP, and two blow jobs with the Coon brothers."

"The Coon brothers," Julia couldn't help but moan. "Those guys are hung like fucking stallions."

"It pays a thousand bucks."

"Yeah, but a double penetration, and I still gotta blow them both?"

"I'll give you twelve hundred?" Boyd began to bargain.

"How about the DP, one blowjob, and I'll jack the other off?"

"Fine, but I can only pay you nine fifty."

"And everybody's wrapped, none of that bare-backed shit" Julia threw in as a rider.

"That'll work," Boyd lit his own smoke on the other end of the line. "Now about that friend of yours? She still looking to film a little scat?"

"Yup."

"Well, I called a couple dumpers I knew, and the only guy filming scat right now is Siggy."

"Siggy? I don't know anybody named Siggy."

"Sure your do. Sigmund, you know, Manny's older brother."

Julia silently nodded.

"So, can you be here by noon? We'd like to get this wrapped up today."

"Sure. Give me the address," Julia quickly scribbled down the information. "And just so there's no confusion, I film today, I get paid today."

"We're both pros," Boyd chuckled on the other end of the line. "I promise that the Coon brothers will be the only ones fucking you."

———————

Coffee cup firmly clenched in her hand, Julia snuck out of the house and quickly ran over to her neighbor Martha's.

"Please," she begged. "I know it's for a really long time, but I'll give you double. I'll pay you eighty bucks."

"Shit, for eighty bucks, I'll even clean your house, too."

"Perfect, so can you come over in half an hour? I'd like to explain Serena's medications to you before I gotta go."

Martha nodded, suddenly deciding that it might be a good idea to pack herself a little picnic lunch for her extended stay.

Julia ran back down the sidewalk, and straight into her bedroom, only stopping for a minute to pick up the wads of tissue Serena had tossed down on the floor throughout the night.

"Honey, I'm going out, but I'll be back before bed," Julia tried to explain. "Martha, the woman who stayed with you before, she's gonna be back. You like her, don't you?"

No response.

"Well, I'll have my phone, as usual." Although Serena wouldn't answer, Julia could see she was still breathing by the rising and falling of her chest. A time would come to worry about her psychological therapy, but right now, Julia just needed to take care of life's basic necessities. "When I come back, I'll bring you some sour cream potato chips. I know how much you love them."

Serena's only response was a huge sigh as Julia turned to strip her clothes off, before stepping into the shower.

"You bitch," Serena suddenly sneered, the pounding water of Julia's shower drowning out the venom escaping from her lips. She couldn't believe that Julia would just flaunt that perfect body when she was reduced to lying in bed, like a piece of rotting flesh.

She had no life, and no future. Julia, on the other hand, she had it all. She still had her body, and all the men who wanted to touch her. When Julia stood exposed in front of a mirror, people didn't flinch, they didn't have to turn away to hide their disgust.

But that would soon end. Serena had a plan. Just because her mouth hadn't been working, didn't mean her brain had been idle too.

———————————

"I got cold chicken," Martha called out to Serena.

"No, thank you," she smiled sweetly. "I don't know if Julia told you, but I haven't been able to really hold anything down lately."

"Oh child, that's just terrible," she returned to the bedroom.

"I know," Serena grimaced. "I'm just so hungry, but my stomach turns flops every time I think of real food."

"We gotta get something into your belly," Martha argued. "How about some chicken noodle soup?"

"Julia tired that. I just threw it up all over the floor."

"Well then, I don't know."

"I have an idea," Serena nodded her head. "I've been craving a strawberry shake. I was wondering if you could help me get dressed and I'd just walk to the grocer on the corner and get myself one. They have an ice cream machine in the back of the store."

"Ice cream, huh? Well, that kinda makes sense."

"It does to me too." Serena struggled to sit up. "I think I'll be able to get dressed, I'll just need a little help with my shoes."

"No," Martha suddenly changed her tune. "I don't think you should leave the house. I'll run and get it for ya. Strawberry?"

"Yeah, I just love pink," she continued to ramble. "But Martha, could you help me get dressed before you go. I'm so sick and tired of sleeping in this nightgown. I just wanna sit up on the couch for a couple of minutes while you're off at the grocer's."

Dressed in one of Julia's grey sweatshirts, a pair of pink bikini panties, and a matching pair of baggy grey sweat pants, Serena allowed herself to be led to the couch.

"Can you please hand me the remote control. I think I need to catch up on my soaps."

"Damn girl, when I get back, I'll fill ya in. I know what's happening on every show."

Serena flashed Martha her most appreciative smile, settling back onto the living room couch as the woman slowly began to waddle off down the front steps.

She waited another obligatory ten seconds, and then Serena carefully pulled herself up and shuffled over to Julia's *dope bin,* hidden amongst the kitchen canisters.

"Fuck me," she groaned, extracting the last two hand-rolled joints from the metal tin. Not willing to waste what little time she had, Serena sparked up the first joint while quickly dialing for a cab.

The way she figured it, she had probably no more than twenty to twenty-five minutes before Martha realized the grocer didn't sell ice cream and managed to drag her fat ass home. If the cab hadn't arrived by then, she'd be hooped.

With each drag, Serena felt a little bit better. The weed must have been top grade even to touch her pain, so she gratefully continued to inhale the marijuana smoke, puffing on the joint as she slowly stumbled through the house.

By the time the cabbie rang the doorbell, Serena was packed and ready to go.

"Where to?" He asked.

Serena recited the address from memory; carefully leaning back into the seat to count the small amount of cash she'd manage to grinch from Julia's purse over the past few days.

"That's a pretty rough area of town," the driver caught Serena's eye in his rear-view mirror. "You sure that's where you wanna go?"

"Just drive," she snapped. "Or do I need to call," she stopped to look at his ID, "Sunshine Cabs and report driver five ninety-seven?"

"Never mind." He returned his eyes to the road, silently kicking himself for even bothering to give a shit.

After paying the driver his fare, Serena gingerly pulled herself out of the car and slowly shuffled toward the front door.

"Who's that?" a voice yelled out as soon as her foot hit the first wooden step.

"It's me," she answered, confident that the sound of her voice would do the trick.

As the front door swung open, Serena was immediately hit with the smell—a combination of rotten food, dead air, and unwashed bodies.

"Where's Keith?"

"Sleeping?"

"Can I come in?"

"Suit yourself." The girl stepped aside to allow her entrance. "You wanna a beer?"

"Why not," Serena shrugged, not as if she cared whether the booze reacted with her meds.

"So, you Serena?"

"Yeah, that's me," she nodded, nervously tucking a strand of hair behind her ear.

"I thought so. Keith has a picture of you by his bed. I think it was a party or something."

"My seventeenth birthday, a couple months ago." She dropped her eyes, digging for the remaining joint she'd tucked in her bag.

Passing the weed back and forth, both women took the opportunity to mellow out, letting the drug work its magic.

"Nother beer?" the girl asked, standing up to grab a fresh drink.

"Actually, you guys got any heroin? I'm looking to buy."

"I got some," she shrugged. "How much you wanna buy?"

Reaching down, Serena pulled out Julia's small collection of gold jewelry, letting the handful of pieces tumble out onto the couch.

"Let's see what we got," the girl returned to inspect the merchandise. Truly only interested in the emerald ring with the tiny diamond baguettes, she decided she might as well take it all.

"I got a bag of *sealies*. They're ones. You interested?" She offered Serena a plastic sandwich bag of ten, pre-filled syringes. Each sealed work was preloaded with a 1cc dose of heroin.

Serena knew she was courting death. Most dealers picked up used needles left behind by junkies, refilled them, and then resealed the bags for sale. She was taking a major risk, but at this stage, she really didn't give a shit.

"You know it's *Poison*." The girl tried to tempt her with the drug's street name. "Really top grade shit. Sorry I don't have any *Cash* left, but I sold all that two nights ago. So, we dealing, or we drinking beer?"

"We're dealing, but can you throw in a tie off? Mine's ripped."

Returning from the basement, the girl dropped a two-foot length of surgical tubing in Serena's lap before carefully handing her the bag of pre-filled syringes.

"You're good to go."

"Thanks Babe," Serena slowly stood up, the pain in her chest a constant reminder of her condition.

"What about Keith? He'll be pissed that he missed you."

"Tell him thanks for the introduction," she slowly waved the bag of needles. "Tell him I wouldn't have been able to do it without him."

"I'll tell him," the girl laughed, walking off to grab herself a fresh beer.

Chapter
Thirty-Nine

*"Fasten your seatbelts. It's going
to be a bumpy night."*

—*All About Eve, 1950*

"How ya feeling now?" Justice quickly pulled off his work boots before rushing over to check on his wife.

"Mommy sleeping," Mary sat up on the edge of the couch, rubbing her eyes from her position underneath the shared quilt.

"Sarah," Justice gently stroked her face.

"I'm so groggy," she moaned. "And my head's pounding all the time."

Justice reached over and picked up his wife's prescription bottle, quickly counting out the pills to make sure she'd swallowed only the one dose since he'd left for work.

"Mommy snores."

Justice plucked his daughter off the couch and walked straight to the kitchen, pouring Mary a glass of milk before rummaging in the fridge for something to fill his own stomach.

"Sorry I didn't make you lunch," Sarah appeared, hanging onto one of the kitchen chairs for support. "I didn't even hear you leave this morning."

"Don't worry. I can take care of myself. Besides, Dr. Clifford said the pills would make you drowsy. So don't worry about it, he said it would only last for another two or three days."

"I don't know Justice, I think I feel worse than…"

"What'd you say, sweetie?" He pushed the juice aside to reach for the jar of jam.

When Justice turned around, his wife was lying on the floor, blood beginning to trickle out of her nose.

———————

Starting to feel the exhaustion creep up through her body, Serena knew it was time to find herself a place, somewhere nice and peaceful. Somewhere pretty, where she could shoot up and not be bothered. Last thing in the world she needed was to get jumped, or worse yet, gang raped when she was in the middle of fixing.

"Nice." She slowly started to climb the embankment, her muscles screaming in pain every step of the way. "Almost there," Serena encouraged herself, forced to take a thirty-second break before continuing her climb. When she finally reached the top of the dirt mound, she took a couple minutes to analyze her surroundings. The entire neighborhood was bustling with action, laid out street by street below her eyes as if waiting for some giant kid to sit down with a fist full of matchbox cars.

"Hey lady," a construction worker yelled up to the top of the man-made pile. "You can't be up there. You better get off this site before you get hurt."

Serena flipped him the bird, turned around, and continued onward with her trek toward the tree line. Exhausted with the effort, but satisfied that she'd sufficiently removed herself from harms' way; Serena picked a grassy spot and carefully lowered herself down to her knees, mindful not to crush a small patch of wild daisies that had managed to cling to life through the early morning frosts.

Ripping open the plastic bag to access her cache of syringes, she took the time to line up the ten little soldiers on the grass. They were her little heroin army. Not brought along to fight against her, they had come to do battle for her.

She'd only shot up a few times before, always with Keith around to monitor her needlework, but she was a quick learner. She was completely confident that she could command the army all on her own.

She took a deep breath, determined to succeed more than ever. Serena slid the first needle with little or no fanfare into the soft upper flesh of her forearm. Forcing the plunger down with one swift movement of her thumb, her first soldier was deployed. Instantly rewarded with the desired effect, a pea-sized subcutaneous heroin blister, she continued her mission.

Shaking off the burning sensation, Serena reached for the second syringe and repeated the procedure. Within a few minutes, her left forearm had the same texture as a blood-streaked piece of bubble wrap. The blisters were on fire under her skin, their absorption taking hours instead of the instantaneous rush of a vein injection. But she didn't mind, it was all part of the master plan.

"One left." The young girl slowly kissed the remaining syringe before ordering her last soldier into the field.

She quickly tied herself off with the length of new surgical tubing; Serena carefully angled the needle so it was almost flat against the thin layer of skin covering her bulging vein. After inserting the tip lengthwise, she was careful to make sure it ran down the length of the vein, and not across it.

Satisfied that the needle was probably in deep enough, Serena slowly pulled back the plunger. Leaning in closer for a final check, she focused her eyes and watched for the telltale trickle of blood to enter the syringe, careful not to allow more than roughly a quarter inch of air to bubble in with it. Finally, she tilted the syringe upwards so the air floated toward the plunger. Serena took a second and looked up to the clear sky before closing her eyes to the reality of her world. Taking one last breath of clarity before depressing the syringe, she kissed all her worries goodbye.

Standing over his wife, Justice couldn't believe that they were back at the clinic in less than twenty-four hours.

"Tell me more about where you live," Dr. Clifford turned to Justice, suddenly wondering if Sarah's condition might be external, rather than internal.

"It's a three-bedroom house. We only just moved in." He shrugged his shoulders, not sure what the doctor really wanted to know.

"Do you work out of the house, Sarah?" He turned back toward his patient as he checked on the bag of electrolytes being pushed into her arm.

"No," she whispered, the mere act of conversation sending stabbing pains through her temples.

"Well, it looks like the blisters are receding," the doctor checked the ink marks he'd dotted around a few of the perimeters. "But I can't guarantee they won't return until we establish the cause."

"Tony, come here," the doctor called out the minute his assistant walked through the examination room. "I want you to have a look at this patient."

Tony stepped around Justice as he cradled his young daughter in his arms. "I've seen this before," Tony said, as he peered at Sarah.

"I have too," the doctor nodded his head in confirmation. "Tell me, has anyone else in the family been experiencing the sudden onslaught of unusual medical conditions?"

Justice instinctively looked toward Tony for clarification.

"What the doctor's wants to know, is if anyone else in the house has been sick lately? Maybe somebody came down with something they never had before?"

"Mathew," Sarah struggled to follow the conversation. "He's had really bad nosebleeds."

Tony and the doctor both stepped away from the table, turning their backs to confer silently.

"Justice," the doctor was the first to return. "I think I might have an idea what's wrong with your family"

"What is it?" he couldn't help but spin his head to watch Tony's sudden departure.

"Pull up a chair," the doctor motioned toward the stools lining the back wall.

"Here it is," Tony reappeared, handing the doctor the manila file.

Dr. Clifford took a second to review a few of his notes before pulling up his own chair and taking a seat.

"I have seen this a few times before," he admitted, disappointingly shaking his head. "I'm going to name off a few symptoms, and you tell me if anything rings a bell."

Justice set Mary down on the floor and leaned forward, giving the doctor his undivided attention.

"Migraine headaches, chronic nosebleeds, rashes, and excruciating blisters."

"We have those," Justice rose to his feet and walked over to his wife's side as she quietly continued to moan.

"There's more," Tony reminded everyone.

"Tony's right," the doctor read. "The first range of symptoms can escalate into painful liver infections, stomach distress, ulcers, and even diabetes."

"What in the hell is it?" Justice demanded, no longer interested in taking a passive role in his wife's diagnosis.

"Well, we've only run into this twice before, although I hear it's getting more and more common all the time."

"What is it?" Justice demanded, his patience wearing as thin as rice paper.

Dr. Clifford closed his file, stood up, and walked over to the examination table.

"I can't be absolutely positive without definitive testing, but this resembles the symptoms of people who work or live around methamphetamine labs."

"I don't understand." Justice reached up to stroke his wife's dampened forehead. "We're not drug dealers. Sarah and I don't even smoke cigarettes."

"Okay," Tony relented. "So maybe you aren't cooking meth. But you were exposed to it somewhere."

Pulling out a stack of papers, the doctor began reciting from a typed page of information. "There are eight main ingredients in crystal methamphetamine labs. Let me read their side effects.

"*Iodine Crystal*—vapors can cause eye and skin irritation, and breathing problems. *Hydrogen Chloride*—inhalation can cause chemical burns to the eyes, nose, skin, and severe respiratory problems. *Acetone*—inhalation or ingestion can cause severe gastric irritation, and comas. *Lithium Metal*—contact can cause severe burns."

Justice stood motionless, attempting to digest the glut of information as the doctor continued his lecture.

"*Anhydrous Ammonia*—inhalation can cause severe respiratory problems along with eye and mucous membrane damage. *Red Phosphorous*—vapors can irritate the nose, throat, lungs, and eyes. And finally, *Freon*—inhalation can result in sudden cardiac arrest and severe lung damage. Of course, this is all mixed with our ever popular over the counter drug—available to anyone with a few spare bucks—*Pseudoephedrine*, common in most drugstore cold medicines. And here's the scariest fact of all," the doctor paused to make sure everyone was paying attention. "There isn't a single ingredient that you or I couldn't pick up at our local hardware store, pharmacy, or farm supply store."

"I've been listening to everything you said, but I don't understand a damn word," Justice wiped his eyes, squeezing his wife's hand in a show of strength.

Tony stepped in, hoping his homeboy logic might make a little more sense. "Justice, nobody is accusing you or your wife of being drug dealers, or even of touching the stuff. What we're saying is that someone used to cook up the drugs in your house, before you moved in. When they cooked it, the chemicals stuck to your walls, your floors, and even the wooden doors. You can't wash it away; it's embedded right in the two-by-fours. And those really toxic vapors, and leftover residue, are slowly poisoning your family."

"But Sarah cleaned," he argued in their own defense. "You should see how my wife washed and scrubbed before we even moved in. All them germs were definitely gone."

"These aren't germs, and you can't wash them away." The doctor decided to reclaim the floor. "But the good news is that most patients inflicted with the contamination recovered, almost immediately after moving out of their contaminated house."

"Move where?" Justice's eyes flicked back and forth between Tony and the doctor. "We just moved in. We ain't got the money to move out."

"You have to," the doctor demanded. "Your family's lives depend on it."

Justice watched his wife close her eyes in total exhaustion.

"How come I ain't been sick like my wife and kids? I live there too, you know?"

"It's a simple case of exposure," Tony walked over and handed Mary a candy sucker, not sure if she'd even be interested, now that her cheeks also appeared flushed. "You work out of the house, and from what I understand, time off is usually spent in the yard, right?"

"I got a lot to do," Justice began to make excuses. "The yard's a mess, and the fence, it's near ready to fall down."

"No one's blaming you," Dr. Clifford picked up his ear thermometer to check on Sarah's temperature.

"So, what do I do now?' he threw his hands up in the air.

"You find out if it's true," Tony simply stated.

"How?" he looked straight into Tony's eyes.

"I'd start with the cops. See if they have any record of a meth lab bust at your address. At least you'll know for sure."

Justice nodded; absolutely terrified at the prospect of having to take his wife and daughter back to that house.

———————

Buck naked, tubes sticking out of his arms, Freddy felt himself begin to shake underneath the thin cotton blanket.

"Excuse me," he called out to the nurse busying herself with what looked like some form of chemical sterilization. "Umh, I was wondering if I'd get to meet the doctor before surgery?"

"Si señor," she grinned. "Surgery today," the nurse repeated in almost a singsong voice.

"Doctor, por favor," he begged, his Spanish about as good as his Klingon.

"Si," the nurse patted him on the shoulder before leaving the room.

"Señor Nally," a man walked into the room, eyes glued to a handful of paperwork.

"Yes, Freddy Nally," he worked up the courage to smile. "Do you speak English?"

"Yes I do," the doctor chuckled. "I take it you don't speak any Spanish?"

If he hadn't been hook up to a thousand IVs, Freddy would have leapt up off the table directly into the doctor's arms.

"This is not what I expected," he started to ramble. "I thought I was going to be operated on in a big hospital, with a cafeteria, and a gift shop."

"This is not the Estados Unidos," the doctor reminded him. "If you wanted American style surgery, you should have booked an appointment in the US."

Freddy finally heard the doctor's message loud and clear. "Sorry, but I'm just a little scared. I'm not really sure what to expect."

"You downloaded our post surgery information, didn't you?"

Freddy nodded.

"Well, then you know that most of your energies in the next three days will be spent on pain management."

"I read that," Freddy admitted, "but I really didn't understand what it meant."

Slipping his arms into a surgical gown, the doctor took a second to walk over to his patient's bedside.

"If means you're going to wake up and be fairly uncomfortable after surgery, and our job here will be to make you as comfortable as possible."

"That sounds good," Freddy smiled.

"You're flying home upon release?" The doctor struggled to recall the patient's personal information.

"Yes, my friend Callie is waiting for me at our hotel. Actually," he suddenly remembered his promise, "can you please have a nurse call the hotel as soon as I'm out of surgery? The name and the number are both in my file."

"Not a problem," the doctor smiled. "Now, do you have any more questions before we begin our procedure?"

"Did anybody ever wake up, regretting what they'd done?"

"No." The doctor turned up the patient's IV drip, watching Freddy's eyes began to flutter in response to the influx of sedative.

Chapter Forty

"A boy's best friend is his mother."

—*Psycho, 1960*

E ven after downing downed three quick shots of tequila mixed with lukewarm cans of ginger ale, Callie found she was still vibrating. No matter what she tried, she just couldn't relax, and every minute spent away from Freddy was just making her feel worse. "That's it," she announced. She grabbed her wallet, and suddenly ran down the stairs in hopes of flagging a passing cab.

Grateful that the evening temperature had eventually dropped a few degrees, Callie still found the car's re-circulated air to be little more than stifling.

As the cab fought the oncoming traffic moving toward them on the Avenida Revolución, the driver worked to keep his car in a free-flowing lane.

"Excuse me, can you please turn on the air conditioning?" she politely asked.

"Too much gasolina," the driver shook his head, left arm hanging out the window as he intermittently hand-signaled his turns.

"Oh no, it looks closed," Callie muttered to herself the minute the cab pulled in front of the darkened building.

"Clinic closed," the driver echoed her sentiment. "Where to now?"

She handed him ten pesos, the cost of her last trip, and Callie hoped out of the car and ran up the main path.

"Hello, anybody here?" She hammered on the door's wooden frame. "Please unlock the door; I know you're in there!" She changed her tone and began shouting as loud as she could. Callie was determined to draw someone's attention, anyone—especially since she'd spotted a small sliver of light creeping out from underneath one of the inside doors.

"Lady, hey lady," the driver yelled from his passenger's window. "The clinic is closed, you gotta come back tomorrow."

"My friend's in there," she began to wail, resorting to brute force as she wrapped her fingers around the wrought iron bars covering the glass door and yanked with all her might.

"Oye chica, just relax," the driver stepped out of his car and casually lit a cigarette. "Look, I can get you some pills."

Dropping her hands, Callie suddenly realized just how frantic she must have appeared for the driver to assume she was some kind of desperate pill freak. "I don't need your drugs." She shook her head and stomped to the back of the building.

In the back alley, no one had bothered to landscape with succulent plants, or even to slap a pleasing yellow coat of paint over the concrete blocks. It was flat grey, with mounds and mounds of plastic garbage bags lining both sides of the metal door.

Something had already gotten into the lower ranks of garbage, tearing open the plastic and dragging out piles of blood-soaked bandaging and discarded medical supplies.

"Oh my God!" Callie dropped to her knees, instantly puking the contents of her stomach, a grainy paste comprised of tequila shots and granola bars.

"Tourists," the cabbie muttered, leaning against the rear corner of the building as he watched the teenage girl gag and spit. He decided to bide his time until it looked like she'd recovered her air and was able to speak.

"Oh Freddy." She pulled her hands up to her face. "Where are you?"

"He ain't here." The driver slowly stepped forward, pulling his cigarette package out of his breast pocket to offer her a smoke.

"No thanks." She shook her head, wiping her mouth and then her eyes.

"You can't wait back here." He nodded toward the fallen chain link fence. "When the sun goes down for the night, the pack of stray dogs that made this mess will come back. They're hungry; don't want them thinking that you're food."

"But I *really* need to find my friend, Freddy Nally. He checked in for surgery today, and I can't find anyone who'll tell me how he's doing."

"This ain't a hospital, this is just an office. They'd put him under; then drive him over to where they operate and stuff."

"Why?"

"Break ins, hold ups. Don't want no-one—locals or tourists—to know where they keep their drugs and supplies. Too much trouble."

Brushing the powdery soil off her knees, Callie stood up and looked back toward the rear of the building, suddenly noticing a set of tire tracks leading from the back door straight to the main street.

"Can you take me to their hospital, where Freddy is? I can get you cash." She hoped to tempt him.

"I told you, I don't know where it is. Nobody knows. That's what keeps the doctor safe."

"But all the bloody garbage," she sniveled, pointing to the open bags of refuge.

"They bring it back; throw it down here for pick-up. I guess if they left it for pick-up at their secret place, everybody would know the location, and nobody would be safe."

"Safe," Callie mumbled. "Do you think my friend is safe?"

"What kind of surgery was he having?"

"It's kind of embarrassing," she shrugged.

"This is Tijuana, Chica. People come here to take care of embarrassing little problems," he knowingly shook his head

"So, you're telling me that I just have to sit and wait 'til Freddy is brought back?" Callie waved her hand at the dilapidated building.

"Well, you could come to a party with me. Have a few cervezas, and blow off a little steam," he winked.

"No, I'll wait." She turned and trudged back to the parked car.

"Where you going?" the driver picked up the pace and hustled after her.

"Back to my hotel. What in the hell else am I supposed to do?"

"There's an extra eight-hundred dollars in the patient's money belt," the nurse reported to the doctor as he sat back with his coffee and Marlboro lights.

"Eight hundred, eh?" he mulled over the amount. "Take half. The kid will need a few bucks for cab rides and food."

"Where's the drop off?" his wife continued to mop the bloodstained floor underneath Freddy's unconscious body.

"He's at the Palacio de Color Rosa."

"I like the Palacio," his nurse smiled. "They have that large freight elevator, and for a couple bucks, the desk clerk always flips me the key.

Rising up from his chair with a lit cigarette still dangling from his bottom lip, the doctor walked over to have another look at his work.

"You know, this turned out pretty good."

"And he's so young." His wife straightened her back, slowly leaning across the operating table, shifting most of her weight to the wooden mop handle. "He's gonna heal up nice; his skin so elastic and forgiving."

Repositioning himself at the foot of the table, the doctor once more evaluated the symmetry of his breast implants. "Don't think they're too small, do ya? Cuz I'd have liked a bigger size, but these," he waved his hand at a pesky flying bug, "and two more sets of 500s, are all that's left in stock."

"Absolutely not," the nurse-in-training stepped up to the table. "Look at the patient's shoulders. He's a small frame, so going any larger than a 300cc implant would have been ridiculous."

"I agree, besides," the doctor shrugged, "he can always come back, and have them changed out after his skin has stretched at little more."

Setting down her mop, the doctor's newest wife/nurse-in-training, left the room for a minute, quickly returning with a box of stents, ranging in size from one, to one and a half inches in diameter. Ten inches long, with four to six inches of length for insertion—they appeared quite menacing—but they were a necessary evil of post-op care, required to keep the new constructed vagina from healing closed.

"I'm thinking this one," she held up a mid-range size."

"Don't forget the instruction package." The doctor handed over a photocopied page.

"I never do."

"Well, I should pull up the van." He crushed his cigarette on the concrete floor, nudging it with his toe toward the sloped floor drain.

"Give me another fifteen minutes," his wife bargained. "I still wanna wipe him down and throw on a gown.

"You got five." He snatched the four-hundred dollars off Freddy's naked belly and walked outside the garage's side door.

───────────

As she handed the driver another ten pesos for her return ride, Callie refused his offer to party for the tenth time, and quickly slipped out of his back seat.

"Here's my card," he yelled out, frantically waving his left hand. "Call me next time you need a cab."

"Thanks for the information," Callie forced herself to smile, dying to get upstairs and take a shower.

He finally relented, blowing her a silent kiss goodbye and pulling away from the curb.

It was nearly eight p.m. and Callie hadn't eaten anything other than tequila and a couple of granola bars, which she'd thrown up behind the clinic anyway. It was definitely time to put something in her stomach before she got a migraine.

Showered and changed, she forced herself to put one foot in front of the other. She wandered out of the hotel and looked for the first hamburger or pizza joint she could find. Not in the mood for any of the local cuisine, she just wanted to stuff down a few carbs, and hit the sack. Tomorrow was going to be hell, and waking up with a splitting headache wasn't going to make it any easier.

With her mission accomplished, a pizza box tucked under her arm, she slowly made her way back to the hotel. Without even realizing it, the evening air was somehow clearing her head, the walk almost rejuvenated her spirit.

Pulling one knee up toward her chest, Callie managed to balance the pizza box and two cans of soda on her leg while working the worn hotel key into her door.

"Come on, baby," she whispered, relieved when the tumbler finally clicked over and allowed her entry into her own room.

"Holy shit," she muttered in disbelief, the cardboard box and aluminum cans all falling to the floor with a tumbling thud.

"Ahhh," Freddy moaned, as his bloated form lay motionless on one of the hotel beds; his chest and lower abdomen swollen to unnatural proportions.

"Freddy?" Callie shrieked, her voice piercing the air and embedding itself in the smoke-stained walls.

As the first light of morning started to filter through the hotel room's curtains, the surrounding transformation became obvious. Callie had an impromptu intensive care unit set up, and was doing her absolute best to care for her roommate's post-operative needs.

"Just keep watching the drainage tube," the hotel desk clerk/ medic had carefully pointed out. "If you see any dark black clots, we might have a problem, but if this stuff just keeps draining out," he pointed to the wash basin of bloody fluid, "then your friend will probably be fine."

"How much longer will it drain?" She picked up her pad of paper to make yet another note.

"Usually twenty-four to forty-eight hours. So," Juan quickly calculated in his head, "I think it's safe to say that we can pull the tube out tonight, or tomorrow morning at the latest."

"Will you be around?" Callie quickly raised her head, terrified that she might be left alone to struggle with Freddy's care.

"I'll be working the front desk 'til four this afternoon, and I promise not to leave without checking in with you."

"Thank you," she wearily nodded her head.

"Now, about his fluids," the man began to carefully explain. "He's lost a lot of blood and it's still draining, so while his body makes more, he's gonna get dehydrated. As soon as he's awake, give him small pieces of ice pops to suck on. The sugar and the water will do the trick, and they're only a couple pesos a box."

"Ice pops," she continued to record. "What about his bandages? They're getting really soaked, especially the ones around his crotch."

Juan dug through the two small bags of medical supplies perched at the foot of Freddy's bed, and confirmed the usual contents. "Don't touch the bandages until I come up later. We really don't wanna expose any of the incisions to the air unless we have to. Twenty-four hours in the same wrapping won't hurt him, as long as it's clean underneath."

Turning her back to dig into her suitcase, Callie pulled out one hundred dollars, gratefully handing the man the cash payment.

"Gracias, señorita." Juan quickly folded the two fifties in half and shoved them down into his uniform pocket.

"I don't know how someone could do this." She walked over to Freddy's unconscious form. "How can you operate on a person, and then just dump them in a hotel with no one around to make sure they're fine?"

"This is Tijuana, miss. You tend to get what you pay for."

"You've seen this before, haven't you?"

"I let them up the freight elevator," he shrugged his shoulders.

"Who are they, and why all the secrets?"

"Don't know for sure." He retreated to the washroom to scrub the blood off his hands. "But even if I did have those answers, I'd still be keeping them to myself."

Callie checked her notes one last time, taking a second to locate the pill bottle of pain medication she found in the delivery bag.

"Two pills every two hours," she repeated for clarification.

"Yep, that's what it says. And don't let him talk you into more. Don't want your friend overdosing right before our eyes."

Nodding, Callie noticed that beads of sweat were beginning to form on Freddy's forehead.

"I think he's got an infection," she started to panic. "Is he gonna die?"

"Bonita, you gotta relax if you're gonna be any help to your friend," Juan gingerly patted her shoulder. "That is just a case of cold sweats, very common with people who've been put under for five or six hours. His body's just pushing out the anesthetic is all. Nothing to worry about, nothing you can do."

"Do you think he's in really bad pain right now?"

"He's sleeping now, the time for pain will come when he wakes up, so I suggest you let him sleep as long as you can. The longer he sleeps, the more time he has to heal."

"I can't thank you enough." She wiped her eyes. "And somebody wanna tell me what I'm supposed to do with this?" She waved the single page of photocopied post-op instructions that had been furnished by the clinic.

"You'd have been fine," Juan comforted her.

"I guess I probably would have," Callie turned her attention back to Freddy. "But what about him? What if he had come here alone?"

As he struggled against the bright light burning his eyes, Freddy fought to speak, mouth as dry as a handful of cotton.

Callie, what's happened to me? Why am I in this hotel room instead of a hospital bed, and why does everything hurt so bad... just came out as a barely audible, "Caaaaa."

"Freddy!" Callie's head jerked up from her task before immediately rushing over to his side. "Can you hear me, Freddy?"

He blinked, his eyelids the only voluntary muscles presently under his control.

"You're safe," Callie gently stroked the back of his right palm, the skin still swollen and bruised from what appeared to be intravenous lines.

"I... I... I caaaa," his eyes closed, exhausted from the effort, his brain once again fading off into another drug-induced sleep.

Callie returned to her position on the second bed, digging through the assorted contents of the post-operative bag.

"Cotton padding, gauze, medical tape, and two large tubes of antibiotic cream," she announced to no one in particular, setting aside the supplies that she would need to change Freddy's dressings. The two extra-wide tension bandages, tweezers, and the small butterfly bandages were obviously intended for his return trip home.

Everything appeared to make sense; everything except for the long plastic tube, cone shaped on one end, and open on the other. Marked off in ten, one-inch measurements, Callie turned it over and over, attempting to figure out exactly what it was supposed to be used for. "Duratek Plastics, Canada," she read aloud off the side, wondering if it was maybe some kind of rudimentary measurement for a liquid medications. Digging back down into the second bag, Callie was unable to find any vials or bottles, concluding that it had been packed by mistake. Ready to drop it back on the bed, she finally noticed two small words printed in raised plastic circling the base. "Vaginal Stent," she read aloud, lifting the white plastic up to her eye just as someone inserted a key in her hotel's lock.

"It's just me," Juan announced, walking in with a tray of fresh supplies. "I brought you a little supper," he nodded toward the plate of tacos, topped off with a huge scoop of rice and beans. "Staff supper," he shrugged, "but it's free."

"I appreciate it." Callie watched him gently set down the tray, surprised that a young man in his late twenties or early thirties would have such a tender bedside manner. "We've been kind of trying to make this trip on a bit of a budget."

"I figured." After he arranged the tray of food, he turned and plucked the stent out of Callie's hand.

"You know, I've been trying to figure out exactly what that's for. Do you know?"

"It's a stent."

"Yeah, I know that, but I still don't know what it's for," she nervously giggled.

"Well," Juan dropped down into one of the empty chairs, "it's used after sex reassignment surgery to stretch out the neo-vaginal cavity. You know," he pointed toward Freddy's groin. "During recovery, the patient must constantly dilate to gradually widen and maintain the vaginal opening."

"Oh," Callie's face flushed a deep crimson red. "I never knew."

"Don't freak out." He slipped the knapsack off his shoulder and pulled out two cold bottles of Corona beer. "Unless you've been through it, how in the hell would you have known?"

"Have… well… are you… umh," she stammered, unsure of how to word her next question.

"No, I'm not saving up money for a sex change. I was actually training to be a physician back in Texas until my parents were killed in a house fire. I left university to come back home to Mexico, and help support my two sisters until they're old enough to be on their own."

"I'm sorry, Juan. I think you'd have made an excellent doctor. And your English is so…"

"My parents moved to Mexico from the United States to teach English before I was even born. My mother home-schooled my sisters and me. She hoped that one day she could convince my father to move us all back across the border. But the fire..."

"Cal... llliiieee," Freddy groans interrupted Juan's personal revelations.

Instantly checking his watch, Juan looked into the young woman's eyes. "Your friend is awake. Now stay calm. He's going to be very agitated from the pain, and disorientated by the move. He may not even remember his surgery."

"Will he remember me?'

"Let's go see," Juan helped Callie up off the bed.

Chapter
Forty-One

"As God is my witness, I'll never he hungry again."
—*Gone With the Wind, 1939*

Offered a chair in front of the detective's desk, Justice sat, nervously balancing his daughter on the edge of his knees.

"This is the complete list?" Detective LaBreque looked down at Dr. Clifford's handwritten letter.

"Yes, but me and my family are only having the ones with checkmarks," he announced, clearing his throat in an attempt to stay calm.

"Well, I can tell you that this is nothing new to us. We see on average about one contaminated household a month."

"So what do we do now?"

"Get the hell out of there, plain and simple."

"But I can't afford to right now. Maybe after a month, but right now I spent the damage deposit money on extra's for fixing up the place."

"What'd you say the owner's name was?" the detective searched through his papers.

"Murray, Murray Brown."

"Oh yeah," he stood up to pull a file out of a neighboring cabinet. "How about you let me make a few calls, and I'll get back to you later tonight?"

"Sure, you can call me anytime. I'm heading home straight away," Justice promised. "I need to check on my wife Sarah."

"And stay out of that basement," detective LaBreque waved his finger. "The police report says that the meth lab busted in your house was confined to the lower level. I suggest you nail up the basement door and make sure nobody goes down there until we get to the bottom of this."

"Thanks," Justice stood up, thrusting out his hand.

"You did the right thing coming in here. Your landlord had no legal right renting out that condemned house, and I think he might even be responsible for a little compensation. A few bucks for your pain and suffering. You know a good lawyer?"

"I don't think so," Justice shook his head.

"Don't worry," the detective raised his hand. "There'll be plenty of time for that later. First, I need to investigate this situation. Go home, Mr. Mallory. I'll call you tonight. I promise."

The minute Julia turned on the power to her phone it began to ring, simultaneously beeping in her ear to let her know she also had a fresh batch of messages. "Hello," she answered, as she wiped a fresh gob of cum off the side of her neck.

"Julia, where you been, child?"

"Working. Who is this?" she barked, not impressed with the caller's tone.

"It's Martha. I... I can't find Serena. I went to the grocer's right after you left, but they didn't have any, so I just bought a couple drumsticks, but when I got home, she wasn't there," the woman summed up in a flourish.

"Slow the fuck down," Julia turned her naked back toward the bathroom mirror, slumping back against the counter. "What's this about Serena?"

"She's gone!" Martha cried, this time her simple message was received loud and clear.

Julia told the woman just to sit tight, disconnecting the line as she simultaneously bent down to grab her clothes.

"Nice job, Babe." Boyd walked unannounced into the bathroom. "You wanna come with me and Pete, maybe grab some ribs or something else? You've gotta be starving after a workout like that."

"Can I just get my cash?" Julia jumped around in circles on her right foot, attempting to shove her left down into the denim of her pant leg.

"What's the rush? I'm offering you free eats, and you're blowing me off."

"Emergency." Julia finally buttoned up her jeans.

"What kind of emergency?"

"Why?" She stopped dressing long enough to look Boyd in the eye, genuinely surprised that he'd take such a personal interest in her problems.

"I don't know, you just seemed so stressed, and you don't strike me as the type of chick who flies off the handle for fuckin' no reason."

"It's my friend, Serena." Julia pulled her tee shirt down over her naked breasts. "She's been really sick, laid up in bed with a bad infection. I hired a lady to sit with her, and now the lady called to say she'd run off."

As he watched Julia throw her belongings into a duffle bag, Boyd grabbed his cell and barked a few orders over the phone. "Alright,

Pete's gonna finish up with everything here. You want some help? Cuz I'm free for a couple of hours."

"What?"

"You want some help?" Boyd barked. "What's the matter, you got cum in your ears?"

"No," Julia shook her head, "it's just that I'm sure you've got about a thousand other things you'd like to do first."

Leaning down to pick up Julia's bag, Boyd suddenly straightened his back. "I'm going to my car, you coming?"

Settled in the front seat, Julia began mumbling to herself, trying to figure out exactly where the girl might have run.

"This the chick who wanted to film scat?"

"Kinda." She quickly lit a smoke, sucking hard on the cigarette's filter in a frantic attempt to flood her bloodstream with nicotine. "To be honest, Serena's already filmed one. That's how she got so messed up. I was just trying to find out who might have abandoned her down at the Crystal Palace in such bad shape."

Boyd continued to drive, wondering just what he'd gotten himself into.

"Unfortunately, I don't know a lot about Serena," Julia admitted. "Shit, I don't even know where she came from."

"So what's the problem then? Don't sound to me like you owe her anything."

Turning her head sideways to look out the passenger's window, Julia debated her next statement. "Technically, I don't owe her anything, but I was the one who pierced her nipples one night when we were stoned on crack. Then only a couple days later, she went out and let some guys cover her body in shit. Serena picked up such a bad infection during that scat movie, that the doctor down at the Changeroom had to cut off her nipples and gouge out chunks of her tits just so she wouldn't get gangrene and die from it." Julia swallowed hard to extinguish the disturbing memory.

"So what now?" Boyd grabbed a smoke from Julia's package. "You *kinda* owe her, but you don't have a fucking clue where to look for her, am I right?"

"Yeah, you're right."

Boyd continued to drive, his mind whirling as he racked up the blocks.

"What she been saying lately? What kind of mood she been in since the doc cut up her tits?"

"She doesn't talk much, I was keeping her pretty stoned on painkillers and shit."

"Well, what kind of mood would you have been in?" He turned to Julia. "If somebody had cut off your tits before they rotted off their chest? What would you have done as soon as you got out of the house?"

Julia nodded, his point hitting home with a definite thud.

"We can't drive around to every crack house in the city," she realized. "Fuck, there's gotta be at least a thousand places where she could have gone to score. Besides, I don't really know any of her old friends."

"But she was living with you, right?"

"Right."

"Well, then I suggest you go home and wait. You know junkies, they're like a fucking stray cats. They eventually manage to drag their asses home."

Sitting back and waiting seemed absolutely useless, but Boyd was right, Julia really had no other option at this point.

Sipping a second cup of instant coffee, Justice continued to prowl the house. With Sarah sleeping and all three kids glued to the TV, he just couldn't settle himself down.

"Dad," Mathew suddenly appeared in the kitchen. "I need to go to the basement, but the knob won't turn, and I can't get it open."

"Don't you go there!" Justice barked, "I told you it's off limits. Don't you ever go down there again." He stomped over to make his point.

"Why Dad? I need my pajamas. Mom left them in the wash, and I ain't got nothing clean to wear to bed."

"Sleep in your sweatpants, I don't care, but you ain't going down there." He turned away from Mathew's face.

"Dad?"

"Git!" he yelled, rarely having raised his voice at his eldest son.

"What's all the screaming about?" Sarah appeared from the bedroom. "I thought you was trying to kill somebody in here."

"Sorry, honey," he absentmindedly patted her on the shoulder as he walked over to the back door, alarmed to see a shadowed figure run through their backyard.

"Go sit with the kids, Sarah."

"Why?"

Justice never answered, he just pulled out a wooden baseball bat from behind the back door and stepped out into the darkness. "Who the hell wants a beating?" he yelled, rationalizing that a good offense was his best defense.

"Justice Mallory, this is the police. Please drop your weapon," a man's voice commanded from somewhere behind his back.

"Like hell," he yelled, raising the bat up to swinging position, prepared to protect his family with brute force if necessary. By the time the scuffle was over, not only was Justice restrained in handcuffs, but two of the officers had bloody noses, and a third was nursing what appeared to be a broken rib.

"We're taking him in for assaulting a police officer," one of the cops informed Sarah minutes before they loaded her husband into the back of a police car.

Down at the station, Justice was thrown into a locked room, left to pace angrily in circles while the officers tended to their wounds.

"Mr. Mallory," Detective LaBreque said as he casually strolled into the interrogation room, throwing a small stack of paper files down on the metal desk. "Take a seat."

"I don't feel like sitting."

"It wasn't a request," the detective barked.

"Why you got me here? My wife's sick, I gotta get home and take care of her and the kids."

The cop waited for Justice to take a seat before he moved to open the files and take out a few sheets of the papers.

"I did a little checking, like I promised." Detective LaBreque began to read off his own reports. "It seems that your co-worker, Mr. Murray Brown, wasn't even aware that you had moved your family into his property. He signed a statement that he'd only promised you a couple bucks in cash for some renovation work on his condemned house. As far as he knew, you and your family were living in some kind of crowded little apartment, but he wasn't sure of the address."

"That's bullshit," Justice slammed his fist down into the table. "We had an agreement. He rented us that house, fair and square."

"Do you have any cancelled rent checks, or you going to tell me you paid cash?"

"Cash," Justice muttered.

"Well then, show me some kind of agreement, tell me where one of the officers can find it in the house."

Suddenly, Justice was scared. He started to see a pattern, and he didn't like the picture that was starting to form.

"It was done on a handshake," he continued to mutter; embarrassed that he'd been such a trusting hick. "Me and Murray worked together down at Jupiter. He said we didn't need any kind of contracts. Said those kind of papers were just for people planning on suing each other."

"What about the utilities, Mr. Mallory? If you were renting the house, why hadn't you transferred them over to your name?"

"They were included," he shook his head, "along with the cable TV."

Closing his file, Detective LaBreque rose from his seat, casually turning to wink at his captain who was listening to every word of the interrogation through the two-way mirror.

"Let's forget about the house for a moment. Why don't we talk about your truck?"

"What about my truck?"

"We found this in the glove box." The detective opened another file, carefully plucking out the Arctic Cat sales brochure, securely sealed in a clear plastic evidence bag. "You recognize this?" He slid the magazine across the table.

"Yeah, it's mine."

"Well, our lab tested it, and it came up positive for acetone and red phosphorus."

"I know!" He threw his hands in the air. You already told me that my house used to be one of them meth labs. Everything we's got is probably covered in that crap."

"Well, Mr. Mallory, that's where we have our problem. You see, your magazine isn't covered with crystal meth. It's covered with the residue released during the exact *cooking* process. These papers were present *during* the manufacturing of crystal methamphetamine. Do you understand what I'm saying?"

"You saying that I was down in the basement when they were making the dope, even before the police busted the lab and cleaned it all out?"

"Exactly," LaBreque smiled, crossing his arms on his chest. "And we have reason to believe that you were more than just a casual visitor."

"Why?"

"Cuz you were hiding a copy of the cook's recipe in the glove box of your truck." The detective reached across the table and flipped the magazine over, his beefy index finger slamming down onto the notes scribbled all over the back cover. "What's this then, a shopping list for your kid's science project, complete with glass beakers and copper tubing?"

"I didn't know what that was." He looked straight up into the two-way mirror. "I can't read those words," he admitted to an absolute stranger for the very first time in his life.

———————

With Martha cleared out, Julia took the opportunity to turn her bedroom upside down, looking for anything that might hint at Serena's whereabouts.

"I called a few of the guys I know, but they swear they didn't sell any shit to your friend today. Just regulars so far," Boyd reported.

"Well, as far as I knew, Serena was broke. When I brought her home from the Crystal Palace, she didn't even have a penny on her. Fuck, she was totally naked and covered in dried shit and cum."

"They dumped her dirty?"

"Yeah." Julia suddenly had a thought. Returning from her bedroom, she opened a small wooden box and turned it upside down over Boyd's lap. "The bitch took all my jewelry. That's how she paid for her score."

"Great, now we can add all the pawn shops to our list of crack houses."

"I'm fucked," Julia dropped to the couch. "She could run for days on my stuff. Hell, I paid six hundred bucks for my emerald ring alone."

"She stole your shit and ran, so you're even now, right?"

Julia wasn't so sure. "I lost my jewelry, but that girl lost her looks.

Shit man, she's really fucked. You should have seen it. Her chest was one of the ugliest damn things I'd ever seen. She kinda looked like a giant tiger had taken bites out of her tits, and then just left her behind, to die."

Realizing that Julia wasn't going to let it go, Boyd had one final idea. "I think we should head down to the county morgue and register Serena in their data base. If she turns up anywhere, dead or alive, they'll call you. It's kind of like a giant lost and found box for actual people."

"How'd you know about this?"

"Sometimes my brother Pete goes missing. I check for my ma." He stood up from the couch, pivoting his hips to yank Julia up to her feet. "So come on. Just get your ass in the car and I'll drive us down."

Having filled out all the appropriate forms with the limited information at her disposal, Julia walked back to the front desk and handed in her clipboard.

"Have a seat." The desk clerk scanned the form. "With a specific injury like hers, it shouldn't be that hard to cross reference our database."

"I'll stand," Julia held her position, watching the man punch information his computer.

"I've got fourteen possibles," he suddenly announced. "Let's narrow our search just a little bit more before I send you out on a wild goose chase. So tell me a little bit more about her appearance. Did she have any tattoos or body piercings that you know about?"

Julia began to answer all his questions, trying as hard as she could to be precise.

"Alright, I think we have a winner." The man stood up, and pulled a page from his printer.

"Is it Serena?" Julia demanded; bouncing on the balls of her feet as the clerk quickly scanned the document.

"It's a Jane Doe." He looked over to Boyd, silently signaling that Julia might need a little support. "She wasn't carrying any ID, but your physical description and description of her injuries match."

"Is she alive?"

"For now." He reluctantly handed Julia the report, "but I think you better hurry."

———————

Before stepping out of the decontamination shower, Sarah quickly wrapped her body in a bleached white bathrobe, silently nodding at all three of her children as they sat waiting in matching attire.

"We've set aside sweat shirts and pants for you and your children, Mrs. Mallory. You'll find them in the men's and ladies changing rooms down the hall. Please dress, and then I'll have another officer show you to a conference room."

Sarah nodded, her blinding headache hampering even her simplest of replies.

"Come children," she whispered, leading the way past the bright yellow trash bags stuffed full with their personal clothing and shoes.

Finally dressed, each child was allowed to choose a pre-wrapped sandwich and a can of soda. While her children ate, Sarah took the opportunity to rest in one of the plastic chairs circling the conference table.

"Want some?" Mark stopped eating long enough to offer his mother a bite of his sandwich."

"No thank you, honey, I'm not really hungry."

"Where's Daddy?' Mary suddenly began to whimper, sliding off her chair to crawl up onto her mother's lap.

"I don't know," Sarah turned toward the far wall, catching her own reflection in the two-way mirror.

Within a minute, three officers silently entered the conference room.

"Mrs. Mallory, my name is Detective LaBreque. I was wondering if we could have a little talk about your husband, Justice Mallory. Detective Dawson here will be happy to take your children to an adjoining room that has a DVD player, where they can watch a movie and finish their snack, if that's all right with you?"

Sarah nodded her agreement, setting Mary on the floor and motioning for Mathew to take her hand.

"Mind your manners," she softly ordered the children.

"Mrs. Mallory," Detective LaBreque jumped right into the interrogation, the minute the children had cleared the room. "Your husband wrote a very simple statement regarding his side of the assault on one of our officers. I was wondering if you could please read it over and take a minute to decide if there's anything you'd like to add."

"My Justice?" Sarah sat up and repeated her husband's name. "My Justice wrote out a statement and you want me to read it?"

"Yes ma'am. Can I ask why you seem so surprised?"

"Well," she nervously raised her right hand up to her face, unconsciously shielding her mouth from the mirror. "My Justice can't read nor write. He never learned how. But if you tell him something twice, I guarantee he won't forget it."

LaBreque looked over at his partner, and then back at Sarah.

"Mrs. Mallory, we want you to tell us in your own words how you came to live in your present house."

Chapter
Forty-Two

*"Life is a banquet and most poor
suckers are starving to death!"*

—*Auntie Mame, 1958*

"You know," Tony looked over at Marcus as they walked down the grassy knoll toward the parking lot. "I think we've closed the clinic doors more in the last couple months than we did all last year."

"I agree." The doctor dug into his suit pocket for his car keys. "And that's something I think we need to talk about."

Waiting for his boss to unlock the car doors, Tony took one last opportunity to look back at Martin and Olga's gravesites. Dug side by side into the slope of the hill, they seemed to have the best view in the city, surrounded by majestic oaks, and manicured flowerbeds.

"You know, even with all Dr. Hood's money, up in that big beautiful mansion, I don't think I ever really heard him laugh,"

Tony mused. "Doesn't seem like that money did him all that much good."

"Martin laughed a lot when he was young, back when he and Olga were a couple, sneaking time together in the locker room, back of the doctor's lounge. They thought none of the staff knew, but we all did. They were so much in love. You just can't hide something as powerful as that."

"Speaking of love," Tony interrupted his boss's train of thought. "What you gonna do about Teresa? Brushing her off as if she didn't fit into your life just wasn't right, especially since you and I both knew it wasn't true."

"I didn't have a lot to offer the woman," he argued.

"But you do now," Tony alluded to their inheritances. "You can pack up, move to Teresa, and start over by opening a proper medical clinic. You have enough capital for trained nurses, truckloads of supplies, and a proper advertising budget. No more word of mouth, through junkies and hookers."

"And what about you?" he shifted the conversation to Tony. "I don't want to think you're going to squander your money on loose women and worthless stock tips."

"Mine's already spoken for."

"Oh Tony!" The doctor slid in behind the wheel, waiting for his passenger to join him. "You didn't get yourself involved in some cockamamie scheme, did you?"

"I don't think so. You know Karen, the girl I just started seeing? Well, she's an accountant, and she's agreed to help me work out a business plan. Karen wants me to make sure all my money is being funneled into the right places. You know, just because I'm not a doctor doesn't mean that I can't run a good clinic."

Marcus nodded his silent agreement, secretly thrilled that his assistant and closest friend was considering keeping the doors open for the underprivileged in the community.

"You sure you wanna dump your inheritance into that old money pit? It'll never make you rich," he warned, "especially if you have to hire a doctor. Nobody's gonna work for what little I pulled out."

"I give you the impression that I need to be rich?"

"No," Marcus shook his head. "But you did give me the impression that you might make a good male nurse."

Tony pointed to the first donut shop he spotted on the side of the road. "How about we stop for a coffee? I wanna pick your brain about the contracts with the linen company. I mentioned it to Karen, and she figured if we're trying to cut costs, we might be better off leasing a sterilizing washer and then process the linens ourselves."

The doctor nodded. The Changeroom wouldn't be closing, and he'd finally be free to retire and enjoy his golden years.

———————

As Boyd waited in the hallway, the nurse escorted Julia to a rear section of the county's emergency room.

"That's the Jane Doe," she pointed to a gurney tucked discreetly between two portable curtains.

Slowly making her way toward the bed, Julia carefully stepped around the monitors hooked up to the patient's body.

"Do you know her?" the nurse politely inquired.

"Yes," she wiped her eyes. "Her name is Serena. She's my friend."

"I'll get the doctor on call. He'll wanna speak to you."

"Is she going to be alright?" Julia asked without taking her eyes off Serena's face.

"I'll be right back with the doctor," the nurse evaded the question and slipped out of earshot.

"Hello, my name is Doctor Watts. I understand you know this patient?" A tall man walked up to the bed, not wasting any time as he quickly scanned the nurse's latest chart notations.

"Her name's Serena," Julia finally reached forward to pick up the young girl's lifeless hand. "What's happened to her?" she motioned toward her bandaged forearm.

"She was found on a construction site by one of the workers. The grass was littered with drug paraphernalia, and according to the notes, the paramedics administered large doses of naloxone, but it was already too late."

"Too late? But she's alive," Julia's eyes flittered to the pulsing monitors. "What do you mean too late?"

"The patient had already administered numerous subcutaneous injections of heroin into her left forearm before directly injecting her blood stream with a final dose. I've seen it before. She has effectively committed suicide through a slow release system. Your friend obviously knew that she'd never stay conscious long enough to inject each syringe one by one into her veins, so she set herself up first, before fixing with her final hit."

"But she's alive," Julia began to shriek. "Quit talking like she's already dead!"

"Let me explain," the doctor reluctantly set down his chart. "Subcutaneous injections form pockets of fluid directly beneath the skin, also known as blisters. Although it can take hours to dissolve, the drugs do dissipate throughout the system, and every drop is absorbed as efficiently as if you'd injected it directly into the vein."

Without warning, as if being electrocuted by an outside source, Serena's body began to twitch, her sudden movements quickly escalating into a rash of violent tremors.

"Nurse!" the doctor yelled. "Remove the visitor. It looks like our patient is seizing."

As Julia was quickly shuffled from the emergency room, Boyd stood up and silently threw his arm around her shoulder, gently guiding her down into one of the waiting chairs.

"Was it her?"

"Yeah."

"Is she going to be okay?"

Julia looked up just as the attending physician stepped out into the hall, his head bowed, and his eyes searching the floor as he mentally prepared his speech.

"No. Serena's dead," Julia dropped her face back down into Boyd's shoulder. "She died of a heroin overdose."

Frantically pulling open every drawer in the motel room, Sarah continued her search.

"Sweetie, what's the matter?" Justice sat up off the edge of the bed and walked over to his wife.

"A bible. I need a bible. Every motel has a bible, but I can't find the one in this room."

"Sarah." He turned and slowly spun his wife in toward his chest. "You don't need a bible to pray. We'll just pray together." He motioned for all three children to join him at the foot of the queen-size bed.

"Dear heavenly Father," Justice started off the family prayer.

After ten minutes of heartfelt thanks for all their blessings and prayers for the future health of their children, Sarah finally closed the prayer with an, "Amen," and rose back to her feet.

"Can we really order whatever we want?" Mathew and Mark rushed back to the room service menu.

"That's what Detective LaBreque said." Justice smiled at his sons. "But don't go crazy, try and show a little appreciation for the help."

"I can't believe we'd moved our family into a condemned house," Sarah reached for a hairbrush, and motioned Mary to crawl up onto her lap.

"I'll tell you what I can't believe." Justice walked over to the window, running his hands through his hair. "I can't believe we're starting over with nothing. No furniture, no clothes, and no place to live."

"God will provide." Sarah felt a wave of confidence suddenly wash over her. "We were so busy trying to make things easier, that we didn't take the time to question where the help was coming from. We'll be more careful next time," she vowed.

"You know," Justice turned back toward his family, "The hardest thing I had to do today was admit to those cops that I couldn't read. I never thought I'd have the courage to do that."

"But you did," she winked.

"I need to learn, Sarah, and I'm not sure how. But I gotta make sure something like that don't happen again. I need to go to school."

"I can teach you, Dad." Mathew turned to face his father. "I'm really good at English. My teacher said I'm the best reader in the class."

Justice nodded, finally realizing that no matter where they lived, they'd all be fine.

———————

After three back-to-back appointments, Wally was exhausted. He'd been up late the night before, filling out his sales reports for the past week, and it had been after midnight before he'd finally crawled into bed.

"I think I'm gonna swing by the cleaners and pick up my suits while I'm on the south side of town. You need anything before I head home?" he questioned his wife over the phone.

"No. Well, there *is* that bakery with the chocolate cupcakes that the kids just adore. I think it's called Bee Bee's." She scrambled through the kitchen's junk drawer for her address book.

"Okay, where is it?" Wally groaned, already sorry that he'd bothered to call.

"It's on Tenth and Marquee. And since you're there, you might as well pick up a couple loaves of white bread. But make sure it's sliced," she reminded him. "Last time I tried to slice it myself, it came out so fat, that I couldn't even fit the pieces in the toaster."

"Got it," Wally prepared to hang up the phone.

"I was thinking of making cannelloni for supper," Annette hoped to entice him. "Or maybe you'd just like a bowl of tomato soup?"

"Gee, homemade pasta or canned soup? Let me think," he paused on the line.

"Fine, I get your point," Annette walked over to the stove to stir the boiling pasta tubes. "You gonna be home by seven?"

"Seven, seven thirty. Depends on traffic."

"I love you, Wally."

"I know you do," he teased, making a mental note to see if he could spot a florist anywhere along his route.

Three suits, one dozen cupcakes, two loaves of sliced white, and a bouquet of wild daisies all loaded in the van, Wally found himself on the last leg of his journey home.

After he pulled into the back alley behind the neighborhood liquor store, he carefully picked the bouquet of daisies off the front seat and set them gently in the back just as a kid hopped in through the passenger door.

"Twenty?" Wally asked, pulling the folded bill out of his suit pocket.

"Twenty," the young man snatched the money and shoved it down into his pocket.

Smiling to himself, Wally leaned back, simultaneously unzipping his pants and pulling out his cock as the kid leaned across the consol and dropped his head down into Wally's lap.

Epilogue

"I'll be back."

—*The Terminator, 1984*

"Do you like this one, sweetie?" Sarah held up another dress in front of her daughter's chest, inspecting the material for rips or stains.

Mary nodded her head, tickled to have a closet full of new clothes, oblivious to the fact that they came from second hand charity bags donated by the local shelter.

"We're gonna need to make sure you kids have boots. In another month, it'll be Christmas, and then the snow will really start to fly."

"I want snow," Mary smiled, pulling out a pink sweater from amidst the pile of children's clothing.

"Mark, show me what you've got," Sarah called out to her youngest son as he continued to dig through the bags in the adjoining room.

"I got sweatshirts, and jeans, and socks. Lots of socks," he pointed to the multicolored pile amassed on the living room floor.

"That's good, now go find your brother and tell him it's his turn to come inside. And, if you see your father, tell him dinner will be ready in an hour."

Settled around the table, Sarah was the first to bow her head, waiting for her husband to offer their dinner blessing.

"Dear heavenly Father," Justice prayed. "Please bless this food, and bless our family. We gather around this table in our brand new house trailer and thank you and the court judge for seeing fit to award us with all them damages. We're so thankful for all our returned health, and for my new job as delivery manager down at Jupiter Greenhouse. Please bless my wife, my children, and my tutor Miss Amy, who's been working real hard to teach me to read. Amen."

"Amen," Sarah and the children echoed his prayers.

Carefully making her way up the bedroom stairs, Lucy Nally balanced the cordless telephone on her son's lunch tray, forced to nudge the bedroom door open with her toes.

"Freddy," she whispered, not wanting to wake him if he was already sleeping.

"What?" he demanded, his voice barely audible over the low hum of his bedroom's humidifier.

"It's that girl again." Lucy set down the tray before handing her son the phone.

"Don't want it." He turned away from his mother.

"Well, then you hang up." She placed the phone on the blanket bedside his right hand before turning to walk out of his room.

"Hello? Hello Freddy?" A girl's voice could be heard shouting from the receiver.

"Hello," he reluctantly picked up the handset.

"Freddy, it's me Callie. Sorry if I woke you, but I just was studying for my exams, and I thought I'd take a break and give you a call."

"It's alright." He struggled to reposition his head a little higher on the mound of pillows.

"I keep checking my E-mail, hoping to hear from you, but…"

"I still don't have a new computer. Dad says he'll buy one, but money's a little tight right now with all the hospital bills."

"How was your last surgery? Did they give you that special bag?"

"Yeah," Freddy smirked. "They did the colostomy, and now I've got a *shit bag* for the next three or four months."

"Well, you can drink soda and eat chips all night, and still never have to pause the movie to go to the bathroom," Callie announced, trying to make light of the situation.

"Oh yeah! That's a bonus."

"If you don't wanna talk about your surgery, we can always talk about something else."

Freddy reached over and yanked a handful of tissue off his nightstand, taking a second to wipe his eyes before clearing his throat.

"I'm sorry to be such a bitch," Freddy apologized. "It's just that after the doctor operated on me to fix my vaginal-rectal fistula. He told me that I wouldn't be able to dilate my neo-vagina for at least sixty days."

"I don't know what a vaginal-rectal fist… fistula is," she took a second to remind Freddy.

"Well," he sighed. "I found out its one of the most feared complications during sex reassignment surgery. It sometimes happens during the operation when the doctor is dissecting the vaginal cavity. Essentially," he summed up in layman's terms, "when he was slicing me open to make a hole for my new vagina, he accidentally nicked or possibly sliced the wall of my rectum."

"Oh, I see."

"Now it seems that the cut, or fistula, lets feces and liquid excrement leak into my new vagina. As long as it leaks, it'll never heal properly, and I run a really high risk of infection. So," he reluctantly summed up, "the doctor gave me a colostomy bag."

"But that doesn't sound too bad."

"Not too bad, eh? Well," Freddy began to sob. "Like I told you, Callie, I can't dilate with my stent for two or three months. If I can't keep stretching out my new *neo-vagina*, it's gonna heal closed. And down the road, I'll need a complete redo with skin grafts and everything, that is, if I ever have the guts and the cash to try and have the whole reassignment surgery again."

"Oh Freddy, I didn't realize," she felt like breaking down into tears.

"And now I have these two little-girly breasts, no penis, no vagina, and a colostomy bag hanging off the edge of my bed to catch my shit and piss. What have I done to myself, Callie?"

"It'll be okay," she tried to soothe him.

"How? Mom and Dad are always fighting about having to sell the house. I hear them when they think I'm sleeping. And Dad... Dad won't even look at me anymore," he let out a painful sob. "You know that none of this is covered by his insurance? Sex changes are considered cosmetic."

"I know, your mom told me that," she mumbled.

"You should have let me die," he stated simply. "Just the repair work from my botched surgery alone is going to suck my parents dry. And after all is said and done, I'll still be a *nothing*. I won't be a man, and I certainly won't be a woman. I'm just some kind of... kind of... post-operative freak." His sobs echoed off his bedroom walls.

Wiping the tears from her own eyes, Callie struggled to say

something comforting, anything to give her old roommate the slightest semblance of hope.

"I'm gonna be just a big deformed *it,* with no sex organs, and no way of ever getting it fixed." Freddy summed up his entire situation in one final thought.

Appearing out of nowhere, Lucy Nally plucked the phone from her son's hands, slowly lifting the receiver upwards toward her own mouth.

"I'm sorry, dear, but this is much too upsetting for Freddy. I think it would be much better if you called back another day."

Callie agreed; apologizing one last time before the receiver went dead in her hand.

"How about some lunch now?" Lucy Nally suggested to her son. "I think a little tuna fish on sourdough bread might lift your spirits. I put chopped pickles in with the mayo."

Freddy slid both his arms under the duvet cover and just closed his eyes, praying that he could just fast-forward the next fifty or sixty years and not wake up until the day he was fortunate enough to die.

———————

"Tony DeMarco, please?" Julia announced to the young woman dressed in a pale blue uniform manning the clinic's freshly renovated front desk.

"Please have a seat," she chirped. "I'll tell Tony he has a visitor." She rose from her chair. "And your name?" the girl added as an afterthought."

"Tell him it's just Julia." She smiled, instantly drawn to the beautiful statue mounted on a corner table.

"Well there, *just Julia,*" Tony strolled out from the back wearing a white lab coat, tan trousers, and a light blue tee shirt. "I'm glad you stopped by. You have time for a coffee?"

"I do. But first, you gotta tell me where you got that beautiful angel statue. It's exquisite. It's so…" She stumbled, looking for just the right adjective.

"Lifelike," Tony offered.

"Yeah. Where'd you buy it?"

"It was a gift from Karen." Tony motioned for Julia to follow him into the back. "An artist created that statue from Karen's likeness. I think that's why it looks so real."

"I like it." Julia stepped forward and helped herself to a coffee. "That's a pretty nice piece of art to leave sitting in a public waiting room. Aren't you afraid it's going to get damaged or maybe even stolen?"

"I was at first. But it's become a little bit of a charm for many of the Changeroom's patients. They rub the base for luck, or leave pennies in the bowl beside the angel's feet. I don't know. It just seems that moving it now would be kind of insulting to them."

"Coffee?" Julia picked up the fresh pot, somehow uncomfortable with the entire conversation.

"Sure. So what brings you by?"

"Well, it's time for another HIV test, and I wanted to give you this."

"What's this?" Tony ripped open the small purple envelope and carefully unfolded the delicate insert.

You are cordially invited to share in the wedding ceremony of
Julia Anne Meyers & Boyd Earl Giovanna
This Saturday at 5 o'clock at the Italian Cultural Center
Cocktails: 6:00 p.m.
Supper: 7:00 p.m.
Dance: To follow.

"We're getting married." She walked over and flashed Tony her engagement ring. "I can't believe that I'm finally settling down and going to play the little woman."

"Your ring is beautiful, and you look really happy. But why bother with the HIV test if you're leaving the business?"

"Who said I was leaving the business. Boyd's gonna bankroll me in a special project, a complete series of movies, starring only me. Isn't that great?"

All of a sudden, Tony wasn't so sure which new development was truly the source of Julia's excitement. "I thought you were itching to get out? I thought that after Serena died, you swore you'd had enough of the drugs, and the raunchy sex? I thought…"

"Enough, please." She waved her hand, using the moment of silence to turn her back and fill her coffee mug with cream and sugar. "Well, I thought you were going to take your inheritance and go to med school?"

"I will," Tony shrugged. "But taking over the clinic after Dr. Clifford retired was more work than I thought. Now that we're trying to incorporate doctor's visits to the local shelters into our weekly routine, it's been a scheduling nightmare."

"Relax," Julia grabbed a chair. "You're doing damn good work here, Tony. Dr. Clifford would be really proud of what you're accomplishing. I was just teasing you cuz you were riding my case, is all."

"So you're getting married." He smiled, bringing the conversation back to a friendly tone. "You know, that'll be two weddings for me in the same month. Karen and I just got back from Marcus and Teresa's wedding last weekend."

"How was it?"

"The wedding was great, and it was our first trip away together."

"I see. Well, tell me stud. How was it?"

"Karen's quite the woman. I can see her as a long-term part of my future. I sure hope she sees me as part of hers."

Julia stood up; reaching for the coffee pot as she carefully chose her words. "Boyd stood with me through Serena's funeral, when I kicked the hard stuff, and then he even bailed me out when I jumped Siggy and was charged with assault. I owe him."

"Sure you do," Tony agreed." But owing someone, and loving someone are two different things. Don't you think?"

"I don't think women like me always find that magical love that everyone talks about. I think that sometimes all you can hope for is a man who genuinely cares for you and won't beat your ass when he's had a few too many beers."

"No," Tony shook his head, "I don't agree."

"Honey, I've had more cock in me than most women have had tampons. Very few guys can handle that. I think I'm damn lucky to find a man like Boyd."

"Well then, if you're sure, I'll be glad to come and watch you tie the knot."

"And bring your girlfriend. I think it's time Karen met a few of your buddies from the old days. What do you think?"

Tony thought about it for a minute before replying. "As long as we continue to divide this community in half, we doomed. We've got to stop talking about *them* and *us*. Nothing will ever change until we do. It's bad enough that our communities are already separated along economic divisions—the haves and the have-nots. We have to come together as people."

"Let me ask you something, Tony. If you're not ashamed of your past history in the porn business, and you think we should bring all our communities together, why did you blow such a big chunk of your inheritance buying up all the negatives for your old films?"

"How'd you know?"

"Where do you think Boyd got his sudden injection of cash

from? When he heard you were paying big bucks for all the old rights, he went ahead and bought them up ahead of you."

"He's behind the numbered company who was holding my titles?"

"Yup."

Setting down his cup, Tony stared into Julia's face.

"Why didn't you tell me? You could have saved me tens of thousands of dollars that were already earmarked for this clinic."

"It was my future, too," Julia argued. "Just think of it as sharing the wealth."

Just before Tony turned to leave the lunchroom, he had to stop and share one last thought. "People like you and Boyd are this community's worst enemies. Not because you make porn, but because you are determined to beat down anyone else who manages to claw their way out of your shit hole."

"That's not fair," she argued back. "You know me better than that."

"Good bye Julia, and good luck with your movies. I hope you and Boyd are very happy together in your new venture."

"Do you mean it, Tony?"

"Good bye Julia. I have patients who need whatever help I can give them."

As Julia watched Tony stroll out of the clinic's lunchroom, she suddenly felt so small and insignificant. God, how she needed to get back to work. She needed to feel like she was contributing something again. Even if her contribution was little more than a faked orgasm and a series of uninspired moans, it was still her contribution, and no matter what, she'd always be remembered for it.

The End

If you have enjoyed reading *Cures For Cash* by Lynne Martin, I'm confident you will also enjoy her novel *Ready, Set, Action!*

Catch up with Julia and Boyd five years later as they take their combined experience in the porn industry and open the financially lucrative venture, Giovanni Films. Experience the undying commitment connecting Dr. Martin Hood and Nurse Olga Heinz, as her debilitating condition leads Martin to a very heart wrenching decision. And don't forget the Changeroom, a community clinic still treating the downtrodden and forgotten members of a society.

In this raw, gritty tale that exposes a dark and realistic glimpse into the porn industry, only time will tell if Julia, a headstrong entrepreneur, can rescue her company—and all those she loves—before it is too late.

To view future release dates for upcoming novels, and a complete list of titles for LYNNE MARTIN, please visit her website @ www.lynnemartinbooks.com

Lynne Martin is an avid movie collector, an animal lover, and a staunch supporter of sexual education. She currently resides in Alberta, Canada, with her husband and their large extended family.

To learn more about LYNNE MARTIN, she can be reached through her website and blog @ www.lynnemartinbooks.com